FORTY ACRES

Phyllis R. Dixon

Beatha,
Best wishes!
Phyllis R. Dixon
6/5/07

New Generation Press
Memphis, Tennessee

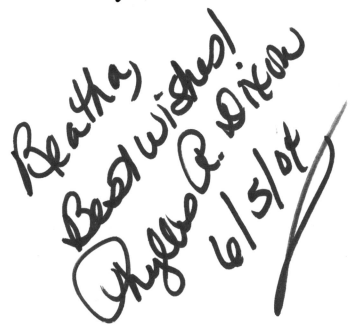

ISBN 0-9749540-5-5

Library of Congress Control Number 2004103868
Printed in the United States of America

For information address:

New Generation Press
P.O. Box 750024
Memphis, Tennessee 38175-0024
www.newgenerationpress.com

Cover design by Phyllis R. Dixon
Cover art by Ruth Russell Williams

Printed in the United States by Morris Publishing
3212 East Highway 30
Kearney, NE 68847
1-800-650-7888

In memory of

Buena Vester Lee, Timothy D. Jackson and Uncle Bubba

Acknowledgements

The fact that I am writing this page is a testimony to the awesome workings of the Creator and I give Him all the glory. There are many people to recognize, but I must first thank my husband, Fitzgerald, for your love, enthusiasm and support. Special thanks go to Mrs. Richmond, my first editor; and to Denise Pines, the first person to say yes. I am grateful to the Milwaukee Alumnae Chapter of Delta Sigma Theta Sorority Inc. for showing me that authors are real people. To Ruth Russell Williams, for graciously allowing me to use your definitive painting on the cover. I appreciate Angela York, Tanya Beckley, Sheryl Dean, Crystal Maddox, Juel Richardson, Clarence Hale, Mary and John Randolph, Pat and Bill Goree, Annie and Caesar Slade, and Betty Washington for being there.

I am forever indebted to Evelyn Palfrey, for your invaluable help and unselfishness. You are living proof that nothing happens by accident.

A special thank-you goes to my children, Trey, Candace and Lee, for sharing me with books and the computer.

And last, but certainly not least, I thank my mother, Maggie Jean Jackson-Hale for Everything. We did it!

Tell ye your children of it, and let your children tell their children, and their children another generation.

The Book of Joel 1:3

The islands from Charleston, south, the abandoned rice fields along the rivers for thirty miles back from the sea, and the country bordering the St. Johns river, Florida, are reserved and set apart for the settlement of the negroes now made free by the acts of war and the proclamation of the President of the United States. ... Whenever three respectable negroes, heads of families, shall desire to settle on land, and shall have selected for that purpose an island or a locality clearly defined, within the limits above designated, the Inspector of Settlements and Plantations will himself, or by such subordinate officer as he may appoint, give them a license to settle such island or district, and afford them such assistance as he can to enable them to establish a peaceable agricultural settlement. The three parties named will subdivide the land, under the supervision of the Inspector, among themselves and such others as may choose to settle near them, so that each family shall have a plot of not more than (40) forty acres of tillable ground, and when it borders on some water channel, with not more than 800 feet water front, in the possession of which land the military authorities will afford them protection, until such time as they can protect themselves, or until Congress shall regulate their title.

BY ORDER OF MAJOR GENERAL W.T. SHERMAN:

IN THE FIELD, SAVANNAH, GEORGIA
JANUARY 16, 1865

SPECIAL FIELD ORDERS, NO. 15

Contents

Prologue

"What do you mean you're not going?" Cecelia yelled into the phone. "You have to go. You told Mama and Daddy you were coming."

"I can change my mind, can't I? Something has come up," I answered, wondering why I was defending myself in the first place. "The Washington Family Reunion will survive without Carolyn Washington."

"Remember, our plan to talk to Mama and Daddy about selling the farm? The reunion will be the perfect time."

"Cecelia, I already told you I feel uncomfortable talking to Daddy about the land. It sounds like we're anxious for him to die," I said as I put the Tae Bo video on pause.

"That's not it. We just don't want him to work himself into another stroke. I've already spoken with a representative from Consolidated Farms. You won't believe what they're ready to offer Daddy. He should cash out and relax."

"Well, it sounds like you have all the answers. Why do I need to be there? I have other plans."

"What plans could possibly be more important than your family?" Cecelia asked.

"I did not say it was more important. I just plan to do something else this year."

"Just a minute, let me put you on hold," Cecelia said before I could object.

Why did I even mention my plans to Cecelia in the first place? I should have known better.

Family reunions are almost a religion in the African-American family. Ever since *Roots*, families have been reuniting and meeting long lost relatives, trying to find Kunte Kinte. It's an admirable tradition. But if Alex Haley had found some of my relatives, he would have quit his search. Don't misunderstand, we're not dysfunctional. Well, not too much. I'm the sixth of eight children and the youngest girl. It's challenge enough to keep up with my nuclear family, without adding cousins, aunts and uncles to the mix. Between a wedding here and a funeral there, I get my requisite dose of kinfolk. And I have my sister, Cecelia, the *Jet* magazine of our family to keep me posted on the drama, whether I want to hear it or not.

"Carolyn, are you still there?" Cecelia asked. "I have Mama on the other line. Mama, Carolyn is on the line, too."

"Chubby, how are you? You know you don't call enough. I worry about you."

Mama and Daddy and relatives over sixty-five are the only ones allowed to call me Chubby. They say I was doing the twist like Chubby Checkers as soon as I learned to walk, so they started calling me Chubby.

"I'm fine. Did you get the Valentine's Day present I sent?"

"Sure did. The fruit basket was so lovely; I didn't want to open it. Then your cousin Sheryl came over and her kids begged so much I ended up giving them most of the fruit. I didn't let you kids embarrass me like that. You all knew better than to ---".

"Well, I really need to go now. It was good talking to you," I said.

"Be careful going home by yourself. We got cable now and I see on that Chicago station there's always somebody being murdered or raped. It warms my heart to know that you visit each other and support one another. Lord knows my sister never has time for me. She didn't even have time to come to her own mother's funer---."

"Mama," Cecelia said, "Carolyn is at her place. I have you on a three-way call."

"Lord, the things you can do nowadays," Mama marveled. "Isn't that expensive? I hope you're saving money for a rainy day, and not wasting it on fancy doo-dads. Them phone people call all the time trying to sell something. One of them even sent us a check for one hundred dollars for some long distance mess. Your Daddy cashed that check the same day. But we still don't do no long distance calling, unless it's an emergency of course. I may call a little on the weekends when the rates are lower. You should have waited until this weekend to call---"

"Mama," Cecelia interrupted again. "Carolyn says she's not coming to the reunion."

"What do you mean you're not coming?" Mama asked.

"Well, Mama, it's just that … You see, I wanted to try… " I stammered.

"She wants to do something with her boyfriend," Cecelia tattled.

Warren and I plan a romantic getaway this Fourth of July to start some fireworks of our own. But I couldn't tell that to my mother.

"Well, bring Willie with you. We'd love to meet him."

"He bought her diamond earrings for Valentine's Day," Cecelia reported in a singsong voice.

"Oh really? Is he my future son-in-law? It took me almost fifty years to get diamonds. Can you believe your father bought me a diamond necklace for Valentine's Day? I told him he shouldn't have spent that kind of money. You should have seen the rock Paul bought his little wife. You missed the wedding. It was gorgeous. But I'm glad we didn't have to pay for it. You don't need anything that elaborate at your age. Although Sister Carter remarried last year and she had ---"

"Mama *please*," I said. "No one is talking about marriage."

"Well, you should be talking about marriage. You're almost forty. I bet if you told him he couldn't get the milk free, he'd want to buy the cow. He's more than welcome, but you know you can't sleep together here. You're grown and I can't control what you do out in the world, but under my roof---."

"Mama, don't worry about it. I'm not bringing him. Why would I subject anyone to Eden, Arkansas?"

"If he cares about you, he'll follow you anywhere, and, there is nothing wrong with Eden. It's a nice, quiet town. We know our neighbors and people care about each other."

Eden is twenty miles south of Cotton Corner and ten miles east of Forrest City. Those bustling metropolis' aren't familiar to most folks, so I usually tell people I'm from just outside of Memphis, omitting the little detail that it's about sixty miles outside of Memphis. And Mama's right, people know their neighbors. Most of them are related. Eden has come a long way and paved county roads, cable and less overt segregation make it more palatable than it was during my youth. But even so, my relationship with Warren hadn't reached the 'home to meet the parents' stage.

"Mama said you can bring Wendell. Why don't you invite him?" Cecelia said.

"If he can't appreciate where you're from, then he can't appreciate you," Mama said. "We won't embarrass you this time. Charles has cut back on his drinking and Sheryl's husband ain't selling Amway no more, so he won't be bugging every body. Although I think he's selling some kind of legal mess now, anything to keep from getting a real job. But I told him I'm blessed to have two children with law degrees, so we don't need nothing he's selling. Chubby is an attorney with the IRS and Paul works for a firm in California. He even got white folks coming to him, so you know he's good. I wasn't bragging, but I just had to let him know ---"

"Mama, you should know I'm not ashamed of my family. You and Daddy are the best."

"Then are you ashamed of him? What kind of beau do you have that you're ashamed to introduce to your family? If he's ugly that's okay. Good-looking men is too much trouble anyway. Women won't let 'em rest, even if they wanted to do right. As long as he has a job and isn't too whorish, he'll do. It would be good if he knows the Lord, but you can work on that. Somebody like Michael would be perfect."

"Are you calling my husband ugly?" Cecelia asked.

"No baby. I didn't mean it that way. I'm just saying ---"

"Look, I haven't said one word about *Warren*. I just thought I would do something else this Fourth of July. Can't I miss one reunion?"

"You've missed most of them," Cecelia stated.

"This will be the first reunion in Arkansas and your Daddy was looking forward to having all of you home. I know you all got your own houses, but this land will always be your home. C.W. say it's important to know you got a place to come home to. You know we almost lost him last fall. He was helpless after that stroke. But the Lord spared his life and restored his health. He has use of all his limbs and his mind is as sharp as ever." Mama lowered her voice. "I can tell you girls this since you're young women, I mean all of his limbs. Since he's been taking them pills, he's like a new man, a new young man, if you know what I mean. Lord, it's almost scandalous the way he---"

"Mama, okay, we get your point," I said shaking my head.

"Well, the least you can do is come see him. Paul and Julia are coming all the way from California. You haven't even met your new sister-in-law. If you don't come, you will be the only one missing, other than Carl of course. But Carl may get a parole hearing before then, so it's possible all my children will be home. You know you don't visit often enough. Seeing you would really give your father a lift."

"Is something wrong?" I asked. "I thought the doctors gave Daddy a clean bill of health."

"They did, but he doesn't have to be on death's doorstep for you to visit, does he? Everyone else is coming."

"That's my point, Mama. Everyone will be there, so we won't get to spend that much time together anyway. I'll send plane tickets for the Labor Day weekend."

"Your Daddy won't leave then, the soybeans will be coming in. You would think he could finally relax with Charles running the farm. But he's more intense than ever. Besides, Labor Day won't be the same. It won't be the Family Reunion."

"Then why don't I come visit you Labor Day? There will be fewer people around and we can spend more time together," I said.

"You said that last year," Cecelia said.

"What's wrong with coming for the reunion and Labor Day? You know tomorrow is not promised. Me and your Daddy won't always be here. I know if my Mama and Daddy were livin'---"

"All right, all right. I'll come," I said.

"Well don't come, if you have that attitude. If you're too busy---"

"Mama, I said I'm coming." I replied in a softened tone, but she had already given the phone to Daddy.

"Hey, Chubby," Daddy said. "Your Mama says you can't make it to the reunion. You're going to miss some good eating. We're having a barbeque and fish fry, with homemade ice cream, black berry dumplings, you know, all the things the doctor doesn't want me to eat. All of your brothers and sisters are coming. Carl may even be here. But I know you're a hard worker and you'd be here if you could. When will you be home? I need you to review my taxes."

So much for my romantic holiday. How could I resist the double team? My getaway with Warren would have to wait. "Tell Mama I'm coming. And be sure to have plenty of ice cream and dumplings."

What's Love Got To Do With It?

1

The numbers on the caller ID device glared as the phone rang for the third time. I knew it was my sister and I debated whether or not to answer. I was in the middle of last minute packing and didn't have time for a long conversation. Warren was due shortly and my clothes were still strewn across the bed. We were going to need that bed for the romantic tryst I planned.

"Hello," I said as I picked up the cordless phone.

"What took you so long? I was about to hang up," Cecelia said.

"I'm doing ten things at once and I couldn't find the phone," I said.

"Well, I won't hold you long," Cecelia promised. "I have to go to work soon. I just want to tell you one more time how important this is. Carolyn, the future of our family rests in your hands."

"You've called me every day this week. I'm well aware of your opinion. And like I told you yesterday, and the day before that, what Daddy does with his property is for him to decide. I'm just looking at his taxes."

"See, you've got it messed up already," Cecelia said. "This isn't just my opinion. It's in Daddy's best interest to sell the farm. He doesn't need to work so hard at his age. That stroke was a wake up call. If he doesn't slow down, he's going to farm himself into his grave."

"Maybe the farm is what keeps him going. Daddy is not the type to sit around and watch television," I said as I straightened the red and white comforter on my bed. "Let's just leave him alone."

"We can't afford to do that. Raymond is down there filling Daddy's head with black power nonsense, telling him the race will suffer if he sells the land. And Beverly said Charles and his lazy wife have been spending a lot of time with Daddy lately. They're up to something."

"You're over reacting. Look, it's almost 9:30, and Warren will be here soon. I still haven't watered my plants or finished packing."

"I thought your flight wasn't until 2:30. Why is he coming so early?"

"None of your business." I said. Cecelia has been married almost twenty years, yet she thinks she's an expert on dating. She says it's a waste of time to date any man for more than six months unless marriage is on the horizon. She just doesn't understand how it is out here. The men I meet are either "between jobs" or have so many women they can't remember my name. Warren has his faults, and I know marriage is not an option, but he treats me better than any man has ever treated me. We've been dating almost two years and we have a comfortable relationship. That's enough for me right now. I don't need the drama and phony pledges of undying love. In the words of Tina Turner, 'what's love got to do with it?'

"If you want to waste your child bearing years in a futile relationship, that's your prerogative. I didn't call to talk about him anyway. Look, I really need a favor."

"And I thought you were calling to wish me a safe trip," I said.

"You know I wouldn't ask if I could avoid it."

"Don't worry about it."

"I feel terrible asking you this."

"What is it Cece?"

"I need two hundred dollars. I'll repay you as soon as we get back from the reunion."

"Didn't you just get paid?" I asked.

"We had to buy new tires before we put the van on the road."

"Are you sure you're not---"

"Do you want me to bring you the tire receipt? Or should I take an oath and sign it for you? I paid you back last time."

"Okay, don't get touchy. I'll loan you the money. Michael's office is on my way to the airport. Do you want me to drop if off?" I asked as I checked to see how much cash I had.

"No!" Cecelia said. "I'd prefer if you wouldn't mention this to him. You know how proud he is."

"All right. I'll see you tomorrow, I can give it to you then."

"I would rather get it from you before we leave town."

"You still have my key. I'll just leave the money in the breadbox. Get my mail too while you're here. But Cece, remember what I told you. You have everything; a loving husband, two healthy children, and a meaningful career. I'd hate to see you throw it away," I said softly.

"Don't worry. Everything's under control, and I promise to pay you back next week. Have a safe trip and don't eat all of the dumplings before I get there."

I took four fifties from my purse and put them in an envelope for Cecelia. I sure hope she pays me back, I thought. I'll need it for my American Express bill. The fee to change my return flight from Tuesday to Monday, will be on my next bill. Warren's friend has a condo in Lake Geneva and we're going there Monday and Tuesday. At least we can spend part of the holiday together.

I leaned on my suitcase, and pulled the stubborn zipper closed. How can one little dress keep this suitcase from closing? I guess it was a mistake to reopen the suitcase to add my white dress. There probably won't even be anywhere to wear it. A family reunion in Eden commands shorts and sandals more than a silk, sleeveless dress. But this dress is the first size ten I have bought in fifteen years, and someone is going to see me in it.

I finally resolved to lose twenty-five pounds when I found myself shopping in Lane Bryant. Or should I say when Cecelia found me shopping in Lane Bryant. Cecelia can wear the same clothes she wore in college. Even after having two children, she was still a perfect size eight. When we were in grade school, I was proud to be bigger than my big sister. By high school, I was jealous of her petite frame. The one hundred thirty pounds I carried at graduation would have looked better if it had been stretched over a taller frame, like my oldest sister Beverly. But on my five foot three inch frame, it looked like my nickname; chubby. Since then another twenty pounds had crept on my frame and I had gone from chubby to plump. I decided to lose weight before I went from plump to fat. Beverly and I made New Year's resolutions to lose weight and joined Weight Watchers this year. The dress was a sign of progress and proof that the crunches, leg lifts and salads had paid off.

I bought the dress to wear to an O'Jays concert with Warren. They were playing in Milwaukee, and we were going to drive up, have dinner, then see the show. Warren canceled when his son's baseball team made Little League playoffs. I suggested we skip dinner and go to the show, but Warren is always prompt and did not want to miss the beginning of the show. I'm usually prompt too, but I would have made an exception to wear my new size ten dress.

"At ten o'clock I heard the front door open. "What's the password?" I asked as I unlatched the chain and flipped the deadbolt.

Warren took his key out of the door and pushed it open. "That's the password," he whispered, after he kissed me.

"Hmmm, I'm not sure I understand. Can you tell me that password again?"

This time he pecked my cheek and walked in. "We'll have to practice that password later. Are you ready? I'll take your luggage to the car."

"We have a little time. Can I get you something to eat? My flight's not until 2:30," I said.

"Then why did you tell me to be here at 10:00?"

"So we can spend a little time together before I leave. I want to give you a proper good-bye," I said as I unbuttoned my slacks and smiled.

Warren turned and walked toward the door. "Next time, let me in on your plans. If that's what you wanted, you should have said so."

I walked up to Warren and blocked the door. "I don't know what you're getting so mad about," I said while putting my arms around his neck. "If you'd told me it was an imposition, I could have gotten Cecelia to take me. I suppose I could have endured another lecture about why we should get Daddy to sell the farm."

"Baby, it's not an imposition, you know I don't mind. It's just that I planned to take the kids to Six Flags this morning, so they could hit the rides before it gets too hot. Their mother went on one of her tirades when I told her we couldn't go until this afternoon."

"Terri is going?" I asked, taking my arms from around him.

"Yeah. Since it's a holiday, she thought we should have a family outing."

"You didn't mention that their mother was going."

Warren patted me on the behind and said, "You're cute when you're jealous. You'll be gone anyway, and rides make you sick."

The vision of the four of them walking along holding hands, eating cotton candy was making me sick.

"As long as you're pouting, I have some other news for you. I have to cancel our plans for Monday. I tried to get out of it, but Terri bought tickets for the UniverSoul Circus. The kids are really looking forward to it."

"But I spent five hundred dollars to change my ticket. Why couldn't you tell me this sooner? Are you sure you have to be there?"

"Look, I don't want to go through this third degree. I told you I tried to get out of it."

"I guess it's a good thing I'm going to Eden. Otherwise, I'd end up spending another holiday alone," I snapped.

"Is this all of your luggage? Let's go." He didn't even wait for my answer. He was on his way to the car while I struggled with my garment bag.

This one time I was tired of being understanding. He had all weekend to be with his kids. It's not like it was Christmas or Thanksgiving. Monday was supposed to be our night. I could have stayed with my family one more night. I thought about calling Terri and telling her this holiday, she could sit alone. But I only thought about it briefly. After all, she is his wife.

Lucky me. We made it to the airport in record time, ensuring me extra time to sit around and conjure images of Warren and Terri's delightful afternoon. This was the one day of the year with light traffic and minimal construction on the Dan Ryan Expressway. So instead of melting in Warren's arms, I was sitting at the gate flipping through magazines. I should have bought *Time* or *Forbes*, I thought. I was not in the mood for the articles in *Essence* and *Cosmopolitan; "How to Make Love Last", "Plan the Perfect Wedding", "Ten Signs That He's the One for You."* Even the newspaper headline, *"Record Crowds Expected for Lakefront Fourth of July Festivities"* reminded me of the afternoon Warren and Terri had planned. I don't think about Warren's wife very often. If I thought about her, I would have to think about myself, and listen to the voices in my head. There's a little voice that chastises me for being with Warren, and nags me to think of his wife, children and my home-training. Then there's a louder voice that tells me to grab whatever happiness I can; to put Carolyn first. I know I should feel guilty, but I don't. I guess that means I'm going to the super-hot section of hell. But, they had problems long before he met me.

He and his wife were separated when we met. Really, they were. I even checked his tax records to be sure. He and his wife filed separately, from different addresses. He was attractive, intelligent, employed, and, a good kisser. I should have known he was too good to be true. We were inseparable for five glorious months. Then, he and his wife got back together. His boys began to have problems in school, which the counselors attributed to their parent's separation. Warren grew up without a father and didn't want his sons to suffer, so he went back home. I'm glad he's concerned about his children. Too many men walk away from their families. I don't have time for a "real" boyfriend anyway. I work long hours and travel frequently. I can't have some man waiting for me, grilling me about where I've been and when I'm coming home. Warren suits me just fine.

I know all the warnings. "You'll never meet anyone else, while you're involved with a married man." "What goes around, comes around." "He's just having his cake and eating it too." "He's never going to leave his wife for you, and if he does, he'll cheat on you too." "You're too smart to let yourself be used." Well, I don't think it's too smart to sit around and wait for Prince Charming. And, to quote Bill Withers, "if it feels this good getting used, just keep on using me..." Most women are sharing anyway, they just don't know it.

Warren even encouraged me to date. He told me I deserved someone who could give me his full attention. We broke up several times, but after a few tortuous weeks he would show up on my doorstep, or I would call him and we'd take up where we left off. We played this break-up, make-up game, until Daddy's stroke made me declare the game over.

It was last Columbus Day, the start of the second week of yet another break-up between Warren and I. The phone rang and I almost didn't answer it. I didn't recognize the number on the caller ID and I had already hung up on two telemarketers. But I answered, and it was Beverly's dog, I mean husband, Anthony. He told me Daddy had a stroke and was in the hospital in Memphis. I jumped out of bed and searched for Cecelia's direct work number. Getting through to a live person at Cook County Memorial Hospital is harder than winning the lottery. It seemed to take an eternity, but I finally reached the third floor nurse's station.

"Girl, what's wrong? I know its bad news if you call me at work."

"Cece, it's bad. Anthony called, and said Daddy had a stroke. They rushed him to a hospital in Memphis, and the doctors say it's touch and go. I didn't talk to Beverly, she was with Mama. They don't know what happened. Tony found him slumped over at the kitchen table."

"Good thing he was there. Time is precious with a stroke. He may have saved his grandfather's life. I'll call the hospital and see what information I can get," Cecelia said. "But it doesn't sound good if they took him to Memphis."

"Well, I'm going to take the next flight. Call Raymond and Paul, and I'll call you when I get there," I said.

Within four hours, I was in the cardiac wing of Baptist Hospital in Memphis. They had just moved him from the intensive care unit. I found Daddy's room, knocked on the door and walked in. The odor in the room was strong as the sweet scent of flowers clashed with the hospital's disinfectant smell. Even though Daddy had been in the hospital less than twenty-four hours, flowers and cards lined his side of the room. Daddy drove a school bus for years to supplement his unpredictable farm income and many former students had already sent flowers.

They said Daddy's vital signs were getting better, but he looked mighty sick to me. Tubes crisscrossed his chest, and a beige solution from an IV bag trickled into his wrist. His usually glistening, milk chocolate skin, looked ashy, the color of dried leaves. Even his moles looked darker. Beads of perspiration dotted his forehead, despite the frigid temperature of the room. His every breath wheezed like Reverend Handley at the climax of his sermon.

I stood in the doorway and watched my parents sleep. I don't know when it happened, but sometime when I wasn't looking; my parents had gotten old. Mama's hair was pulled back and her white roots were showing. Daddy was aging gracefully like Paul Newman and Harry Belafonte, but today he didn't have his teeth in and he looked older than his seventy-seven years. The deep laugh lines in Mama's face showed clearly even now, when she wasn't laughing.

Daddy had never seemed old before. His hair was more salt than pepper, but at least he still had hair. He still drove, cut his own yard and was even known to wink at the ladies every now and then. He said there was no law against looking. The pillow seemed to swallow him up, and my father who rarely even caught a cold, now looked frail. I had always thought of my parents as a package deal and never considered having one without the other. They had been together so long most folks said their names, CWandLois, as if it was one word. I tiptoed across the room and kissed Daddy, then walked up to Mama and took the newspaper out of her hand that she had fallen asleep reading.

"Oh Chubby, it's so good to see you," she said softly as she sat up.

"How are you both doing?" I asked.

"We're doing okay. They may let him come home next week," she whispered.

"Mama, you've got to be tired. Why don't you let me stay tonight?"

"I'm okay, really. If I left, I wouldn't rest anyway. Why should I go home to an empty house? He might need something. He can't reach the call button and they take forever to answer when you do ring it. I need to be right here," she said as she adjusted his pillow and spoke softly. "C.W., Chubby is here to see you." He raised his twisted fingers and waved. I kissed the white stubble on his usually smooth cheek and wiped the sweat off his brow.

I joined Mama's vigil at Daddy's bedside, and we informed the steady stream of visitors of Daddy's condition. The doctor came and I interrogated him with a list of questions from Cecelia's list. By nine o'clock, they had removed some tubes and Daddy's breathing had quieted. Visiting hours were over, but Mama had no intention of leaving. She let the recliner back and I draped a hospital blanket over her.

"I'll be at Beverly's if you need me," I said and kissed her and Daddy before I left.

I noticed other couples as I walked toward the elevator. One lady was helping a man take baby steps down the hall. A man in 210C was helping the orderly change sheets. Visiting hours were over, so they must have been spouses like Mama, keeping an eye on their partners. Who would be there for me? I wondered, as I walked through the lobby. It was a depressing thought, but I knew the answer; no one. I have sisters, brothers, parents and other relatives, but they all had their own partners. I was dancing through life without a partner.

So I decided to dance while I had the chance. Warren may not be my permanent partner, but a dance can be fun even if you go stag. Why should I waste my life waiting for someone to ask me to dance? I realized that tomorrow is not promised. Daddy's roommate was only fifty and this was his second stroke. When I got home there were several messages from Warren. I called him and told him of my decision to live each day as though it were my last. I decided to stop waiting for my life to happen, and searching for Mr. Right. I decided to enjoy Mr. Right Now. I'm not saying, I relish being the "other woman". I was looking forward to spending part of the holiday with Warren. But on the bright side, I can use the day to catch up on work.

So rather than lament about Warren and Terri or worry about the money I spent to change my ticket, I'm going to focus on my family and enjoy my trip. At least the circumstances are happier than my last trip home. Daddy's last doctor visit was positive and he's back to his old self. I haven't been to a reunion in years and it may even be fun. Mama will have plenty of mouth-watering, calorie-laden delicacies to greet me. I'm getting out of the stifling heat of the city to a place with open spaces and fresh air.

I've been spending too much time thinking about Warren anyway. This Independence Day, I'm reasserting my independence. I've vacationed alone, don't mind eating alone in a restaurant and I have money in the bank. This is the twenty-first century and I don't need a man to make my life complete. I threw those magazines in the trash and headed to the gate, but I made sure my cell phone was on, just in case he called.

2

"Ouch, chile' you burning my edges! You may be grown, but I can still give you a lick or two."

"I'm sorry, Aunt Belle. I'm out of practice with this pressing comb. I'll be careful," Beverly said, as she sipped her Diet Coke. She made it a policy not to do relative's hair. She'd tell them she was booked and would refer them to Sharon or Tanya, her best stylists. Then they knew they weren't getting a free deal. She even stopped keeping supplies at home.

Aunt Belle never asked Beverly to do her hair. She called and *told* her when she would be in Memphis and what time she was coming to the salon. Then to top it off, she wanted a press and curl. Beverly could not convince her that relaxers today were milder than they used to be. Aunt Belle still remembered the perm she got in 1967 that took out all of her hair, and she was not ready to try one again. She wanted her hair hard pressed and curled in fifty small curls, like she'd had it done for the last fifty years. When Beverly's best friend Wanda opened a shop in Eden, Aunt Belle went a few times, but switched back to Beverly after Wanda accidently swept her feet with a broom as she sat under the dryer. She was upset for weeks, saying everybody knows its bad luck to sweep someone's feet. "I will go bald before I let that evil woman touch my head again. Her spirit is deceitful," Aunt Belle prophesied. Beverly asked Tanya to do Aunt Belle's hair once when she had several paying customers waiting. Tanya used a blow dryer and styled her silver gray hair with a side part and loose waves. The style showed off her almost wrinkle-free, bronze skin. But Aunt Belle had worn her hair in the same style for the past half century and saw no reason to change.

"I don't like that girl, and I don't want her to do my hair again. You need to watch that heifer, she's trying to take over."

"It looks pretty, you look ten years younger," Beverly said.

Aunt Belle replied, "At my age, ten years don't make that much difference," and demanded that Beverly press and recurl her hair.

Despite Aunt Belle's demands, Beverly enjoyed her visits. She didn't come to Memphis often and it was a way to get Mama and Daddy to venture out of Eden, since they usually brought her. Aunt Belle lived in Memphis during the 1950's with her second husband, a musician who never made it past the starving artist stage. She told countless stories about Beale Street and the musicians they knew who went on to become famous. Mama said Aunt Belle made up half of that stuff, but it was still entertaining.

Aunt Belle was our grandfather's youngest sister. She was just seven years older than Daddy, but she practically raised him. She helped Grandaddy Beau raise Daddy, Aunt Ethel, Aunt Pearl and Beau Jr. when their mother died in childbirth. She could be nosy and cantankerous, but she was also a trustworthy confidant with a sense of humor. She was a heavy-set woman with a laugh that seemed to emanate from deep within her chest. You found yourself laughing along with her, without even knowing what was funny. We relished her stories about Daddy's childhood.

Beverly didn't like to press hair, but like riding a bike, it all came back to her. The smell of the hot comb reminded her of singed hair, and Royal Crown grease. On Saturday nights, Mama's kitchen became a beauty salon and they all got their hair fixed, then tied it up in a scarf so it would still be straight for church. Beverly always wanted to be a beautician; or a salon owner, as she preferred to be called. As a teenager, she made extra money doing hair. She started pressing her mother and sisters' hair when she was only ten years old. They had long, thick hair. Beverly always wondered where she was when God was handing out hair to this family. Her hair never seemed to grow longer than four or five inches. Back in the day, if you weren't light-skinned, the least you could do was have a long head of hair. Being dark-skinned with short, nappy plaits was a curse. She missed out on the hair, but made up for it in the curves department. She was a tall, "healthy" girl and wore a C cup in the ninth grade. Healthy was the term black folks used to describe big-boned, thick-legged women. She took pride in the fellas' references to her as a "brick house". But at forty-three, her "brick house" was now a "barn". While the years had not been kind to her figure, her cocoa brown skin remained clear and smooth as velvet. When they were growing up and her sisters wanted to be extra mean, they teased and insulted her for being dark skinned. Now they were jealous of her ageless complexion. She had a new appreciation for Aunt Belle's declaration that "black don't crack". Remembrances of Aunt Belle's pearls of wisdom usually brought a beam to Beverly's spirit. But today, it would take more that a witty phrase to calm her troubled spirit.

"Girl, you burned me again," Aunt Belle cautioned. "Don't take your troubles out on my head."

"I'll be more careful," Beverly said, wiping her brow. The heat from the pressing comb was starting to heat up the salon. The weatherman predicted another day of triple-digit temperatures, and even at this early hour, the heat was relentless.

Aunt Belle held center stage, telling the three waiting customers of her days as a civil rights activist in Dwight County, when she and her third husband, registered folks to vote amidst threats from white folks. Her audience was so enthralled with the living history lesson, they didn't mind being patient while Beverly tried to do her customers, her stylists' customers and Aunt Belle. It was early and she already had customers backed up. "How in the world will I be able to leave here and go with Daddy to the airport to get Carolyn?" she wondered.

As Aunt Belle continued her storytelling, Beverly let her mind drift through the events of her morning. Her day started on a sour note and went downhill from there. She woke up mad, still seething from Anthony's late arrival the night before.

Beverly glanced at the clock when the garage door opening awakened her from a light sleep. The red digital display screamed 2:45. For the second night this week, Anthony had come home late. She turned her back to the door and didn't stir as Anthony slipped into bed. He began snoring within minutes.

Beverly was unable to go back to sleep and arose at sunrise. Not her usual considerate self, she turned on the lights, television and radio.

"Is all of that necessary?" Anthony grumbled as he pulled a pillow over his head.

"Maybe you wouldn't be so sleepy if you brought your behind home at night."

"Bev, don't start, okay? I've told you before, me and the guys hang out after work. A couple of drivers are on vacation, so I agreed to work their late shift. If I got off work at five o'clock and came home at seven that would be no big deal. So I get off at eleven and get home around one."

"Make that two forty-five. And it's a big deal because the only thing open at that time of the morning is legs and bars. You don't need to be in either one of them," Beverly retorted.

"Look, we've been through this before, just---"

"And I don't intend to go through it again."

"What does that mean? You're getting jealous and worked up over nothing," Anthony said calmly. "I tell you what. You pick me up from work tonight and we'll go out for a little while. We both deserve a break."

"Anthony, you know Carolyn is coming tonight. I'll probably be in Eden this evening. There's still a lot to do for the reunion."

"Well, if I can leave early, I'll come down there. But don't say I didn't ask," Anthony said and turned over.

Beverly slammed the door and went downstairs for a quick breakfast before going to the salon. She made coffee and poured cereal and Equal in her bowl, only to discover the skim milk had spoiled. She wrinkled her nose at the sour smell and poured the cereal down the garbage disposal. She grabbed her purse and went to the salon to do paperwork before opening. The phone was ringing when she walked in. It was Tanya; she had a toothache and probably wouldn't be in.

Then Raymond called and asked her to pick up some beer for the reunion. Raymond didn't drink and figured anybody that wanted liquor could bring his own. But Daddy said we should have some. Dwight County was dry, and beer was cheaper in Memphis anyway. So would she mind asking Anthony to stop and get some? "No problem," she replied.

No problem until Anthony called and said he wouldn't be coming to the salon today. A driver couldn't come in and Anthony was going to drive his route. Then he was going to help a friend move, so he wouldn't go to Eden until tomorrow.

"Why do *you* have to go?" Beverly asked. "Can't he find someone else to take his route? I'm sure if you told him your wife's family reunion was this weekend, he would understand. I need to help Mama and Raymond wants you to bring beer. Besides, I thought we could go together for a change."

Lately they had been more like roommates than husband and wife. When she was at the salon, Anthony was at work. He still maintained a full-time schedule as a bus driver, even though he now had a barber's license and worked in the salon. When he was at the salon, she taught classes at the beauty school. Saturdays in the salon were hectic and they barely saw each other since the barbershop was on the other side of the wall. Since Daddy's stroke, she spent most Sundays in Eden, and it was her only chance to see their son Tony, who was helping Charles with the farm. The salon was closed on Mondays, but Anthony was working, so they still didn't spend time together. They were doing well financially, and she had even repaid most of the small business loan Daddy had co-signed, ahead of time. Their business partnership was prospering, but the marriage partnership had hit a dry spell.

"Baby, we'll be down there all weekend, even Monday. I'll bring the beer to the fish fry tomorrow. I'll be tired tonight, after working all day. I'll get an early start and meet you down there tomorrow."

"Let me get this straight. You'll be too tired to sit around Eden, but not too tired to move furniture?" Beverly's voice was rising.

"Look, I need to get to work. I'll call you on my break. You can wait and go tomorrow with me, they'll survive. Gotta go." Anthony hung up before Beverly could respond.

Anthony was a bus driver and worked a split shift. His first shift was from eight in the morning until noon, and his second shift was from three until seven. Most of the drivers didn't like those hours, but they were perfect for Anthony. In between, he would come to the salon and cut hair. Lately, he was even working the late route, nine o'clock until eleven o'clock. Anthony said he didn't mind making money for sitting on his behind. He said the young guys were lazy and he would be happy to make the money if they didn't want it.

The next phone call was from Aunt Belle. She didn't even say hello. "Your Daddy is coming to Memphis today. He and Raymond will drop me off at your shop. We'll be there in a couple hours, baby."

"Yes, ma'am," Beverly said contritely. She had planned to go the airport, too. Daddy looked like he was fully recovered, but the idea of him driving around in Memphis during rush hour didn't sit too well with Beverly. At least Raymond was coming with him.

The next phone call was from Sharon. She was due in at ten o'clock, but would be late. Her baby's daddy didn't come home last night. She would try to catch up with her sister and get her to babysit. Could Beverly call her customers and reschedule? Sharon was one of those people always in a crisis. Either she was sick, or one of her kids was sick. Half the time her car wasn't running. When it *was* running, she let some sorry boyfriend use it and he was always late bringing it back. She was undependable, but she could work miracles with hair and her customers loved her. She could make Buckwheat's hair look good. Anthony kept telling Beverly to let Sharon go. He thought she was too country and unreliable, but Beverly wouldn't consider it. Sharon had been with her when she was working in her garage and had to choose between having lights or a phone. Sharon was loyal, and usually got along well with everyone. The last few weeks there had been tension between Sharon and Tanya, but Beverly attributed it to jealousy on Sharon's part because she had given Tanya more new customers. Beverly was just trying to ease Sharon's load, since she had a new baby.

Beverly usually understood when Sharon went through one of her crises. But she couldn't believe Sharon would leave her high and dry on the weekend of her reunion. Sharon was the one that convinced Beverly not to close for the weekend. Maybe Anthony was right. Sharon's ongoing problems were costing them time and money.

Beverly glanced at her watch and tried to quicken her pace. I hope I get caught up before Carolyn gets here, she thought. She hadn't seen Carolyn since October. They had been preoccupied with Daddy's health and hadn't spent much time together during that visit. Beverly was looking forward to seeing her brothers and sisters under happier circumstances.

Just as Beverly was starting one of Sharon's customers, she burst through the door. "Girl, I am so sorry. I know this is the worst possible day for me to be out. I got here as soon as I could. I brought the baby with me. He's still sleep, so I'm going to put him in the bed in the back room. He'll be good. I promise."

Beverly usually did not allow stylists to bring their children to work. It was distracting and unprofessional. But today she would have to make an exception.

"The devil is busy," Aunt Belle said. "He attacks at the weakest moment. We need to slow down and remember God is in control. No use hurrying and worrying, things work themselves out. Give me that baby," she said, taking him from Sharon.

That's easy for her to say, Beverly thought as she opened one of the Snickers bars in her drawer, and waited for Aunt Belle to sit back down. She doesn't have three customers sitting in the foyer tapping their feet. Or a husband helping someone move for the third time in a month. Maybe I need to find out exactly what he's moving.

3

"I'm sorry, I can't come back," Cecelia said as she unlocked her sister's condo. "I'm going out of town tonight and I still have errands to run. I'll be back Tuesday." Cecelia felt guilty as she put her cell phone in her Fendi bag. Her hair appointment wasn't until this afternoon, but she knew if she went in to work she wouldn't be able to get away. The oncology ward was already short staffed. Combine that with the weekend and the holiday, and Cecelia knew her coworkers had a hectic schedule ahead of them. She usually went in when her supervisor called. But she worked Christmas, New Year's and Memorial Day. Cook County Memorial Hospital would have to struggle through the Fourth of July without her.

Cecelia stepped into her sister's foyer and felt like she had just entered a furniture store showroom. A faint aroma of jasmine potpourri filled the air. The foyer floor was done in cream terrazzo tile. Then there were two steps down into plush white carpet. A cream butter leather sofa sat in front of a new cherry wood entertainment center. Glass end tables flanked the sofa and held Thomas Blackshear collectible figurines. If not for the doll collection that filled a rocking chair in the corner, you wouldn't know anyone lived here.

Why can't my house look this neat? Cecelia wondered as she inspected the entertainment center. She hadn't visited since Carolyn's new entertainment center had arrived. It definitely made the room look more elegant without an ugly television as the focal point. Cecelia made a note to ask her where she got it.

She usually visited more often but was still offended by remarks Carolyn made on her last visit. Cecelia had stopped by to repay the money she had borrowed.

"I have your five hundred dollars," Cecelia said. "But I would appreciate it if you'd let me hold two hundred of it until next week."

"Is something wrong?"

"It's not an emergency. Sheree made an appointment to get her hair braided tonight. I wanted her to wait until next week, but she acted like I was ruining her life. Seventeen year olds are so self-centered."

"Cece, don't take this the wrong way, but I'm worried about you," Carolyn said.

"What do you mean?"

"I know how much nurses in Chicago make and I can estimate how much your bills are. You shouldn't be having money problems."

"I'm not having money problems. This is only a slight cash flow crunch. If you don't want me to keep the money ---"

"The money isn't the issue. I just can't believe you don't have two hundred dollars to spare," I said.

"That's easy for you to say. All you have to worry about is Carolyn. It's different with a family to take care of. Children are expensive."

"Don't blame your kids. They aren't the problem."

"Just forget it. I don't need a lecture from you. It's nice to know who I can depend on."

"I'm not lecturing you. But I can see it plainly. You're getting hooked on gambling."

"Aren't you being a little extreme? Next, you'll want me to go to Gamblers Anonymous."

"That's a good idea. If you listen to their stories, they started out just like you. You need to stop now before it gets out of control."

"When I want your advice, I'll ask for it. Mind your own business," Cecelia said.

"Well, it is my business when my money is involved."

"Then keep your money." Cecelia placed five hundred dollar bills on the counter, picked up her purse and left.

Carolyn called to apologize the next day. "I just want what's best for you. You wouldn't believe the number of people that get into tax trouble because of gambling. I don't want that to happen to you."

"Don't worry," Cecelia said. "The casino is just a way for me to relax and forget my sick and suffering patients. I'm sorry for being so sensitive."

That was a month ago and neither mentioned it again. Their conversations centered on the upcoming reunion and their parent's property.

She looked in the breadbox and found the money her sister left for her. She knew service would be slow at the Friendly Payday Loan Office, and was relieved she didn't have to go there today. She pulled out her checkbook and wrote out her mortgage payment. She tore off the bottom of the bill and placed it in the envelope. She tore the top part of the bill in tiny pieces so no one could decipher the red past due warnings across the notice. As she licked the envelope, she calculated the days until the check would hit the bank. The holiday would give her one extra day, so the check wouldn't arrive until Tuesday. It would bounce on Wednesday and be represented on Friday, which was payday.

She had become adept at this juggling act. Her paycheck was three hundred dollars smaller now that deductions to repay loans from her 401K plan were being made. There just didn't seem to be enough money to go around anymore. But this time next week the pressure would be off. She would repay Carolyn and catch up on all of their bills.

Cecelia watered the plants then headed to her van. She pulled on her seatbelt, then remembered she hadn't checked Carolyn's mail. She dashed back and fished a phone bill, Money magazine and an envelope with what felt like a credit card out of the mailbox. She stashed them in her pocket and got back in the van. As she searched for her RayBan sunglasses she found a fifty-dollar coupon the casino had mailed her. It was only good from Thursday to Monday, for the Fourth of July weekend. She had curbed her casino visits since school was out and hadn't been in almost four weeks. She checked her watch, and calculated that she had three hours before her hair appointment. She decided to visit the casino for a couple hours to unwind and take advantage of their offer. "I'll start my vacation a little early. Maybe Lady Luck will welcome me back."

Going Home

4

"Thank you, Jesus," I mumbled under my breath as the plane sped down the runway, and screeched to a halt. Flying is one of my least favorite things to do. My head aches and my stomach turns flips from takeoff to landing. I trust the Lord and I know he has the whole world in his hands. I just feel better trusting him on the ground.

I felt someone grab my purse from behind as I stepped on the escalator. "Hey, what do you think you're . . . Raymond, I mean Malik!" I yelled as I whirled around and grabbed my chest. "Boy, don't play with me like that. You're going to give me a heart attack."

"Hey Carolyn, I couldn't resist." Raymond laughed and hugged me. "And I gave up on Malik. I got tired of trying to explain it to everyone. It's back to my slave name."

Raymond is between Beverly and Cecelia, but you would think he was the oldest. He is a walking black history book and the last holdover from the sixties. He took eight years to graduate from college and majored in black studies. Daddy couldn't understand why anyone would go to school eight years for a degree in something that wouldn't get you a job. Raymond ended up working for Chicago National Bank after they promised local groups they would hire more blacks and establish more branches in black neighborhoods.

"Well, whatever your name is, you were almost history. I could have been packing heat." I said, still holding my chest.

"They check for guns before you even get on the plane. Anyway, you're too scary to carry a gun," he said, as we reached the baggage area. "Looks like you dropped a few pounds. It looks good."

"Thanks. I'm glad to see you, but what are you doing here?"

"Mama sent me and Daddy to get you. She wanted to come, but said something about baking more pies," Raymond said.

"I specifically told her I didn't need anyone to meet me. I've reserved a rental car."

"You know your mother is the last of the big-time spenders. She said you can drive her car and save your money."

"I was planning to go straight to Beverly's before I drove home. She's going to do my hair."

"Sorry, I already have my orders. I took Daddy and Aunt Belle to Beverly's earlier. She complains that I never visit her, so we'll hang around while you get beautified. Then it's off to Eden," Raymond recited. "Let's go, madam, your carriage awaits."

"I appreciate your picking me up. But I'll be here almost a week, and I don't want to ask Mama for her keys every time I want to go somewhere."

"You're talking to the wrong person. Mama gave the orders. I followed them. Besides, you'll be in Eden, where can you go? I thought you were coming to see your family, not wander all over the countryside," Raymond said.

"I guess you have a point. There's not much going on in Eden. I just prefer to have my own transportation. Everyone else will want to use Mama's car too."

"Well, 'Miss Independent, I Can Pay My Own Way', since it means that much to you, you can rent my car. I'll drive my truck. I won't even charge mileage."

I punched him in the shoulder. "Rent? What happened to all that family jazz, you were talking a few minutes ago?"

"What can I say? I'm a bid'nessman."

Raymond handled Daddy's shiny black Sedan Deville with ease. It still had the new car smell. The car was Daddy's present to himself after the specialist referred him back to his family doctor. Daddy always said paying more than ten thousand dollars for a car was foolish. But, after the stroke he loosened the knot around the purse strings. He even took Mama to Hot Springs for their anniversary.

"Well have you come to your senses yet?" I asked. "Are you coming back to Chicago with me?"

"No way. You couldn't pay me to live in that rat race again. Eden is cool. It's a little slow, but I'm slow too, so it's a good fit. If I feel the urge to party, I'm just an hour from Memphis. The casinos book great entertainment. Anything I need, I can get at Walmart. If they don't have it, you don't need it. Plus I can always order off the Internet. I don't have to deal with snow and ice six months of the year, and I get to see Mama and Daddy all the time. What more could you ask for?" Raymond said sounding like the Chamber of Commerce. "I've visited Carl several times. I think I've been able to keep his spirits up. I've been helping to keep an eye on Tony too, trying to make sure he doesn't end up where Carl is. I like being close to family."

"So Cecelia and I aren't family?"

"You know what I mean. Cecelia has her own family to deal with. And you were always wrapped up in the boyfriend-of-the-month. We rarely saw each other. I miss my kids, but I'm building a future for them. I hope Geneva will let them come stay with me."

"What if she doesn't? You always said you'd never leave your kids."

"Things don't always turn out like you plan. Whatever happened to your law practice?"

I thought about Raymond's comments, as the Cadillac floated down the freeway. I looked out of the tinted windows as if seeing Memphis for the first time. Every time I come to Memphis I'm amazed at the city's growth. It is shaking off its segregated past and overcoming the stigma of the assassination of Dr. Martin Luther King Jr. The National Civil Rights Museum and the Smithsonian Rock and Soul Museum are tourist attractions that draw visitors from all over the country. When I was in law school, the airport was on the outskirts of town. Now the city has grown past the airport.

Some classmates and I had even talked about opening a law practice in Memphis. But by the time I graduated, I had so many student loans to pay, I could barely afford to open a bag of groceries, let alone a law practice. Maybe I would have found a husband if I had stayed here.

Raymond pulled into Beverly's driveway, but left the car running.

"Carolyn, wait before you get out. I need to talk to you. We may not have any time alone this weekend after this," he said as he turned off the Al Green CD.

"I'm almost afraid to hear it. It's Daddy, isn't it?"

"No, no, nothing like that. He's probably healthier than I am. Since I've been here, I've been involved in some exciting things. I've met some brothers who are serious and want to act, not just talk. Did you know the black farmer is almost extinct? There's no one coming along to take up where Daddy and Charles leave off. Not only are there no farmers; black people are losing their land."

"Oh, I know, I've seen hundreds of cases at work. People lose their land for unpaid taxes. Most of the time, it's a small amount of money, but heirs can't be located. The government gets it and some big corporation buys it at an auction for a fraction of its value. Or, the heirs fight over the land and end up paying twice the value of the land in legal fees."

"I knew you would understand. There's a group here interested in opening a bank. They want me to run it. We're soliciting investors now."

"Are you serious? That's fantastic. But is there enough black capital to sustain a financial institution in Eden?"

"We are an equal opportunity investment. We have a few white investors and the Shamir brothers, who own all the convenience stores between here and Dwight County have made pledges. We already have two million dollars committed and we're trying to raise three. Cousin Shawn and several of his teammates have promised to invest. You know he's with the Clippers now. I'm going to ask Paul to get some of his clients to invest. Most of the churches made pledges, even some white ones. The multinational banks are gobbling up the independent banks, freezing the small white guy out, too. They scale back services in small towns, keep the deposits and make very few loans. Can you believe there are four payday loan offices in Dwight County? Those are just a legal form of loan sharking. We're going to be a real bank, for local folks, run by local folks."

"Listen to you. You really have gotten involved in things around here. I'm happy for you Raymond, I hope it all works out."

"Well, I need a little bit more from you than good wishes. I want you to subscribe to some shares."

"I don't have that kind of money. You're talking about millions of dollars."

"You know, that's what we've had to tell people over and over. If we all put our little money together, we'll have big money. A former slave in Virginia opened the first black bank in 1889. The bank eventually reached over a million dollars in deposits! Now if they could do that back then, surely we can pull together now." Raymond reached under the center console and pulled out a large envelope. "Don't say "no" before you look at this," he said, handing me a large envelope. "This contains the business plan, feasibility studies, and state application."

"Raymond, I don't have that kind of money."

"Your money is green, isn't it?"

"You know what I mean. I used most of my savings to refinance my condo and I'm still paying credit cards that Carl ran up. I don't have a lot of money. What little I do have, I need to save. I don't have anyone looking out for me, but me."

"That's precisely why you need to get in on the ground floor. The people that started with Sam Walton and Bill Gates were set for life within ten years."

"That's different."

"What's different about it? Only difference I see is I'm black and they're white."

"Don't play the race card. Black or white, I'm not going to give thousands of dollars to people I don't even know. Who are these serious brothers you're talking about?"

"Their resumes are in the envelope. At least look at it."

"Daddy wants me to look at some papers for him this weekend. I don't know if I'll have time."

"My deadline isn't until the end of this month, so take it home with you. Please look at it. Then tell me it's a crazy idea and the numbers won't work. I won't accept "no" for an answer if you haven't even looked at it."

"Boy, you missed your calling. You should have been a salesman," I said as I put the envelope in my bag.

Beverly swung open the screen and ran through the door. "Hey you two! I thought Money was barking at that black cat that's been hanging around here. Aunt Belle almost wouldn't come in because she didn't want to cross it's path."

"I'm surprised you could even see a cat around here. Your grass is so tall, you'll need a machete to cut it," Raymond said.

"Tony was the gardener in this family. My yard hasn't been up to par since he left," Beverly said, waving him off and turning toward me. "Check out my baby sister. You look good," she said as she hugged me and spun me around. "I guess you see I didn't keep our New Year's resolution. You've lost weight and I found it."

Daddy was behind Beverly and I rushed to hug him. "It's so good to see you. You shaved your head!"

"If it's good enough for Michael Jordan, I figured it's good enough for me. Chubby, you look so thin. You haven't been sick, have you?"

"No Daddy. I finally decided to get rid of those extra pounds I've been carrying around."

"What did you cook?" Raymond asked. "I'm hungry and I know Carolyn didn't eat on the plane. Nowadays, you're lucky if they serve peanuts."

"I didn't cook today. Run over to the Fish Market and get some catfish for you all. I had Slim-Fast," Beverly said.

"Slim-Fast? You must have drank a six-pack," Raymond quipped, as he and Daddy got in the car.

"Very funny," Beverly said. "Come on in, Carolyn." Beverly led me past the scraggly hedges onto a screened-in patio next to the garage. "You can sit and catch your breath a minute before I start on your hair. You know I wouldn't do this for anyone but you. I have a strict rule about doing hair at the house. Once your relatives know you'll do their hair at home they begin to drop by unannounced, or want to make appointments before or after hours. Then they don't want to pay. So don't tell anyone I did this."

"I won't tell a soul. I could have come to the shop, though. I haven't seen it since you remodeled."

"I'm proud of it, but we're already outgrowing it. Now that Anthony is working with me, we need more space. I was hoping you could put in a good word with Daddy," Beverly said lowering her voice.

"What do you want me to do?" I asked.

"Well, Daddy cosigned my small business loan. Now, I want to move into a larger place and have it professionally designed. I've already been to the bank and even though I never missed a payment, they want Daddy to cosign again. Just mention it to him and see what he says."

"What would you do with the shop next door?" I asked.

"Anthony and Tanya can manage this shop. His clientele has really grown, but he doesn't want a second barbershop. So he'll stay next door. He won't be home until later. Too bad you'll miss him."

Yeah, too bad, I thought.

"I would take you to the salon, but I know after sitting on a plane the last thing you feel like doing is sitting in a beauty salon. Aunt Belle is over there getting in every body's business. We can have more privacy here, and you can tell me all about, what's his name. Is it Willie?" Beverly said. "Mama says you may be getting married."

"Mama is in denial. She doesn't want to accept me being single. Warren and I aren't that serious. We have an understanding."

"Well, I bet that was his idea. 'Understanding' in man language means he's free to do what he wants to do, while you sit around and wait on him. I'll tell you what I told Tanya," Beverly said as she massaged my scalp. "Get a new hair do, or rent some comedy videos. Don't sit around waiting on him. Tanya and her boyfriend broke up a few months ago and she was pitiful. I took her shopping and we started working out together just to get her out of the house. She's much better now."

"I'm not sitting around. I know not to build my life around a man. And if I remember, Tanya was very pretty. Men like petite women. She'll find someone soon," I said as I closed my eyes and sat back in the chair.

"She's been a godsend. I've started teaching classes at the beauty college and Tanya can run the place like it's her own. I was gone a lot when Daddy was sick. Sharon was on bed rest, so she was out. Can you believe her old behind had another baby? Her kids are almost grown, but she met this man and he never had any children. They eloped and she was pregnant within two months. I tell you what, I won't be having any more kids, I don't care if I meet Denzel Washington, Shemar Moore and Billy Dee rolled into one. Anyway, Sharon was out. Tanya worked my clients, hers *and* Sharon's. She was practically at the shop from sunup to sundown. She and her boyfriend were just breaking up, so I think that was her way of dealing with it. She's overcome a lot of setbacks and is a determined young lady. You know it's hard to find good workers. I don't know why black folks are so trifling."

As if on cue, Raymond appeared in the doorway. "I know I didn't hear what I think I heard. Black folks worked free for two hundred years. Now you want to complain because you can't find someone highly motivated to transform naturally curly, Nubian hair into stringy, white folks hair?"

"Raymond, you need to quit. I don't see you wining and dining no nappy-headed women. I heard you were dating Gloria Stewart. She's the lightest thing in Eden. Now that I think about it, Geneva is high yellow, too. You are color struck."

"I am not color struck and what does skin color have to do with anything?" Raymond asked.

"My point exactly. Trifling is trifling. I just happen to deal with trifling black folks. I'm sure there's some white beauty salon owner somewhere complaining about her trifling white staff. Sometime I think it was easier when it was just me doing hair in my kitchen."

"You're in the wrong end of the business anyway. Vertical integration is the solution to the black man's economic problems," Raymond said, as he searched her refrigerator.

"Newsflash, we already had the civil rights movement. And what did integration get us?" Beverly said.

"Girl, you need to read something other than the *Enquirer,*" Raymond said. "You all are cannibalizing each other by putting a beauty shop on every corner. You need to open a beauty supply business and get all the beauticians to buy from you, instead of from foreigners. Vertical integration is an economic strategy that establishes a network of linked businesses ---"

"There you go throwing that college stuff in my face," Beverly said. "You think you're so smart."

"This doesn't have anything to do with college. Stop being so touchy about everything. I'm just trying to tell you ---."

"Memphis sure is growing," I interjected to change the subject.

"Sometimes I think it's growing too much," Beverly said. "Traffic and crime are getting really bad."

"Well, it's still ten times better than Chicago. I don't know how I lived there so long," Raymond said.

"Don't start bashing Chicago," I said. "I followed you up there after you said Chicago was "the place to be." And what do you do? Desert me."

"I still like Chicago, in the summer, but this southern hospitality will spoil you. Coming home has been the best thing I ever did. Have you thought about moving home?"

"No way. Believe me, the thought of going back to Eden has never crossed my mind."

"I understand the prospect of not being within five minutes of a mall is unsettling to you. But you could move to Memphis. It takes just as long to get here from Eden as it took to drive across Chicago. I know Mama and Daddy would be thrilled."

"Some of my biggest tippers are lawyers, so I know they do well," Beverly said. "You could open your own office like you always wanted to."

"I don't think private practice is for me."

"Well, the IRS has an office here," Raymond said as he soaked his fish in hot sauce. "Just think about it. There are drawbacks to being near family, but the good outweigh the bad. I think Daddy's considering selling the farm. If you were here, he may feel more of us are interested in keeping the farm."

"But Daddy always said he would never sell his land," I said.

"I think he always planned for Charles to take over. And now he wants me to work with Charles. When I told him I didn't think Charles and I were a good team, he said maybe he should sell."

"Why can't you and Charles work together? He can probably teach you a lot. Mama told me Charles was doing such a good job since Daddy had been sick. According to her he should win 'Farmer of the Year'."

"Well, Mama doesn't know the whole story. With Charles at the helm, Daddy has lost thousands of dollars. Daddy always presells part of his crop at the beginning of the season to Jackson Grocers. He said they offer him a lower price, but its insurance against prices falling, which they have. Charles didn't do that this season. Then, Charles tried to fix the irrigation pipes himself. Now they need to be replaced. The lights were even cut off because Charles forgot to pay the bill while Daddy was in the hospital. He does a good job with the help and the crops, but there's more to farming these days than planting seeds and praying for rain. You almost need a P.H.D. just to deal with the paperwork and technology. Charles is my brother, and I love him, but he doesn't have the business acumen to run an operation like Daddy's."

"Have you discussed these things with Charles?" I asked.

"I've tried. I showed him software that produces detailed maps that pinpoint which plots need more fertilizer, herbicide or pesticide. It tracks yields by acre and monitors irrigation. Charles dismissed me and said you can't use a computer to run a farm. He thinks I'm trying to sabotage him and take over."

"Charles has also been spending a lot of money," Beverly said, as she opened a Diet Coke. "He bought a new tractor while Daddy was sick. Not just any tractor; a new John Deere with the enclosed cab and air conditioning. Those things cost over fifty thousand dollars."

"We suggested that to Daddy years ago. He always said being outside was part of being a farmer, and if you wanted air conditioning to stay in the house," I said.

"Cecelia says Daddy should sell the land. She wants us to talk to Daddy about it this weekend," Beverly said.

"We can't let him do that. If more of us were involved, Daddy would be less likely to consider selling out. Black people will never prosper if we don't own land. The black family must come together if our people . . . "

I nodded my head as Raymond began one of his soliloquies on the future of the black race. My reasons for considering a move to Memphis were not as noble as the uplifting of the race or saving the family farm. I could get a raise and make a clean break from Warren. I made a mental note to start watching the job postings for the Memphis office again. My heavy eyelids closed as the cool water soothed my tender scalp.

"Okay, tell me what you think!" Beverly said, as she wheeled me around to face the mirror.

"Beverly, you said *trim*. You scalped me!" Curls framed my face, and she tapered the back to the nape. My hair had been a comfortable shoulder length that gave me several options on bad hair days.

"This works better for you," Beverly said. "I layered your hair and added copper highlights to brighten your face and camouflage the gray that's peeking out around your hairline. After a certain age, short hair looks better on a woman. This haircut and your weight loss make you look ten years younger."

"I guess I'll get used to it," I said eyeing my hair from all angles in the mirror. "And it *will* be low maintenance. But that's not the point. Say the words 'cut' or 'trim' within earshot of a beautician, and the scissor demon takes over. If you weren't my sister, I could sue you."

"If I weren't your sister, I'd let you continue to walk around with that old Aunt Jemima hairdo. You'll thank me when the men start beating a path to your door."

Daddy came in from the patio where he, Raymond, and Aunt Belle were watching a Braves game. "I hate to cut your time short, but we need to be moving on," Daddy said. "I want to get home before dark. I don't like to leave your mama alone at night."

"I'm ready. We better get out of here before I'm as bald as Daddy," I said as I brushed hair off my collar.

As we were leaving, Aunt Belle picked some of my hair off the floor and carefully packed it in a tissue. "Chubby, you keep this and when you find the man you're sure you really want, put this under his bed or under one of his rugs and he'll be yours," she confided, pressing the hair into my hand.

"Aunt Belle, I doubt this will do the trick, but I'll save it in case I'm ever in Morris Chessnut's house."

"You'd be surprised how many of my customers want to save a piece of their hair," Beverly added.

"I bet they don't have problems getting no man, either," Aunt Belle said, reaching for her cane. "You'd better listen to your elders. I can tell you how to get a husband. I done buried four of them."

I wasn't sure if that was an enviable endorsement or not. But to humor her, I put the tissue in my purse. What could it hurt?

5

We finally left Memphis around 8:30. Eden is ordinarily a fifty-minute ride, but Aunt Belle insisted Raymond drive just under the speed limit and not pass any cars.

The last twenty-five miles were on a two-lane road. Drooping power lines on old-fashioned utility poles flanked the highway. This road paralleled the Mississippi River along the Arkansas side of the Delta and intersected with back-roads that led to woods that only residents dared venture in to. Some woods hid juke joints that offered Daddy and his generation their only recreation from a slave-like existence. They worked from sun up to sun down, six days a week to make others rich. They *lived* the blues. All Daddy's friends claimed they were in Twist, Arkansas when the fight broke out over Lucille, the namesake of B.B. King's guitar. Never mind, that the place couldn't have held that many people. The King Biscuit Flour Hour radio show broadcast the blues all over the South and it originated right up the road in Helena, Arkansas.

Daddy and Aunt Belle reminisced about the heyday of the blues as Raymond inched above fifty-five miles per hour. "Slow down, boy. Everything will still be there when we arrive. We don't want to get the police on our tail. They see black folks riding in a fancy, new car like this and they'll stop you just for sport," she said.

"That doesn't go on anymore, does it?" I asked.

"Not as much. But you still have some racist police out there. Sheldon County is the worst. Tony was pulled over there," Daddy said.

"I heard about that. It didn't help that he was speeding and had beer in the car. He was just asking for trouble," I said.

"Wait a minute," Raymond said. "You mean he asked to get his head bashed in? If he was wrong give him a ticket, or call his Daddy. That's what they do for the white boys they catch joyriding."

"The boy took Daddy's new car, without permission, and, he was drinking and driving. It's probably a blessing that they stopped him. He could have had an accident," I said.

"He had an accident all right. His black face ran into a white fist. They had no right to touch him. I wish Beverly and Anthony had pressed charges," Raymond said.

"Pressed charges for what? That would be a waste of money. Why bother with lawyers, when Tony was wrong?" I asked.

"We have two lawyers in the family. You or Paul could have handled it."

"Take my name out of that. Tony has been in and out of trouble and Beverly is always bailing him out. He's going to end up just like Carl. If someone had beat some sense into Carl, maybe he wouldn't be locked up today. I think Tony got what he deserved."

"The Lord has a way of fixing things. Maybe that beating was the Lord's way of getting Tony to see he was heading down the wrong path," Aunt Belle said.

"No disrespect ma'am, but you have been brainwashed. What kind of God would subject a person to that? And what kind of God would put Carl in jail for an illness? If that's your God, you can have him," Raymond said.

"Watch your mouth boy," Aunt Belle warned. "Don't go questioning God. He takes care of us, but he also gives us a free will to make decisions. Carl made some bad decisions and now he has to live with them."

"Maybe I should have gotten a lawyer from Memphis or Little Rock."

"C.W. you done all you could," Aunt Belle said.

"But Carl said he wasn't involved in the robbery. He was only---."

"Daddy, please. Jails are full of innocent people, to hear them tell it. You know good and well Carl was there. He wasn't hanging with a bad crowd. He *was* the bad crowd."

"Carl was a good boy," Daddy said quietly. "He just got on that dope and it changed his whole personality. He forgot who he was."

Carl is my younger brother. He's two years older than Paul, but you would think he was the baby of the family. Carl had rheumatic fever as a child and was near death. He was on medication for years and Mama and Daddy spoiled him. Carl had no chores, always had money and didn't make the grades Mama and Daddy demanded from the rest of us. He eventually grew out of his illness and excelled in sports. He and our cousin Shawn led Lincoln High School to their last state championship. We should have known Carl was heading for trouble, the signs were there. But it wouldn't have mattered if Carl was Attila the Hun reincarnated. Daddy couldn't see it.

"You're right Daddy. This is supposed to be a joyful reunion. We shouldn't dwell on the past. Let's change the subject," I said.

"So we just throw Carl away?" Raymond said. "If the person doesn't meet our approval, we act like they don't exist? That is so hypocritical."

Raymond, like Daddy, always had a soft spot for Carl. He was devastated when Carl went to prison and Raymond felt partially responsible. Raymond gave Carl his first joint when they were in high school. Carl always did everything his big brother did. Raymond's drug use was a passing phase, but it became part of Carl's life. He snorted cocaine, graduated to freebasing cocaine and the last stop on his ride to self-destruction - crack.

His heart murmurs resumed in college and he had to stop playing basketball. He got married, moved to Little Rock, and had three boys. He hid his addiction well and maintained what we saw as a normal life. A licensed plumber, he made good money and tried to get Raymond to give up his shirt and tie and come work for him and make some 'real money'. We suspected he was using drugs, but Carl appeared to have things under control, so we looked the other way. Eventually, his facade crumbled when crack won the battle for his soul. His wife had to hide her money and anything else of any value. She said the last straw was Christmas morning when she found Carl had pawned the boy's bikes and video games. She changed the locks, packed his clothes, got a restraining order and filed for divorce.

Carl stayed away about a month, then came back to claim his territory. He couldn't get in the door, so he broke a window. His wife knew the restraining order wasn't worth the paper it was written on, so she had a human restraining order waiting for him. Her brothers met him and whipped him like he was a child. They called Daddy to come get him, and warned the next time he tried to break in they might kill him. It was not an idle threat. Carl's in-laws were a large, tight-knit family and didn't take no mess. Daddy and Charles brought him back to Eden where he worried Mama and Daddy. Raymond eventually went and got him and brought him to Chicago. It was harder to get in the plumber's union in Chicago and Carl seemed to give up. It wasn't long before he ended up back in Arkansas and in Cummins prison.

"Well I think Cummins saved Carl's life. I don't say that lightly, because my second husband spent some time there and I know it ain't no picnic. That boy was headed for an early grave from dope, or getting shot trying to rob somebody. Everybody said Mama Mary was just old and forgetful, and she couldn't remember where she put her billfold. But she swore Carl stole it from her pocketbook, and she was right. Only reason he didn't go to jail then was because it was family," Aunt Belle said.

"How can you say that? If it weren't for racist sentencing, he wouldn't even be in jail. Did you know the penalties for crack are ten times more severe than for the same amount of powder cocaine? That's because more blacks are sentenced for crack use."

"Raymond, don't blame it on racism. No one made him use crack," I said.

"Paul and I are going to visit him this weekend," Raymond said. "His parole hearing was postponed until September. But Paul says he may be able to get the sentence reduced."

"I'm glad to hear that," Daddy said. "We don't know why things happen, but Carl is still your brother."

"Do you want to go with us, Carolyn?" Raymond asked.

"I'll let you know," I lied. I had no intention of visiting Carl. I feel bad about his situation, but it's a situation he created. He has no excuse. I know drug addiction is an illness, but nobody made him do drugs. He didn't grow up poverty-stricken or in a drug-infested neighborhood. Daddy was the best role model you could ask for. Carl had more opportunities than any of us and he threw them away. He took advantage of everyone, including me. What he's done to Mama and Daddy is selfish and I can't forgive him for that. Mama and Daddy have both aged ten years in the three years he's been in jail. He broke Mama and Daddy's hearts and they haven't recovered yet.

"So, you couldn't get Mama to come for the ride?" I asked.

"No, she was busy making sweet potato pies. We have enough food for an Army, but she said Paul always looks for her pies, so she wanted to make sure she had extra," Daddy answered.

"When is Paul getting here?" I asked.

"They're taking the last flight tonight," Raymond answered. "They should be arriving shortly. He and Julia are renting a car, so they don't need to be picked up."

"He's bringing Miss Ann with him?" I asked.

"Yes, he's bringing his wife and I expect you to make her feel welcome," Daddy admonished. "This is a family reunion and we want everyone to feel at home and have a good time."

"Of course, Daddy, I wouldn't dream of upsetting Miss Ann."

"That's what I mean. I didn't raise you like that. Just because some white folks is bad, we don't reject the whole race. Now, her name is Julia. You wouldn't want her family to call Paul, Sambo."

"I'm sure they call him much worse than that."

"Actually, Paul says they've been to visit her family several times and they get along well. I met them at the wedding and they seem like nice people."

"Don't worry Daddy, I won't embarrass Paul. I can't help how I feel, but I will be civil," I said.

Now, I'm not prejudiced. I believe love can be color-blind and we're all God's children. But as a Black woman, I am disappointed. It's like discovering your Dad cheated on your Mother, or having your sister-in-law tell you how trifling your brother is. It's just so typical. If Paul was working at the paper mill, she wouldn't have looked at him twice.

Paul is the baby of the family. Like Carl, he was a talented athlete and went to college on a basketball scholarship. He was the first in the family to graduate from the white high school and always mixed well in both worlds. He played for a CBA team, but got cut when he hurt his knee. When Shawn went to play for the Clippers, he invited Paul to live with him while he rehabbed his knee. Paul went to Los Angeles, but gave up on basketball and decided to go to law school. He and Miss Ann met while they both worked for an entertainment law firm.

"I bet H. Rap Raymond had a fit when Paul delivered the news. What's your opinion about your new sister-in-law?" I asked.

"I don't have too much to say about who a brother sleeps with. He's grown. It's what he does when he's on his feet that concerns me. In fact, my experience with black women hasn't been that good, so I say go with the one that's going to help you be your best," Raymond said.

"Now who is being hypocritical?" I asked.

"That's a woman thing, equating sex with everything. Thomas Jefferson and our esteemed founding fathers had no problem sleeping black, while they profited from black labor. Our problem is economic. Sex is not the issue."

"Raymond, you need to quit. Our so-called founding fathers raped us. We had no choice. Paul had a choice and he chose Miss Ann."

"All right you two," Daddy interjected. "You haven't been together one hour and you're already at it. This is a family reunion, not Family Feud."

This family reunion business is way overrated, I thought. Miss Ann was pissing me off already and I hadn't even met her. Carl was still causing confusion in the family from behind bars. Raymond was trying to make me feel guilty because I didn't want to entrust him with my life savings. And Beverly chopped off all my hair.

"Glad we're finally here. Drop me off at Mr. Ben's house," Aunt Belle said as we entered Dwight County and passed cousin Booker T's barbeque stand.

"All right now young lady," Daddy said. "You and Mr. Ben are getting mighty cozy. I need to talk to him to see what his intentions are. I want to make sure he's a good man."

"Any man my age is a good man," Aunt Belle said.

"Who is Mr. Ben?" I asked.

"He's my new neighbor," Raymond said. "His wife died last summer. He came to visit his niece for Christmas and she talked him into staying with them."

"So he's your new boyfriend, huh?" I asked Aunt Belle. "Do I need to have *the talk* with you?"

"You hush chile'," she said with a smile, as she got out of the car.

We turned off Main Street, crossed the railroad tracks and quickly reached the western edge of town. There were no streetlights, but I knew the way blindfolded. Spaces between houses increased and our house was the last one on Route 4, before the road curved and ran into the highway.

Raymond honked at Champ, who stood in the middle of the driveway barking at us. Champ was Grandmother Jean's dog, and Mama and Daddy took him in when she died. Daddy complained the dog was too spoiled and couldn't hunt. But it was obvious he was still a good watchdog.

"It's about time you got here," Mama said as I stepped on the porch. "I was starting to worry."

"Aunt Belle made Raymond drive so slow I thought we'd never get here," I said, giving her a tight hug.

"Come on and eat. I know Beverly doesn't hardly cook anymore, so you must be hungry."

I dropped my bags on the bed and followed the smell of nutmeg to the kitchen. Mama had cooked my favorite meal - chicken and dumplings. Dumplings were a no-no on my maintenance diet. But, I didn't want to hurt her feelings, so I made the sacrifice and ate. I sacrificed again and ate a slice of sweet potato pie, still warm from the oven. Once Paul arrived there would be no chance for leftovers.

"I haven't been home two hours and I'm already breaking one of my rules. No eating after seven at night," I said as I licked my fingers.

"I'm glad to see you eat," Mama said. "You have lost too much weight."

"If I'm not careful, I'll gain it all back at this one meal. I am stuffed."

"I was worried about you. Cecelia told me that you were losing weight. A little is okay, but I see girls on TV that die from not eating. You know Erica's daughter had that anoreck. Little thing wasn't big as a broom."

Erica Kane, on All My Children, is like another member of the family. Mama religiously watches soap operas, or 'stories' as she calls them. She didn't have much use for most of the presents we bought her. The lace nightgowns, designer perfumes and housecoats were packed away, saved for some unnamed special occasion. The blender, answering machine, coffeemaker, and crock-pot were all in the cabinet in their original boxes until she 'needed' them. The one gift she did enjoy was a small, portable television that she kept in the kitchen and moved to the porch or the quilting room. She could do her work and still keep up with Erica, Vicki, Monica, Montel and Oprah. She didn't care for prime-time shows, other than wrestling, but we were all on a first name basis with the characters in her daytime shows.

"Mama, I doubt if I am at risk of developing anorexia. I like to eat too much. In fact, that's my problem."

"Well then, we have come a long way. I can remember a time when getting enough to eat was a problem."

"Mama, I don't ever remember a time when we didn't have enough food. We didn't have a lot of junk like the kids do now. Potato chips and candy were special treats, and we only had Kool-Aid on Sundays. But we never missed a meal."

"No, you didn't have to worry about food. Your Daddy always kept the refrigerator and freezer full. Now, when I was growing up things were different. We didn't go hungry or miss a meal either. But we didn't eat meat every day, and dinner may have been a pot of beans or rice. And we were glad to have it. Apples, oranges and cheese were treats reserved for Christmas. If things were tight at our house, Mama Mary always had something to eat. If Mama Mary didn't have it, Miss Millie next door did. And, when she was low, she was welcome at our house. Folks were more helpful to each other then. When Aunt Clara took sick, Larry and his sisters stayed with us. We thought skinny folks were sickly, and people *wanted* to carry a little extra weight on them."

"Mama, I have enough extra weight to hibernate the whole winter. I can't eat like this every day that I'm here," I said setting my plate in the sink.

"Let me do that," Mama said. "Go on and get yourself settled. I changed the sheets in your old room and moved Tony's clothes to the front closet so you can put your things in there. I'm going to wash these few dishes."

"Mama, I was going to stay at the motel."

"Child, you know we want you to stay here with us."

"But there will be so many people here this weekend. The house will be crowded."

"We got couches, and we can make pallets on the floor for anybody that wants to stay here. But this is my children's home and your beds are always here for you. Besides, if Ethel Fay and Henry think we have extra space, they'll be trying to stay here and I don't want to be bothered with them. Go on to your room. And get the door on your way, I hear someone knocking. It's probably Paul and Julia. He should know it's not locked."

I really don't feel like being Miss Ann's welcoming party, I thought. "Come on in Attorney Washington," I said as I opened the screen door, expecting to see Paul. It was dark on the porch, but I knew it wasn't Paul. This was a figure I didn't recognize, although I had to admit it was a nice-looking figure.

"Hi Carolyn. I see Chicago agrees with you," he said.

It's always frustrating when someone knows you and addresses you like you should know them. I couldn't place which cousin this was.

Just then we heard footsteps on the porch. "I hear a sweet potato pie calling my name," Paul said as he opened the door for his wife. "Hey, Derrick, how did you beat me here?"

"You went the long way and got caught by the train. You've been gone so long, you've forgotten the shortcuts."

"After driving in L.A., nothing around here will seem like the long way. Can you believe this, Carolyn? I ran into Derrick at the gas station. Oh, excuse my manners. Carolyn, I want you to meet Julia."

"Nice to meet you," I quickly said to Julia. "Derrick? Otherwise, known as Bucky?" I said incredulously.

"No fair. I didn't call you Chubby."

"Sorry about that. I didn't recognize you." The years hadn't added many pounds to his six-foot frame. His hairline was receding slightly, and showcased his smooth mahogany skin, trim goatee and mustache. He had retired his black, plastic-frame, coke-bottle eyeglasses for sleek gold, designer frames.

Derrick lived down the road from us when we were growing up. He was an only child, raised by his grandmother. He and Carl were classmates, and both tagged behind Raymond. Daddy always included him on hunting outings or other male activities. He was like family. It was bad enough that I had two younger brothers to pester me, with Derrick, I had an extra pest.

He was two years younger than me, which seemed like a lifetime back then.

"I don't know whether that's good or bad," Derrick said, his smile showcasing a perfect set of teeth. No trace of the trademark overbite for which he was named was evident.

"It's good. You used to be . . . I mean . . . "

Luckily, Mama and Daddy came in to save me from putting my foot further in my mouth. "Well, what have we here?" Mama said as she hugged everyone. "All my children are coming home. Even Bucky is here. Carolyn, can you believe this is Bucky?"

"It's been a long time," I said as I extended my hand to his.

"It sure has," he said.

"I know you can do better than that," Mama said. "You two were raised almost like brother and sister. Give him a hug Carolyn."

Derrick pulled me toward his broad, firm chest. It wasn't a brotherly hug.

6

Memphis 489 miles. "What a depressing sign," Cecelia said as she pushed her rimless Ralph Lauren glasses up on her nose. "Just as you've left the city lights and settled in for the drive down home, that sign taunts you and reminds you how far you have to go. I should have followed my first plan and flown to the reunion like we always do. Driving is so tacky. All we need now is fried chicken."

"It will be fun, Cece. Since we're not in a hurry, we can stop along the way. Maybe even get a motel room. Remember the diner in Carbondale that had the fluffy pancakes? If it's still open, let's stop there," Michael said.

"I see nothing fun about driving thirteen hours after working all night, then packing all evening because your hardheaded children didn't wash and pack the right clothes. I thought the whole point of driving was to save money. If we stop at a motel, we need two rooms since Rayven and Malcolm are with us. It's better to drive while the kids are sleep, it will be cheaper and more peaceful. If we stay at a motel, we'll have to buy breakfast and lunch tomorrow. That defeats the whole purpose of driving to save money. Besides, we used to stop in Carbondale to avoid problems farther south. From Cairo on to Memphis was not too much better than Mississippi for black folks."

"Mama, it's not like that now. Lots of kids from my school go to the University in Carbondale. It has one of the largest black populations of any state school. I'm thinking about going there," Sheree informed them. "If it's daylight when we go through there, can we visit the campus? It's on the way."

"Girl, I know that campus has a reputation as a party school. I'm paying for you to get an education, not to party."

"Mama, you always assume the worst. If you're worried about me partying, why not send me to a convent?"

"Don't tempt me," Cecelia responded. "Honey, my head feels like someone is pressing my temples with a vise. Can we talk about this later? We'll keep Carbondale on our list of schools, but I think another school may have more to offer you."

"Whatever." Sheree answered and turned to look out the window at the black shadowy landscape.

"Maybe we should tour the campus," Michael said. "The college guides say it's a good idea to visit several campuses. She wouldn't have to pay out-of-state tuition at Carbondale."

"Michael, why do you do that? You heard me tell the girl I thought she should consider other schools. Then you go against me and make me look like the bad guy. Did any of those books tell you parents should present a united front?" Cecelia asked, as she adjusted her seat to a reclining position. He knows we don't have money to send her way down there to school. I planned to steer her to a school near Chicago, she thought. She had a plan to get Sheree's college money, but she hadn't told Michael yet.

"Excuse me for having an opinion. It's obvious you are determined to be a drag on this trip. This is my last vacation this year, so I plan to have a good time. Why don't you go to sleep? Maybe you'll feel better after you get some rest," Michael said.

"Maybe I'd feel better if you had helped me get ready. I asked you to get the kids packed and go to the bank before I got home, and you didn't do either one. I had to do the dishes, because Sheree didn't get around to it and I left my watch and rings on the counter. I feel naked without my jewelry. I only asked you to do a couple things to help me out. I should have known I couldn't depend on you."

Sheree and her brother, Mike, exchanged glances as their parents resumed their incessant bickering. Mike put on his headphones to drown out their familiar tones.

"Well, I had a few things to do, too. These kids are old enough to do their own packing. The line at the bank was too long, so I figured we could stop at an ATM machine on our way out of town. You know what it's like at the bank, before a holiday weekend. I didn't know you wanted me to make a deposit, too," Michael explained in a controlled voice.

"I told you to deposit your check before two o'clock. Our checks will be bouncing like rubber by the time we get back." Cecelia took two pills out of her Christian Dior coin purse.

"We'll cover them when we get back. I'll go to the bank myself first thing Tuesday morning," Michael said.

Cecelia wished it were that simple. She mailed their American Express and Discover bills by next day mail yesterday, to make sure they arrived today, the final due date. She knew she was cutting it close, but planned to cover those checks with Michael's paycheck. They were bumping the limit on the other cards and she wanted the American Express card available for the trip. She had hoped only the mortgage payment would bounce. Good thing she had run by the casino. She initially turned her fifty-dollar coupon into six hundred fifty dollars. Then she hit a dry run and was down to the last fifty Carolyn had given her before her luck turned again. She was back up to four hundred when she had to leave for her hair appointment. Her winnings, plus the money she borrowed from Carolyn should be enough for the trip.

Michael reached for her hand. "Let's leave the bills and worries in Chicago, and enjoy the ride and the reunion." He fumbled through the center console for a CD. "This will relax you." Smokey Robinson and the Miracles Anthology was one of her favorites.

"I *know* I'm going to sleep, now," Sheree said. "Do we have to listen to that old stuff?"

Michael feigned a heart attack a la Fred Sanford. "Forgive her Lord, she's young. Little Girl, you don't know what good music is. That junk you listen to is almost pornographic. The only stuff worth listening to is remakes of the old music."

Michael and Sheree debated the merits of rap and hip-hop vs. rhythm and blues. Somewhere along the way the suburbs turned to farms and stretches of nothingness. Mike fell asleep before they reached Kankakee. Rayven and Malcolm were asleep, too. Cecelia put her head back and reveled in the crooning of 'Baby Baby Don't Cry' and 'Second That Emotion'. Too bad they can't put Smokey in a bottle. A surefire way to get rid of a migraine, she thought.

Michael was always able to calm her. That was one of the things she liked about him when they were dating. He had that "What? Me, Worry?" attitude that complimented her high-strung personality. Part of it was his faith. His credo was 'Worry, don't pray. Pray, don't worry.' Cecelia would rant and rave. Michael would just say, "It'll work out" and go on about his business. He was usually right. Things worked out and the consequences were never as dire as Cecelia predicted.

Her headache was dissipating, but Cecelia still couldn't sleep. Michael thought she was asleep when he switched to a Ramsey Lewis CD. We've been so concerned with the day-to-day bills; we haven't considered money for Sheree to go to college. It always seemed so far away. I thought we would have time to save. Now, she's a senior in high school and we have less than two thousand dollars in the bank. The government will say we make too much money for financial aid and the bank will deny our student loan because our credit is weak. Why can't we ever get ahead? Cecelia wondered.

They had an attractive two-story home, a car and a van, and took vacations every year, but Cecelia wanted more than that. It didn't help that Michael was talking about changing jobs again. He'd been with AT&T eight years, the longest tenure he had with any employer. In the eighteen years they had been married, he had been an insurance adjuster, a cable installer, computer salesman, and clothing store manager. They were good jobs and he was always employed. But they were entering their 40's and it was time to start thinking about retirement and stability. As she tried to sleep, thoughts of bills, money and more bills swirled in Cecelia's head like a trailer in a tornado.

"Daddy, can you stop at the next station? I need to use the restroom," Sheree announced.

"Are you sure you can't wait?" Cecelia asked. "We've barely been gone an hour."

"I'm sure, Mother, I know when I have to go. I'm not a kid."

"I made the kids use the bathroom before we left. Looks like I should have included you in that ritual. I see I can forget about getting any rest. As soon as we stop, everyone will probably wake up," Cecelia said, sitting back up.

"Why do you make such a big deal out of everything? I can't help it if I have to pee. You should have left me at home like I asked, then you wouldn't have to be bothered with me."

"What's the point of going to a family reunion, if you don't bring your family?" Cecelia asked.

"Mama, we see the same people every year. They have some tired fashion show or dinner. Uncle Nap tells some tired jokes and they have a tired picnic or barbecue and make everyone wear the same tired shirt. It's a bunch of old folks and little kids, no one my age. I'm almost eighteen. I'm old enough to stay home alone."

"I doubt that Greg would let you stay alone," Cecelia said.

"I knew that was your reason for not letting me stay. I guess you think I'd let Greg stay there. It's a wonder I even have a boyfriend. You never let me do anything. You treat me like a kid."

"You are my kid, and I'm trying to keep you from having one before your time."

"Why don't you lock me up, then?"

"Be careful what you ask for," Cecelia said.

"Time out, you two," Michael interrupted. "There's a gas station at the next exit."

After a brief stop they were on their way. Thankfully, none of the other children had awakened. Michael put the Smokey Robinson CD back on, and Cecelia reclined her seat again.

"You know Cece, they're offering a buy-out at work."

"Yeah, I read it in the paper," Cecelia answered.

"Well, I'm thinking about taking it."

"Oh, you are? Where did this bright idea come from?" Cecelia let her seat up and reached in her make-up bag for her nail clippers. She broke a nail at work and would miss her appointment this weekend.

"The severance package includes, health insurance for a year, and six months salary in a lump sum. I can keep my stock options. John and I are going to start a consulting firm to help businesses monitor Internet intrusions."

"What kind of crazy idea is that? Michael, I have gone along with all of your schemes. I have a basement full of photography equipment from your short-lived photo studio. We have a lifetime supply of detergent from your Amway career. You have a real estate license and you've never sold anything. We can almost see the light at the end of the tunnel and you want to turn around and go back. You can't keep bouncing from job to job. You're not getting any younger."

"Thank you for that vote of confidence. I want to create my own living, then I won't have to bounce from job to job."

"You have a job. You don't hear me saying, I think I'll go and start my own hospital. Then I can guide my own future. Michael, you're not being realistic. Idealism at twenty and thirty is expected. Idealism at forty is the mark of a fool. Is John quitting his job?" Cecelia asked without looking up from doing her nails.

"Not right away. I wouldn't either if not for the buy-out. The Internet --- "

Cecelia cut him off. "Maybe John doesn't have as much faith in this as you do. He's being responsible to his family and thinking about their future. You're the one taking the risk."

"Well, he may miss the opportunity of a lifetime. I'm doing this with or without him. Once I get the business plan together and you look at it, you'll agree. I know this is a lot to hit you with suddenly. The buy-out offer is good until year-end, and I can work for ninety days after that. So it will be this time next year before---"

"Michael, I don't want to argue about this. But I don't think this is a good time for you to leave your job. I don't care how many business plans you develop or what *Black Enterprise* magazine says. We're just getting our credit back together, and we need to think about Sheree's college. We need to get on more stable financial ground first ---"

"That's backwards. You don't work or save your way to wealth. If we were on stable financial ground, we wouldn't need more money. That's the reason to become a businessman- to make money. Ray Kroc was over fifty years old before he started McDonald's. Sam Walton sold vacuum cleaners before he started Wal-Mart. This will work, Cecelia."

"Oh Michael. You're making my headache come back," Cecelia said as she reclined her seat again.

"I'm glad we didn't borrow against your 401K. It will take a while for the business to get established and we may need to use the 401K for Sheree's college. But I know this business is a sure thing. I wouldn't do this without your agreement, but I know you'll be convinced, once you learn more about it. Promise me you'll keep an open mind, and we'll both pray about it," Michael said.

Yeah, I'll pray for the Lord to send you some sense, Cecelia thought.

Michael turned up the Smokey Robinson CD.

I don't think Smokey in the flesh could calm me right now. Well, maybe in the flesh . . . she thought and smiled.

Cecelia opened her eyes, surprised to see a glimmering sun already on the horizon. She had planned to take over driving before sunrise, so she could see the world wake up. All the kids were asleep.

"Where are we?" she asked, as she wiped her eyes.

"We're about fifty miles from the state line. I have a quarter tank of gas left. That will get us to Blytheville. I'll stop there. Do you want to sit down and eat or drive through McDonald's?"

"With this bunch, McDonald's is all we can afford. Geneva only gave me fifty dollars. Old tight Raymond won't be getting up off any cash either. Those two were a perfect pair. How can you expect someone to take your children half way across the country for fifty dollars? We spent that much on gas going up to Downers Grove to pick up her kids. And I told her in the cafeteria at work what time we were leaving. You would think if we're nice enough to take her kids to see their father, the least she could do is bring them to our house so they wouldn't further inconvenience us. Then, when we got there, they weren't even ready. Is it me? Why are such simple courtesies so difficult for everyone? All I want is a little consideration. Is that asking too much?"

"Then McDonald's it is," Michael said, passing over Cecelia's latest tirade. The kid's Mickey D radar must have gone off. Within five minutes, they were all awake.

Cecelia ordered breakfast, as the kids went to the restroom. Michael took the van to the truck stop next door to get gas. Rayven pushed through the other customers in line and jerked Cecelia's arm as she was about to pay for their food. "Aunt Cece, Sheree is sick. She's throwing up in the bathroom." Cecelia left her order on the counter and rushed to the ladies room.

Sheree was doubled over the toilet retching and crying. She was standing in a pool of lumpy pink and white vomit. "Sheree, what happened? You were fine a minute ago."

"Mama, I feel so bad. I felt bad when I got out of the van, but I thought it would go away once I started moving around. Can you give me something to make me feel better?"

Cecelia wet some paper towels and wiped Sheree's face. Last night I didn't know anything, now I'm Mama to the rescue. I guess that's what having teenagers is all about, Cecelia thought.

"Does your stomach ache like you've been punched or do you feel nauseous? Are you dizzy when you stand up? Cecelia's nursing training was kicking in. "Rayven, go tell the manager we had an accident in here and ask for a cup of ice water."

"I suddenly felt sick to my stomach. I guess I'll be all right."

Cecelia looked up to see Michael standing in the door. "Everything all right in here?"

"My diagnosis is too much junk food and car sickness. She'll be okay. Can you get our overnight bags? We need to change. And can you get the kids breakfast? I forgot all about them," Cecelia said.

An hour later, they were finally on their way. Cecelia drove, and Michael stretched out in the back seat. Sheree sat in the front passenger seat. Cecelia said she wouldn't be as susceptible to carsickness in the front.

The late start and the stop at McDonald's meant it would be midmorning before they arrived. Cecelia hoped to avoid driving through the heat of the day. She also wanted to avoid a lunch bill. Cecelia's stomach growled as she turned onto the highway. With all of the commotion over Sheree, she hadn't eaten.

"Mike, turn that down," Michael said.

"Mike," Michael yelled. "I'll never get to sleep sitting back here with you. Turn your CD player down. I can hear it clearly and I don't even have headphones. What is that mess you're listening to?"

Cecelia watched Mike put the CD in its cover. "Michael, take that from him," she said pointing to the CD cover. "I told you I didn't want you listening to music with all that cursing."

"Dang. Sheree you should have stayed in the back seat," Mike muttered.

"Hand it over," Cecelia said. "And dang is not a word."

Cecelia had been driving since they left McDonald's. She turned off the interstate on to Highway 62. This two-lane road would lead them directly to Eden. Eden was one of the few towns on the highway big enough to warrant a traffic light. For the first time, a sign included Eden on the list of destinations. "We're in the home stretch now," she said.

"Mama, its hot back here, can you turn on the air?" Mike asked.

"I turned the air on, but you're right, it doesn't seem to be cooling." Cecelia moved the knob all the way to high.

Lukewarm air drifted out of the vent. "Mike, nudge your father. I don't know what's wrong."

Cecelia pulled over and left the van running while Michael came around to the driver's side. "I can't figure out the problem. We'll just have to ride like this. I'll ask Charles to look at it."

"Daddy, you mean we have to drive without air? Can't you do something?" Sheree asked.

"You know, Little Girl, cars didn't always have air conditioning. It's a relatively new invention. You'll survive, " Michael replied.

"We may survive, but I know my hair won't," Cecelia said. "I guess I can get Beverly to do it for me. There's some advantage to having a beautician in the family."

"Do you want me to drive now?" Michael asked.

Cecelia figured she would keep on driving. At least in the front she had the vent and the window. The heat in the back would be unbearable, particularly with those musty boys.

"No, I think I can take us on in."

Good thing they had done most of the driving at night, Cecelia thought. I sure hope Charles can fix the air. Lord knows we don't need a car repair bill. Why can't we ever get ahead?

Their debt had gotten out of control like smoke in a summer wild fire. Last summer they remodeled the basement into a family room. Michael had asked her to wait, but what was the point? If they waited much longer, the kids would be grown and they wouldn't need the space. Since she'd gotten the new living room set, she was even fussier about lounging on the furniture.

She remembered Michael asking, "Why do we need new furniture?"

"We've had that pit set ever since we got married. Styles are totally different now," Cecelia answered.

"Prices are different too. I can't believe you spent that much money on something we can only look at. Why don't you get covers like my mother has?"

"Michael, I know you're not suggesting I get those ugly, hard plastic furniture covers for our living room? That's from the 1960's. People don't do that anymore. Don't worry about it. We don't have to pay any money until March. We'll have our tax refund by then and we'll pay it off. What's the big deal?"

"The big deal is, have you ever heard of saving? The big deal is we don't need new furniture. Your children and I have a right to be comfortable in our own home. Why get something you don't want us to sit on? Our furniture was fine until Carolyn got new furniture. She can afford this stuff. She doesn't have any kids."

"Well, we can afford it too. I plan to get the basement fixed up after the first of the year. Then we can keep the living room nice and have the family room downstairs. Payments for a home improvement loan to remodel the basement will be tax deductible, so it won't be so bad. Besides, I didn't see you making any sacrifices for your children when you got a new car."

"Here we go again. It's not the same thing. Fifteen-year old furniture is different from a fifteen-year-old car. We needed a new car. Since the payments were affordable, why not go for the top of the line?"

The top of the line BMW was only three months old when someone rear-ended Michael on the way home from work. They had a sixty-month loan to keep the payments affordable and they did not make a down payment. The insurance company settlement didn't cover the loan balance and they ended up owing the credit union. On top of that, they still needed a car. So much for the tax refund.

They now had a furniture payment they hadn't budgeted for and a higher car payment than they had planned, on top of home improvement loan payments. The home improvement loan was a sore spot between Cecelia and Michael because he claimed a friend of a friend could do the work cheaper.

"Do you know these people?" Cecelia asked.

"No, but I saw the job he did on Larry's house. He has good references."

"I don't want some nigger-rig job. I want a professional, with insurance and guarantees, so I can call them if something isn't right," Cecelia said.

"Now why does the brother's job have to be nigger-rigged? What makes you think he doesn't have insurance, or that he's not professional?" Michael asked.

Michael rarely got upset, but Cecelia knew she had touched a nerve. "I'm sure he's very good, but you can't compare him with Sears."

"I bet you can't compare the price either. You'd rather pay Sears twice as much for the same thing you can get for less, and you would be helping a black business."

"Oh, Michael, you sound like Raymond. I'm not trying to prop up the black economy. I just want my basement remodeled. Is that too much to ask?"

"Well, is it too much to ask that you let him give you a quote and show you some examples of his work? Give him a chance. How did Sears get started? By people using them based on word of mouth. They didn't start as a billion-dollar company. Nobody wants to give the black man a break."

"We gave the black man a break. Remember your cousin Wino-Willie, the plumber? You missed a day of work because he missed his appointment. Then when he did come, he didn't have the right tools. You ended up buying tools and spending almost as much as if you had called Sears. No, thank you. I don't want any more jack-leg repairmen."

Michael shook his head. "You've had unsatisfactory experiences with white repairmen haven't you? I don't hear you saying you won't deal with them anymore. You chalk it up to a bad apple and move on. Why can't the black man get the same benefit of the doubt?"

"Look, Michael, I don't want to fight about this. Tell him to come on over and give us a quote."

In the end, Sears was much higher, but they used them anyway because they could charge it to their credit card. Cecelia told Larry's friend about the contract out for bid at the hospital. He secured a six-figure subcontract job and made good contacts. He was so grateful, he offered to do a job for them free. Too bad he doesn't work on vans, Cecelia thought. Hopefully after this reunion, our money woes will be over.

Cecelia planned to find time during the reunion to talk to her father about selling the farm. She'd heard that Cousin Jackie's dad just sold his land to some big company for almost four hundred thousand dollars. He'd given Jackie and her sister fifty thousand dollars each and put money aside for their kid's college. Daddy had three times as much land as he did. Daddy also had more children, but would surely be as generous, if not more so.

Money wasn't Cecelia's only concern. The doctors had ordered C.W. to slow down. Most men his age had retired years ago. Daddy can't run that farm forever, she thought. Charles was doing the best he could, but good workers have been scarce since the casinos opened. It's better to take the money, and invest it. Let the money work, instead of my family. Daddy always said he'd never sell the land, but he also said he'd never pay twenty thousand dollars for a car. He's changed his mind about a lot of things since the stroke.

"Mama, are we there yet?" Mike asked from the back seat.

"We're not too far. We should be there in a little over an hour," she replied. One hour from a cool drink of Mama's sweet tea. Just an hour from a soft bed and air conditioning. And, just a few days away from the ticket to financial security.

Selling the land was the cure for Daddy's health and Cecelia's sick finances. Surely he would see things her way.

7

Raymond heard Milton, the neighbor's rooster, crow and knew it was about five o'clock. A light orange sun was peeking over the horizon, but by Daddy's standards it was late. By sunrise, he'd had two cups of coffee and was out in the fields. Though he had cut back since his stroke, he still rose early to make sure Charles had everyone on their job.

Raymond had a restless night. Cecelia was bringing his kids to the family reunion to spend the rest of the summer with him. He hadn't seen them since he left Chicago last year.

He had hoped to see them during their Christmas and spring breaks. He sent money both times for plane tickets. Both times their mother changed her mind and wouldn't let them fly unaccompanied, though at twelve and thirteen, they were old enough. He and Geneva had separated three years ago. They even dated each other for a while. Raymond hadn't been ready to join the dating scene. He didn't feel like wading through the silly women who were only interested in how much you made and your title, and the prospect of AIDS terrified him. The arrangement with Geneva was working, until she started pressuring him to move back home. He told her he liked things the way they were because he needed his 'space'. Then Geneva did the unthinkable, she started dating someone else. Raymond hated to admit he was jealous. He couldn't live with her, and couldn't live without her.

To further complicate his life, Chicago National Bank had been sold. Rather than start over in another division at less pay, that is *if* the new bank kept him, he took the buy-out. It was a decent severance package since he had been there ten years. Raymond inherited his parents' thrifty genes, so he'd be okay for a while.

The notion to relocate surfaced after Daddy's stroke. Raymond came to help Mama while Daddy was recuperating. Mr. Phillips visited Daddy and mentioned he had two rent houses for sale. His wife was ill and they were moving to Phoenix. He needed to sell quickly and thought Daddy might be interested. By the end of the conversation, he'd agreed to sell one of the houses to Raymond with a small down payment. The lease expired in December, and that coincided perfectly with the end of Raymond's job.

He returned to Chicago just long enough to pack and break the news to Geneva and the kids. "Raymond, I know I didn't hear you right. You did what? You didn't think we should talk about this first? I didn't say anything when you shaved your head and pierced your ear. You joined the Muslims and changed your name without asking me. I supported your decision to eliminate the Christmas tree and celebrate Kwanzaa. But this?" Geneva asked.

"You're the one that filed for divorce," Raymond said as he looked for his keys.

"You're the one that moved out. And it's not a divorce, it's a legal separation. I have to think about my future and I need to increase my deductions and file as head-of-household," Geneva said.

"So that's what this is all about? The money. I give you money all the time. I take care of my kids."

"Your kids need more than money. They need you."

"I agree. I think they should move with me to Eden. Chicago is no place to raise children."

"Now I know you are losing your mind. You think I'm going to let you take my kids down to those prejudiced white folks and cotton fields?"

"Those white folks aren't any different than the ones in Chicago. Besides, they're my kids too."

"Then you should think about them. You're just trying to get back at me for dating Brent. They shouldn't suffer because you're being selfish."

"Call it a midlife crisis. Some men buy sports cars, some date young women. I'm moving. I need a change."

"As usual, it's all about you. Whatever you're looking for, I doubt that you find it in the back woods of Arkansas. Or maybe you have found it. Have you met someone?"

"This is getting us nowhere. I've got to go," Raymond said.

Geneva didn't understand. Chicago was eating away at him. Black people were moving backward and didn't care about each other. He couldn't find the motivation to get another job. He and his brother-in-law discussed starting a business, but Cecelia didn't want Michael to borrow from his 401K. They had argued about letting Carl live with them. Raymond didn't understand how Geneva expected him to turn his back on his brother. Geneva wanted to buy a house in the suburbs and Raymond wanted to stay in the city. Geneva wanted their children to go to private schools; Raymond disagreed. Geneva wanted to keep working nights to make more money. Raymond wanted her to switch back to days. He and Geneva were in limbo and he didn't know how to fix it.

So when he saw the opportunity to move, he jumped at it. Didn't think on it, didn't sleep on it, didn't discuss it with anyone. The bank had already gone through two mergers in three years and his branch was going to be closed. It was one of the few branches in the inner city. It was not viewed as a fast track position, but he liked working in the community. With his tenure, he would probably get a position downtown, but he had no passion for that assignment. After managing a branch and being a big fish in a little pond, Raymond didn't want to go back to being a little fish in the big pond; a big white pond, at that.

Instead, he decided to go back to his original little pond: Eden. He was part of a growing trend, the migration of black baby boomers to the South. Blacks had left the South in droves generations earlier to escape Jim Crow, the fields and Miss Ann's kitchen. Now they were moving back, escaping long winters, the concrete and density of northern cities. The factory jobs were gone, and black people were moving away from black people in the inner cities just like whites were.

In Eden, Raymond loved sitting on his porch and waving to passersby. At night he would sit on his porch and look at the stars like a man who had just gained sight. After living in Chicago, he had forgotten there even were stars in the sky, and it wasn't too safe to sit outside at night looking for them in Chicago. The night sky in Eden was black and still. The sounds of crickets and the kildee comforted him. When he first moved home, their continuous bleating kept him awake, but now their even tones lulled him to sleep, and Milton's triumphant crow was his alarm clock.

He liked going to his mother's for Sunday dinner and being able to sit and talk about anything and nothing and not have to cram a whole year into a ten-day visit. He liked it when people called him 'C.W.'s boy', even though he was forty-two years old. It made him feel youthful, like his best days were still ahead. It was this feeling of hope and anticipation that he wanted to pass to his children. He hoped they would like his house and want to stay. He told his young cousins they could watch movies and play their music at his house during the reunion. He thought this would help his kids get acquainted with some young people in town. Maybe Geneva would change her mind if the kids asked to stay. They were almost teenagers and required close supervision. Geneva worked a lot of nights at the hospital and this was the perfect solution.

His house had three bedrooms, a screened front porch and hardwood floors. His nephew Tony had trimmed the overgrown hedges and pruned the trees in the large back yard. The house needed work, but was liveable. He could have hired someone and gotten it fixed up faster, but he enjoyed fixing it himself. Some repairs, he and Malcolm could work on together. If the kids stayed, he'd add another bathroom. The neighbors were friendly and looked out for him. He ran errands for the elderly ones and they kept him supplied with vegetables and preserves canned from their gardens. And, he didn't need bars on his windows or doors.

Few people in Eden called him Malik. His friends and associates in Chicago respected his wishes and acknowledged his name change two years ago. Carolyn and Cecelia usually remembered and only slipped in family gatherings, but the people in Eden didn't play that. They didn't think twice about calling you PeeWee, Bubba, or Tashinikqua, but they acted like it was blasphemy to take a meaningful name from the mother country. Even though they wouldn't acknowledge his chosen name, Raymond enjoyed being around his extended family. He and his sisters were so busy with their respective lives; they rarely saw each other in Chicago except holidays. He had visited more with his relatives in the ten months he had been back in Eden than he had all his life. Reunion planning and researching the family's roots had consumed him and made the time pass quickly. This was the best part about moving home, the chance to reconnect with his extended family and enjoy his parents.

Just as he was falling back to sleep, the sound of a key in the front door startled him. He slipped on his gym shorts and met his nephew in the hall.

"Sorry Uncle Ray, didn't mean to wake you," Tony said. "Now before you get upset, me and a couple of my frat brothers went over to Pine Bluff for a step show. We met some honies and well... what can I say? She couldn't resist my charm," he said laughing.

"I thought we had an understanding. I know you're over eighteen, but if you're going to stay with me, you have to follow my rules. You can't stay out all night."

"Aw, Uncle Ray, I thought we were cool."

"We are cool. But, I'm still responsible for you. I'm way past grown and I would never come in my parent's house at this hour. You need to show some respect."

"Now you sound like my father. Man, I could have stayed home for this."

"I'm not trying to give you a hard time. I know how it is. Me and my Dad used to butt heads when I was your age. But life is not one frat party after another. If you want to be treated like an adult, you need to act like one. I let you use my car and you're staying in my house. The least you could have done was called."

"Sorry, Uncle Ray. I meant to come back, she was just so fine..."

"Just remember, all that glitters ain't gold. Follow the head on your shoulders, not the one in your pants."

"You're right. But if you had seen her ---"

"Boy, you are hopeless," Raymond said shaking his head. "I hope you had condoms. Now, go change your clothes so you can go with me to Uncle Edward's place. We're getting ready for the fish fry tonight."

The phone rang as Raymond and Tony were walking out the door.

"Raymond, this is Brenda. Can you come jump-start my car for me? Paul and Julia are coming for breakfast, and I need to go to the store. Charles and C.W. went to run an errand and I don't want to bother Miss Lois."

"But you don't mind bothering me?" Raymond teased. "No problem, I'm on my way out the door."

Since Raymond was near his extended family, they called on him so much, that he wondered what they did before he got there. But what about his own family? He thought about his son. In less than ten years, Malcolm would be Tony 's age. Geneva was a good mother, but a boy needs his father. Who would be there to talk to him about condoms, or teach him how to jump-start a car? Who would screen Rayven's boyfriends, to protect her from the Tonys of the world? Maybe he should have stayed in Chicago. Geneva said he was selfish for leaving. Maybe she right.

8

Even though I have my own condo, no place is as comforting as my old room. Walking into this room was like traveling back through time. The twin beds stood in the same places, but carpet now replaced the oval shag rug between the beds that had been the unofficial boundary between my side of the room and Cecelia's. My fourth and fifth grade spelling bee trophies were on a shelf over my bed. My teachers said I should have represented Eden in the district spelling bee, but the winner from the white school was selected. Even Cecelia's stringy, wilted, cheerleader pom-poms were still crisscrossed and stapled to the wall in an 'X'. The blue and gold of Lincoln High School had long ago faded into turquoise and beige. Mama had the room painted, but she returned the pom-poms to their spot on the wall. I suppose it was sentimental value that made Mama leave them there. After all, I hadn't moved them either when Cecelia graduated.

That was a happy day. She was going to Chicago to stay with Aunt Ethel Fay and attend nursing school. I was happy because I finally had my own room.

My Smokey Robinson album covers were still on the top bookshelf. Cecelia tried to claim them and we had one of our last knock down, drag-out fights over those albums. She packed them with the things she was taking to college. I protested because we shared our record collection. Both of us had bought albums and forty-fives. Now, she was picking all of the good ones to take with her. She thought she won, but I smuggled the records out of her suitcase. She didn't discover my heist until she unpacked in Chicago.

My books were still on the shelves. I read Agatha Christie and Nancy Drew mysteries and tried to solve the endings. I was also an Earl Stanley Gardner fan. I'd help Perry Mason catch the crook. That is when I decided I to be a lawyer. The IRS is not exactly the drama of Perry Mason, but it pays the bills. All of my James Baldwin books were still on the shelf. He was one of a handful of black authors I had been exposed to. The Dwight County Library was desegregated without fanfare in the late 1960's, but their collection had very few books by black authors. *The Autobiography of Malcolm X* also rested on my shelf. Raymond gave it to me, on one of his visits home from college. The book awakened in me a new sense of pride and curiosity about my race. The civil rights movement was just something on television to me. Eden was not the site of any freedom rides, sit-ins or marches. I've heard stories of skirmishes and threats between local blacks and whites, when black people started voting in the sixties, but I was too young to remember any of it. Whites held onto as much power as they could for as long as they could, and blacks went along to get along. Those that didn't want to conform, left. I devoured Malcolm's story like a starving man. He described a world so different from mine that I couldn't wait to escape Eden and taste it.

My radio was still on the dresser, next to my prom picture. Marvin Handly and I wore matching Afros. I hadn't seen him in years, although I'd heard that he retired from the Air Force and was preaching at his father's church.

It's difficult to imagine that I am old enough to know anyone who's retiring. Even though a person can retire with twenty years in the military, and Marvin did join right after high school. Talking of retirement still seems strange. My image of retirees is gray-haired, stooped-over, bifocal- wearing, hard-of-hearing old souls. I am starting to see more gray in my own hair and changed the part in my hair to camouflage the stubborn gray patch that refuses to stay hidden. I even noticed gray in a private spot. Another reason to favor dark, candlelit evenings.

Some of my classmates are already grandparents. I suppose it's fulfilling to watch your offspring grow and hopefully become responsible adults. I enjoy spending time with Sheree and Mike, although twenty-four/seven might be a bit too much. Everyone else seems to have some sort of accomplishment to point to. Even others that are still single have exciting careers where they travel, or have started their own businesses. What had I done in my years since graduation? My law degree was supposed to be my ticket to easy street, but other than a couple of degrees on my wall and a vested retirement plan, I don't see anything tangible. I don't even have much money in the bank, because I'm paying bills left by my loving brother and a trifling ex-boyfriend.

I began unpacking and changed from my large travel bag to my canvas summer purse. As I put my cell phone in my purse, I noticed that I missed two phone calls from Warren.

Daddy peeked his head in the door as I was dialing Warren's number. "You all settled in? How does it feel to be in your old room? Seems like just yesterday, I was peeking in this door telling you girls to turn out your lights and go to sleep. You grew up so fast. "

"Come on in, Daddy. I guess I was thinking about old times too," I said as I put the cell phone back in my purse.

"Here are the papers I want you to review for me," Daddy said as he handed me three shopping bags, two shoeboxes and some loose papers. "Ask me anything you want, but let's keep this between you and me."

"Okay. But beware, I charge by the hour."

After two hours of sorting through papers, I already had one recommendation for Daddy. He needed folders, labels and a file cabinet. So often clients bring their important papers in flimsy sacks and tattered boxes. Sometimes people owed taxes just because of poor record keeping. One of the drawbacks of working for the IRS is everyone wants you to tell them loopholes and advise them how to avoid an audit. I advise them to document everything. People interpret that as save everything, but it doesn't do any good to save papers and receipts and then keep them in disarray. I've had wealthy people that could afford an accountant come to the office with drawers of papers, not even separated by year. Here I am, this big-time government attorney and my own father's stuff is disorganized.

I pulled a few papers out of the bag to get an idea of what was there. I became so intrigued that I went through everything and didn't finish sorting papers until after midnight. I placed stacks on the dresser and on the floor, and listed each item. I attempted to organize my thoughts and keep all of my unanswered questions straight. I thought Daddy's taxes would be simple. But he brought me insurance policies, loan documents and other papers. When Daddy was sick, he had given Charles Power-of-Attorney. I wondered if Daddy meant to rescind it now that he was better. This was a major project and I decided to ask Paul to help me. I planned to rest my eyes for a few minutes to get my second wind, then write a list of questions for Daddy.

That wind never came. In what seemed like minutes, the sun was up and Mama was knocking on the door. "Good morning Sleeping Beauty. It's after nine o'clock. We've eaten already, and your Daddy and I are going to Wal-Mart." She stepped over the stacks of paper around the room as she came in to open the blinds. "You brought work with you?"

"I'll have these papers up in a little while. Don't put yourself to any trouble, Mama. I'll just get some coffee."

"It's no trouble, I'll fix you a little bite to eat. Breakfast is the most important meal of the day, you know. It will only take a minute."

I showered and dressed and followed the aroma of homemade biscuits to the kitchen. "Where's Daddy? I need to talk to him," I asked, surveying Mama's "little bite to eat" of homemade biscuits, sausage, eggs, grits, preserves and sliced honey dew melon.

"He's on the porch. But sit and eat, while the food is warm. It's so good to see you at the table. I can remember you as a little girl in that exact spot," Mama said while washing breakfast dishes. "You're not eating much, though. I've never seen you turn down plum preserves. Don't tell me you're trying to lose more weight. Remember only a dog wants a bone."

The food was tasty, but I could only nibble. It still hadn't sunk in, but based on what I'd seen so far, Mama and Daddy had an estate worth at least a million dollars. They received ten thousand dollars when my oldest brother, Walter, died in Viet Nam. From 1983 to 1995 they received twenty thousand a year from a government subsidy program, which paid Daddy not to farm some of his land. Daddy saved the payments and lived on his bus driving salary. He signed up for direct deposit for his Social Security checks, and they haven't made any withdrawals from the account since they set it up ten years ago. He has rent houses in town and 600 acres of unencumbered land. He loaned Ozell Moore some money and received a partial interest in their funeral home, which eventually expanded to four homes. Mr. Moore died two years ago and none of his children wanted to return to Arkansas to run the business. They sold it and Daddy's share was forty thousand dollars. It was incredible.

What was even more incredible is that all of this money was parked in savings accounts and certificates of deposit earning a piddly amount of interest. I remember Daddy saying he wouldn't invest in the stock market, because he wouldn't buy something he couldn't control. But I didn't think he had any money to invest. I figured it was just one of those conversations he always has where he solves all of the world's problems without leaving the kitchen table.

There were several solicitation letters from Consolidated Farms, or CFI as they called themselves in the letters. Some of the letters hadn't even been opened.

The most surprising document was a letter from the Department of Agriculture, stating his case was being mediated and offering a settlement of three hundred thousand dollars. The Black Farmers Association had been working with farmers regarding loan discrimination lawsuits. I remember seeing reports of the Black Farmers protests on BET news. But I never imagined they would be successful, or that my own Daddy was involved. I wonder if Mama knows, I mused, as I watched her wash and dry a baggie.

"Carolyn. Carolyn? You didn't hear a word I said, did you? What in the world is on your mind, child? You used to daydream when you were a little girl. I can remember --- "

"Excuse me Mama. Thanks for breakfast. I need to ask Daddy something."

I found Daddy on the porch reading the newspaper.

"Good morning, Chubby. Did you sleep well?"

"No, Daddy, I didn't. I was up late looking over your paperwork. I thought I was just going to look over your taxes." I leaned over and said in a low voice, "You didn't tell me you were wealthy."

"Oh, I've managed to put away a few pennies," he said, without looking up.

"When did you get all this money? I don't remember these bank accounts when I did your taxes."

"I had my own bank. I didn't put it in Eden National Bank until Carl moved in."

"You had all this money around the house?"

"I'm not saying where it was. But I never have trusted the bank. If my Daddy had trusted a bank, we wouldn't be sitting here now."

"Daddy, the bank is safe as long as ---"

"Yeah, that's what them white folks thought back in '29. My Daddy had been saving money all his life. The officers of both of the banks in town were members of the White Citizens Council, so he didn't trust the banks. He hid his money in the outhouse. When the white folks' depression came, both of the banks failed. Daddy said folks lined up to get their money out of the bank, only to be told it was gone. Yes sir, depression was the best thing ever happened to this family. White folks needed money and they wasn't so particular about who they sold their land to. My Daddy bought the thirty acres he was sharecropping plus ten more. Old man Rhodes claimed my Daddy stole the money and organized some of those good ole'boys to come out to our house and start trouble. My Daddy was in the outhouse with his shotgun, waiting for them. It rained so hard that night, the dirt road to the house turned to mush. Them fellas had to turn around and go home. Once the rains stopped, everyone was so busy recovering from the flood they forgot about my Daddy. That outhouse saved this family."

"I always wondered why you never tore that old raggedy building down."

"My Daddy left it up as a reminder of what he went through to get this land. So I did too."

This is going to be a tough sales job, I thought. I was going to recommend mutual funds, annuities and estate planning, and he just started using banks.

"Daddy, this will take more time than I thought. It took me all night just to organize your papers. I'd like to take them with me and get back to you when I ---"

"No. I need you to go through them right away."

"What's the rush? I want to do a good job. The deed for the first forty acres is in Grandaddy Beau's name. Since you and Aunt Ethel Fay and Aunt Pearl are his heirs, they need to sign their rights over to you. Do you think they'll be opposed to doing that?"

"No. I got a Quit Claim deed from them around here somewhere."

"We need to make sure you specifically name who you want the land to go to. Just leaving it to your 'heirs' is too general. Black folks have lost millions of acres because of 'heirs property'. I need to go to the court house and get copies of all of your deeds, then ---"

"Good, good. That's what I want you to do. Go through everything and make sure things are in order. I'll pass first because your mother's going to smother me to death, so make sure she's provided for. After she passes, I want you kids to split everything. Remember Walter's daughter and don't forget Carl."

"Daddy, it's not quite that simple. First I need to know ---"

"Hey, I think that's Cece coming," he said as he stood next to Champ who was barking and wagging her tail. "Yeah, it's an Illinois license plate. We'll have to discuss this later, Chubby. I don't want to talk in front of the others. Keep it between us until we can talk later."

Cecelia was driving. As they got closer, she honked the horn and the kids leaned out of the windows, waving. She turned into the yard and drove up to the porch step. Driveway usage was a formality rarely observed in Eden.

"Go tell your mama Cece is here," Daddy said, as he opened the porch door.

Cecelia and her brood filed out of the van. She did not look like a woman who had been riding all night. Her golden brown skin looked flawless even without makeup. Her light blue

Donna Karon pantsuit barely had a wrinkle. The belted style showed off her trim waist and hips. Even her short hair, which was not as curly as usual, still flattered her round face. "Daddy, you look good," she cried as she opened her arms for a hug. "You shaved your head and you even had some moles removed. Bald is sexy now, Mama better watch out."

The kids made the rounds of hugs and kisses from their grandmother and grandfather. They were already headed for the kitchen.

Daddy went to help Michael unload the suitcases. "Hey you guys, not so fast. Come help with the bags."

I went to relieve Cecelia of part of her load. "How was the drive down?" I asked.

"You wouldn't believe it. We left late, then had to go across town to get Rayven and Malcolm. Girl, Geneva didn't even have them ready and only gave us fifty dollars for the whole trip. Then Sheree got sick. The air went out ---"

"You two act like you haven't seen each other in months. I'm pulling rank," Mama said as she stepped between us and hugged Cecelia.

"I haven't seen this Carolyn," Cecelia said. "I can't believe you let Beverly cut your hair."

"Doesn't she look cute?" Mama asked patting my hair. "Beverly is always itching to cut my hair, but I learned to keep an eye on those scissors. You all are just in time to eat. You get settled in and I'll fix more eggs. The kids are going to stay with Raymond. You and Michael take the back bedroom," Mama said as she walked between us with her arms around our waists. "It's going to be so much fun having all of my babies together. I wish you didn't live so far away. Wouldn't it be nice if we could have a reunion every month?"

"Sure would," Cecelia and I said, almost in unison. We smiled at each other and crossed our fingers behind Mama's back.

9

Beverly stepped out of the shower and dried herself. As the steam dissipated from the mirror, she saw a body she didn't recognize. Her upper arms jiggled when she moved them, her waistline had long ago disappeared under rolls of skin and her breasts hung to her navel. She had stopped weighing herself when she went over two hundred pounds. That's what heavyweight prizefighters weigh, she thought. She always felt her height helped her carry more weight than average. She was 'healthy' or 'big-boned'. But now, there was no polite term. She had gotten fat. She still turned a few heads when everything was girded and covered up. She knew how to dress to compliment her generous curves and cleavage, and she didn't wear cheap clothes. But she felt depressed when she viewed her birthday suit.

She felt a draft and rushed to cover herself with the towel as her husband opened the bathroom door. "I'm on my way to work," he said.

"Okay. I have a meeting, and then I'm headed to Eden. You're coming later. Right?"

He leaned over and pecked her cheek. "I'll be there," he said as he playfully jerked the towel off of her. He stood back and whistled. "Um, um, um. I better get going before you tempt me, woman."

"Hush. You're just saying that. I have really got to get this weight off. I need to start working out with Tanya again."

"Baby, you look good to me. Most people gain a little weight when they quit smoking. I'm proud that you finally quit.

If I had time, I could help you burn a few calories," he said with a smirk.

"Anthony Townsend, get your mannish self to work."

Beverly smiled as she put on her housecoat and walked into their bedroom. She looked out the window and saw her husband pulling out of the driveway. After twenty-five years, Anthony still made her heart quiver. He was the love of her life, and though he could give her the blues, he always managed to make those blues go away. She saw a customer go into the salon and hurried to get dressed. She was meeting a beauty supply sales rep this morning before going to the reunion. She liked having her salon next door. When the house on the corner went on sale, she and Anthony bought it and renovated it. She had the best of both worlds. Her house faced a residential street, and a few steps away; the salon faced a busy street. But now she was ready to expand again. Since Anthony had gotten his barber license, the barbershop had just as many customers as the beauty salon. They had started looking for commercial property for a second location.

Beverly skipped breakfast, packed clothes for the weekend and went to her meeting. She could hear Tanya and Sharon fussing as she walked in the backdoor. "What do you two think you're doing?" she asked. "Why are you back here carrying on, when you should be out there with your customers?"

Tanya rolled her eyes and went back to her station.

"Do you want to tell me what that was all about?" Beverly asked.

"No," Sharon said. "She can't help it if she's a scandalous wench."

"Is it safe to leave you two this weekend?" Beverly asked. "You know I'm going to Eden for my reunion."

"Yeah, girl. Go have a good time. You deserve it."

Beverly shook her head and went to her office. She wrote out her order and gave it to Tanya to give to the sales rep. "You have my cell number if you need me. You're in charge."

Why can't those two get along? Beverly wondered as she turned out of her parking lot. They were her two best stylists, and she didn't want to be forced to make a choice. Tanya was the most professional and profitable, but Sharon was like a sister to her. Maybe they'll work it out. I'm not going to worry about them this weekend. I'm going to enjoy a peaceful weekend with my family. She slammed her brakes as a black cat ran in front of her Ford Expedition. Good thing Aunt Belle isn't with me, she thought. She would make me turn around and go another way, just to avoid crossing the path of a black cat. How silly.

We Are Family

10

The Dwight County courthouse was musty with high ceilings and the halls echoed Paul's footsteps. It did triple duty as the post office and jail. The cornerstone was dedicated in 1898 to the memory of the valiant Confederate soldiers from Dwight County. County officials had only stopped flying the Confederate flag a few years ago. The building was on the National Historic Register and despite being more than one hundred years old, was in better shape than many buildings constructed since then.

Even though the building was well preserved, the operating systems were ancient. It's been ages since I've researched records manually, Paul thought as he sifted through sheets of microfilm. To make matters worse, the documents were in chronological order, not alphabetical. "I'm glad I told Julia not to wait for me today," he murmured to himself. This will take forever.

Julia and Brenda were gone to Graceland. This was Julia's first trip to Eden, and first on her 'to do' list was to tour Elvis' home in Memphis. She was disappointed when Paul told her he needed to help Carolyn and couldn't take her, but he wasn't too sad about missing the trip. He and his wife were color blind on most issues, but most African Americans, including Paul, did not revere Elvis Presley. Elvis was a white boy, with the voice, flair and moves of a black man, loved by an America that scorned the real thing.

Carolyn had divided the papers into farm and non-farm related items. She kept the records related to the farm and asked Paul to look into everything else. Paul started with an envelope marked 'Beau'. It contained three Series-HH bonds and an insurance policy originally issued by Southern Life and Home Insurance Company. The bonds were issued in 1944 in the name of Beauregard Nelson Washington, Daddy's older brother, and matured in 1969. Paul called his broker and found out Series HH bonds were no longer issued. In the 1980's, the government stopped accruing interest on the bonds. They had to be worth at least ten thousand dollars, but every minute they weren't reinvested was like giving money away. The insurance policy had a death benefit of two thousand dollars.

Paul organized his thoughts and came up with a 'to do' list. The bonds would require going through a lot of red tape to resolve. Uncle Beau never had children, so Daddy and his sisters were next of kin. Another company had taken over Southern Life and Home. Paul added 'research survivor company' to his list. Also, this company may have been one that routinely charged black customers higher rates than whites. A lawsuit had been filed on behalf of the policyholders. Paul made a note to research this. Next Paul wrote 'Betty?' The policy was issued to Charles and Betty Washington. Daddy must have forgotten how these instruments were titled, because Betty, his first wife, was still listed as the beneficiary. Paul wondered if this had been changed when the new company took over the policy.

Paul decided to obtain Daddy's divorce certificate. He would need it for any correspondence with the insurance company about changing the policy. The courthouse records department closed at one o'clock on Fridays and Paul was running out of time. He had asked the lady behind the counter for assistance twice already. She looked like she had been working there since the building opened, and acted like the records were hers personally. Even so, Paul decided to try one more time.

"Ma'am, I hate to disturb you again. I am having a problem finding some documents. I'm here from California and I'm leaving this weekend. I won't be able to return next week, so I really need to find these things before you close. Do you think you could help me? I'd appreciate your help."

"What was it that you needed, son?" she asked in that Southern twang that made the hairs stand up on Paul's neck. It reminded him of his high school teachers. His was the first integrated class to graduate from Eden High School. All black Lincoln High School was closed after his freshman year. He had attended black schools all his life and the abrupt immersion into Eden High had been traumatic. Paul was one of the smartest students at Lincoln. At Eden High, the teachers were pleasant but obviously didn't think much of the Lincoln students. The Lincoln teachers had been dispersed among the other schools in Dwight County. None were transferred to the high school. Her tone was a flashback to those teachers telling him he was more suited to basketball when he voiced aspirations of being a lawyer.

"Ma'am, I need a divorce decree."

"What year?" she asked.

"I don't know what year exactly. It was in the early fifties."

"Well, no wonder you can't find it. All records before 1960 are still paper only." She disappeared into the basement and returned with several boxes. "These are all the divorce records for 1950 through 1960. Amazing isn't it? This was when wedding vows meant something. People stayed together in those days. These days, the divorce records for one month would fill these boxes. Me and my husband been together forty-eight years. It hasn't been easy, but we stuck together. Are you married, hon?"

Sometimes Southern hospitality was irritating. Paul didn't care to discuss the sociological changes of the last fifty years. He had one hour to sift through those boxes, and this lady wanted to carry on a conversation.

Paul managed to politely excuse himself from her desk and resume his search. He never found the decree. Then he began to think the unthinkable. Maybe Daddy had never gotten divorced. Surely that couldn't be. He rarely mentioned Betty's name. We all knew she was his first wife, and Charles' mother. We didn't know much else about her. She had a drinking problem and that was part of the reason she and Daddy broke up. They stayed together six years until Daddy got fed up with her and Detroit. He met Mama and the rest, as they say, is history.

Betty even showed up at Mama and Daddy's house a few times. Eventually, she realized he was not leaving and she quit bothering them. Daddy didn't have much contact with Charles after that. She called for money a few times, but Daddy figured she would just drink it up. He would send clothes and shoes. A couple years later, people were telling Daddy that she was neglecting Charles. Her sister called Daddy to ask him for money. Betty had asked her sister to keep Charles and hadn't returned for weeks. Her sister was willing to keep Charles, but she had six kids of her own and she needed money. This wasn't the first time Betty had disappeared. Daddy got in his car and drove to Detroit. He gave the sister fifty dollars, that was a lot of money then, put seven-year old Charles in the car and drove back to Arkansas. Some say Charles wasn't really even Daddy's child, but he didn't question it. By this time, Walter was born. Mama raised Charles as her own, and they never said another word about it.

"Son, we'll be closing in a few minutes and I need to return those boxes," the clerk said. "Be sure to put everything back like you found it."

Paul gathered his papers and returned the boxes. The clerk was standing at the door with the keys in her hand, waiting for Paul to leave.

Carolyn was waiting in their mother's green, 1985, Delta 88. "I should have come down here with you earlier. I probably would have accomplished more. That house is like Grand Central Station," Carolyn said, as she pulled out of the parking space. "Aunt Ethel Fay and Uncle Henry are here. Willie and his wife came on the bus. He had barely said "Hi Cuz" to me, before he was asking me questions about his taxes. Sheryl brought her wild kids over, then claimed she forgot something and would be right back. That was three hours ago. Aunt Pearl and Veronica are here too. I should have stayed at the motel like you," she said as she stopped at Eden's one traffic light.

"How many kids does Sheryl have now?" Paul asked.

"I think five. I've lost count," Carolyn said. "Listen, I didn't have much time to look, but I found something strange. There was a security agreement filed using part of the farm as collateral."

"What's strange about that?"

"It was filed last October, ten days after Daddy had his stroke. He wasn't conducting any business then."

"You said Charles had power-of-attorney, maybe he did it."

"But why? Planting is over by October," Carolyn said. "It wasn't from Daddy's regular bank and Daddy never uses the land as collateral. He may pledge equipment, or crops, but never his land."

"You think Charles did something without Daddy's permission?" Paul asked.

"That's what it looks like to me. And Beverly said Charles bought a fifty thousand dollar tractor while Daddy was sick. I wonder what else Charles has done."

"Carolyn, you may need to consider visiting more often. Daddy's not a young man and he needs help keeping track of his affairs. Charles has all he can handle running the farm, and Beverly has her own empire in Memphis. You and Raymond could be a big help to him."

"I have started thinking about a transfer. The office in Memphis always has openings."

"I know I should be more involved too, but this isn't a good time for me. I haven't told anyone, but I'm opening my own office. I've been helping Shawn with his contract and he told some of his teammates. He'll probably only play a few more years, and then get his license to be an agent. Sports and entertainment are where the money is."

"All right, Johnny Cochran better watch out," Carolyn said. "I'm just glad you made time for us little people. Daddy told me not to mention this to anyone, but I wasn't prepared for anything complicated. I don't know what I would have done without your help."

"I haven't been much help." Paul said. "I tracked down the Treasury information on the bonds. They're worth over ten thousand dollars. But I couldn't find a divorce decree. The clerk said if it was done in this county, they would have it."

"Maybe they filed it in Detroit," Carolyn said.

"Or maybe they never filed it at all. I did find Mama and Daddy's marriage license and it stated this was the first marriage for both of them," Paul said.

"It's possible he and Betty were never married," Carolyn speculated.

"I don't know, but you need to ask Daddy about this. He probably hasn't thought about it for ages."

"Paul, what if Daddy never got a divorce? Does that mean he and Mama aren't married?"

"Don't ask me. I didn't specialize in family law. It's possible he and Betty were never married. Charles could be a love child," Paul said and laughed.

Or maybe we are, Carolyn thought.

11

Raymond scheduled a visit to Eternal Rest, the old Dwight County Colored Cemetery, on the reunion agenda. Cecelia and I tried to dissuade him, but Raymond insisted on this ritual. He said the cemetery held history that would benefit the youngsters, and held memories for older relatives. He said it was our turn to clean it up and this way we could get more people involved in the upkeep.

I tried to talk my way out of the visit by saying I had to look over Daddy's papers. "Oh no," Cecelia said. "If I have to go, you're going."

A two-acre tract of land just past Cousin Edward's place is what's left of the Colored cemetery. We drove as close as we could, then hiked beside railroad tracks for about two hundred yards to a clearing surrounded by rows of soybeans and cotton. Mama Mary led the way. She is our grandfather's sister, and at ninety-eight; our oldest family member. We should send her picture to *Essence* or *Oprah* as an example of looking good at any age. She wears a short, snow white afro and always smells like Jergens lotion. Her husband and son died from consumption in the 1930's and she never remarried. She does her own cooking and walks to the bayou behind her house to fish at least twice a week.

Mama Mary has never been more than seventy miles from Eden and is the expert on our family history and the history of Dwight County. According to Mama Mary, the land next to the cemetery was the site of the church her brother, Simon pastored. The church burned in the early 1900's. Mama Mary said a group of whites set the fire as a warning to Uncle Simon to stop helping sharecroppers leave their plantations. They rebuilt the church closer to town, but kept using the cemetery. The original church trustees signed the deed in such a way that the land couldn't be sold without their signatures. Some said the land belonged to the heirs of Uncle Simon. Some said it belonged to the heirs of the trustees and some said the land belonged to Mr. Richmond, the white man that let his sharecroppers build the church on his land. He sold his land to Cousin Edwards' daddy during the depression, so some said the land belonged to Cousin Edward. That was at least four generations ago and no one was sure who owned the land now.

Once Forest Lawn opened to blacks, they stopped using Eternal Rest. No one had been buried there since the late 1960's. There was no caretaker and the land fell into disarray. Daddy and Uncle Nap organized a group to take care of it and keep it groomed. Whenever a family had relatives come to town, they made it a point to go to the cemetery and clean up. On the first Sunday of the year, all the black churches took up a collection to pay the taxes.

. "I can't believe you woke me up from a sound nap for this. I should have stayed with Daddy," Cecelia said. "Who but my brother would think people want to spend their vacations traipsing around a graveyard?"

"Cece, would you stop whining?" Raymond said. "Daddy wanted to come, but Mama said it was too hot and too much walking for him. Besides, we're taking our children to touch history. There are graves of former slaves out here. The kids should see this."

"That's right," Aunt Belle said. "You got to know where you been to know where you're going."

"All I see are weeds, weeds, weeds. Can't we pay somebody to come out here to do this?" Cecelia asked.

Raymond ignored her whining and assigned duties to the children. He brought Daddy's riding lawn mower on his truck and Mike was excited about driving it.

"I don't think it's a good idea for Mike to drive that mower. It's not a toy," Cecelia said. "Where is Charles? He should be driving the mower."

"Mama, it ain't no diff'rent than ridin' a bike. Don't be making Uncle Ray change his mind," Mike pleaded.

"Boy, will you listen to your English? In five hours, you've forgotten everything I've taught you in your eleven years on this earth." Cecelia threw up her hands and shook her head.

"Lighten up, Cece," Raymond said.

"Broken English and double negatives may be acceptable to you, but Mike knows better," Cecelia said.

"Give him a break. The boy don't have to talk white around us," Raymond said.

"It's not a matter of 'talking white'. It's a matter of using correct English."

"Correct according to who? According to white folks? When will we stop trying to---"

"Raymond, it is too hot to argue. Just worry about your own children. They can say 'dis', 'dat', and 'dey', all day long. Let them major in Ebonics. They won't be able to compete, and they will end up calling Mike saying, 'I ain't got no money'. Let's get busy so we can get out of here. This place is spooky."

Cecelia joined me by one of only two trees in the clearing. I kept quiet rather than risk being branded a whiner like Cece, but she was right. It was hot. Too hot to do anything other than sit on a porch and sip water or Kool-aid from a Mason jar. Sweat rolled down my neck and beneath my blouse. I knew Arkansas would be hot in July, but I didn't expect to be hiking through a graveyard with no shade in the middle of the day.

I was supposed to be picking weeds, but I was doing more reading than picking. I'm sure most of the deceased were related to me somehow. I can't recite the exact relationship. To get that information you had to talk to Aunt Belle or Mama Mary. Raymond called Mama Mary the family griot. She didn't particularly care for that name even after he explained to her that it was a position of respect and reverence in many African cultures. Mama Mary said "I don't know nothing about Africa. You got to speak American when you talk to me, and don't call me nothing but a child of God."

I walked up to Raymond and Mama who were standing over Mr. Simms' grave. Mr. Raymond Simms was principal of the colored elementary school for almost forty years. "I named you after him," Mama said. "He was an important man around here for a long time."

"We may have had old, worn textbooks and leaky roofs, but everyone learned. Being sent to Mr. Simms' office was like walking the plank. I guess being named after him is an honor," Raymond said.

Raymond's cell phone rang and startled Mama. "I will never get used to folks' pockets and purses ringing. Can't hardly concentrate in church, for phones ringing and beeping," she said. "I'm going to check on Beau's grave. I promised C.W. I would make sure it looks real nice."

"That was Daddy, he asked us to stop at the drug store and pick up his prescription. He also said you had a phone call from Warren. I told him I would give you the message, even though I don't want to," Raymond said.

"What are you talking about," I asked.

"Isn't Warren the guy I saw you with at The Shark Bar last year?"

Warren was helping me celebrate the end of another tax season. We were about to order, when I noticed Raymond and his date at the entrance.

"You were with some lady named Leslie. See, I can keep a boyfriend for more than a month."

"Is he still with his wife?"

"What?" I asked, looking around to see if anyone was listening.

"Come on Carolyn. You may have everyone else fooled, but I know the game."

"I never told you he was married."

"You didn't have to. Remember when I argued with you that Leslie's hair was real? You knew it was a weave, but I couldn't tell. Just like you knew about Leslie, I knew about Warren. I just figured it was a phase and you'd get through with him quickly. I didn't think you would keep seeing him. I thought you were smarter than that."

I was about to defend myself, but then we heard rumblings of thunder. I guess God didn't like what I was getting ready to say.

"I'm glad to hear the rain coming. Maybe it will cool off some," Cecelia said as she walked over to where we were standing.

"It's just a sun shower. It won't last long," Raymond predicted.

"They say if it rains while the sun is shining, the devil is beating his wife," Aunt Belle said as she fanned herself. We tried to get her to stay at the house, but she insisted on coming.

"Lord, I haven't heard that one in ages. Can you imagine we used to believe all that stuff? I wonder where those silly sayings came from," Cecelia said.

"Call them superstitions if you want to, you'll find it's usually right," Aunt Belle snapped.

"Belle you need to quit hanging on to all that ole' timey stuff," Uncle Henry said. "We used to be practically scared of our own shadows."

"I didn't see you calling it old timey when you asked for some garlic out of my garden to take back to Detroit," Aunt Belle countered.

"That's diff'rent. Garlic is a natchall' remedy. Ask your doctor," Uncle Henry said.

"I don't need no doctor to tell me what I been already knowing. You think you so---"

"Well, let's hurry and get busy before the rain starts," I interrupted, leading Aunt Belle toward a shade tree. Raymond winked at me and led Uncle Henry with him.

We broke into groups of two or three. We pulled weeds, trimmed grass and read the headstones. Some brought flowers to place on the headstones. It was an indescribable feeling to walk among those graves. To think of the obstacles they faced on a daily basis was humbling. Some headstones didn't have names. Some graves didn't even have headstones - just a cross.

I stopped at my great-grandparent's graves. Great-grandfather Otis died when Mama was young. They named me after Great-grandmother Carrie. She always seemed old to me and I didn't appreciate her or have time for her. She lived with us the last two years of her life and all I remember is the nasty Prince Albert spit can, she kept for her snuff. Mama would make one of us empty it and wash it out.

"Cecelia, Paul, I found our great grandparents. Come here," I beckoned.

Cecelia bent over to pull grass out of her sandals. "I wish I had driven. I'm ready to go," Cecelia she said.

"You're here, now. Just make the best of it. Look, here's someone that died in 1910. The writing was done by hand. It just says Stella. Died 1910," I said.

"They may not have even known when she was born. Some certificates in the courthouse as recent as the 1950's had estimated birth dates. I had a hard time finding---" Paul stopped in midsentence. He looked like he looked thirty years ago when he got caught using his church offering money for candy.

"Okay, don't stop now. I knew something was going on. Why were you at the courthouse?" Cecelia asked.

Paul looked at me. I should have known. He never could hold water.

Paul was opening his mouth to speak when I said, "Cecelia, let it go."

"Let what go? If something is going on, I need to know."

Paul was opening his mouth to speak when Mike interrupted. "Mama! Mama! Sheree is sick again."

We turned to see Raymond fanning her. "I think she got too hot," he said as Cecelia rushed to see what happened.

"She has on too many clothes. I guess she was trying to keep the mosquitoes off. Does anybody have any water?" Cecelia asked.

Raymond went to his truck to get his ice chest.

"Mama, I'm all right. I just needed to sit down. I'm not used to this heat," Sheree said.

"You city kids," Cecelia said. "When we were coming up, we stayed outside as long as we could. These kids can't handle anything that's not air-conditioned."

Paul and I offered to take Cecelia and Sheree back to the house.

"Really, I'm all right, Aunt Carolyn. You don't have to leave on my account," Sheree said.

"Hush, girl. You're messing up my get-away excuse," I whispered.

"We still have some unfinished business. I'll catch you two later,'' Cecelia said as she and Sheree got out of the car in front of Raymond's house.

"Not if I see you first," Paul said once she was out of earshot. "That was close."

"We're not clear, yet. You know how Cecelia is. She'll be on us like white on rice until we tell her something," I said.

"Should we tell her?"

"I guess it wouldn't hurt. She may even know something about Betty," I said. "I'm sure Daddy just forgot her name was still on some documents. And I'm also sure Daddy doesn't know about that loan Charles signed for. Daddy was fighting for his life, why would he be bothered with a loan? I wonder what else Charles has done? We need to find time to talk to Daddy before Monday."

"Julia had some ideas that may be helpful. Why don't you come over to the motel and we can talk about it?"

"You told her?" I asked, turning the air conditioning knob to high.

"Yeah, I had to let her know why I was gone all morning. She won't say anything. Hardly anyone talks to her anyway. You haven't really had a chance to get to know her. Come to our room for a little while."

"I don't think so. Just drop me off at the house."

"Carolyn," Paul hesitated, "I just want to say, I've enjoyed spending the day with you. You never call anymore. I forget about the time change and you're half asleep when I call you. I was beginning to think you were mad at me or something."

"No, I'm not mad at you. We'll catch up later, okay?" I said, looking at my watch. I wanted to get to the house and call Warren.

"We wouldn't have so much to catch up on, if you kept in touch. You didn't even come to my wedding."

"I told you I had to work."

"I know what you told me, but I don't believe anything at the IRS was that critical. It wasn't even tax time."

"I guess you think you're the only one with a demanding career?"

"No, that's not it. What I really think is that you're mad about Julia."

"Why would I be mad about Julia? She hasn't done anything to me."

"I'm not stupid, Carolyn. I just thought you would have gotten over it by now. You have to accept the fact that Julia is in my life."

"Why do I, make that we, have to accept it? Of all the places in the world, Los Angeles is the 'fine sister' capital of the world. You couldn't find one that met your criteria? I'm sure Julia is a nice girl. But do you honestly think she would be interested in you if you weren't a lawyer? I get tired of white girls always getting our brothers with money."

"Carolyn, I cannot believe you. You say 'we' but you're the only one with an attitude. Mama and everybody else likes Julia. Why can't you just be happy for me?"

"Look, you started this conversation. I've been nice to Julia. What more do you want from me?"

"I want us to be like we used to be. You've had boyfriends I didn't approve of, but I didn't cut you off. Raymond says you're even seeing a married man. But I'm not judging you. I sent you a ticket for the Soul Train Music Awards and you wouldn't even come. We could've had a ball. How could you let this come between us?"

"You don't understand. It's different for men. I have nothing against her personally. I'm glad you're happy and I'm proud of you. I'm *not* proud that my brother saw nothing in the four women who raised him that he thought good enough for himself."

"Carolyn, wait. It's not like that at all. You think I woke up one day and said, ' I'm gonna find me a white girl, by golly?' Julia and I worked together six months before I even realized I wanted to see her outside work."

"Spare me, please. I don't need to know the details."

"What you *do* need to know is that she is most like the four women that raised me than anyone I've met. She's patient and tolerant like Mama and she's feisty and funny like Beverly. She's smart like you and Cecelia. Other than you and Beverly, she's the only woman I know that likes to fish." Paul drove his rental car up to the porch, but left the motor running.

"I told you, I have nothing against her personally."

"Then I don't understand why you won't give her a chance. Mama, Beverly and Cece love her. She knows how close you and I are, or at least used to be, and she wants to get to know you."

"Save the violins. I told you before, I have nothing against her. It's just what she represents that I can't stand," Carolyn said, as she unfastened her seat belt.

"Then you're no better than any KKK member, if you dismiss a whole race based on what a few did to you or your perception of them," Paul argued.

"Perception is reality. I'm not Raymond and I don't want to debate the socio-political-economic impact of who you screw. That's your business. Just don't ask me to be happy about it. I'm going in the house before you use up all your gas sitting here with the motor running. You need to get back. You don't want to keep Miss Ann waiting."

"Well, I'm glad we had this family talk," Paul said. "Next time, tell me how you really feel."

12

The first official event of the reunion was the fish fry at Cousin Edward's place. Raymond smiled to himself with each hug, kiss and greeting exchanged as family members saw each other for the first time this weekend. Months of planning, endless errands and weekly crises had paid off. Despite being thrown into the role of Host Committee Chairman at the last minute, Raymond pulled everything together. Things couldn't have been smoother if Martha Stewart had planned them herself.

This was the first reunion he had actively helped plan. His position helped him adjust quickly to life in Eden and become reacquainted with family members he had only interacted with superficially while living in Chicago. He coordinated everything from purchasing toothpicks to preparation of the family tree.

He was relieved that things were going well. Yet this was a bittersweet occasion for him. The picturesque gazebo in the yard had been the site of countless barbecues, weddings and impromptu get-togethers through the years, but this would be the last family gathering at Cousin Edwards' place. Cousin Edward was selling his land to Consolidated Farms, Inc. This was a blow to the organizational efforts of the East Arkansas branch of the Black Farmers Alliance. Cousin Edward was a founding member of the Dwight County chapter. Cousin Edward encouraged Raymond to get involved and nominated him for treasurer at their last election. Raymond initially felt betrayed by

Cousin Edward's defection, and their exchange at the last meeting had been contentious.

The BFA met bimonthly at Mama's church. Cousin Edward stood immediately after Rev. Handley opened the meeting with prayer. "Before we get to old business, I have an announcement to make. I know some of you have heard rumors about me selling to Consolidated and I want you to get the facts from me. We signed the contracts yesterday, and they will take over on August 1. It was a hard decision to make, but I couldn't turn down their offer."

Several men rose and shook Edward's hand. "I hope this doesn't mean you're leaving town," Rev. Handley said.

"What are you going to do with your equipment?" Booker T asked.

"Hey, now you can pay me back that five dollars you owe me," Uncle Nap said.

Raymond stood and spoke over everyone else, "What are you all doing? You're congratulating him like he won the lottery or something. You should be mourning the death of another black farm. Why didn't you let one of the members buy you out?"

"I contacted a few people, but CFI didn't give me much time. You know I lease most of my land now, and with crop prices down, the tenant farmers have trouble making their payments. I talked to your daddy and a couple other fellas around here. No one could match their offer."

"So you sold us out? Black people need to become more self-sufficient and we're turning over what little land we still own. You owe this community ---"

"You're out of line, young blood," Edward said quietly in his raspy, bass voice. "I don't owe nobody nothing. That's what being a farmer is all about. Being free to determine your own living, with the help of the good Lord. I cut back a few years ago and been renting out most of my land. I'm not selling out. I'm retiring. I was farming before you was even thought of. You talk a good game, but I don't see you riding no tractor or irrigating no crops cause the rains didn't come. So don't go telling me about being self-sufficient."

"Don't mind Raymond. You do what you got to do," C.W. said. "I wish I could buy your land. With crop prices being what they is, I just can't meet their price. I can barely find fellas to work the land I got now. Young folks ain't interested in farming no more. I thought about selling, but I believe if they want it that bad, it must be worth ten times what they're offering, so I'm going to try to hold on. I want to keep my land in the family."

"I wasn't going to say nothing, but CFI contacted me too," another gentleman said. "Emma's boy, Lester, works with them. Me and him talked a long time and he made me a good offer. I got til' next week to give them my answer."

Raymond sat and shook his head. "Can't you see what they are trying to do? People laugh when I say there's a conspiracy, but it's obvious to me. It's the oldest trick in the book. They send Lester- probably the only black man in the whole company-, to talk to us. Once you have all sold your land, I wonder if Lester will still have a job? I guess I'm the only one not blinded by dollar signs."

"You're the only one that ain't got his living tied up in this deal. You're a smart boy, but you ain't no farmer. I ain't seen you plant nary a seed nor crop," Edward said as he moved the wad of chewing tobacco to the other side of his cheek.

"Mr. Edward is right, Raymond," Derrick said. "I hate to lose another farmer, black or white. If it makes you feel any better, CFI is buying out the white farmers too. It's not a black vs. white issue. It's big vs. small. What Walmart did to Main Street merchants, CFI and others like them are doing to farming. Cotton and soybean prices have hit bottom and stayed there the last two years. A lot of small farmers are getting out."

"But Daddy is one of the largest landowners in the county," Raymond said.

"He may be the largest black landowner. But he's still classified as a small farmer. Farms these days are thousands of acres," Derrick said.

"Well, you're the County Agent. Can't you do something? Don't they have programs to help these guys stay in business?" Raymond asked as he paced the floor.

"Sure, there are lots of programs. But they're designed to help farmers increase their yields, or resist disease or repay the bank. They aren't designed to put money in these men's pockets, like CFI is doing. Look around you. I don't mean any disrespect gentlemen, but only a few of us in this room aren't senior citizens. Realistically this may be their last chance to cash out," Derrick said.

"There may be snow on the roof, but there's still fire in the oven," Uncle Nap quipped.

"Derrick is right. It's different for C.W." Edward said. "He has you boys to take over. Charles has worked side by side with your daddy for years. I even saw Beverly's boy over there driving a tractor. When my boy got locked up, I knew I would end up selling this place. My girls don't know nothing about farming and their husbands ain't interested."

"If they made me a good deal, I would sell too," Booker T. said.

"Because of my job, I'm supposed to be impartial," Derrick said. "I will tell you this. Make sure you get a fair price. Your land is worth a lot of money. I can't tell you what other farmers have gotten, but you know which white farmers have recently sold land. Go down to the courthouse and check the tax records for sales prices because I have seen biased pricing. Also, get the advice of an accountant. The timing and terms of your sale impacts your taxes significantly. There's a guy in West

Memphis that will come to your house and go over the figures with you."

"What about the black farmers lawsuit settlement?" Raymond pleaded. "The government has already settled the Pigford v. Glickman lawsuit for millions of dollars."

"Boy, that was the biggest lie ever told," Uncle Nap said. "They wrote it up in the paper like it was a lot of money. But they only offered each farmer fifty thousand dollars. That will barely buy a good used tractor."

"Much of that is earmarked for loan programs that most black farmers can't qualify for. They're not profitable enough," Derrick said.

"The only people happy with that settlement is the lawyers. They got millions," Edward said. "A few farmers got debt relief, and then had to turn around and pay taxes on it."

"Most of the people that did get paid don't even farm anymore," Booker T said.

"You know how the government works," Uncle Nap said. "We'll be dead and gone before they settle with everyone. A few have been paid, but I think they're just trying to wait us out."

Raymond paced and shook his head. "The Nation of Islam has been buying land. Maybe I could talk to one of the brothers in Chicago. Can't you all just hold out a little longer?" Raymond asked.

"Boy you're getting into other folks business," C.W. warned. "These men know how to handle their affairs. Leave them alone. I always said I would *never* sell my land, but I may be calling CFI too. Maybe three generations of farmers is enough, and it's time to move on. Sometimes things don't work out like you plan."

The agenda then turned to more mundane things like dues and weather reports. Raymond managed to offer Cousin Edward best wishes at the end of the meeting, but he still felt a loss over Cousin Edward's announcement.

That feeling lingered now, as he watched his children playing in the tire swing with their cousins. Enjoy it while you can, he thought. This may be the end of an era.

"It's been ages since I've been out here, but if I were lost, I would follow my nose. I smell garlic and onion," I said as I lowered the window on Beverly's Ford Expedition. "I remember all we used to smell out here was hog poop. When we were kids, I dreaded coming out here. Some houses even had outhouses until the 1970's. The television reception was poor and their well water left a nasty, metallic aftertaste."

"Well times have changed. This is prime land now. All Cousin Edward's neighbors - if you want to call them that, the houses are about a mile apart - are white. Black people sold out when their children grew up and left the farms," Beverly said. "Some land has frontage on Council Lake, and whites have been buying the land for vacation homes and hunting lodges. Cousin Edward and Daddy are one of a few remaining blacks that still own any sizeable tracts of land in Dwight County."

"The last time I came out here, the roads were still gravel. Back then, you had to watch for cows, and get out of the car every one hundred yards or so to open the gate that crossed the gravel road. Only six families lived on this road off Highway 29, and you had to watch closely for the opening or you would miss the turn," I said.

"We thought this was really the boonies. We may have been in the country, but at least we had city water and our roads were paved," Cecelia said.

"I have a new appreciation for this land after seeing Daddy's papers. As kids, we couldn't wait to grow up, graduate and leave. Daddy and other farmers had a lot of land, but as far as we were concerned they had a lot of nothing. We couldn't have been more wrong."

"That fish sure does smell good," I said as we got out of the SUV.

"You know it's probably not on your diet. I wonder if they used shortening or peanut oil," Cecelia said.

"Girl, you nag too much. I don't see how your husband stands it. By the way, where is Charles?" I asked. "I haven't seen him since I've been here. Have you?"

"No. I think he's boycotting this event. He still thinks Raymond took over so he's not coming," Beverly said.

The original plan was for Charles to coordinate the fish fry. On one of our three-way long distance calls, Beverly and Raymond told Cecelia and me that plan wasn't working.

"I need each of you to send about seventy bucks so we can get this fish fry together. I usually try to take up for a brother, but Charles is really making it hard," Raymond said.

"Just admit it, Raymond. The boy screwed up," Beverly said.

"What happened?" I asked.

"We've already sent more than our share. We're not serving lobster. Just go out to the lake and catch some fish. What's so hard about that?" Cecelia asked.

"Charles got a deal on some fish last month. He gave Jesse Stevens the money and Jesse agreed to store it in his deep freezer. Well, Jesse's wife left and took all the money. His lights got turned off and all the fish spoiled," Raymond explained.

"Then Charles should make him reimburse the money," Cecelia stated.

"Get real. The man can't keep his lights turned on. How is he going to pay for fish that wasn't even his?" Raymond asked.

"Looks like that's not all he couldn't keep turned on. I heard his wife ran off with their next door neighbor," Beverly said.

"Is that the Jesse Stevens that used to run the cafe?" Cecelia asked.

"Yeah, girl. Everybody knew his wife---"

Raymond interrupted Beverly, "You can gossip on your own dime. Let's get back to the business at hand."

"I'll send the money Monday," I said.

"I don't see that we have much choice," Cecelia said. "We've already told everyone we were having a fish fry. Make sure you collect seventy dollars from Charles. This is all his fault."

"Cecelia, it does no good to cast blame at this point. We just need to get the situation resolved," Raymond said.

"Yeah, yeah. You just get some money from Charles. You would think a person would have a little more wisdom once they past the half-century mark. Don't try to let him off either. I'm going to ask him when I see him," Cecelia said.

Raymond recovered from Charles' fumble and pans overflowed with catfish, crappies, buffalo, and bass. Gallons of spaghetti, and coleslaw, and platters of sliced ruby red tomatoes, cucumbers and scallions lined the picnic tables. There was no remnant of the chaos that reigned just a few days ago.

Raymond always came through in a crisis. He organized a parent's security group after a shooting outside his kid's school. At the bank he had been the trouble-shooter for the computer system. It was Raymond to the rescue when his parents needed help after his father's stroke. Everyone was always appreciative of his efforts. Everyone but Geneva. He caught himself staring at Rayven. She had vanilla colored skin and dimples like her mother. She had graduated from the training bras she had worn when he left and it looked like she was going to be well-endowed like her mother. This was his first reunion without Geneva. She got along well with his family, and his parents loved her like their own daughter. He always thought he would have a marriage like his parents. But marriage in twenty-first century Chicago was hard. Most of his peers were divorced and those that weren't, were miserable, or had a woman on the side. He had never been unfaithful to his wife and didn't like dating. He thought about the reunion in Orlando, when he and Geneva organized a side trip to Eatonville to visit the hometown of Zora Neale Hurston. He thought about their trips to Eden when they always stopped at the Civil Rights Museum in Memphis. Even though relatives surrounded him, something was missing.

We gathered around the tables to bless the food. This was the first official event of the reunion and Mama Mary said we should start it off right. We held hands and bowed our heads while she prayed. "Master, Lord, Jesus, we thank you for the safe arrival of those gathered, and we ask you to bless those on their way. We pray for those that desired to come but couldn't make it. You have brought this family from a mighty long way. We know we couldn't have made it without you. You have been our shelter in a time of storm, a bridge over troubled waters . . . "

I peeked at the table and made a mental note to avoid the side of the spaghetti platter where two flies hovered. I caught Raymond's eye and he smiled. We were used to this routine. Mama Mary's tone rose and fell to a chorus of 'amens' and 'yes, Lords'. Mama Mary prayed longer than some ministers preached. She was well known for her praying ability and was always asked to pray at church meetings and other gatherings. Her resonant praying voice was stronger and deeper than her speaking voice. She was our own Barbara Jordan. Surely if God heard anyone, he heard her. She was long-winded, but out of respect for her age no one ever told her to keep it short. You never knew when you might need her to pray for you.

Finally, we lined up to heap food on our plates. We were hungry and grateful Mama Mary had finally finished the prayer. "Everything looks so good. I don't know what I want to eat first," I said to Cecelia.

"You know, if you scrape off the breading, the fish won't be as fattening," she informed me.

"Are you kidding? That's the best part. I don't get a treat like this often. I'll just spend more time on the treadmill next week."

People were steadily arriving, and hugs and kisses were in abundance. Everyone was in good spirits. Well, almost everyone. Leave it to Cousin Veronica to rain on everyone's parade.

"No wonder black people have so much high blood pressure," she commented with disdain. "Baked fish is so much better for you. Why is everything fried?"

"I think that's why they call it a fish fry." Uncle Nap snickered.

Uncle Nap was Aunt Belle's son by her first husband. His name was Napoleon Roebuck Wilson. His father died in a mill accident, shortly after our grandmother died. She and Grandaddy Beau moved together and Uncle Nap and Daddy were raised as brothers. He was a quick wit and always had a joke to tell. He was funny as long as you weren't the object of his jokes. He could talk about you so bad, he'd make you cry. But you didn't want to cry, because then he would talk about you even worse. Mama and Daddy made old times sound depressing and hard. Uncle Nap's version sounded altogether different. He made picking cotton and sharecropping sound fun. He said it was hard, but you had to laugh to keep from crying.

Uncle Nap fixed his plate and returned to the men's corner. These events were supposed to be reunions for the entire family. Invariably the men ended up on one side and the women on the other. Daddy, Uncle Nap, Uncle Henry and others were sitting near the porch catching up and trying to out-lie each other. This was the first time many had been back to Arkansas in decades.

Each new relative brought another round of, "Chubby, look at you. I remember when you were just a little girl. Now you're a grown woman." Or I heard, "You've lost so much weight. Have you been sick, baby?" Of course, my cousins closer to my age were delighted. Jackie is one of my favorite cousins and I finally saw her at the fish fry. "Girl, who are you and what did you do with my cousin?" she exclaimed and hugged me.

I joined Beverly and Cecelia at a table and was reaching for the hot sauce when Derrick appeared. "I haven't seen you for twenty years, and now I've seen you two days in a row. Lucky me!" he said. "Mind if I join you?" he asked, sitting before I could answer.

Beverly and Cecelia were chatting like they hadn't seen each other in years. I see Cecelia all the time and Beverly and I caught up yesterday. So Derrick and I caught up on each other's lives. More accurately, I caught up on his life. I was surprised to find out he already knew what I had been up to for the last twenty years.

His grandmother was in a nursing home in Eden and he came over to visit her for the holiday weekend. He tried to get her to move to West Memphis, so she could be closer to him. But she felt better being near her friends, even if it was in a nursing home. She fell and broke her hip last year and it never healed right. She couldn't get around too well and moved in the nursing home the first of the year. Derrick was single, with no children and worked for the State Agricultural Department.

Everyone's attention was drawn to the glistening, pearl, white Lincoln Continental coming up the road toward the house. We all knew who it was, without reading the SAW personalized license plate. Uncle Sill stepped out of the car wearing a tan suit, matching snake skin shoes, a tan and white Panama hat, dark, tortoise shell sunglasses and a ring on every finger.

"Boy, you're cleaner than the Board of Health," Uncle Nap said as they hugged each other.

Uncle Sill's real name is Sylvester Archer Washington and he isn't really our uncle. He's our cousin, but he's so much older than we are, we call him uncle. His mama was Daddy's youngest sister Henrietta. Aunt Henrietta died when Uncle Sill was a teenager. They say her old man shot her because he heard she was messing around. That was grown folks' talk so we only heard the story in bits and pieces. Sill went to live with Daddy in Detroit, but it wasn't long before he struck out on his own.

No one really knows what Uncle Sill does for a living. He has no visible means of support, and I think we're afraid to ask. He worked in the Ford plant a few years. Other than that, no one ever knew of him holding a job. He buys a new Lincoln every other year, and they say he pays cash. He always has a new woman with him, and he always comes bearing gifts. He pulled packages out of the car for Mama, his aunts and Mama Mary along with a Toys-R-Us bag that he let all the kids reach in and pull something out of.

We were watching the 'Christmas in July' exhibition when Beverly announced she was ready to go.

"We haven't finished eating yet. What's your hurry?" I asked.

Cecelia looked up from picking bones out of her fish. "Is that who I think it is? She has a lot of nerve coming out here."

"Who and what are you talking about?" I asked as I licked my fingers.

"Don't turn around, but Wanda Ann just drove up. Can you believe she had the nerve to show her face?" Cecelia said.

"She figured I wouldn't kick her butt out here in front of everybody. I should go pull that raggedy weave right out of her head," Beverly said. She had stopped eating and was standing up.

"Have some class girl. You will embarrass Mama and Daddy to no end if you clown Wanda out here," I said.

"Don't worry, this will be short and sweet." Beverly walked toward Wanda.

"Cecelia, we've got to stop her," I said.

"What you mean ' we'? My name is Bennett and I ain't in it," Cecelia said.

Now, she says she's not in it. Cecelia was the one who started this mess in the first place. Well, actually Anthony started it by messing around with Wanda. Cecelia heard about it and called Beverly. Beverly didn't believe it at first. Wanda and Beverly were close friends growing up. They used to do each other's hair. Wanda's husband, and Anthony were best friends so they often double dated in school. Wanda had divorced a few years ago and Beverly stuck with Wanda through all her emotional changes. She even gave her some equipment and supplies so she could open her own beauty shop in Eden. Wanda took Beverly's generosity too far and helped herself to her husband. Angela Phillips, who is Cousin Cookie's sister-in-law, saw Wanda and Anthony together at the movie theater in Forrest City. She told Cousin Cookie, who told Sheryl, who told her sister, Jackie, who told Cecelia, who told Beverly.

Now, here we were about to have the showdown at the OK corral. Everybody knew about Wanda and Anthony. Luckily, Uncle Sill was still holding center court and most eyes were on him and the Diahann Carroll look-a-like with him. A few were trying to see what Beverly was going to do without being obviously nosy. Beverly was marching toward Wanda. Wanda was greeting Cousin Edward and had her back toward Beverly.

"Cecelia, come on. We can't let Beverly make a fool of herself out here," I said. "Anyway, Anthony is the one she should be mad at."

"That's a different kind of mad. Wanda was supposed to be her friend. That is unforgivable and she deserves to get her butt kicked."

"Then, she needs to find a different forum. Go on Jerry Springer and ambush her, not here."

Beverly had reached Wanda and tapped her shoulder. I lowered my head. I didn't want to witness the carnage. Beverly could always fight. Nobody messed with any of us, because they knew Beverly could beat everybody up, boys included. Good thing Cecelia was a nurse. Somebody was going to need medical attention when this was through. It might even be me because this drama was going to give me a heart attack.

I hadn't heard any shouting yet. I peeked from under my eyelids to see Beverly and Wanda hugging and laughing like old friends. Beverly hugged her again and whispered something in her ear, then came back to our table. "You ladies ready to go?" she asked us sweetly.

It wasn't really a question since Beverly was driving. Derrick handed me a business card with his home phone number written on it. Cecelia, Beverly and I made a graceful exit and headed toward Mama's house.

"What did you say to her?" I asked.

"I told her we discovered Anthony has herpes-B and she should see a doctor."

"Is that true?" I asked.

"Of course not," Cecelia said. "There is no herpes-B and herpes doesn't lay dormant. If that were true, she would have known it by now."

"That stupid heifer won't know that. It'll mess with her mind all weekend until she can get to a doctor. Revenge is sweet." Beverly said with a satisfied smile, as she turned onto the main highway.

"I wish you had waited until I finished my catfish before making your dramatic exit. I've denied myself fried foods for two months, just waiting for this day. I sure hated to leave it behind."

"Get over it, Carolyn," Beverly said, as we parked in front of the porch. "We needed to leave early anyway. The barbecue is here tomorrow and I told Mama we would help her with the cole slaw and potato salad."

"Don't volunteer me for work. I say just order it from the grocery store."

"Girl, you will make your mother the laughing stock of Eden with store bought potato salad," Beverly said.

"It's too muggy to be sitting outside anyway," Cecelia stated. "I can't wait to get in the house and crank up the air. I'm glad Raymond finally talked Daddy into getting central air."

We entered the front room to find Sheree sitting in the dark watching television. "Why are you cooped up in here?" Cecelia asked. "I thought all the young people were going to Jackie's."

"I didn't feel like going," Sheree said. "I told Grandma Lois I would stay here and peel potatoes for the potato salad."

"Oh, Lord. Now I know my child is sick. You offered to do some work?"

"Yes I did, and it's a good thing I was here. Daddy called and said he's going to spend the night with Grandmother Juel. Uncle Anthony called and said he won't be down here until tomorrow."

"Did he say he had to work?" Beverly asked.

"I didn't ask. I just took the message. Oh, yeah. Aunt Carolyn, some guy named Warren called."

"Warren who?" Cecelia teased. "The way she was talking to Derrick, I thought Warren would be a faint memory."

"Um hum. That Bucky did turn out pretty cute. You go, girl," Beverly said.

"Don't even try it. You know Derrick is like a brother to us. Besides, he's younger than me."

"Don't *you* try it. Bucky *was* like a brother to us. But Derrick is fine, F-I-N-E, and he is not your brother," Cecelia said.

"He's only a couple years younger and age doesn't have a thing to do with anything. You know what they say about an older woman and a younger man. Look what it did for Stella!" Beverly stated.

"Yeah, girl, go ahead and get your groove back!" Cecelia laughed.

"Who said I lost my groove?" I asked with my hand on my hip. "You all are too bad. If you'll excuse me, ladies, I need to return a phone call," I said.

"Carolyn, don't bother to call him back," Beverly said. You can always tell who a man is serious about, by who he spends his holidays with."

"That's right. Don't let him think you're sitting around waiting for his call," Cecelia said.

"Why are you both all up in my business? I don't recall asking for your opinions."

"Don't get mad at us," Cecelia said. "You know we're right. We're only trying to keep you from wasting your time. Men will tell you they know right away when they meet the right woman. It doesn't take years of dating."

"Derrick seems promising, " Cecelia said.

"He is cute, with a good job too," Beverly commented. "A few years younger than you, but that's okay. Women live longer than men anyway."

"I think he and Karen Jones dated for quite a while, but I heard they broke up. So now is your chance," Cecelia reported.

"I heard he caught her with Booker T.'s son. She knows she messed up big time and has been trying to get him back ever since."

"She can probably chalk that one up to experience. Men can mess around all they want, but they rarely forgive a woman for stepping out," Beverly said.

"Long distance relationships are hard. But Derrick would be a good catch," Cecelia said.

"He may be a good catch, but I'm not fishing. I've made it this far, I think I can handle things myself."

"Yeah, you can handle things all right. Let's see, there was Antoine, your coworker who was working overtime on more than just tax returns," Cecelia said. "There was Marcus, the mailman. He was all right as long as he took his medication."

Beverly piped in, "What about Jeffrey? Wasn't he the one who lived with his mother and was always 'between jobs'? His mother wanted them to get married so she could get him out of the house."

"Then there was Lorenzo. That courtship was so quick, you probably didn't even hear about it. She met him on Monday. They were engaged by Saturday and broke up three weeks later. He was so jealous, she couldn't even go to the grocery store alone," Cecelia said. "Don't forget Jerome. The reason she left here in the first place was to be with him. I begged her not to move in with him, and as soon as she did, the romance fizzled."

"And I remember you telling me about some old man she was dating," Beverly said.

"Girl, that man was older than Daddy. Now he did have money, but he couldn't remember where he put it."

"Cecelia, stop lying," I laughed. Even I had to chuckle at the mention of some of the losers I had tried to forget.

"I've been trying to get her to go out with a man from my church. He would be perfect."

"No more men from your church, please. I let you fix me up once and I ended up being stalked by the church lady. Cecelia gave my phone number to that man and I had to get my number changed. His girlfriend, a 'good sister' from the church saw my number on his caller ID and harassed me for weeks."

"I thought he and Sister Harris had broken up."

"Well, apparently Sister Harris didn't think so. I visited your church one Sunday, and the woman practically cursed me out in the church parking lot."

"I introduced Geneva and Raymond," Cecelia said.

"We see how they ended up," I said.

"That's just because Raymond is so stubborn. They were a good couple," Cecelia said.

"Let's go out tonight," Beverly said. "You might meet Mr. Right."

"The men in clubs are not my type. All the nice fellas are at home."

"How do you know? You're nice and you'd be there. You may meet one of these good ol' Southern men. That's what you need."

"I think she's already met one," Cecelia said.

13

Friday evening, my sisters and I sat on the porch and snapped peas for Sunday dinner, just like we did when we were growing up. Mama always cooked her Sunday dinner ahead of time, so on Saturdays, there was extra cooking and dishes to wash. While my brothers were off fishing, or playing basketball, we had kitchen duty. Women's lib didn't exist in our house. Beverly, Cecelia and I did the cooking and housework. But there was a benefit to the kitchen chores. If we were having something special like ham or banana pudding we would sneak and get samples. Daddy would sneak, too. Mama fussed at us, but never at Daddy. He always said he might not wake up tomorrow, so he was getting his while he could.

Sundays were filled with church activities. After Sunday School and church service, we rushed home to eat, change clothes and returned to church. There was always an auxiliary program, anniversary or choir program to attend on Sunday afternoon. This was supposed to be Mama's day of rest. These activities were even more hectic than the weekly routine, so it didn't seem like a day of rest to me.

"Are you taking these to the banquet Sunday?" I asked.

"No, this is for us to have at home after church. I got a small ham and some corn on the cob in the freezer, and I made some black berry dumplings just for us. God blesses the child that has his own. So we will have our own," Mama said.

"Mama, we have so much food already. Do we really need these peas?" asked Beverly.

"There must be a million peas here," whined Sheree. "We'll be here all night."

"Girl this is nothing. We used to do bushels full at a time, pack them and freeze them. We used to shell peas for hours." Cecelia said.

"I know that's right," Beverly said. "I remember shelling purple hull peas and then I couldn't get the stains off my hands. I had a date with Anthony that night, who was only the finest boy in the County. I couldn't have messed up hands, that would be just too tacky. I went to town to the white beauty shop. The black ones didn't do manicures then. That was when I decided I wanted to own a classy beauty salon. I didn't want to keep doing hair in my kitchen or a garage. I wanted a shop just like that one, that gave facials and manicures, with color coordinated fixtures and furniture. The women in there looked at me like I was from the moon, but they did my nails. The next year, I was the first black person to work there."

"I haven't seen my son-in-law today, where is Anthony?" Mama asked.

"He has been working a late shift," Beverly replied.

Cecelia and I cut our eyes at each other. Anthony's absence was a good thing as far as I was concerned.

"Well you're not going to drive back tonight are you? Why don't you spend the night?" Mama asked. "Folks drive crazy on a holiday weekend."

"I didn't bring any clothes with me. I thought Anthony was going to bring them. Maybe Carolyn and Cece can ride back with me tonight. We're going shopping in the morning in Memphis anyway. We can drive tonight instead of in the morning," Beverly said.

"You and Uncle Anthony knew each other in high school?" Sheree asked.

"We sure did. He graduated before I did and worked at the tire plant. Mama and Daddy didn't like him though."

"It wasn't that we didn't like him. We didn't want you two getting too familiar," Mama stated.

"It was too late to be worrying about that," Cecelia said.

"We thought we were keeping close tabs on you. I was putting your clothes away and found a box of starch in your drawer. I knew then you were expecting. I was glad you weren't too far along and were able to graduate with your class."

"What does starch have to do with being pregnant?" Sheree asked.

"A lot of rural women claimed to crave starch when they were pregnant," Cecelia said. "It's very unhealthy. There is no nutritional value and the woman is full so she doesn't eat healthy foods."

"Aunt Beverly, you and Uncle Anthony were doing the wild thing back then?"

Cecelia cleared her throat. "I think this conversation may be too grown for mixed company."

"Oh, please. This child can probably teach us something, " Beverly said.

"Beverly, if you had a daughter you would understand. It's not like it was when we were coming up. There's more to worry about than getting pregnant. There's AIDS now. And you can't get welfare like you used to," Cecelia said.

"What are you talking about? I was never on welfare. If I did have a daughter, I would tell her the real deal. I would tell her to protect herself. And I wouldn't tell her to come to me when she's ready, like so many of you do. Sheree will never come to you. Think about it, would you have gone to Mama?" Beverly asked.

"Sheree and I have a good relationship. We can talk. Don't you think so honey?"

"Don't put the girl on the spot. Besides, I always knew what I wanted. I wanted Anthony and I wanted a salon," Beverly said.

"Then I guess you've been successful," I said. "You've gotten what you wanted. Cecelia always wanted to be a nurse. She always wanted a boy and a girl. I guess we all can't get everything."

"What kind of talk is that?" Mama said. "You finished law school. Do you know how special that is? I know you probably want children, but you still have time. The right man will find you. There is someone for everyone. Maybe it's Willie."

"No, he's not the one," I said without bothering to correct his name. Somewhere out there, someone has more than their share of male attention, because my someone hadn't found me yet. I had been so busy; this was the first time I had even thought about Warren. "I doubt if I get married. I don't feel like going through the changes men take you through these days."

"Well I never liked him anyway. Even Michael said there was something about him he didn't trust," Cecelia said.

"You need an older man," Mama said. "Your Daddy is almost ten years older than me. He had already done his running around and was ready to settle down when we met."

"Mama, I've dated older men, joined singles groups, met men over the Internet and had blind dates. They don't make men like Daddy any more."

"Carolyn, baby, have you asked God?" Mama asked, as she pulled peapods out of the basket. "I was the last one of my friends to marry. They were having babies and I was still living with my mother. I didn't think I would ever get married. I just prayed and then I met your Daddy. He found me at the Café. I was working and he would come in every day and sit at one of my tables, and order a fried egg sandwich. Folks didn't eat out as often as they do now, so I had an idea he was sweet on me."

"But you were only twenty-two," I said.

"That was an old maid in those days."

"You know, Mama, I pray all the time, but it seems petty to ask God for a man when there are children starving in Somalia."

"That's not petty. The Bible tells us, 'you have not because you ask not'. Where else would you go for a man or anything else, other than to the One who holds everything?" she asked.

"Yeah, girl. It is written that you cannot live by bread alone. You need some *beef*," Beverly said.

Cecelia and I laughed. "Beverly, you are crazy, girl," I said.

"All right. Don't go taking the Lord's word so lightly," Mama chastised above our laughter.

"Lighten up, Mama. You're the one who told her to pray for a man. Maybe that will be Reverend Handley's sermon topic on Sunday," Beverly laughed. "Touch your neighbor and say 'a man.'

"She's not just praying for a man. She's asking for inner peace and contentment, so you will feel whole until he sends the right one your way. And you need the will not to have sexual relations. I seen it on Oprah. That's the reason men these days don't feel the need to marry. You girls give it up too easily."

"Let's change the subject," Cecelia said as she stood. "There's a minor in the room."

"She needs to hear this too," Mama said. "Stay a virgin, baby."

"Mama, I watch Oprah too, and a seventeen year old virgin is as common as a honest politician," Beverly said.

"You obviously have my daughter confused with some of the hot-tail girls your son runs around with. My daughter is a lady."

"May I be excused?" Sheree asked as she stood and dumped her peas in Mama's bowl.

"Is that all you've done? Girl, you're lucky you have cans at home. You would be here all night at your pace," Mama said.

"Yes, Lord. Hallelujah for cans." Sheree stomped her foot and raised her hand in the air.

"See how easily children can be corrupted? Now you have her blaspheming the Lord," Cecelia stated. "We'll leave so you all can finish your X-rated conversation." Cecelia dumped her peas in my bowl and went in the house with Sheree.

"You girls go talk to Cece," Mama said. "I wanted all my children here so they could have fun and fellowship with each other. It hasn't even been twenty-four hours and you're fighting already."

"We're not fighting, Mama," I said. "Cecelia is always so dramatic. She *wants* us to come after her."

"I think she's irritable because she and Michael are having problems. I noticed she wasn't wearing her wedding rings," Mama said. "I hope they aren't splitting up. Folks don't want to work on their marriage anymore. Go talk to her."

Beverly grabbed my arm. "Let's go talk to her." Then she whispered to me. "At least we get out of shelling peas."

"I'm not sure that's a fair trade off," I whispered.

Beverly and I followed Cecelia to her room and found her unpacking a long nightgown.

"Put that gown back in your suitcase," Beverly ordered, holding up a peace sign. "Let's call a truce. Carolyn and I want to go out."

Cecelia looked at me skeptically and said, "I find that hard to believe. Carolyn can't even stay awake for the ten o'clock news."

I had to admit she was right. Driving an hour to some sweaty club and getting my hair full of smoke did not appeal to me. I was looking forward to getting some rest and snacking on leftovers. I've been on the go since I arrived, and we left the fish fry before I got my fill. I also planned to sneak in a call to Warren. I knew I couldn't talk to him, but I was going to leave a message on his cell phone.

"Well, she's on vacation now. I know a club in Memphis with an oldies night that I've wanted to check out. Anthony and I haven't been able to synchronize our schedules to go."

Cecelia shook her head. "Beverly, I don't feel like it, it's already late. I know you're trying to show us a good time, but---"

"Hey, this isn't just for you." Beverly said. "I want to have a good time too. I work like a dog and never go anywhere. I went out with Tanya a few times, but I felt so old. She picked a club and I felt like I was partying with Tony. When I picked a club, she was bored. I went out with Sharon once and that was one time too many. Her motto is 'a hard man is good to find'. If I wanted to be alone, I could've stayed at home. We haven't done anything like this in years. We can spend the night at my house and have a pajama party. It will be fun. Don't you think so, Carolyn?"

"I don't know if I can keep my eyes open that late," I answered sarcastically. "Besides, I need to get back to Daddy's papers."

"Tell him Mama wanted us to spend time together."

"I don't think this is what Mama had in mind when she encouraged us to fellowship and spend time together," I said.

"Well, it beats shelling peas. We won't stay too late, I promise. That settles it. Watch out Memphis, the Washington Sisters are headed your way!" Beverly sang while snapping her fingers and singing *Let's Groove Tonight.*

If Beverly had known what was waiting in Memphis she would have sang a different tune.

14

Summer days were longest and hottest in July. It was almost nine and the sun was just setting. As we left Eden, the highway landscape had not changed in twenty years. Just outside town there stood a stretch of rickety shotgun houses with dirt front yards. A woman was taking clothes off the line and waved as we passed. Folks on the porch, waved as well. It was amazing that the houses were still standing, much less that people still lived in them. Those houses marked the end of town and the landscape was now farmland as far as the eye could see. The furrows of cotton and beans resembled moving stripes as we sped east. Closer to Memphis, billboards enticed travelers to turn south and try their luck in the Tunica casinos. We crossed the expansive bridge that stretched across the Mississippi River to link Arkansas and Tennessee. In our minds, this bridge was our passage from the stifling boundaries of Eden to the rest of the world. We thought Memphis to be as grand as the Egyptian capital it was named for. The Pyramid Arena arose on the riverbank and held lively memories of concerts and basketball games. For fear of giving away our humble roots, we acted unimpressed. In reality, we were amazed that The Pyramid held more people than lived in all of Eden.

We exited the freeway onto Martin Luther King Drive and arrived at The Turning Point. The club was in a strip shopping center, and the parking lot was packed. Beverly put Daddy's handicapped tag that he refused to use, on the rear view mirror and parked next to the door. We paid our money and squeezed past a woman in an outfit two sizes too small who was blocking the doorway.

"I *can not* believe my eyes," Beverly whispered.

"I know, girl. Who told her she looked good in that?" Cecelia said.

"Just because it comes in a size eighteen, doesn't mean you should wear it," I said. "I've lost weight and I still wouldn't fold my flab into spandex."

"No, I'm not talking about girlfriend," Beverly said. "I'm looking over there, next to the bar. That's Kenny. He and his wife are close friends of ours, but that's not his wife that he's hugged up with."

"Has he seen you?" I asked.

"I don't know, but he will. I intend to go over there and speak to him and his little ho'."

"Now don't go calling her names. He's the dog. She may not even know he's married," I said rising to my single sister's defense.

"Well, if she doesn't know, then she's a stupid ho'. Even if they don't tell you, it's not hard to tell if a man is married. Women know, they just don't care," Beverly said. "He feeds them some line like, 'he's separated' or 'his wife doesn't understand him.'

"Or he's just staying for the kids," Cecelia piped in.

"Or he lies that his wife isn't interested in sex anymore," Beverly said.

"Some women prefer a married man," Cecelia said. "I work with ladies who say a married man treats them better and spends more money on them."

"I'm going to make sure I keep an eye on Anthony when he goes out with Kenny," Beverly said.

"I could never get that desperate. I'd rather be alone than with someone's husband," Cecelia said. "I'm not playing second fiddle."

Their words stung like a wasp. That was me they were talking about. But I'm not desperate, or a stupid ho'. Besides, Warren and I were different. Although, he did say he was separated. And he did say he was staying for the kids. Maybe he wasn't any different from the other cheating men, and I wasn't any different from the other desperate women out there. But I am different. I'm not asking him to leave his wife. I know we can't go on forever, and when I'm ready, I'll break it off. Most single men come with too much baggage and act like I'm trying to trap them. I wish I could make them understand my side, but I knew they wouldn't, so I kept quiet.

We nabbed a table near the buffet counter. Happy hour was over and they were clearing the trays as we sat down. I could smell the spicy buffalo wings as they took the pans away. I fought the urge to grab some grapes off the tray as they walked past me to the kitchen. A hunger pang hit me as I remembered that my dinner had been interrupted. We ordered a drink and sang along as the DJ mixed in some Denise LaSalle.

"I had tickets to go see her at the Blues Legends concert last year, but it was the same week Daddy had his stroke so we didn't go. I hope she comes back," Beverly said.

"Warren and I saw her at Summerfest in Milwaukee," I said. It had been fun going away for weekends to Milwaukee or Lake Geneva. Now I realize I was just fooling myself. The only reason we went away was so he wouldn't be seen in public with me. "She really put on a jammin' show. Girl, we *must* be getting old, talking about going to a blues concert. I hated that old timey music Daddy used to play," I remarked.

Mama and Daddy felt buying records was a waste of money. Occasionally they would splurge and buy something by Ray Charles, Bobby Blue Bland or B.B. King. While all my friends were jamming to Motown and Stax, we had to suffer through '*Georgia*', '*I Pity the Fool*', and '*The Thrill Is Gone*'.

Time brings about a change, as Mama Mary says. Now, the highlight of my week is the Friday night blues show on the radio.

"Well, you two can get old all by yourselves. I prefer Beyonce, myself," Cecelia teased.

"I'm glad you talked me into coming." I said, yelling over ZZ Hill's ' *Down Home Blues'*.

"I'm glad you came, too. You're the designated driver," Beverly laughed. She was on her third rum and coke and feeling no pain.

Even Cecelia was loosening up, as she nursed her glass of white wine. She was singing along with the record and kicking me under the table whenever a good-looking guy walked by.

"Carolyn, you should go to the bar and get another drink," Beverly advised.

"I don't feel like wading through the crowd. I'll wait for the waitress to come back this way."

"Dear, dear Carolyn, you're not just going to get a drink. You're walking around so you can be seen. If you don't want a drink, go to the ladies room. You'll never going to catch anything sitting over here hidden by the tables," Beverly said.

"Good. That's what I'm trying to avoid."

"Three fourths of these men are probably married like your friend," Cecelia said.

"What does she care? She's not trying to marry any of them. They buy you a few drinks, you dance a little, then you go home."

"I can buy my own drinks. And I'll wait for the *Electric Slide* to come on, then I'll dance."

"Carolyn, you are hopeless," Beverly said. "So don't talk to the married ones. According to Cecelia's calculations, twenty-five percent are still available."

"Available for what? A club is the worst place to meet a man. Now if you don't mind, I will go to the ladies room. Not to be seen, but because I have to pee. Can you move your chair, Cece?" I scooted around Cecelia and escaped from the table.

"You know, I think Carolyn has the best of both worlds right now," Cecelia said. "She can come and go when she pleases, spend her money on herself, call Warren when she's horny and send him home when she doesn't want to be bothered. I know the Cinderella story is to marry Prince Charming and live happily ever after, but that's not real life. Are you happily married?"

"Girl, please! That's an oxymoron, isn't it? Didn't know I knew big words, did you? And I didn't even go to college," Beverly said.

"Why do you always do that? I'm not the one always bringing up college. You act like I should apologize for getting an education. You already said you got what you wanted. Don't take it out on me that you got yourself knocked up," Cecelia said.

"You two could have fought in Eden," I said returning to the table. "We're supposed to be having a good time."

"I told you I didn't want to come in the first place. I rode twelve hours last night, I worked ten hours the night before that, and I've been up all day. I'm tired."

"Well you're here now, so you might as well make the best of it. You can sit here if you want. I'm going to dance," Beverly announced. She got up, tapped an unsuspecting man on the shoulder and headed for the dance floor.

"I wish I could do that," I said. "It does seem silly to dress up to go out and then wait for someone to notice you and ask you to dance."

"Michael doesn't really like to dance. I have to practically beg him and that takes all the fun out of it. He says he doesn't mind if I dance with other men, but they won't ask because I'm with him, " Cecelia said. "Men can be so contrary."

"You're reading my lines. I'm the spinster in this group. I should be doing the male bashing. You have a husband who adores you. Okay, so he doesn't dance. You can't have everything."

"Why not?" Cecelia said. "Why can't I have everything, or at least most things? I'm tired of waiting for *my* life to start."

I ordered another drink as Cecelia continued her diatribe about life's unfairness.

"You two look too serious," Beverly said as she and three men walked to the table, laughing and talking. "These are my sisters, Cecelia and Carolyn. They're visiting from Chicago. I want you gentlemen to show them a good time tonight. The Whispers' '*And the Beat Goes On*' came on, and Beverly and her dancing partner turned around and sashayed back to the dance floor. The tallest of the three reached for Cecelia's hand.

"I'm sorry my sister dragged you all the way over here, but I really don't feel like dancing," Cecelia said.

"She said you would say that. She told me not to take 'no' for an answer," the Richard Roundtree look-alike said. "You're tapping your feet so hard, you're going to put a dent in the carpet. Come on," he said reaching for her hand.

Cecelia relented and slid out of her seat. By the time they waded through the crowded dance floor, they missed most of the record. The DJ continued in the Whispers groove and segued into "*In the Mood.*" Cecelia turned to head toward her seat.

Her dance partner stepped in front of our table. "Oh no you don't, that one didn't count. You still owe me a dance." Cecelia winked at us and headed back to the dance floor.

"Check out your sister," Beverly said nudging me. Cecelia was following his lead and swaying to the music. When the DJ moved into "*Just Gets Better With Time*," I saw Cecelia rest her head on his shoulder.

The DJ picked up the pace and the three of us danced for several more songs. Beverly and I came off the dance floor at the same time. I reached the table first and picked up my drink. Beverly pushed the man in front of her aside, rushing back to the table. "Carolyn, don't drink that," she said, practically knocking the drink out of my hand.

"Why not?"

"That's how they slip that date rape drug in your drink. Where have you been? It's been on Oprah. They say don't ever leave a drink on a table and don't accept a drink from a stranger unless you open the bottle or can yourself."

"People sure can think of some despicable things to do," I said.

"I know," Beverly nodded. "There are so many willing women out there, why would a man rape a woman? I just don't understand. He would have to really be sick. They should castrate all rapists."

If you only knew, I thought. I wonder if she would feel that way if she knew my secret. The rape was something I had never discussed with anyone. I shoved it far back in my mind, and rarely acknowledged that it happened. A psychiatrist would probably tell me that wasn't healthy, and I needed to let it out. But I refused to even let it be part of my reality.

At the end of the song, Tall, Dark and Handsome led Cecelia back to the table. "Can I get you ladies a drink?" he asked in a sultry voice.

"I'll have White Zinfandel," Cecelia said.

"Okay, I'll be right back."

Beverly gave Cecelia a sly look and smiled. "You go, girl."

"Don't get any ideas. What is his name anyway?"

"I don't know," Beverly replied.

"You don't know? I thought you knew these guys. You picked up some strangers and brought them over here? "

"Well, I know Nate. He comes in the barbershop. I told him I wanted you and Carolyn to dance and he brought those guys over."

Cecelia shook her head. "You can't pick up men in a club. These men could be serial killers or terrorists," she whispered under her breath.

"Relax, it's just a dance. Here comes your drink. Carolyn, let's go to the ladies room," Beverly said.

The Richard Roundtree look-alike pulled a chair to the table and handed Cecelia a drink.

"Thank you. I didn't catch your name."

"I never threw it. My name is Maurice Wesley. I live in Memphis. I'm from Taylor County, Mississippi. I work for Federal Express. I'm divorced and have two children. I'm drug-free, AIDS-free, heterosexual, and I'm not a serial killer or a terrorist. Anything else?"

"Not right now," Cecelia said with a smile.

I was comfortable in my seat, but took Beverly's hint and left the table. "Do you think we should leave her alone with him?" I asked Beverly. "Someone might see them, get the wrong idea and tell Michael."

"Cece will be fine. She's been under some serious stress, a little dancing and flirting will do her good."

We bought a drink and stood at the bar for a few songs. A Tupac-James Brown remix drew us to the floor like ants to a picnic. We danced up a sweat, then went to the ladies room. It was brightly lit, with a towel girl inside displaying a selection of perfumes. I dabbed on some *Passion* as we walked out. On the way to our table, Beverly turned to me and whispered, "Your admirer is sitting at our table."

"I hope that snaggle-tooth, no-deodorant-wearing, clown doesn't hound me all night," I said, trying to look without being seen. "I knew I shouldn't have danced with him. Let's go back to the bar. Maybe he'll go away."

"You don't want this one to get away," Beverly said.

As my eyes readjusted back to the dim dance floor, I saw Derrick sitting at our table. "Do you think he's here with someone?" I asked.

"I think he's looking for you, baby sister. Go on over there. I can find something to keep myself amused."

"How did he know we were here?"

"Girl, please. People in Eden know you have gas before you fart," Beverly tapped a well-dressed man on the shoulder and headed for the dance floor.

Derrick stood as I approached the table. "I'm beginning to think you're following me," I said.

"I'm doing my best," he said.

Derrick grabbed an empty chair from another table and motioned for me to sit in it.

"You know, I feel funny sitting with you. Are you sure you don't have a girlfriend lurking around anywhere? I don't want to start any mess," I said.

"No girlfriend."

"I find that hard to believe."

"I have a good friend, but it's nothing serious."

"Okay, now the real story is coming out. What do you mean by 'nothing serious'?

"It means we're friends. We enjoy each other's company, but we're not madly in love or anything."

"Does she know this is the type of relationship you have?"

"Time out. Am I on the witness stand or something?"

"No, I just know how men like to have it both ways. I bet your good friend thinks of you as her man." By this time, Cecelia and Maurice joined in our conversation and we had a friendly battle of the sexes.

The rest of the evening flew by. I danced so much, my wrist ached from popping my fingers. We went to eat after the club closed. It was almost four in the morning before we called it a night. We said our good-byes and Derrick said he'd see me at the picnic. Nate offered to follow us home, but Beverly said we would be okay.

"Are you sure you can drive?" I asked.

"I'm fine. That burger and milkshake absorbed any lingering alcohol in my system. I need to stop by the salon for a minute, then we'll go in the house."

Beverly navigated the short ride to the beauty salon. We drove up and parked next to Anthony's truck. "I wonder why his truck is over here," she said.

"Do you think we should call the police?" Cecelia asked.

"Everything looks all right. He probably left his truck over here and walked to the house. He's been having problems with it lately. Both of you look like you're going to need a few curls in the morning. I'm going to run in and get my curling irons now so I don't have to come over in the morning. I can never run in and out during shop hours. I always get hung up doing something and we don't want to be late meeting everybody at the mall in the morning. I'll be right out," Beverly said, shooing away the black cat that sauntered past the truck.

Beverly unlocked the door, and was surprised that the alarm was off. She figured Tanya forgot to turn it on when she closed. Even so, she got the pistol out of her drawer. She wasn't going to be like those silly white girls in the movies who go investigating in high heels and eventually trip and scream. She also let Money out of the back room.

Just then Beverly noticed the bathroom light on. " I guess people think utilities are free. I'll have to remember to address proper closing procedures in our next meeting," she mumbled. As she walked to the bathroom, something in the back room caught her eye. She turned the light on and was shocked at what she saw. She stood frozen in place before she screamed.

She startled Anthony from a deep sleep. He awoke to see Beverly standing over him with a nickel-plated, thirty-two pistol three inches from his nose. "Aw' hell!" He untangled his legs from Tanya's and jumped to his feet.

Tanya turned over and shouted. "Are you crazy? Put that thing away."

"*You* must be the crazy one, sleeping with my husband, in my place, leaving my lights on. I'll show you how crazy I am." Beverly pulled the trigger and shot twice. Tanya screamed and pulled the cover over her head.

Beverly snatched the blanket off her and pulled her to the floor by her hair. Beverly kicked her in her size six butt.

Money barked and jumped on the couch.

"Leave her alone," Anthony said, as he tried to pull Beverly off Tanya.

"Money, sit," Anthony commanded.

"Are you defending her?" Beverly asked, turning to aim the gun at him.

"Baby, let's talk about this."

"Talk to this," she spat and shot his reflection in the mirror.

Tanya rolled off the couch as shattered glass flew everywhere. "You could have killed me. I'm calling the police," she said as she searched for her shirt.

Cecelia and I looked at each other. "Did you hear something?" Cecelia asked.

"I'm not sure. Maybe we should go in. She said she was coming right out." Then we heard gunshots and barking. "Oh, my God," I said as I reached for the door.

"No," Cecelia said. "You can't go in there. Do you have your cell phone? Call 911."

"This is a black neighborhood on a Friday night. We can't wait for the police. Let's go," I said.

Cecelia and I stormed through the door like Batman and Robin. I picked up one of the firewood logs stacked by the door and began beating the man on the back of his head. When he turned around to protest, Cecelia sprayed him with mace from her key chain.

"Hey, hey!" Anthony cried as he waved his arms. "Chubby, Cecelia, it's me!"

Cecelia rushed to Beverly, who was holding Money back. "Anthony?" Cecelia said.

We had been in attack mode and didn't notice his bare feet and unzipped pants. We hadn't even seen Tanya, who was practically naked.

"You know these crazy freaks?" Tanya asked as she was searching for her skirt.

"Don't you talk about my sisters," Beverly said and aimed the pistol at Tanya's legs. "Get out of here right now."

"I don't have my car here. Anthony brought me."

"I don't care if you crawl, just get the hell out of here," Beverly said and shot the floor next to Tanya's legs.

Tanya jumped like she was playing hopscotch, as Beverly shot again and again. "I said get out!"

"Beverly, this is between you and me. Let me call her a cab," Anthony said.

"I'm going to count to three and then..." Beverly said.

"Beverly, quit shooting that gun. You might hurt somebody," Anthony said calmly.

"One, two..."

"You all are crazy. I'm getting out of here." Tanya cried as she ran toward the door with only her panties on. She was clutching her purse, her shirt and her shoes as she ran down the street.

Cecelia and I took our cue from Beverly, who started laughing. We went to the front door and we could see her still running down the street. Money was at the edge of the driveway barking. We were laughing so hard, we didn't see the policemen come in.

"We're responding to an emergency call. We received a report of gun shots fired at this address," one of the officers said.

"Everything is fine, Officer," Anthony said. "My wife thought a burglar was in here."

"Well she seems mighty happy about it," the policeman said, as he watched Beverly struggle to contain her laughter.

"She spends a lot of time here alone and I've told her to shoot first, ask questions later. This is all a misunderstanding," Anthony said.

"I need to get some information for my report. I'll have to keep the gun and run a check on it," the officer stated.

Beverly and Cecelia answered the policeman's questions. Anthony finished dressing and I searched for a broom, careful to step over the shattered glass.

"You have never been one of my fans and you may find this hard to believe, but I really love your sister. We have a good marriage. Tanya was just something to do."

"Spare me your remorse, I'm not buying it," I said without looking up from sweeping. "Save it for Beverly, I'm sorry she missed."

"She didn't miss. She wasn't trying to shoot anybody. That woman can hit a running deer 150 yards away in the woods. She was just trying to mark her territory and scare Tanya off. It's a shame. Tanya was very good with the customers."

"Why does she put up with you?" I asked, more to myself than to him.

The officers reentered the room to get additional information from Anthony. Once they left, Anthony walked toward the dryer where Beverly was sitting. As Anthony sat, Cecelia stood.

"Let's go Beverly," Cecelia said. "Let him clean up his own mess."

"I don't think it's a good idea for you to come to the house tonight," I said to Anthony. "You know my sister is an excellent mark, and she may not miss next time."

We left Anthony in the shop and walked over to the house. Once inside, Beverly turned down the covers on the twin beds in Tony's room for Cecelia and me, then went to her bedroom and closed her door.

"So much for the pajama party," Cecelia said. "Can you believe what just happened?" she whispered.

"That bastard. She *should* have shot him. She could've used a burglar defense and there probably wouldn't have even been a trial," I said softly.

"Will the police do anything?" Cecelia asked.

"I doubt it, but if I were Anthony, I'd sleep with one eye open. I never told anyone this, but I know something he did a long time ago. Beverly was so crazy about him. She was pregnant, so I didn't say anything. They've managed to stay married longer than most folks, so I figured it was a youthful blunder and he was making her happy. But if she isn't happy, maybe I should tell her."

"It wouldn't make any difference. This isn't the first time she's caught him with his pants down, so to speak," Cecelia said. "Maybe she *will* leave him this time. I know I wouldn't stand for it. They say 'boys will be boys', but there are too many diseases out there these days, and you can't cure them with a pill or a shot. There is a matter of respect. To have an affair with someone right under her nose is a bit much," Cecelia said. "I'm going to go talk to her and make sure she's okay."

"Tell her to get Aunt Belle to put some roots on him. That will straighten him out," I said.

"What in the world will I say to Anthony?" Beverly wondered as she lay in bed staring at the ceiling. According to the sistergirl code, she should be burning his clothes or throwing them out the window and calling the locksmith. Don't even give him time to lie. But part of her wanted to hear what he had to say. What did she lack that he found in other women?

That's a dumb question, she thought. Who wouldn't be attracted to a young, shapely, pretty girl? How could I have been so blind?

Just then, Cecelia peeked her head through the door. "Are you okay?"

Beverly turned away from the door to hide her tears. All of this was bad enough, but to have it happen in front of Cecelia and Carolyn was humiliating. Carolyn had never been too crazy about Anthony and never missed a chance to put him down, and Cecelia was married to Mr. Perfect. I'm sure she thinks I'm the Queen of Fools, Beverly thought. How many times had she preached to her clients in similar situations to let the brother go? Why didn't she take her own advice?

"Beverly, I know you're hurt and embarrassed. I want you to know that I'm here for you. Whatever you want from me just ask. Carolyn feels the same way. She'll probably even do your divorce free. It's not her specialty, but it shouldn't be that hard."

"Who said anything about a divorce?" Beverly asked, sitting up.

"I guess I just assumed . . . Surely you aren't going to stay with him?" Cecelia asked.

"Cecelia, I appreciate your concern, but this is a private matter between me and my husband and we need to discuss how we're going to handle it."

"I'm not trying to get in your business, but Beverly, wake up. I know this is not the first time. How long are you going to let him do this to you?"

"These things happen. Couples work through them. Now that I think about it, that heifer was always prancing around Anthony and getting him to help her move stuff or fix something. That damsel in distress bit is the oldest trick in the book. I should have hired Sharon's cousin. She's loud and flat-chested, not Anthony's type at all. Putting Tanya and Anthony together was like putting gas with a match. "

Cecelia threw up her hands. "You're blaming *yourself* because Anthony can't keep his pants zipped? Now I've heard everything. He's a dog. Face it. You could hire Rupaul and he will probably try to get with him. If you want him, fine. But don't blame yourself or Tanya or whoever the next woman is."

"I know how this looks, but you don't know the whole story. He's been under a lot of stress lately," Beverly said.

"And you haven't? Are you trying to convince yourself or me? Just do me one favor, get tested. I don't remember seeing any condom wrappers in their love nest."

"Cecelia, please. Most men are dogs, anyway. Some just hide it better than others."

"Well, your dog is putting your life in danger. We've had to expand our HIV and AIDS wing. Black women in particular are becoming HIV positive at alarming rates from screwing around with careless men. He may even be bisexual."

"Cecelia, just drop it," Beverly said.

"Don't get mad at me. You should be yelling at your no-good husband. Take my advice and invest in condoms," Cecelia said as she left the room.

Beverly fell back on her pillow, and searched her mind for the clues she had missed. She knew Cecelia was right. She should kick him out. The other times, Tony had been small and she convinced herself she was keeping her family together and a father for her son. But Tony was grown now, she couldn't use that excuse. And the possibility of AIDS had never crossed her mind. Anthony was wrong, but she still blamed Tanya. She had pretended to be her friend. Beverly now realized what Tanya and Sharon had been arguing about. How could she have been so blind? She wondered how long they had been seeing each other. Maybe they knew each other before Tanya started working there. Maybe it's been going on for years and he told her to come apply for a job. The more she thought about it, the madder she got. She wiped her tears with the sheet, and vowed not to let him do that to her ever again. She considered following through and calling a divorce lawyer as she had threatened last year. She also thought about calling Nate. He was always flirting with her and it wouldn't take much encouragement from her to heat things up with him. Let Anthony see how it feels to be betrayed. Then she thought of the perfect plan. She was not going to be a fool any longer. This would never happen again. She was going to fix Anthony. She would replace Tanya with a gay hairdresser.

Cecelia and I were at the kitchen table sipping green tea when Anthony came in. "I'm sorry you have to be involved in all of this. Beverly and I will work it out," he said.

"Apologize to your wife, not us," Cecelia said.

"You're right about one thing," I said as I washed out our cups. "You are indeed sorry."

"You got that right Carolyn," Cecelia said.

Anthony shrugged his shoulders and headed for their bedroom.

Cecelia stuck her tongue out at him as he walked toward the hallway.

"What do you think she's going to do?" I asked, as I pulled splinters out of my hand.

"Absolutely nothing. She's mad at Tanya, and me, and everyone except Anthony. She blames herself for hiring her. She thinks Tanya seduced Anthony. Hey, if she wants him, more power to her. Don't worry about it Carolyn, there's nothing you can do," Cecelia said.

"I wouldn't be so sure about that," I said softly as we turned out the kitchen light and headed for our room. Cecelia selected the bed next to the window, just as she had when we were growing up. I turned off the light and climbed into the twin bed. Within minutes, Cecelia's breathing settled into a sleeping rhythm. I turned from my back to my side, trying to settle into a position for slumber to overtake my weary body and mind. Instead my thoughts rewound back to that night with Anthony. Just like Beverly, I blamed myself for what happened. All these years, I've carried this burden, not telling a soul but Jesus. I thought I was keeping the peace, but Beverly didn't seem at peace to me. Maybe now is the time to tell her. She has a right to know. I vowed to tell her tomorrow.

15

"Rise and shine, girls!" Beverly sang as she flipped the light switch. Cecelia groaned, while Beverly bounced to the window and opened the blinds. I pulled the bedspread over my head. "Let's get moving, the mall awaits," she said.

No reunion is complete without a shopping trip. Today we were going to Woodridge Mall and then to the outlet malls on the way back to Eden. Most of us were from larger cities and could surely find whatever we found in Memphis at home. But doing it as a group was fun and those visiting could buy souvenirs.

"After staying up half the night, and committing attempted murder, I know you don't still plan to go shopping?" Cecelia muttered from under the sheet.

"Beverly, we understand if you'd rather not go shopping today," I said.

"Who said anything about not going? I've planned this reunion for a year. I'm not going to let Anthony or that two-faced whore spoil it," Beverly declared.

"Do you want to talk about it?" Cecelia probed. "You don't have to pretend for us. We heard you crying last night."

"Then, hear this. I will *deal* with Mr. Anthony Townsend, but not today. I had fun last night with you guys and I'm going to enjoy my family this weekend," she said as she sat on Cecelia's bed.

"We're not trying to pry, we're just trying to help," I said.

"If you want to be helpful, then let's act like it didn't happen."

"Suit yourself," I said. "Act like I didn't see your husband running around half naked with another woman and that you weren't within two inches of committing murder. Sure, I can do that."

"We're here for you if you need us," Cecelia said. She hugged Beverly to her.

Beverly winked at me as Cecelia hugged her.

"I didn't plan to do much shopping anyway," Beverly said. "Sheree asked me to do her hair, so I'm bringing her back to the salon. We'll meet you guys at noon. Since I seem to be one stylist short, I'll have extra customers to do. "

"Just don't give her one of those ghetto mama hairdos with all those fake pieces and different colors," Cecelia said.

"I was going to dye it blond," Beverly said, rolling her eyes.

Mama, Jackie, Aunt Pearl, Sheree and some cousins I didn't know were waiting at the Sears entrance when we got there. They were wearing their Washington reunion T-shirts.

"Let's stop in the bookstore," I said, as we approached Main Street Books. "You know I can't walk past a bookstore without browsing."

"Girl, please," Jackie said, "this is a vacation. We don't want to look at books." Unfortunately, this was a democratic shopping trip so we didn't stop in the bookstore.

"Mama, let's look at the purses in Macy's. You were admiring mine. Come pick one for yourself," Cecelia said.

"Now you know I don't want one of them fancy pocketbooks. What did you say they called it?"

"A Coach bag."

"I don't need no pocketbook that has its own name. I know they cost a lot of money because Mae Carter was bragging in Missionary meeting about the one her daughter sent her."

"Then let me buy you one, and you can brag too."

"That ain't bragging, that's just broadcasting how big a fool you are. What a waste of money."

"Mama, sometimes you have to treat yourself."

"That's okay baby. I see where I want to go. Ethel Fay, come with me to the One Dollar Store," Mama said.

Cecelia steered the rest of us to Victoria's Secret. "Hey, let's stop in here a minute. I want to buy Mama some Pear Glace lotion, since she liked mine. She said it reminded her of the fruit trees in her mother's yard."

Jackie held a skimpy black negligee up to her ample bosom as we waited for Cecelia to check out. "Ooh, girl, I don't know if my husband can stand this. Now, Carolyn, if you spent more time shopping in here instead of the bookstore, you'd have a husband," Jackie said.

"I don't want a man that would be more impressed by me in a $65 nightie, than what's in my mind," I said. After last night's episode with Beverly, and Cecelia's whining about Michael, I may be better off single.

"Okay, okay, don't be so touchy," Jackie said. "Can't you be smart and sexy? Men may say they admire a smart woman, but they like a little bootie with the brain."

"Girl, you are crazy," I laughed. "Let's get out of here. What's taking Cece so long?"

Cecelia stood at the cash register trying to purchase Mama's lotion. "I'm sorry, ma'am. Your card has been declined. Would you like to pay another way?" the cashier asked, handing back her Visa card.

"Are you sure?" Cecelia asked. "Try it again."

"I've already run it twice," the cashier said.

Cecelia handed her a MasterCard that was declined and another Visa, which was also declined. The two people in line behind her shifted their feet and the cashier tapped her fingers on the counter.

"I don't know what the problem could be," Cecelia said, as I walked up to the counter. "I'll pay cash, since you're having a problem with your machine."

"You girls must be buying the store," Jackie said, as she approached us.

"Never mind, let's go," Cecelia said. "I'll buy some in Chicago."

"Is it time to eat yet? " I asked.

"Eat? We're just getting started," Jackie said. "Let's stop in the shoe store next."

I can shop with the best of them, but I think I may have met my match.

"Thanks, for doing my hair Aunt Bev. Mama says you get tired of mooching relatives," Sheree said, as Beverly massaged her scalp.

Beverly was grateful to escape her sisters' pity. Working in the salon always took her mind off her troubles. "You don't fall in that category, honey. This way I get to spend time with my favorite niece. Besides they don't mooch off me. They have to pay. They know I don't play that. I got bills just like they do. So how are you doing in school?"

"Okay," she said and shrugged.

"That's one of those answers kids give adults that means leave me alone. How are you *really* doing?"

"I'm doing okay. I'm not going to be valedictorian, but I'm not flunking out either. I'm not in a gang and I'm not smoking dope. So things are okay," she snapped.

"Well, excuse me, Miss Lady," Beverly said.

"I'm sorry, Aunt Bev. I guess I've been asked that question so often this weekend I'm sick of it. It seems that's all older people want to talk about. There's more to life than school. They don't really care how I'm doing in school anyway. It's just a way to make conversation."

"Well, this *old* person does care and I am interested in how you're doing in and out of school. Do you have a boyfriend? As pretty as you are, I'm sure you have your pick of the fellas."

Sheree continued to thumb through the hair magazine and ignored Beverly's question.

"You're not answering," Beverly said. "I guess that means 'stay out of my business'."

Beverly was blow-drying Sheree's hair when she calmly asked her, "Aunt Bev, if I tell you something will you promise not to tell Mama?"

"Uh-oh. I don't think I want to know this. All right, I won't tell."

"Do you promise?"

"Yes, I promise. Did I tell when I saw you kissing that Jones boy last summer? What is it?"

"I'm pregnant."

Beverly spun her around in the chair and whispered, "What did you say?"

Sheree stared at the magazine cover and didn't answer.

"Lord, what does it take for you girls to learn? Your mother and father have given you everything. Don't you know this will kill your mother? Can I keep a secret? How long do you think *you* can keep this a secret?"

"Oh, just forget it. I shouldn't have even told you. I just figured after hearing that you were pregnant in school, you would understand."

"It's not the same at all. I was within a few weeks of graduation. Besides, it's different now. You can get birth control pills or Norplant. I heard they even sell condoms in the schools. You're a smart girl. How could you let some little sweet-talking boy blow your mind?"

"First of all, he's not a little boy. He's nineteen, and in his second year of college. He has his own apartment and a job. Secondly, I haven't even decided if I'm going to have it. I thought I would get some understanding and advice from you, but I see you're just like Mama. You want to do all the talking," Sheree said as she snatched the plastic smock off and headed for the door. As she reached the front door and looked in the mirror, they realized her hair looked like Don King without the gray. They both started laughing at the same time.

"Come on back here, girl, and let me finish your head. You definitely get the drama from your Mama. I can't have you walking out of here like that. It would be bad for business. Let's talk."

Cecelia eyed the white sandals in the Nine West display case. They sure would look nice with the sundress I packed. I wonder how much room is on my Discover card, she thought. I should be able to get an eighty-dollar purchase approved.

Cecelia got the salesclerk's attention. "Can I see these in a size eight and a half?"

"Don't even try it. You know you need a nine. With those sandals, you probably need a nine and a half so your rusty heel won't be hanging over the back," Jackie said as she came in the store.

The salesclerk returned. "We have it in an eight and a nine. It doesn't come in half sizes."

Cecelia tried on the nine and it fit.

"What did I tell you?" Jackie teased.

"I have to admit, they do look nice, but I don't think I'll get them." Cecelia modeled the shoes in front of the mirror. "Michael says I'm trying to catch up with Imelda. It's not like I don't have white sandals. I just forgot to pack them, and those graveyard weeds scratched up the tan pair I brought."

"Suit yourself, let's go," Jackie said. "I'll tell you one thing, Steve better not say a word to me about what I buy. I work just like he does. I don't say anything when he brings home some new gizmo for his truck. So he doesn't bug me about shopping."

"Michael doesn't bug me about shopping," Cecelia said. "He just thinks if you have a pair of black shoes, and some tennis shoes you're set."

Cecelia was not at all concerned about Michael's opinion of her shoe inventory. She just didn't want to take the chance of Jackie seeing her credit card declined. She was trying to conserve her cash for the trip home. All her cards weren't at the limit, but she didn't want Jackie to see her try to figure out which one she could use. "You know what? I'm going to go back and get those sandals. You go ahead and catch Mama and everybody. I'll meet you in the food court."

"Okay." Jackie said. "Let me give you a tip. Go ahead and buy the sandals. Then get a pair of black spike heels. Model them sometime when you want to set the right mood, if you get my drift. Once he sees them, he'll be buying *you* shoes."

They both laughed. "I won't be long," Cecelia said.

"Remember to get a size nine," Jackie called over her shoulder.

Cecelia waited until Jackie walked off before she went back to the store. It would take a lot more than shoes to spice up her marriage. She switched to third shift, for the higher pay, but the cost may be higher than she anticipated. She got home in time to wave at Michael as he left for work. Between their schedules, and money problems, their marriage was headed downhill. But she was confident this was just a temporary valley. Once Michael realized he needed to keep his job, and C.W. got his settlement money, they would have some breathing room.

Their money shortage perplexed Cecelia. Private school tuition was a sacrifice, but things were out of control in the public schools. A girl had been gang raped at Mike's school last year and several students were expelled for carrying guns. The schools had already implemented uniforms, see-through backpacks and metal detectors. The place was more like a prison than a school. The kids were on waiting lists for magnet schools in the public school system, but she wasn't too crazy about sending them miles from home either. The last straw was a shooting outside the high school. She enrolled them in the private school near their house, that same day.

Michael was upset that she didn't discuss it with him first. "The possibility that you would oppose this never entered my mind," Cecelia said. "We've got to get our kids out of those dangerous schools."

"We can't afford it. Besides, you can't run away from problems Cece. There are hoodlums and nuts in private schools, too. We just have to pray and instill values and discipline in our kids."

"All the values and discipline in the world won't do any good when there's a stray bullet whizzing by. We'll cut back somewhere else. I'll go on nights. They're giving a graveyard bonus to the third shift. I would never forgive myself if something happened to my babies because we were too cheap to pay for a safe school for our children."

Michael couldn't match that argument without seeming uncaring.

Cecelia knew they were struggling to meet tuition payments, but whenever things got really tight, magically, she would win at the casino. New credit cards also came in handy. At first she threw away the preapproved credit card solicitations. But she had accepted the last few offers they received. Better to have and not need, than to need and not have, Daddy always said.

That last card came in handy today, she thought. Cecelia went back to the shoe store and put the sandals on her new Discover card. She'd forgotten that one. Since she had more funds available, she decided to buy a sterling silver ring and bracelet so her hands wouldn't be bare. She then headed to the food court and was going up the escalator when she saw a familiar face coming down. Their eyes met.

"Wait for me, I'm going to come back up," Maurice said.

Cecelia couldn't believe it. Of all the people in Memphis to see, and he looked even better in daylight. Sometimes people look good in the club with dim lights and strong drinks to camouflage their flaws. Not this man. He wore khaki pants with a perfect crease down the front. His black polo shirt unbuttoned enough to reveal a patch of hair on his chest, while the ribbed short sleeves showcased his muscular biceps. Looking down on him she could see slight waves in his hair and a little thinning in the top. Not that she was looking, of course.

"Fancy meeting you here," he said, as he reached the top of the escalator. He smiled and took her hand.

Cecelia felt self-conscious. Who said black people don't blush? I must be red, or at least reddish brown. If I didn't know better I'd think this man was trying to make a move on me.

"Hello, Maurice. I guess it's a myth that men don't do malls," Cecelia said.

"I'm here with my mother and sister. I should have known better than to let them talk me into this. We were supposed to be buying my mother a new television. She's probably the only person on the planet without remote control. I went to get the car. They were only going to look for a minute, then meet me at customer pick up. That was forty-five minutes ago. I think I've been had, but I won't complain since I ran into you."

"I'm here with my mother, too," Cecelia stammered, looking past him.

"Let's sit over here." Maurice pointed to a bench.

"I really need to be going," Cecelia said. "I'm supposed to meet my mother and the others in the food court in ten minutes."

"Then you have time to sit with me. Ten minutes translates to thirty minutes in mall time. What are you planning to do tonight?"

Cecelia tried to remember if she had told this man she was married. Between the drinks and the shooting, last night was a blur. It had been so long since a man other than Michael, had expressed an interest in her, she'd forgotten the signs.

"Just hanging out with family, maybe go to the casino. We're having a big barbecue today. That's why we came to the mall early, so we can get back."

"I wish there was some way I could see you again. We had such a good time last night. Any chance of you skipping out on your family duties?"

Cecelia stood. "Look, I don't want you to get the wrong impression. I am married, with two kids. I've enjoyed talking to you, ("And looking at you", she thought). But I want to clear the air before you waste your time."

"I don't think I have the wrong impression and I'm not wasting my time. You're on vacation right?"

"Yes."

"You said you liked to dance and you had a good time last night, right?"

"Yes."

"Your husband went to Pine Bluff to see his people, right?"

"Yes." I don't remember telling him that, she thought.

"No need in you sitting around listening to old folks reminisce about days gone by. I'm sure you'll get enough of that this weekend. I'm not suggesting anything out of line. Why don't you and your sisters come to the casino? I was planning to try my luck there tonight, and George Benson is going to be performing in the lounge."

"You're kidding? I love him. We talked about going to the casino, but our plans weren't definite."

"I'll be at the eight o'clock show. Maybe you can come. If not, I'm still glad I ran in to you today. Here's my card. My number is on the front and I'll put my mother's number on the back. Call me sometime."

Cecelia put the number in her pocket, smiled and walked away, conscious of him watching her.

Jackie waved to get her attention.

Cecelia joined her shopping partners. "I told them we have plenty of food at the house, but they insisted on eating." Mama said. "You all sure know how to waste money."

"I'll wait until we get home to eat. I'll just get something to drink." Cecelia put her bags down and headed to the cookie shop.

"You must have really gotten a good deal on those sandals," Jackie said. "You're grinning from ear to ear."

My arm was starting to ache as I struggled through the mall with my bags. I stopped in an office supply store to buy items to help arrange Daddy's papers. The binders and organizers didn't look so heavy at the checkout counter. But those bags added to the gifts I had already bought for Mama and Daddy were weighing me down. I was huffing through the mall, as I rushed to make our meeting time. I should have known not to worry about the time. Even after allowances for CP time, everyone still hadn't made it to the food court at the agreed time. We ate a snack in the food court, while everyone compared purchases and bargains.

I left the group to go back to the bookstore, by way of the ladies room. I planned to duck in there to call Warren. I knew he'd be golfing and I could reach him on his cell phone. But Rita wanted to go to the bookstore with me. She was a cousin from Atlanta that I had never met. We discovered we both loved Walter Mosley's books, and she turned me on to Barbara Neely's mysteries. Even though we just met, I knew I had found not just a cousin, but a friend. We exchanged phone numbers and email addresses and vowed to keep in touch. When we got back to the group, Beverly was back and everyone was ready to go.

"Mama, do you mind riding back with Jackie? I'm not going to stop at the outlet mall," Beverly said. She then whispered in my ear. "I want you to ride with me."

I said okay, even though I was looking forward to going to the Ann Klein store at the outlet mall. The trip back would give me a chance to talk to Beverly about Anthony and about Daddy.

"Beverly, I'm glad we'll have a little time alone together," I said, as we walked to the mall exit. "I need you to keep a secret."

"Two in one day," she said.

"What does that mean?" I asked.

"Don't worry about it. What is it?"

"Now remember, you can't discuss this with anyone. Paul and I have been looking at some of Daddy's papers. Did you know Charles has Power of Attorney?"

"No, I didn't. I knew he was taking care of a lot of the paperwork with the farm. I guess I never thought about it."

"I found a security agreement on file at the courthouse for a five thousand dollar loan last October. Daddy was still sick, so I know he didn't make the loan. Did Charles mention it to you?" I asked.

"No, he didn't discuss it with me."

"I know Charles has always worked with Daddy. But is it a good idea to put that much responsibility in his hands?"

"I'm not sure it would be in his hands," Beverly said. "Brenda handles the finances in that household. I'm not comfortable with my hussy-in-law all up in our business."

"Beverly, this is not about Brenda and Anthony."

"Well, if she would lie about that, she would lie about anything. I thought it was strange that she was so sweet to Mama while Daddy was sick. Then when he got better, she was back to her usual petty self. I bet she just knew, she and Charles were going to get their hands on Daddy's place."

"So do you think Charles should have Power of Attorney?" I asked.

"What does a Power of Attorney do?"

"That means Charles can sign Daddy's name at any time."

"Well, Daddy and Charles have been closer lately," Beverly said as she searched for her keys. "They've been coming over to Memphis quite a bit too."

"Just to avoid any problems later, I think we should ---"

"We'll have to finish talking later," Beverly interrupted. Sheree was waiting when we reached the mall exit.

"You're riding back with us?" I asked. "You know we're not stopping at the outlet mall. I'm going to tell Cece to take you to the doctor as soon as you get home. You must be sick, if you're passing up an opportunity to shop."

Beverly and I sat in the front of her hot Expedition. Beverly turned down the radio. "Sheree I know you told me this in confidence and I promised not to tell your mother and I won't. But I didn't promise not to tell Carolyn. Sheree is pregnant," she blurted out.

"Aunt Bev, you promised," Sheree cried.

I turned around in shock. "Then, it's true?"

She nodded her head and looked out of the window.

"She told me because she figured I would be empathetic since I was a teenage mother," Beverly explained. "I'm telling you because she's thinking about having an abortion, and I know you had some close friends who went through this and you could talk to her. I myself am totally against the abortion idea but it's not my decision."

So this is why I was missing phase two of the shopping trip. What she really meant is that I had an abortion and I could talk to her from experience. I usually manage to put that out of my mind. I rarely think about it. I'm sorry about it, but I don't think I would have been a good mother then.

"Sheree, how far along are you?" I asked.

"If I had wanted to discuss this with you, I would have told you," Sheree said."Look, child, you're not hurting us. Not talking about it won't make it go away. Maybe Carolyn can give you some legal advice. Can she even get an abortion without her mother's consent?"

"There are ways around it if she has the cash. To go to a free clinic, her parents have to be notified. Most girls just give a fake name and address. The abortion and follow up visit cost about $300. "

"I thought you said it was free," Sheree said.

"Nothing in this world is free," Beverly responded.

"It's about $600 at a private physician. There's a recovery period involved, too. I think it's a couple weeks. I'm not telling you what decision to make, but I don't think you need to go through this alone. You should tell your mother. What does the father say?"

"That's why I thought you should know, Carolyn. Since you're there with her, she will still have someone she can talk to."

Great. Just what I need, to be in the middle of Cece's family business. "Sheree, if you were woman enough to have sex, you need to be woman enough to tell your mother," I said, looking for my sunglasses.

"I will, when we get back. She's been edgy lately. I was hoping this vacation would improve her mood."

"I thought it was just me," I said. "She's been jumping on me lately too, so I quit calling for a while. Is everything all right at home?"

"I guess so. She and Daddy have been arguing lately. He wants to quit his job like Uncle Raymond and Mama doesn't want him to."

Kids sure will tell your business. I'll have to remember, if and when I have children, not to discuss certain things around them. "They'll be all right. Back to your dilemma. You promise to talk to your mother as soon as you get back?" I asked her.

"Yeah, I guess," she said with a noncommittal shrug.

"You never did say how the father felt about all of this," Beverly asked glancing in the rear view mirror at Sheree.

"He doesn't want me to have it," she said softly.

"I knew you must have been getting this abortion idea from somewhere. He should have thought about that a few months ago. I know I said I wouldn't nag you about this, but I may not catch you alone anymore this weekend. You need to have your baby. A baby is a gift from God. Just think if I had aborted Tony. I never had another baby. It wasn't because we didn't try. I know you want to go to college. You still can. You can even come to school down here. I'll help you. What good is all that education and a career if you have no one to pass it on to? You're on this Earth to be fruitful and multiply."

I cut my eyes at Beverly. She was talking to Sheree, but she was talking about me. She and Daddy were the only ones who knew about my abortion. Daddy had Beverly go to the doctor's office with me, because we didn't want to tell Mama.

It had been almost twenty years since Marvin Handley and I were in Sheree's position. We ran off to get married, and that only made things worse. Daddy and Reverend Handley almost came to blows as each blamed the other's child for being a bad influence. When Daddy and I left Reverend Handley's house, Daddy asked me "Do you want to have this baby?"

"I don't know," I answered. "I guess I didn't think I had a choice."

"Yeah, that's how you got in this fix, not thinking. Do you want to go to school?" he asked.

"Yes sir."

"Well then, you shouldn't have it. You got a lot of potential. Miss Carter said you can still get a scholarship. None of my kids have finished college. Cecelia's talking about dropping out and getting married, Beverly got pregnant, and Raymond has been in school forever. You're going to be the first. I'm not going to let that bastard Handley take that away from us."

I had never heard Daddy use that cuss word before. I think that shocked me more than his suggesting an abortion.

That Friday, he drove Beverly and me to a Memphis doctor. Mama and Cecelia were at church. When I came out, we drove home in silence. When we got out of the car he said, "Neither of you is to mention what happened today to anyone. Is that clear?" We never said another word about it.

Beverly and I have only talked about it once since then. During her last visit to my house she commented on my doll collection. "Do you think you collect these to make up for not having your baby?" she asked.

"I suppose that's what a therapist would tell me. I just like the way they look. I always inherited your and Cece's leftover dolls with half the hair pulled out and shoes missing. So now I have a whole room full."

"You know I was mad at you and Daddy when he let you get that abortion," Beverly confessed.

"I know you didn't want to come. I guess I've never thanked you for helping me through that."

"No, that's not it. My feelings were hurt when Daddy took a different approach with you than he did with me. He protected you, as though you were too good to go through what I went through. Like, I wasn't going to be anything, anyway, so it didn't matter if I started having babies."

"I'm sure Daddy didn't mean it that way. Anthony was a grown man with a job, and you said you weren't interested in college."

"I was never *expected* to go to college. But I'm not complaining. Tony may be a handful, but I wouldn't take anything for him. And I'm sure I make more money than you or Cece anyway." She walked out and we never discussed it again.

Until now. I know this little sermon about the beauty of motherhood is for my benefit. Beverly is always belittling my life, as though I'm some pitiful, barren woman, moping around, hunting for a husband. Let's see. Beverly has a trifling son and a philandering husband. Cecelia has killer migranes and a pregnant daughter. Right now being single and childless sounds pretty good.

"Sheree, I'll help you in any way I can, and if you want me with you when you tell your mother, just let me know," I said.

"Thanks Aunt Carolyn," she said between sniffles.

Lord, forgive me for that lie, I prayed. I would rather be anywhere, than with Cecelia when she gets this news. She is going to explode and I plan to stay clear of the combat zone.

16

The picnic gods smiled on Eden Saturday morning. The sun was radiant and a slight breeze wafted through the kitchen window. Raymond found a can of tomato juice in the back of his cabinet and opened it, recalling Geneva's reminder last night. She had started him drinking tomato juice every morning for his prostate. He smiled when he thought about their conversation. The kids called her when they got home from the fish fry, and Raymond spoke to her when they were finished.

"Hey Geneva. I'm surprised you're home. It's Friday night and your kids are gone. I figured you would be out on the town," Raymond said.

"You know I never liked to go out. Every once in a while I'll go to the casino with Cecelia."

He told her about all the relatives who had asked about her. She filled him in on her recent promotion and Chicago politics. They talked for an hour and it was the first conversation they had in a long time that didn't turn acrimonious.

The scent of homemade pancakes and turkey sausage permeated the house and drew Rayven and Malcolm to the kitchen. They sat at the card table that served as his kitchen table. Once he convinced them to try Aunt Belle's homemade sorghum molasses, they devoured the feast he had prepared.

Raymond enjoyed watching them eat. They were growing up so fast. He missed these times, when they sat in their pajamas and talked. He found out things they never told him on their hurried phone calls. He found out Malcolm wanted to join the basketball league at church, but Geneva didn't get off work in time to take him to practice. Her 'friend' took him to practice, but he had stopped coming around. Geneva said he would have to wait until ninth grade, when he could play for the school. Raymond promised he would find someone to take him to practice. He found out Geneva had let Rayven get a perm, something he had adamantly opposed. He was relishing this time, but Rayven rushed to get dressed so she could go shopping with her cousins. He didn't even mind when she asked him for twenty dollars. He wondered how much he was missing by living so far away. When he went in the bathroom to shave, he noticed a sanitary napkin in the garbage, and realized just how much he was missing.

Raymond and Malcolm went to his parent's house to help with picnic preparations. Brenda and Julia were busy putting plastic tablecloths over the tables they had borrowed from the church. Smoke from Cousin Booker T.'s barbecue contraption filled the air. The giant black metal barrel looked like a portable junk heap with two chimneys. It wasn't much to look at, but succulent, tender meats emerged from inside. C.W. and Charles came out of the shed to greet Raymond and Malcolm.

"Hey there. I'm going inside to see if Mama needs help with anything," Raymond said.

"Your Mama been gone. Bunch of the womenfolk went shopping over in Memphis. So me and Charles been working on the backhoe. Needs a new battery."

"Farm work don't stop just because you got company," Charles said, wiping his greasy hands on his pants.

"We have to keep a journal about our summer vacation," Malcolm said. "I'm going to write about my Grandaddy's farm. But where are the tractors, the cows and the scarecrow? Daddy said he had to milk cows every morning before he went to school. He said he had to keep the horses fed, and chop wood, and ---"

"That's enough Malcolm," Raymond said patting his son's back. "They don't want to hear about old times."

C.W. and Charles smiled as they looked at Raymond. In the version they remembered, Raymond was always scarce when there was work to be done.

"Come with me," Charles said to his nephew. "I'll show you some of the equipment we use and take you for a quick ride on the tractor."

"Well Daddy, what should I do to help get things set up?" Raymond asked.

"I think we got it all under control. Booker T. been here since four this morning. Paul is bringing ice. It shouldn't take Charles too long to finish changing the battery on that backhoe, then we'll close the shed. You know, I wish you two were closer. I thought when you moved home you'd get to know each other better."

"I've tried, Daddy. Charles won't listen to anything I have to say."

"Why does he have to listen to you? Why can't you listen to each other?"

"I was trying to tell him how to use the computer as a farming tool. You can use it to determine your crop rotation by tracking yield and fertilizer. And if you get crop insurance---"

"When I moved to Detroit I came home one summer and told Daddy and Beau they needed to quit planting corn. It was ruining the land. He told me I couldn't run my business and theirs too. Now this belongs to all of you, but Charles is in charge right now."

"I'm not trying to take over. I'm just trying to help, but he doesn't even want my help."

"Just be patient with him. He always was a little jealous of you cause' you went to college. Let him know you appreciate him."

"I don't know. Sometimes I don't think I'm doing much good down here. Maybe I should go back to Chicago. Did you look at my kids? Did you see how big they've gotten?"

"Yes, it doesn't take long. I remember you and Geneva bringing them down here in diapers. Y'all ran out of diapers and couldn't believe there wasn't no stores open on Sunday."

"I want more than memories. I want to be a part of their lives." Raymond leaned over to whisper in his father's ear. "Rayven has started her period already. Geneva didn't even tell me."

"Sometimes, womenfolk like to keep that kind of talk between themselves."

"But she's just a kid. And Geneva let her get a perm. She's growing up too fast."

"Kids mature a whole lot faster than they used to. Lois says it's the vitamins pregnant women take. You got to face it. They aren't babies anymore."

"When I first moved home I felt like you needed me. Charles was busy with the farm, and Mama was running herself ragged trying to look after you. I've been able to keep Carl's spirits up and even rein in Tony. Now that you're better, I feel like I should tend to my own family. I don't want to just be a vacation dad. But I like it down here. And, I have a chance to not just work at a bank, but to be an owner. What would you do?"

"That's a hard choice son. I'm glad you got to make it and not me."

17

When we returned to Eden, the picnic was in full swing. Cars from Michigan, Illinois, Missouri, California, Florida, Georgia, Ohio and even North Dakota were parked all over the front yard. I didn't even know there were black folks in North Dakota. Several children I didn't recognize were on the porch, chattering and laughing. Aunt Belle appeared at the screen door and told them to stop jumping. Just yesterday, we were the ones playing on the porch and Aunt Belle was scolding us. The difference though, was that we listened. Those kids resumed jumping as soon she turned her back.

We followed the aroma of barbecue to the back of the house. Mama's flower garden, pecan and plum trees outlined the backyard, just as they had when I was growing up. Charles had put in a patio outside the kitchen. Geraniums in old number ten washtubs, that used to be our bathtubs, lined the patio. A cottonwood tree still held our old tire swing. A patch of red dirt in a clearing behind the house, doubled as a basketball court and backed up to the first rows of shoulder high corn. Charles' trailer stood on the east end of the yard. A blanket of red filled the yard, as everyone sported the reunion T-shirts our cousin designed. The shirts had a large tree in the center, with long roots branching out. Roots connected a picture of Africa on the right and of the United States on the left, with a star where Arkansas would be.

There were endless tables of food, with more being added. Dishes of potato salad, macaroni salad, fruit salad, carrot and raisin salad, baked beans, green beans, cabbage, watermelons just picked from Daddy's patch, and every type of cake and pie imaginable adorned the table. Cousin Booker T. presided over the grill. Every man in our family claimed to be a master at barbecue, but his was the best. There were platters of barbecued ribs, chicken, steaks, hamburgers and goat. People always turned their noses up at the mention of goat. But, once they tasted it, they were hooked. It was Daddy's specialty. I even saw Julia get seconds.

We didn't waste any time and headed straight for the food. "There's so much here, I don't know where to start," I said as I heaped some sweet smelling baked beans on my plate.

"Just don't start making it a habit. You worked too hard to get that weight off to let it slip up on you," Cecelia warned. "Get some of the grilled cabbage. It's low in calories."

"I see the food police are out in force. Let me enjoy this holiday meal, please. I'll worry about the calories later," I said.

"You may enjoy it now, but you'll pay later. Look around, I bet half the people here have diabetes, high blood pressure or another ailment related to unhealthy eating. Look at that corn just bathing in butter," Cecelia said, shaking her head.

"Umm, sure does look good. I think I'll get two," Beverly teased.

"Beverly you did good to quit smoking. Now you just need to get your weight under control. Put some sliced tomatoes and beets on your plate. They'll help fill you up," Cecelia said.

"Yeah, you get beets and tomatoes," I said. "I want fried chicken, fried okra and pecan pie. If I'm going to backslide, I want to make sure it was worth it."

"You got that right," Beverly said. "I've got to have some of Aunt Pearl's macaroni and cheese. That dirty rice looks good, too. I wonder who made it? You can't eat every body's cooking you know."

"It does look good," I said as I picked up the serving spoon. "I think Mama said Cookie was bringing the rice dish."

"Then, girl, you don't want to eat that. They may be family, but those folks are so nasty they have roaches in their refrigerator," Beverly whispered.

"It's about time you women folk got back," Raymond said as he walked up and began fixing his plate. "You come all the way from Chicago to go shopping? I don't understand it. All the stores carry the same stuff."

"It's a woman thing," Beverly said.

"Be careful, you are under the watchful eye of Food Police Officer Cecelia Washington Brown," I said.

"Make light if you want. I'm trying to get you people to realize what you eat affects your health. We really should have discussed the menu more. Most of this is very unhealthy," Cecelia said. "Look at Uncle Nap over there sucking that rib bone. He's not even supposed to eat pork, and, look at Aunt Ethel Fay. She's already over three hundred pounds, and she's waddling back for more. It's a sad commentary that we would subject our loved ones to this. We are putting the nail in their coffin."

"I have to agree with Cece about the pork," Raymond said. "But, I think it's inspiring that a people who came here with nothing and were given scraps to live on, turned those scraps into the most delicious food on earth. The white man gave us pork scraps and grease while he ate the best of what the slaves planted, picked and cooked."

"If our ancestors could survive on fatback and beans, we can too," Beverly said as she continued to fix her plate.

"Our ancestors did more physical activity than we do," Cecelia said. "I'm going to check your blood pressure and blood levels before I leave. My bag is in the van."

"There were fewer preservatives in the food too," I said.

"Well, I know how you and Cecelia can contribute something fresh to the menu. You can start cranking the ice cream," Raymond ordered.

"I don't know why we just can't buy ice cream like everybody else. It is too hot to be sitting out here stirring ice cream like this is 1925," Cecelia huffed.

I had to admit, that wasn't my idea of fun, either. We always had homemade ice cream when we came home. The taste is so sweet and rich, it makes the store bought brands taste like water. I would love to top this meal off with some homemade ice cream. But it would taste better if someone else made it.

"Where is the electric mixer? Didn't we get Daddy one for Father's Day awhile back?" I asked.

Raymond looked at us like we had two heads. "That thing is still in the box. Daddy said the cream didn't taste the same, and I agree. We're all going to take turns. You just get us started. This is about more than ice cream. This is about fellowship and history. Black folks are always trying to forget the past. We need to remember---"

"Oh, don't get started on that stuff. You win the Blackest Brother Contest. Okay, Raymond, or I mean Malik or whatever you call yourself these days," Cecelia said, as she pulled up a chair to sit and start turning.

"See that's why black folks can't get ahead. Look at the Jews. They have traditions they honor proudly."

"No," Cecelia replied, "the black man can't get ahead because he is sitting somewhere turning a 1925 ice cream machine. Meanwhile the white man uses his electric mixer, or he buys ice cream. Then, he spends the time he saves to plan a way to make more money," Cecelia said.

"I can't believe you two are related," Beverly said, shaking her head.

"Cecelia, just turn the crank please." Raymond said and waved us off as he walked away.

"All that boy needs is an Afro and a dashiki. He is ready for the revolution," Cecelia said.

At least we were in the shade. From our turning station, we had a panoramic view of the picnic. A group had a volleyball game going on near the shed. Julia was spiking the ball relentlessly. Daddy and Uncle Nap were holding court, playing bid whist under the pecan tree. They were playing 'rise and fly', and so far no one had beaten them. Mama seemed to be everywhere. She was putting dishes on the table, then she was turning meat on the barbecue pit, then she was sitting with Mama Mary and Aunt Ethel Fay drinking iced-tea. She would complain about being tired, but she was enjoying her role as hostess. Children were everywhere. Despite my lack of contribution, the Washington bloodline would be around for many generations to come.

The kids from the porch moved to the back yard. They were dancing to somebody's CD player, when Mama Mary marched right in the middle of their group. "What kind of dancin' is that?" she asked. "Lord, all these children know how to do is shake they tail. Yo mamas oughtn let y'all perform like that. It ain't cute, not one bit."

"But Mama Mary, this is what they do in the videos," Rayven whined.

"Well, no wonder. Them videos is plain nasty. They shouldn't even be on TV."

Daddy came to the rescue. "I'll show y'all how to dance." He started doing his favorite dance. Actually, it was the only dance I had ever seen him do. It looked like a slow motion version of the mashed potatoes with a stomp thrown in every other beat or so. He grabbed Mama Mary's hand and twirled her around. The kids were laughing and pointing.

"Lord have mercy, I have seen it all," Mama laughed.

"All right now, don't break nothing," Uncle Nap said.

"Hey, I got some real music," Raymond said. He put on an O'Jays CD and started a soul train line. Daddy even got Mama to go down the line. She had a little jerk thing working. Jackie and her kids came down next. Aunt Belle and Mr. Ben strolled down with their canes. Raymond then broke out B.B. King's 'Let the Good Times Roll'. This brought everybody to the patio, turned dance floor. Cecelia and I abandoned the ice cream machine and joined the party. Even Aunt Millie was clapping from her wheelchair. After two songs everybody headed for the ice chest. "Okay, we've shown you how to do it, you young people try it now," Daddy said as he fanned himself with his Braves cap. "You can put your Snoopy Cool J back on."

The kids thought this was hilarious. "There is no Snoopy Cool J, Granddaddy."

We returned to our post turning the ice cream. Daddy made his way over to us wiping the sweat from his face and sat down. "Whew, I'm not as young as I used to be, but I can still shake a tail feather every now and then."

"Just make sure you don't break your tail feather while you're shaking it," I said.

"Don't you worry about me. I got some shaking left to do," Daddy said.

I saw Cousin Willie head toward our table and began hitting Cecelia under the table. Willie is the king of multilevel marketing. He is always pushing some plan that will make everyone rich, as long as you sign others up to sell too. I had managed to avoid him, but now I was trapped.

"Hey Chubby, Hey Cece, I've been looking for you two," he said, as he sat next to Daddy. "I've got a great investment I want to tell you about."

"What's that boy?" Daddy asked.

"It's a new company called Nutrimins. Not too many people have heard of it yet, so you can get in on the ground floor.

We have vitamins, weight loss products, supplements, everything to keep you young." Willie was passing out brochures when Uncle Nap walked up.

"C.W. we're up next. We got to go reclaim our bid whist crown," Uncle Nap said. "Willie, leave them girls alone. You're slowing down the ice cream progress. Boy, when are you going to get a real job?" he asked as they walked away.

"Thank goodness for Uncle Nap," Cecelia said.

"You got that right," I agreed.

Call it a mother's radar, but Beverly noticed Tony as soon as he arrived. Everyone else was dancing or cheering, while Beverly walked over to the food table that her son was surveying. She kissed him on his cheek as he began loading ribs on his plate. "Be sure to get some vegetables," she said.

"Hey Mama."

"Hey sweetie. You look thin. I hope you've been eating."

"Now Mama, have you ever known me to miss a meal? I'm just getting lean," he said flexing his tatooed muscle. "Working with Uncle Charles is better than going to the gym."

"I know. You hardly call home, you're working all the time. But it's good to keep busy, and I hope you're saving your money for school. The semester starts next month."

"I'm not going back to school," Tony said as he grabbed three slices of bread.

"What are you talking about? We've planned for your college all your life. I know you didn't like school in Memphis. I thought you wanted to go to the college in Pine Bluff with some of your friends."

"Naw. I just like to party over there."

"We decided a smaller school would be better---"

"No Mama, *you* decided. I'm not interested in college," Tony said licking barbecue sauce from his fingers.

"What do you think you're going to do? It's hard for a black man, you need every advantage you can get."

"Well, I was thinking about staying here. I like working with Uncle Charles. I like being outside, working on my own."

"Son, this is just a summer job. I didn't work like a dog and scrimp and save for you to be a field hand," Beverly said, as she put her hand on her hip.

"It's not like that. Farming is a business, Mama. It's more than just dropping seeds in the ground."

"This is not a career for you."

"Why not? Grandaddy has been successful."

"He didn't have many choices in his day. He worked hard so his children could have choices. Daddy didn't even graduate from high school. He was proud of Charles and me when we graduated. And when Raymond got a scholarship, Daddy vowed to send the rest of his children to college too."

"Mama, I appreciate all of that, but I'm just being honest. I don't want you and Daddy wasting your money when I know that's not what I want to do. Grandaddy and Uncle Charles have to pay somebody, why not me?"

"Well, Daddy will be selling this place soon. Then where will you be?" Beverly asked.

"That's not what Uncle Charles said. He said he's going to be taking over and he and Aunt Brenda are getting ready to build them a house."

Beverly sat at the table while her son went back for seconds. Her eyes scanned the yard looking for Carolyn and Cecelia. She couldn't wait to tell them about Charles' plans.

Cecelia and I had only gotten a brief respite from our ice cream duties. We were back on the job, when Paul came by with the video camera. He spoke in his Walter Cronkite voice, "Here we have two of the Washington sisters stirring the famous

Washington ice cream. The ingredients are a well-guarded secret. Would one of you like to share your family recipe with America?"

"The secret is in the wrist. You try it," Cecelia said as she offered Paul her seat.

Paul did a 180-degree pivot and headed toward the house. "Next, we will move on to the grill . . . " Paul said, as he walked away.

"Now we know how Henny Penny felt. No one wants to help until it's time to eat," I said to Cecelia.

"Carolyn, look, there's the Twins," Cecelia whispered. Their names were Yvonne and Yvette, but we could never tell them apart, so we called both of them Twin. "I can't believe they are still dressing alike. Did they ever get married?"

"Why is that the first thing people want to know about someone? You haven't seen them in twenty years. Where do they live? What kind of jobs do they have?" I asked.

"Don't get an attitude. It was just a question. We can talk to them later. Listen, we never finished our conversation yesterday. When are we going to talk to Daddy about the farm? Jackie said CFI paid Uncle Edward two hundred fifty thousand dollars for his land. Is Daddy thinking about selling his land? Is that why you and Paul were at the courthouse yesterday? How are we going to handle this?"

"Cecelia, *we* have nothing to do with it. I'm not going to say another word about it. I already feel bad that I told big-mouth Paul," I whispered, looking around making sure no one overheard us.

"Why are you and Paul in on everything and the rest of us left in the dark? That doesn't seem fair."

I decided to give Cecelia a little information, just to get her off my back. "The government is about to settle with Daddy on his discrimination case. Paul and I were just looking over the terms."

"How much is he going to get?" she asked.

"Now you know not to ask me that," I said. "I've told you too much already."

"Well I've been reading about it in the paper. I think the government's initial offer was fifty thousand, but those who held out are getting more. I bet Daddy is getting hundreds of thousands!"

"Cecelia, hold on," I cautioned. "It's no where near that much."

"You're just trying to throw me off track. Girl, can you imagine, we are going to be rich!" Cecelia said. "The first thing I'm going to do is get a new house. If Daddy gives me enough money for a down payment, I can move out of the city. What are you going to do?"

"I'm not making plans for Daddy's money. And, I'm not going to talk about this with you anymore," I repeated.

Beverly pulled up a chair next to us. "I see you two are still stuck with ice cream duty."

"And you are just in time to unstick us," Cecelia said.

Cousin Jackie came to the table. "What are you gals whispering about?"

"We were talking about you, but since you came we'll have to stop," Beverly laughed.

Just then we spotted an unidentified fine brother hugging Mama Mary.

"Ooh, please tell me we are not related," Jackie said.

"Calm down, girlfriend. Remember that man you brought here? I think he's called your husband," Beverly said.

"I can still look. Anyway, I was checking him out for Carolyn."

"Just check somewhere else then," I said.

"He's not Carolyn's type," Cecelia announced.

"He looks fine to me. What is Carolyn's type?" Jackie asked.

"I'm not into looks. I'm interested in a man that treats me good," I said, although I don't know why I was even explaining myself to her.

"Uh'oh," Jackie said. "That means ugly. But that's okay. I dated a few ugly ones myself. You remember Johnnie Ray? He was ugly and a half. He had that gold tooth in the front of his mouth and those chicken pox marks on his face. But I tell you what, them ugly ones can really hit it."

I had a puzzled look on my face as she and Beverly laughed and gave each other high fives.

"Carolyn, girl, you are so slow," Beverly said. "Let's just say they are very skilled in the bedroom. Everyone has a talent. He might be able to get some sparks flying. It *is* the Fourth of July weekend, you know."

"Well, a little birdie told me you're getting some sparks started with Bucky," Jackie teased, as she nudged me with her elbow.

I forget that everyone knows everyone else's business around here. "We are just old friends. And I can find my own men, thank you very much."

"If you don't want him, maybe I'll turn him on to my sister. He has to be better than the dregs she's been dating. He can't be family, he doesn't favor anyone here," Jackie said.

"You all can stop drooling. Boyfriend is gay," Cecelia announced.

We looked at her in disbelief. "You're kidding," Jackie said.

"How can you tell?" I asked. It always amazes me how Cecelia is such a repository of information.

"He came with Cousin Bryan from Atlanta and Bryan is gay. So I put two and two together. I figured if they're traveling together, they must be a couple. You all really need to be more observant," Cecelia said.

I shook my head. Two more fine brothers out of circulation. I noticed Bryan earlier, but hadn't had a chance to speak to him. Bryan is Uncle Nap's oldest son. He and Paul grew up together.

"I wonder if Paul knows," I said.

"It's not a secret. Everyone knows," Cecelia said. " You would too if you came around the family more often."

"I'm not exactly around the family now, sitting over here stirring this ice cream," I said.

"Good afternoon ladies," Anthony said as he walked up behind us. He had just delivered several cases of beer and made his way to our table.

Cecelia stood and cleared her throat, "Something is making me sick," she announced. "Let's get some fresh air."

Jackie and I dutifully followed. At least Anthony was good for something. He could turn the ice cream now. Jackie whispered as we walked away, "I heard what happened last night."

"I don't know why she won't leave him," Cecelia said.

"What for?" Jackie asked. "These women down here are so pitiful, they don't respect your marriage. And look at Anthony, he just seems to get better with age. I tell Steve all the time he needs to stay in shape like Anthony."

"He needs to respect his own marriage. It's called self-control," Cecelia said.

"Well Beverly knows what she's doing. As long as Anthony brings his money home, she's not going to let some tramp tear apart her home. My mama says they eventually settle down and decide to do right."

"Yeah, when they get too old to vote. I don't want you when you're all bent over and used up," Cecelia said.

"Maybe you have the one faithful man out there. But the majority of men mess around. It's just a fact of life," Jackie said.

"Carolyn, you need to get your single sisters to respect themselves and find their own man," Cecelia said. "I hate to see my sister mistreated."

I nodded in agreement, wishing I could get them to see the other side.

"My sister definitely needs help in the 'man' department. I'm going to find her and get Bryan to introduce her to boyfriend. He is too fine to be gay," Jackie said.

Cecelia and I walked to the front of the house to get our shopping bags from the van. Rayven and three other girls were playing double dutch on the carport.

"Marquis and Lanisha sitting in the tree, k-i-s-s-i-n-g, I'll show you mine, you show me yours, when the baby comes we'll call him George," the girls chanted in a singsong voice.

Cecelia and I looked at each other. "Did they say what I think they said?" I asked her. They answered my question by singing it again.

"Girls, that is not a song that nice young ladies sing. Whatever happened to Mary Mack?" Cecelia chastised.

The girls laughed and rolled their eyes. A girl about nine or ten years old with a head full of braids said, "Aunt Cece, that was a million years ago. Did you even have a jump rope back then?"

"Whose child are you?" Cecelia asked.

"My mama's name is Marilyn," the girl replied.

"I should have known. You look just like her, and you have a smart mouth like her too. I guess I'm going to have to beat you like I used to beat your mother. Come on, let's show them how we used to do it, back when they invented the jump rope."

I looked all around. "You're talking to me? I haven't jumped rope in a million years, like she said."

"It's like riding a bike. You never forget," Cecelia said as she pulled me toward the rope.

We had a rocky start, but eventually it came back to me. Cecelia asked Veronica to jump so we would have an even number. She declined and said she had to speak to someone in the back yard. We all looked at each other when Cousin Linda said she wanted to jump. The girls giggled. She was about five feet two, and two hundred pounds. When she jumped, everything on her body jumped. Her breasts looked like they wanted to break out of their tight T-shirt prison. But she showed us a thing or two. She won.

"Whew, I'm ready for some ice cream now. That jumping should have been worth at least 400 calories," I said.

I took my bags to my room and took out my cell phone to call Warren, but I couldn't find my charger. Cecelia was waiting when I came out of my room.

"We need to talk with Daddy soon," she said.

"Charles Washington Senior has no problem speaking his mind. When he wants to discuss things with us, he will. I am not going to go behind his back and set up a coup. Drop it Cecelia."

The sounds of screams interrupted our conversation. We rushed to the front porch and saw a black, convertible Corvette drive up. It was our cousin, Shawn Lewis. His father was Daddy's first cousin. Shawn plays for the Los Angeles Clippers. He's not a starter, but he still reigns as the family celebrity. I don't see a NBA star when I see Shawn. I see Shawn and Carl running around Eden barefoot. Shawn's family moved to St. Louis for his last two years of high school. He went to college on a scholarship, and the Clippers drafted him in the second round. He didn't get caught up in drugs like Carl did. Everyone was proud of him and rushed to greet him. Malcolm and the boys admired the car.

Cecelia caught me as I headed to the kitchen. "It's not disloyal to discuss Daddy's affairs," she said. "This affects all of us. It's a given that Daddy can't run the farm any more. He needs to make some decisions, and he knows it or he would not have asked you to look things over for him. This weekend is a good time, because we're all here. Do you want Charles and his greedy wife getting their hands on everything after we leave? I refuse to let that happen. We need to get this out in the open, the sooner, the better."

I stepped on the back porch where Sheree sat alone under the ceiling fan. Now, there's something Cecelia should handle, the sooner, the better. How long does Sheree think she can keep her pregnancy a secret? I wondered.

I poured a glass of tea, and reached in the cooler for ice. "Give me some ice too," Aunt Belle ordered. "Whew! It is hot out here. I think I'll go in the house for a few minutes to cool off. Are you going inside?"

"No ma'am. I'm going to sit with Sheree. She has a quiet spot on the swing." It was also a spot out of my sister's view. I felt like an escaped convict trying to stay one step ahead of Cecelia the bounty hunter.

Aunt Belle stood closer to me and spoke softly, "I dreamed about fish last night."

"Maybe your dream was about the fish fry yesterday," I said.

"Chile', don't play with me. You know what I'm talking about."

Aunt Belle 'sees' things. A dream about fish is supposed to mean a new baby. I don't normally subscribe to the supernatural, but Aunt Belle is right too often to dismiss. Her first husband was from Louisiana, so she claims to know voodoo skills. Growing up, we made fun of her old wives tales and superstitions. The older I get, the more I appreciate her wisdom.

"Aunt Belle, I assure you, I am not expecting," I said. When I was growing up it was disrespectful to say "pregnant."

"I don't mean you," she said, as if even the possibility were remote. "I'm talking about Cece's baby, Sheree."

I don't know how she does it, but she's usually right. She advised Mama and Daddy to pray for Walter because he was in danger. We knew that, he was in Vietnam. Well, within a month he was dead. Daddy said when his sister Henrietta was killed, Aunt Belle made them stay in the house for two days. She said death comes in threes and they couldn't go outside until she heard of two more deaths. We were upset when Daddy had a stroke last fall. But Aunt Belle was nonchalant and said he would be fine. A butterfly had landed on her shoulder that day, and that meant good luck. The doctors told us it was touch-and-go and if he lived he may not regain full mobility. Of course, Aunt Belle proved them wrong.

"She hasn't told her mother yet," I whispered.

"I know."

"Aunt Belle, we need to get you a 900 number and make some money," I said as I hugged her.

"That's what my fourth husband used to say. By the way, it's a boy," she said, as I walked away.

"Mind if I join you?" I asked Sheree.

"You're not going to give me a lecture are you?"

"I promise. I just need a place to hide for a minute. Raymond wants me to turn the ice cream maker, Cousin Willie wants to talk to me about his taxes and your mother has been nagging me."

"Well, nobody would even miss me. I should have just stayed home," Sheree said.

"You shouldn't feel that way. You're a very important part of this family. I feel like you're the daughter I didn't have. I know you're anxious about your situation right now. But your mother and father will accept it and life will go on."

Sheree kept swinging. "I don't think Mama will ever accept this," she said, pointing to her stomach. "I don't know how I'm going to tell her," Sheree said.

"If you want me to be there, just let me know." I thought back twenty years, when I was the one wondering how I would tell my parents. I often wondered if I made the right choice. Sometimes I felt God was punishing me for not having my baby. Maybe that's why I keep ending up with the wrong men. I had been afraid for my father to find out, but he ended up being the one to help me. To this day, I don't think he told mother.

"Sheree, maybe you should tell your father first," I said.

"No way! He would be ready to kill Greg. He didn't even want me to date. At least Mama let me go out."

"He may surprise you. He would be mad at Greg, for sure. But once he got over the shock, he'd probably be easier to deal with than your mother."

"I don't know."

"Well, you need to decide soon. Your problem won't go away or get easier. Just remember, I'm here for you."

"Thanks, Aunt Carolyn. I'll be right back, nature calls," Sheree said as she headed for the bathroom.

As Sheree went inside, Derrick came out. "I see you saved a seat for me," he said as he sat in Sheree's spot. "I called earlier, but they said you went shopping. I would have thought you and your sisters would sleep late. I know I didn't get up until almost eleven. I can't hang like I used to. I came in and fell into bed. I don't think a tornado would have awakened me."

I fell into bed too, but I didn't get any sleep. I tried to decide when to tell Beverly my news. Tomorrow after the banquet seemed best. I didn't want to tell her before church or the banquet, and have Mama ask why she wasn't there.

"I hope you didn't mind me crashing in on you and your sisters. It must be nice to have a big family to hang out with. I know my grandmother did her best, but sometimes I think I missed a lot by not having brothers and sisters.

He was missing the opportunity to loan money, be part of a shooting scene, and the chance to be stalked. But I saw no need to shatter his idyllic view.

"I enjoyed last night, but I'm glad for a minute alone with you," Derrick said.

It was only a minute, because Mama opened the screen door slightly. "Hey you two, sorry to be a bother, but I need you to run across the field to Charles' house. We are out of garbage bags and I don't want to go to the store. I would call over there but I can't find either phone. I like the old fashioned phone that's always in the same place, or at least you can follow the cord and find it. These cordless phones are a nuisance. One time C.W. left it in the tool shed. He swore up and down he hadn't moved it. But I knew he had it last. I told him ---"

"I'll go to Charles' house for you," I said as I stood.

"I'll go with you," Derrick said.

"Thank-you," Mama said. "And I don't know why they're fastened up in the house anyway. Tell Charles everyone is asking about him and to bring his rusty behind to the picnic. Sometimes I wonder about my children," she said shaking her head. "Ain't got a bit of sense. My Mama always said to cherish the time with your family, because you never know when it will be the last time. But I guess I can't talk about y'all when my own sister ---"

"We'll be right back Mama," I said, pushing Derrick toward the door.

Derrick and I crossed the stone path to Charles' trailer. Crepe myrtle bushes lined the pathway and a white picket fence surrounded his place. The view of the picnic from this side of the field seemed surreal, like a silent movie.

Brenda met us at the door. "What do we owe this surprise to? she asked.

"Mama wants to borrow some garbage bags and she wants you two to come over," I said.

"I didn't think she'd notice our absence with all those folks over there," Charles said.

"Well she noticed. Although it is nice and cool in here. I can't blame you for taking a respite from the heat," I said.

"I have a big box of garbage bags from Sam's," Brenda said. "I have a big ice chest out there too. Why don't you take it back with you?"

"I'll help you," Derrick said as he followed her outside.

I was surprised at how stylish their home looked. I rarely came over, since Charles was usually at Mama's house. It didn't look like I expected a trailer to look. There were vaulted ceilings and a fireplace. The carpet was as soft as a down pillow. Beverly mentioned a few months ago that they had gotten new carpet. Brenda had done an admirable job of decorating. "Grandma Jean's crystal looks perfect on your shelves," I said. "I know she's pleased that we all have a piece of her to remind us of how special she was. I have one of the quilts she made draped over a chair in my guest room."

"Let's quit the chit chat," Charles said as he opened a can of beer. "You know you didn't come over here for no garbage bags, or to talk about Brenda's decorating. Just say what you came to say."

"Okay. Mama did send me, but since you mentioned it, why do you still have Power of Attorney? Daddy's better now, shouldn't he rescind it? And why did you take out a loan while Daddy was in the hospital. And did you get permission to spend all that money on tractors and who knows what else? You never mentioned these things to any of us. How do you think Daddy would feel about all of this?"

"I knew you were trying to stir up trouble," Charles said.

"No I'm not. I'm just looking for some answers."

"Well, I don't owe you any answers. Me and C.W. been running things just fine for years."

"But that couldn't go on forever. Daddy is not a young man anymore. What's going to happen now that Daddy's not running things every day?"

"I've been running things and I can keep on running things. Nobody was interested in this place until they heard CFI was buying land around here. You're so worried about C.W. How do you think he would feel if he knew you were plotting to sell his land?"

"That's not true," I said.

"Cecelia has made no secret what she's trying to do. She's already convinced Beverly and Raymond just wants to take over."

"I don't know where you're getting all this from. I think I need to talk to Daddy to sort this all out," I said.

"You do that. Tell him about ---"

"Will you lower your voice?" I asked. "Derrick will be coming in at any minute."

"This is *my* house. If you don't like how I'm talking, leave. I didn't invite you in the first place."

"Fine." I slammed the front door so hard, Champ ran under the house.

"Hey, what happened?" Derrick asked as he rushed to catch up with me. "And you forgot the garbage bags."

"Just take me to Walmart. I'll buy Mama some bags. And if you still want some siblings, I can get you a brother, real cheap."

18

Paul had rested his video camera and switched to snapping pictures of everyone. Daddy posed with his sisters Aunt Ethel Fay, and Aunt Pearl. They couldn't even agree on how to pose for the picture. Aunt Ethel Fay wanted Daddy to be in the middle, and Aunt Pearl said they should line up by age. We laughed when Aunt Belle threatened to get her switch. Raymond gathered the grandchildren for a picture with Mama and Daddy. This reunion was the first time all of them were together. Mama and Daddy posed with all of the grandchildren first. Walter's daughter was the oldest grandchild. She was an Army Staff Sergeant, and arranged her leave to coincide with the reunion. Ironically, she decided to give her life to the institution that took her father's life. Carl's sons inherited their father's height and stood behind Mama and Daddy in the picture. Charles' children and grandchildren came over from Memphis and flanked Mama and Daddy in the portrait. Rayven, Mike, Malcolm, and Sheree sat in front. Tony almost missed the picture, because no one could find him. He appeared just in time for Paul to say "cheese," which Daddy changed to "money."

My baby would have been a little older than Sheree by now. I always thought of my baby as a little girl, dressed in pastel pinafores and starched slips, with bows in her hair and ruffled socks to match her dresses. In my mind, she was stuck in time, like the girl on the Morton Salt box, but she would have been almost twenty, in college by now. Questions arose from the tomb I kept them buried in, “I did do the right thing, didn’t I? Did I kill my legacy? Is God punishing me?”

Thankfully, my brooding thoughts were interrupted as Paul ordered, “Come on, Carolyn, we’re waiting on you.” He commissioned Uncle Nap to take a picture of all of us with spouses and grandchildren. Then we took a picture with just the eight of us. Mama and Daddy sat on the picnic table bench. Raymond and Charles sat on the table and Beverly and Cecelia sat on the outside of Mama and Daddy. Paul and I kneeled on the grass. We had a few false starts and Uncle Nap claimed, “It’s too much ugly for one camera.” But he finally took the picture.

“Paul, make sure you send me copies of that picture. We haven’t taken a family picture in twenty years. I’m so happy to have all of you here. If only Carl could be here,” Mama said.

“I know one thing, if Carl was here we’d need more pound cake. That boy loved Mama’s pound cake,” Beverly said.

“He could eat a whole cake and never gain an ounce,” I said.

“Yeah, and he was about the only one who could beat Daddy in cards,” Paul remarked.

“You talk like the boy is dead,” Daddy said.

“Daddy we didn’t mean . . . ” Beverly was talking to the wind because Daddy got up and left.

“I shouldn’t have said anything. I spoiled Daddy’s good mood,” Beverly said.

Mama stood, “You know how C.W. is about Carl, it’s been three years and it’s like it just happened yesterday. We can’t worry about what happened, though, we have to deal with right now.”

Right now, Carl is inmate C46783218 at Cummins Correctional Facility, serving seven years for aggravated robbery. I still can’t believe my brother is in prison. Convicts are mean, profane, scarfaced villains who deserve to be put away. Carl is handsome, sweet, and well mannered and wouldn’t hurt a fly. He lettered in two sports and still holds the basketball record at Lincoln High, for most points scored in a single season. Unfortunately, his good looks, charm and athleticism were a curse that allowed him to sweet talk his way through life, for a while. Then, as the last child left for college, Carl returned home. Mama said she didn't even recognize him at first. He was rail thin with sunken cheeks, dark circles under his eyes and rusty skin. His matted jheri curl had long since lost the curl. This was the clearest evidence that the Carl we knew was gone. He had always been meticulous about his mane and served as early training for Beverly. To see him so unkempt unnerved Mama so that she cried for weeks. Daddy gave him jobs to do on the farm, but Carl would disappear for days then reappear as though he stepped out for only a moment. Mama and Daddy began to miss things around the house and Carl would get phone calls at all times of the night.

Raymond took him to Chicago, to relieve Mama and Daddy. But he became an Achilles heel in Raymond's already rocky marriage. Raymond sided with Carl when Geneva accused him of stealing her jewelry. Then, Raymond caught him rifling through Geneva's purse and said he had to move. Carl said he could never live with Cecelia and asked to stay with me. I said okay, only if he agreed to get help. Cecelia enrolled him in a rehab program at the hospital. He stayed at the rehabilitation center forty-five days and he was back to the "old Carl" when he got out. He got a job at a grocery store and was a big help around the house. He fixed my leaky pipes, painted and installed ceramic tile in my kitchen. We rented movies, ordered pizza, and even went to see Shawn when his team came to play the Bulls. I had just broken up with Antoine, and was grateful to have someone to spend time with. Eventually he met a nice lady and just used my house as a pit stop. Those pit stops started costing me money and I decided to tell him about it.

"Chubby, let me borrow twenty bucks," Carl asked, bringing in a bag of dirty clothes.

"I thought you got paid today."

"I did, but I'm not making that long green like you are."

"You don't have my long bills either. You know I don't mind you staying here. But you are nickel-and-diming me to death," I explained.

"It's only twenty dollars. I'm not asking for blood."

"It's only twenty dollars today. Then it's five tomorrow, then ten on Saturday. I hope you're not . . . "

"I sent most of my check to Pat, okay? She was talking about filing for child support. As long as I send her money, she's cool. I'm not making enough to pay her, help you and save to get my own place."

"Don't worry about helping me. Maybe you should go to court. Then, you can get a set amount and due date. This way she's sticking you up whenever she gets ready."

"I can take care of it. Thanks."

Later that evening Cecelia called. "Where is Carl?" she snapped.

"Hello to you too. He's not here. I think he has those follow-up classes at the hospital tonight," I answered.

"Well, think again. They told me that he hasn't been to a session in almost five weeks and he failed a drug test the last time he did come."

"Are you sure? I can't believe he would do that after all we've done for him."

"I pulled a lot of strings to get him in this program. There was a waiting list."

"He has been borrowing more money lately. He told me he was sending most of his paycheck to Pat for the kids. And I found marijuana papers in the garbage can. He said he cut back his other vices and just smoked weed now."

"An addict can't cut back. It's like being a 'little pregnant'," Cecelia said.

"He's been staying out all night too. I thought he was with his new girlfriend. How could I be so dumb? Let's pick him up from work tonight and talk some sense into him."

"I don't think talking will do any good. He probably needs it knocked into him. But I'll go with you."

Cecelia and I got to Kroger a little after closing. We waited at the employee's side door for thirty minutes. "Maybe he left early today," I mused. I knocked on the metal door until someone finally came and yelled through the door.

"No deliveries tonight."

"I'm here to pick up my brother," I hollered, looking around to see if anyone was watching me make a fool of myself in the middle of the night.

Someone cracked open the door. "Who are you looking for, ma'am?" Now I felt foolish and old. When did I become a ma'am? "Is Carl Washington working late tonight? I'm his sister and I'm here to give him a ride home."

"No, ma'am. He doesn't work here anymore."

"Are you sure you know who I'm talking about? Is the manager here?"

"Yes, ma'am, I'm sure," the young man replied. He looked behind him then whispered, "Carl got caught stealing cases of cigarettes and they fired him. The manager couldn't press charges because he didn't give a valid social security number or address. If I call the manager, he'll try to get information from you to have Carl arrested. I'm sorry to tell you all this."

Speechless, I nodded my head and went back to the car and delivered the news to Cecelia.

"I was afraid something like this would happen. I know we love our brother, but very few people beat crack addiction. The only ones I've seen are those that come to the Lord, and they don't usually do that until they've hit absolute rock bottom," Cecelia said.

"I would call losing your family, getting run out of Arkansas, then being fired from a minimum wage job for stealing, rock bottom."

"No, Carolyn. He still has a place to stay, food to eat, a car to drive when you let him and spending money for his habit. You're going to have to put him out."

"I can't do that. Geneva already told Raymond he can't stay with them. He only stayed with Beverly two weeks before she sent him home. Maybe you could..."

"Don't even think about it," Cecelia said. "Carl has to admit he has a problem and be willing to help himself."

"We can't push him back on Mama and Daddy, he'd worry them to death. Where would he go?"

"That's his problem. He's a grown man. Everyone has tried to help him. We're just helping him kill himself."

"I know you're right, Cece. I don't know why Carl can't see what he's doing."

"He's sick, and we can't make him well."

I stayed up all night rehearsing my speech to Carl. I didn't go to work and was home when he came in.

"Hey Chubby. Is it some President's birthday or something?"

"No. I stayed home to talk to you. I found out you lost your job."

"Yeah, I couldn't work with those prejudiced white folks. I think the white people up here are worse than the ones at home."

"So where are you going to find a job with no white people?" I asked.

"I'll find something."

"Well, until you find a job you can go to your sessions. Cecelia found out you haven't been going to your classes."

"I didn't feel like sitting around with a bunch of losers. Those people are pitiful. The women have been turning tricks and the men are homeless. I know I have some problems, but I don't belong with them."

"That's the whole point of going. So you don't end up like them. I don't think you realize how serious this is. That manager is threatening to press charges against you for theft."

"I should have you sue that white boy for defamation of character. He told you that and you believed it."

"I don't know what to believe. I believed you when you said you needed money because you sent Pat your paycheck and now I find out you didn't even have a paycheck. I believed you when you said you would stay clean and now I find out you failed a drug test. You don't get it, do you? This is the last chance for you. There are 'help wanted' signs all over the place and tomorrow you're going to find a job. You're going to stop coming in here at all hours of the night and you're going to go to those recovery classes."

"I'm not your child. I'm grown," Carl said, lighting a cigarette.

"Then you need to act like it."

"You think you're such big stuff with your government job and your foreign car. I could have had it all. Everybody said I was ten times better than Shawn. I know I would have made it to the pros."

"Carl, you've got to start thinking about here and now. You're not in the pros, okay? In fact, you don't have a job so you can't even buy a ticket to see a pro game. You don't own anything but the clothes on your back so you can't even watch a pro game on TV. Grow up."

"I don't feel like hearing this," Carl said as he put his coat back on.

"I know what you can do to avoid hearing me. You can pack your things and move. I'll buy you a ticket home."

"Don't bother," Carl said as he slammed the door.

At first I was mad that he had the nerve to act like I was wrong for wanting him to be responsible. But as the days stretched into weeks without a word from him, I became worried. "Cece, it's been two weeks. I think we should complete a missing persons report."

"Girl, the police aren't going to do anything. Carl is grown and free to come and go, and call or not call as he pleases."

"I can't keep stalling Mama. She's starting to get suspicious that every time she calls he's not here."

"Just tell her what happened. I'm through covering up for him."

"I hate for her to worry."

"Then do what you want, but if she asks me I'm going to tell her."

The next night I came home from work and found my apartment ransacked. I called 911, then I called my sister. "Cecelia, my place was broken into while I was at work. My computer, stereo, TVs, microwave, jewelry; it's all gone."

I hadn't been in my condo long and I was terrified to stay alone. I spent the next few weeks with Cecelia. Sheree and Mike spent weekends with me. I finally got my nerve up to stay home alone, although I talked on the telephone most of the night, to keep from being alone.

A month after the robbery, a notice came from Best Pawn addressed to Carl. I opened it looking for a clue to his whereabouts. The notice said his redemption period would expire in five days. If he didn't claim the items on the attached list, he relinquished all ownership of the items. The pawn ticket listed my stolen items. That jewelry was all I had to show for time wasted with old boyfriends. They had given him only two hundred dollars for my computer and fifty for the printer. I became lightheaded when I realized the 'old dishes' referred to on the pawn ticket; my antique Wedgewood plates and my original Mammy cookie jar were pawned for fifty dollars. He had even pawned my chocolate brown, full-length, sable coat, which I had saved for over a year to buy. I felt as if someone had stuck a knife in my stomach. A thousand questions ran through my head.

Is it stealing if your brother takes it? Should I drop my case with the police? Will I get in trouble if I take the money from the insurance company? Why should I go pay to reclaim my own things? But if I tell the pawnshop they took the items fraudulently, would they charge Carl with theft?

In the end, I paid fifty-six hundred dollars to go buy my stuff back. It was cheaper than buying new things and there was information on my hard drive I needed. Luckily it hadn't been erased. Two of my Blackshear collectibles were chipped, but I was still glad to get them back. I had to cancel my trip to Jamaica, because Carl ran up my credit cards. I was and still am furious with him. I stuck with him longer than anybody, and I got played worse than anybody.

He showed up unexpectedly in Eden on Mother's Day. Mama and Daddy were glad to see him, but it wasn't long before they saw nothing had changed. Carl promised to straighten up and he moved back with Pat and his kids. But within six months he was arrested for writing bad checks. They matched his fingerprints to two robberies. He pleaded guilty to one charge of aggravated robbery and they dropped the other charges. We all went to the sentencing hearing. I was still incensed, but his attorney said it looked better if he had a supportive family present. It didn't seem to matter too much. They sentenced him to seven years. They wouldn't release him until the next century.

None of it seemed real until the judge pronounced sentence. Mama and Daddy were devastated. Mama howled like a maimed dog and made the bailiff let her hug Carl. We had to pry her away from him so the guards could take him away. Daddy sat in his seat and cried. None of us had ever seen Daddy cry. He didn't even cry at Walter's funeral. The statistics about black men in jail are continuously cited in the media, but it doesn't hit home until it's a family member. I felt bad for Carl, and worse for Mama and Daddy.

Mama used to take the bus to go visit him, or get Charles to take her. Since Raymond has been home, he takes her on the first Friday of each month. Beverly goes sometime and I think Uncle Nap has been a couple times. Daddy refuses to go. He talks like Carl is only away on a trip and doesn't mention prison. Daddy took it hard, because Carl was his favorite. Parents say they love all their kids equally, but we knew Carl was the chosen one.

I haven't gone to see him either. I can't forgive Carl. It's not about the pawn incident. Although, I do get upset every month when I write the check to my credit union to repay the loan I took out to pay off my credit cards. I can't forgive him for what he did to our family. According to Carl, everything that happened was always someone else's fault, not the result of his own actions. We're all grown and free to choose the lifestyle we wish. But when your choices affect my Mama and Daddy, then I become concerned. Daddy has wasted a fortune on Carl, from legal fees to rehab costs. Daddy even borrowed money from the bank and used his spring planting line of credit to pay an attorney and post bond. Carl worried them when he stayed with them and when he left, they still worried. At least in prison they knew where he was.

Carl was the only one absent, yet he was still the center of attention. Daddy's whole mood changed. The smiles we sported minutes earlier were gone. We had come from far and near to be with Mama and Daddy, yet they yearned for the one who was absent.

Family Reunion ?

19

"Uncle Ray, I know you didn't let Charleen score on you!" Tony shouted. They were playing two-on-two on the dirt basketball court near Charles' trailer. Raymond and Malcolm were teamed against Charleen and Tony. Charles' daughter blocked his pass to Malcolm, stole the ball and scored. Charleen had been a star in high school and was attending Tennessee State University on a basketball scholarship. That didn't make them tease him any less about being beaten by a girl though.

Raymond waved them off. "That was just a warm-up. I'll be back," he panted as he headed toward the house, holding his chest. Raymond talked a lot of trash before they started, but wouldn't concede that his legs weren't what they used to be. Instead, he blamed his drubbing on his preoccupation with Cecelia's news.

Cecelia pulled him to the side as everyone danced through the Soul Train Line. "I'm mad at you Raymond. I've talked to you several times on the phone to make arrangements for your children's visit, and not once did you mention Daddy's settlement," she said.

"I don't know anything about a settlement."

"Shhhh, lower your voice," she said. "Carolyn just told me Daddy's going to get at least a half million dollars from settlement of that lawsuit with the government."

"I heard they finally paid some of the farmers around here. I didn't know Daddy was one of them."

"Raymond, you need to get your head out of the sky and be more alert to what's going on around you."

"Don't you mean nosy?" Raymond asked.

"Call it nosy if you want. I'm looking out for all of us. Daddy will need your advice on how to invest his windfall. And we still haven't talked to him about selling the farm," Cecelia said.

"You know how I feel about selling the land."

"Raymond, you're not being realistic. Let's get together to---"

They didn't finish their conversation, because Paul called them to take pictures. Now Raymond was trying to sort out the news. This couldn't have come at a better time, he thought. If he liquidated the rest of his Chicago National Bank stock, and got some cash from Dad's settlement, he'd have enough capital and collateral to be part of the controlling owner group, he calculated. He smiled for the picture, but his smile was for his business plan.

Raymond had become active in the plight of the area's black farmers, that is those who were left. During one of his infrequent visits to church, a representative from the Black Farmers Alliance stood as a visitor. The man asked the congregation to stay for a short meeting after church. Raymond wasn't particularly interested, but sat in since Mama had to stay for a bake sale.

"Good afternoon, everyone. I thank you for staying and I won't hold you long. I know you're looking forward to going home and relaxing after such an inspiring service. I thank Reverend Handley for allowing me this forum to speak to you. I am here to alert you to an emergency. At the turn of the twentieth century, there were over one million black farmers in America, this number dwindled as blacks moved north for better paying jobs and less overt discrimination. Now, there are less than twenty thousand black farms in America, and the majority of those are owned by individuals over sixty years of age. As this generation retires there are few to take their places. In this county alone, acreage owned by blacks has declined from thirty percent to less than three percent. While much of the decline in the number of black farms is due to social and economic forces, the government has played an insidious role. Most of you are familiar with the Federal Farmer's Loan Association. This is the agency that is responsible for lending to small farmers and providing other assistance. Their office is right across from the courthouse. That office approved millions of dollars in loans in the last twenty years. How many of you received a loan from this agency?"

A couple of hands went up.

"How many of you know anyone who received a loan from this agency?"

A few more hands went up.

"Ladies and gentlemen, only a handful of you have ever received anything from this agency that is supposed to help farmers. If you are not the recipients of this money, it is not hard to figure out who is. You are being robbed. You are being robbed of your tax dollars, because that is your money that they're loaning. Your children have been robbed of their inheritance because you can't compete against farmers and corporations funded by the U.S. Government. They are buying your land from you with your own tax money. We cannot continue to sit by and let this happen. The government has already been found guilty of discrimination and offered to settle with you. But they are offering you crumbs."

"You may be saying, what can I do about it? I am asking you to do three things. Number one, join the BFA. I'm President of the Jefferson County chapter. We want to organize a chapter here in Dwight County. Membership is only ten dollars. It is not so much about the money, as it is about gathering a constituency of support for our efforts. If you do not have the money, register anyway and send it when you can. With your membership, you will receive benefits such as legal assistance, tax assistance and exposure to new farming technology. Number two, we ask those farmers in the audience to go the FFLA office and apply for a loan. Apply for a reasonable amount that you believe you can pay back. If you have previously applied, you are eligible to participate in the class action lawsuit. If you have not applied, take your tax returns to the FFLA office and apply for an operating loan. These agencies often use the excuse that no one applied. No one applied because we are tired of the game and don't want to waste our time. However, we need you to apply to help with our third strategy. We are going to lobby state and Federal government officials. We are planning a March on Washington and will do all we can to generate media coverage about this issue. We have other plans as well but I don't want to go over my allotted time, so I thank you for your indulgence. Please take a brochure and sign a registration card. You must do it for your children. Thank you very much."

Raymond made his way to the speaker. "That was very enlightening. I didn't realize the number of black farmers had fallen so low."

"We're trying to reverse the trend. Can we add you to our membership roster?"

"I'm not a farmer."

"You don't have to be a farmer to join. This movement affects us all. Everyone has a stake in the future of black farmers and black land ownership. We can use whatever talents you have."

"Well, if you put it like that, sure, I'll sign up. My background is in banking."

"We definitely need you then. We're planning to open a bank."

"For real? You must have some serious backing."

"We've been very active. Part of our program is to lobby the government to fulfill its moral duty to us as U.S. citizens, but we're not going to wait on Uncle Sam to give us our forty acres and a mule. We were able to get Derrick appointed to the County Land Commission. And, we've been encouraging landowners to prepare wills. I didn't discuss our bank plans today, because we're waiting on a few key investors."

"Count me in. I'll see if I can interest my father and brother in joining. They farm together." Raymond took three registration forms and promised to attend the next meeting.

Over the next months, Raymond became an active BFA member. He directed protests against the banks in Dwight County as well as the FFLA. They began challenging banks' Community Reinvestment Act ratings and lo and behold, a few black farmers actually got loans. One of the banks even hired their first black teller. He helped farmers prepare projections and budgets, and negotiate better terms. Something he learned while doing all this field work, was that many of the residents were pretty well off. They owned their homes and land debt free. They had lived simple lives and managed to save a little nestegg. Never in his wildest dreams, though, did he think his own father fell in that category.

Now that he knew his father could afford to invest, he had to devise a tactful way to broach the subject. C.W. was skeptical after their earlier conversation, but Raymond wasn't giving up. Last year their conversation didn't go too well.

"Dad, did you know the BFA has signed up a lot of members in this county?"

"Sure has. I'm proud of the way you've come back home and jumped right in. We need more young people like you to use their book learning to help our people down here. Some folks are still farming like we did when I was coming up. It's a new day."

"You're right. Not only are we helping with farming, we're going to open a bank."

"Y'all collected that much dues?"

"No, sir. We're soliciting investors. Residents and people from here have money. I've already talked to Shawn and he's going to invest three hundred thousand dollars. He said he would mention it to his teammates. We have a few sizable pledges from doctors, funeral home owners and preachers. Then we're going to solicit one thousand people to invest five hundred dollars, so we have a broad base of support."

"That sounds mighty ambitious, son. I know they got black banks in Chicago and other big cities. But most of these people around here live from paycheck to paycheck."

"They say that Daddy, but all the kids have the latest Nike shoes and the newest video game systems. That's five hundred dollars right there. These good sisters pay that much for a new dress, hat and hair do. We need to get our priorities straight. This is something we can do for ourselves. It has nothing to do with white people. All the marching and protesting in the world will do no good if we aren't ready to put our money where our mouth is."

"Whoa, there, you're preaching to the choir, boy. I'm on your side. Put me down for five hundred. I may even be good for one thousand. Reverend Handley ought to be good for a couple thousand. He swindled at least that much out of your Mama. Ask your Uncle Nap and Charles, too."

"Daddy, I'm looking for a little more than five hundred dollars from you. The farm is free and clear---"

"Now, wait a minute. I know you're not suggesting that I sell this land? This land has been in our family over seventy years. My Daddy and my brother both struggled and died out there on them fields, so we could sit here today on over six hundred acres of fertile Delta soil. I said I would help you, but don't even think about selling this land. I thought you understood that better than anyone."

"Daddy, it's not to help me. It's for everybody. It's an investment. And, of course, I'm not asking you to sell the land. That's just what the white man wants us to do. But you could use it as collateral for a loan. I would pay the loan back from the bank's earnings."

"I'm not selling and I'm not mortgaging it either. If this colored bank thing doesn't work out I could lose everything. I don't know them folks and you don't either. They could be crooks."

"Daddy, what is wrong with us? Black folks will never have anything if we don't trust each other. If a white man presented this deal, there would be no questions."

"I didn't get to be this old and accumulate a few pennies without asking questions. I've seen a lot of hustlers in my time-black and white. I'm not saying your partners aren't genuine. Hell, I helped raise half of them. But I'm not getting a loan against my farm. I never would have a moment's peace. I got a few dollars in the bank I can let you have, but the land is off limits." C.W. said. "I hope it works out. I sure would get a kick out of putting my pennies in a colored bank. It would still be insured, right?"

"Of course, Daddy," Raymond answered shaking his head. Man, how will we ever overcome?

That was last year. They were much closer now to applying for a bank charter and were meeting with attorneys next month. Raymond barely had enough to purchase his qualifying shares as a director. That was with maxing his credit cards, withdrawing from his IRA, selling his bank stock and getting a second mortgage on his house. Daddy could use part of his settlement and not get a loan against the farm. Then, Raymond could be one of the controlling owners of the bank, that's where the power was. Daddy's concerns would be alleviated because everyone would be subject to background checks by the bank regulators. Daddy would also be more comfortable when he found out Carolyn was investing. Surely he could recognize this was a better investment than parking money in a savings account earning a piddly two percent interest. It would also be the start of real wealth for his children. Daddy thought his son should be proud and satisfied to work in a bank. Raymond wanted more and this was his chance to get it. I'll approach him after the reunion, once things have died down, Raymond planned.

"Hey, Shawn," Raymond called, spotting his cousin cutting a slice of watermelon. "I need you to help me show up some folks around here who think they can play ball. Come show them what I taught you." Raymond hummed 'We're in the Money' and drove to the basket for a layup.

20

Cecelia hid the Nine West shoebox in the bottom of her suitcase and zipped it up just as Michael came in the bedroom. "I didn't know you were in here. I'm going to pack a change of clothes and go back to Pine Bluff to see my mother. Your father said I could take his truck," Michael said.

"When are you going to get the van fixed? Mama asked me to pick up Miss Millie tomorrow from the nursing home and take her to the banquet," Cecelia said.

"Charles is going to look at it. He thinks the battery connectors are bad. That won't take long to fix."

"Don't you think you should take care of that before you leave? What if it's not the battery? It may be hard to get parts on Sunday."

"Okay, I'll work on it before I leave. Come sit on the bed with me," Michael said, patting the mattress next to him. "I've got good news. Your dad heard me talking to Raymond and he offered to loan us money to help start our business. Isn't that great?"

Cecelia continued fumbling in her suitcase. Michael walked behind her and put his arms around her waist. "You look mighty sexy in those shorts, Mrs. Brown," Michael said as he moved his hands under Cecelia's shirt and cupped her breasts.

"Michael, not now. What if someone came in?"

"They would say excuse me and close the door. If that's what you're worried about, how about this?" Michael took two suitcases and put them in front of the door. "Now, is that better?" Michael said as he resumed his position and began kissing her neck. "You smell delicious. Whatever you have on is very sexy."

"It's Mama's dollar store lotion. In my haste to pack everything that *you* didn't pack earlier like I asked you, I forgot my toiletry bag."

"I told you, I'm sorry I forgot your stuff. Let me make it up to you," Michael said as he turned Cecelia around to face him. "We've been married seventeen years, and you still turn me on."

"Well, turn yourself off. It's the middle of the day and these walls are paper-thin. Someone will hear us."

"We'll do it quiet. If you're worried about the bed creaking, we can do it on the floor. We used to make love on the floor all the time. We couldn't even make it to the bed."

"I am not going to be flipping around on these hardwood floors."

Michael jerked the covers off the bed onto the floor. "Okay, cushion for your back."

"Michael, my mother has had that spread thirty years. She only brings it out for company. She would have a heart attack if she saw it on the floor," Cecelia said, picking up the chenille bedspread.

Michael raised his hands, "Forget it. I don't think it's the fancy spread, or thin walls, or the creaky bed. Stop making excuses and just say it."

"Say what?"

"You don't want to have sex with me. Don't say, not now. Because it's always not now. If I didn't know better, I would think you were seeing someone."

"I just have important things on my mind. Like how are we going to get home, how are we going to pay the bills once we get home, should I take our daughter to a doctor down here, or can she make it home? Minor things like our home and our family," Cecelia said. "Forgive me if I don't feel like screwing around."

"That's the whole point of a vacation, baby. You can't do anything about those things. Why worry about that stuff?"

"We can't screw our troubles away. One of us needs to worry about it."

"You worry all you want. Knock yourself out. I'm on vacation and I intend to enjoy myself. You have been a drag ever since we left home, just because I didn't run your little errands."

"Excuse me, but they weren't my errands. They were things that needed to be done that I do all the time. Why is paying *our* bills *my* errand? I asked you to do it once and you couldn't even do that. But, I'm not mad about that. I should have known better than to ask you to do anything in the first place. I'm upset that you asked Daddy for a loan, and why did you tell him you were quitting your job? I thought we were still discussing this."

"I didn't ask, he offered, and I'm not quitting. I'm taking a buyout offer, while it's still available. Each cutback gets closer and closer to my department. Their next offer may not be as generous as this one."

"Then why not wait it out? If they're going to cut you, isn't it better to work as long as you can and make as much as you can?"

"No. It's better to take this package than to be cut with nothing but six months unemployment."

"They wouldn't cut you."

"Don't be so sure. Downsizing has affected all of my coworkers. They should call it white sizing, because that's the result. The black managers that are left have had to move or take a cut in pay."

"There you go with that black man stuff. I don't care if they only have one black manager left, as long as it's you."

"Cecelia, you're missing the point. I could work five jobs and it wouldn't be enough. That's the way the system is set up. The only way to get ahead is to work for yourself. I wish you could see that."

"I wish you could see the bills that I pay each month. I could join the circus, I've gotten so good at juggling bills," Cecelia said, as she sat at the desk.

"Let's call a truce. We both know where the other one stands. If it doesn't work out, you can say 'I told you so'."

"No, if it doesn't work out, I get to pay the leftover bills. Again."

"We'll always have bills. Does that mean we won't have sex until the bills get paid up? I feel like some teenager, begging my girlfriend to give me some."

"Oh, grow up, Michael. This is not about sex. It's about you holding up your end of the marriage. I'm tired of struggling. I can struggle by myself."

"Be careful, you might get your wish."

"See that's what I mean. Instead of trying to work our way out of this, you want to give up and run to your mama."

"Cecelia, if I stay, you don't want me. If I go, I'm running away. Nothing is ever good enough for you. I'm tired of trying to please you. Up to now, we've done everything your way. I've made up my mind about this business," Michael said as he changed shirts.

"So I don't get a vote? I'm forty years old, and I still need money from my Daddy. Do you know how that makes me feel? If I need his help, what do I need you for?"

"You know what? Maybe you don't. This is the last time I'll get away for a while and I'm not going to spend it listening to you whine. If you're not going to help, at least get out of the way. I'm going to see my folks. Don't wait up."

Cecelia went to the kitchen to get water to take with her pills. The doctor said the migraines would stop if she got away from work for awhile. Maybe, what I really need is a vacation from my family, she thought.

"It must be the medicine hour," C.W. said as he came in the kitchen. "Your mother sent me in here to take my pills. What are you taking medicine for?"

"Just a headache, Daddy."

"Michael says you get those a lot. He thinks you're working too hard," C.W. said as he hung his baseball cap on the doorknob.

"Well, since you mentioned it, Mama thinks *you're* working too hard."

"I'll tell you one thing, that woman's gonna worry me into another stroke. I'm fine. Just because the doctor told me to take it easy doesn't mean I have to sit around the house all day. I'm not helpless."

"I know Daddy, but I know how you are. You go to the fields to check on things, next thing you're showing someone what to do and before you know it, you're doing it yourself."

"Cece, I believe when it's my time to go, it's my time to go. It doesn't matter if I'm sitting in a rocking chair or dancing a jig."

"You've worked hard all your life. Why not sell this land, take the money and relax? There is no reason for you to work so hard, anymore. Jackie's folks sold their land and bought a house up town."

"Girl, you're talking crazy. Living up town would kill me for sho'. I don't want to hear my neighbors arguing, or smell what they're cooking for dinner. I've been here all these years; I see no reason to change now. I like my little place just fine."

"Daddy, that's the problem. It's not a little place. I don't know much about farming, but I know this is a big responsibility. Do you think Charles is up to the task?"

"He can handle it, and Raymond is home now. Raymond can help."

"I know you're not serious. Raymond knows less about farming than I do."

"Let me worry about that. I'm getting things in order, and I got enough sense to know when I'm tired. I'm not the one with the headaches. You are. Michael's worried about you."

"I'm surprised he's even concerned."

"Of course he's concerned. You're just like your mother. You fret too much. Y'all supposed to be such church-going women, I thought the Lord was supposed to carry your burdens for you," C.W. said as he poured a glass of water.

"I must have more than my share," Cecelia said.

"Girl, you don't know how good you got it. You have a nice home, your children aren't disrespectful like some I've seen. You got a good man. You have your health and a sound mind."

"You're right. I'm especially lucky because I have you," she said, leaning over to kiss his forehead. "I hope I'm lucky tonight, too. I'm going to change clothes."

"Where are you going?"

"I'm going over to Lady Luck casino. Uncle Henry and Veronica are both driving."

"That's something I don't care for. I can play cards all night, but when they put money on the table, it's time for me to get up. Money ain't nothing to play with," C.W. said shaking his head.

"It's fun, Daddy. I bet you'd like it if you went."

"I didn't say I hadn't ever been to the casinos. I said I didn't care for it. I've been here almost eighty years and I've tried most everything. Losing money ain't fun, it's foolish. How much do you spend at casinos, anyway?"

"Not that much."

"You seem to go a lot. I'm sure that adds up."

"Michael asked you to talk to me, didn't he?"

"No, we were talking and he mentioned a few things that troubled me."

"Don't worry Daddy. I won't pawn the family jewels. I don't appreciate Michael tattling to you and I'm going to let him know when I see him."

"He wasn't tattling to me. We were just talking. Michael was telling me about his business plans. Sounds like he has a good idea."

"Daddy, what do you know about the Internet?"

"I know enough to recognize something that can make money. I'll help Michael get started. He's my son too, and I'm proud he feels he can come to me for advice."

"You and Mama shouldn't throw your money away on Michael's latest pipe dream," Cecelia said, as she laid a pink, red and white pill on the table.

"You need to support him Cece."

"So, Michael's been crying on your shoulder?" Cecelia asked. "I suppose he said I'm an unsupportive wife who won't stand by her man. Just because I want my husband to keep his job, I'm not being supportive."

"Nagging about bills and spending money foolishly every chance you get is not being supportive. Black folks need to run their own companies. The man that started *Ebony* started with $500 he borrowed against his Mama's furniture. And he was from Arkansas too."

This man must be an imposter, Cecelia thought. This can't be the same man who drilled the importance of all of us getting a degree so we could get a good job.

"It's going to take a lot more than five hundred dollars to do what Michael is talking about. Besides, I would never consider asking you to gamble on something so uncertain," Cecelia said, throwing her head back to swallow her pills.

"I have a little saved, I wouldn't mind giving you a loan."

"But Daddy, what if it doesn't work? We can barely pay the bills now. We're not kids. We have responsibilities."

"That's exactly why he should do it. Up to now, he would have been too young. Man don't really know what he's about until he's forty. In a few years, he'll be too old. You've got to let him try this, Cece. If he doesn't do it, he'll always hold it against you," C.W. said, shaking his finger at his daughter.

"Daddy, I didn't see you traipsing off somewhere to follow a dream. You stayed here and raised your family. Uncle Henry and all of them left. I'm sure you thought about leaving."

"Thought about it and did it. We used to see those *Chicago Defender* newspapers that advertised all the so-called opportunities up North. I left school and went to Chicago, then moved to Detroit when Aunt Belle told me about the jobs at her husband's plant. I lived in Detroit almost six years. I know how it is to go to the other man's job. I admire Michael, because I couldn't do it. That's why I left. I was making almost three dollars an hour in the Chrysler plant. Believe me, that was big money back then. I came home to bury Daddy and Beau asked me to stay and help him farm. I told him he must be crazy if he thought I wanted to come back to these woods and hateful white folks. I told him if he had any sense he'd leave too, especially since Daddy was gone. I could line him up a job real easy. He said this was his home and he was staying. The more I thought about it and the colder it got that winter, I decided I must be the crazy one. Me and Betty came home for Christmas and stayed. That first year I barely made five hundred dollars. I made that much in Detroit in three months. I worked harder and longer than I did at Chrysler. I didn't mind it though, because I was my own boss. That's the feeling Michael wants. That's the feeling every black man in America wants. Most aren't blessed enough to have the vision, and to act on the vision and to have a woman who can see the vision. Betty couldn't see it and went back to

Detroit after two years. I felt bad when she left, but I couldn't go."

"What about my vision, Daddy? What about my vision of having nice things, and not worrying about bills and sending our kids to college?"

"Michael's trying to do that for you. Some things you have to do on faith. Don't look at what can go wrong. Look at what can go right." C.W. patted Cecelia's hand. "It'll work out, you'll see. Now, I'm not meddling. I want to help. I told him he don't need to look for no partners. That ain't nothin' but a nuisance. I can lend him some money to get started. But I don't want to give him money for you to gamble away."

"Daddy, my job is intense. I work hard from the time I walk in that hospital, until the time I leave. And even when I leave, I'm still thinking about my patients. I don't smoke, drink, do drugs or sleep around. I found one thing I like to do and everyone wants to give me a hard time about it. I won't go. Are you satisfied?" Cecelia said, rinsing her glass.

"Don't be trying to satisfy me. You're grown. I can't tell you what to do. But why don't you try this? When you get home, stay out of the casinos for two months."

"You're making it sound like I go every day. Does Michael think I have a gambling problem? I can't believe he burdened you with this nonsense," Cecelia said.

"Baby, it's not about Michael. Please do this for me. You'll have a little more money, Michael will be off your case and I'll be relieved that you were right."

"Michael and I used to go to Las Vegas all the time. How can he be anti-gambling?"

"It was different when it was an occasional thing you did together. Now it sounds like it's coming between you."

"Daddy, really, this is not a big deal," Cecelia said.

"It's a big deal if your husband thinks it's a big deal. I went through the same thing with Betty. We used to go to juke joints from Friday to Sunday, and have a good time, too. But she got to where she didn't want to wait until Friday or Saturday, and it didn't matter if I went with her or not. Is it that important to you that you can't stop?"

"That's not the point. I can stop any time I want."

"Then prove us wrong. Take a little break."

"Why do I have to prove anything?"

C.W. stood up from the table. "You know, that was the last thing Betty said to me before she went back to Detroit. I asked her to quit drinking for two days, just for me. She never did, and that alcohol devoured her liver and sucked all the life out of her. You think you're having fun, but gambling is the same way. If you don't watch out, it will suck all the life out of you. I don't want to see that happen to you Cece."

"Now who's fretting too much? Don't worry, that would never happen to me."

Uncle Henry's voice boomed throughout the house, "Everybody riding with me better come on. I'm ready to win me some Mississippi money."

Cecelia rushed to the door. "I better get going, before they leave me. And even though you smoothly changed the subject, consider my suggestion about the farm. Don't be so quick to say no, think about it."

"Well, you need to think about what I said, too."

"I will, Daddy. And I promise to take a break, starting tomorrow."

21

Uncle Henry coordinated a casino trip Saturday evening. He and Aunt Ethel Fay were gambling connoisseurs. They played Bingo, went to the horse and dog track, were regulars at the casinos in Detroit, and went to Las Vegas every year. Their attendance at a reunion, was predicated upon how close it was to a casino.

"Lois, come go with us," Aunt Ethel Fay said. "It will be fun."

"Giving away money don't sound like fun to me," Mama snapped.

"You never know. You might win. Beginners always have good luck. Just take about twenty dollars. You could spend that much at the movie," Aunt Ethel Fay said.

"Hummph, I don't waste my money on movies either. Most of it is filth, and that what ain't, I can wait for it to come on TV," Mama said shaking her head.

"Aunt Ethel Fay, save your breath. Mama keeps dollars rolled up in her bra so long, they curl back up when she tries to spend them. They were probably the last people in Eden to get cable, and that was only so Mama could get more wrestling," Beverly said.

Cecelia was helping Uncle Henry gather everyone. "Beverly, are you going?" she asked.

"I hate to leave the picnic. I'd feel bad about leaving Mama with a house full of guests," Beverly said.

"Come on, you can only eat so much barbecue, and we'll be back before ten o'clock," Cecelia said.

"No, that's okay," Beverly said. "I think Cousin Willie and some others want me to take them to Memphis."

"Ethel, you and Henry leave your gas money here. If you lose all your money, you won't be broke," Mama said as she started washing dishes.

"I'm already broke, so I may as well go," Cousin Jesse from St. Louis said.

"You know some people really get hooked on that gambling. It can be as bad as drinking. I see it on TV all the time. Miss Rose and her daughter almost lost their house. They were taking the bus over there three, four times a week, leaving those kids alone in the house all night. At first, they bragged about the money they won. Next thing you know the church was taking up a collection to keep them from losing their house. That don't sound like fun to me. The only ones I see having fun is them Mafia men. They owns the casinos, you know. Besides my Bible says---"

"Okay, Lois, give us a break!" Uncle Henry said. "Anyway, you and C.W. got extra room here. If we lose our house, me and Ethel will come stay with you. Let's go y'all."

Derrick and I had returned from our garbage bag search and collapsed on the porch. It seemed like every resident of Dwight County must have been at Walmart. I had just kicked off my shoes when Beverly opened the door.

"Derrick, if you can tear yourself away from my sister, you need to move your car," she said. "You're blocking Uncle Henry, and they're ready to go to the casino."

"Carolyn, you're just in time to go with us," Cecelia said as she led several relatives onto the porch.

"Girl, I can't hang, I'm going to lay down a little while. I haven't really recovered from our late night. I need a nap."

"Lord, I have heard everything. You all are the tiredest bunch of young folks I ever saw," Uncle Nap said. "When I was your age, I'd work all day, none of that nine to five mess. That was when a day meant sunup to sundown. I'd come home, get clean, and party all night. Then come in and catch me a couple hours sleep and go back to work. I wasn't on no dope neither. Who ever heard tell of a grown somebody taking a nap in the middle of the day? Y'all going to sleep your life away."

"I haven't been to the nursing home yet today," Derrick said. "I'll go see my grandmother. Call me when you get back. Here's my cell phone number."

Beverly and Cecelia cut their eyes at me and grinned. I waved them off, sighed and put my shoes back on.

Casino gambling had given the extremely depressed Tunica, Mississippi area a boost. Some argued that casinos lured money from those least able to afford it. But there was no arguing with the new jobs, new roads and teacher raises made possible from gaming revenue. Tunica County, just south of Memphis, had gone from being infamous for it's abject poverty to the third highest gambling location in the country. The casinos had taken over the cotton fields and welcomed millions eager to part with their money.

Cecelia didn't see anything wrong with it. She and Michael had these same discussions. Cecelia and some coworkers often went to the casino riverboat in East Chicago after their shift. She wasn't sleepy when she got off work. She figured she didn't spend any more money at the casinos than he did at football and basketball games. And he could see those games on television. He paid more than three hundred dollars for Bears tickets without even discussing it with her. And he *didn't* complain when she came in and counted out two thousand dollars just in time to replace the van transmission. She figured she didn't smoke, drink, do drugs or party. So she didn't see why he should begrudge her this one vice.

"I knew we shouldn't have listened to Raymond," Cecelia said as we tried to figure out riding arrangements. "I should have followed my first instinct and chartered a bus."

About ten people were on the reunion planning committee. But the committee turned out to be Raymond, Beverly and Mama on the phones at Raymond's house plus Cecelia and I on three-way calls.

During one of our "meetings" while Daddy was recuperating, Cecelia suggested we charter a bus to the casinos. "A lot of people will be flying in and won't have a car. This way they won't be imposing on anyone."

"You all can have the next reunion in Las Vegas if you want to gamble. I don't think that's a worthwhile endeavor for this family to sponsor. This is supposed to be about family and unity. I don't want to bring my family from across the country so they can go give the white man more money. If you want to charter a bus trip, we should go see Carl," Raymond stated.

"Going to Cummins prison doesn't sound like an appealing vacation spot. Besides only three people can visit him at a time. We were trying to think of something a lot of people would be interested in," Cecelia said.

"It's not like there's a lot of activities to choose from," I said.

"Some people are going anyway. If we had a bus, they could all go together. That would be family time," Beverly offered.

"You all are just trying to sneak something in while Daddy is sick. You know he would never approve of that. Would he, Mama?" Raymond asked.

"No, I don't think he would," Mama said slowly.

That was the end of that conversation. Raymond had played the guilt card.

Cecelia was able to round up three carloads of gamblers. Those from St. Louis rode in Jackie's new Escalade. The rest of the men rode with Uncle Henry. Cecelia, Aunt Pearl, Aunt Ethel Fay and I rode with Veronica. If I had known I would end up in the car with Veronica, I would have passed.

Aunt Pearl's husband died in a car accident and she never remarried. Veronica was her only child. Aunt Pearl sent her to spend summers with us. But of course nothing in Eden was up to par with Detroit. According to her, we were behind with the dances, our clothes were out of style and how could we survive with one AM radio station that went off at sunset? We were as anxious for her to leave as she was to go, but we couldn't say anything rude to her because she would tell Mama and then we'd get a whipping. So we learned to ignore and tolerate her, which we're still doing today.

Veronica drove and her mother rode in front with her. Cecelia, Aunt Ethel Fay and I sat in the back seat. Aunt Ethel Fay reached in her purse and pulled out a cigarette case. I nudged Cecelia and grabbed my neck in a mock choking gesture.

"Excuse me, Aunt Ethel, but I'd rather you didn't smoke in my car. It leaves a bad smell and it's too hot to leave the windows down," Veronica said.

"How you going to a casino and don't want to be around smoke? You going to ask everybody in there to put out their cigarettes?" she asked, as she lit her cigarette.

"I can't control what they do, but I can control what happens in my car."

"Then you need to pull over and let me out of your car. Flash your bright lights for Henry to stop."

"Can't you wait an hour and a half?" Aunt Pearl asked.

"I could if I wanted to, but I don't want to. I been smoking fifty years and I'm not going to have this little heifer telling me what I can and can't do. I knew her when she didn't have a car or a bike for that matter. Now she so high and mighty, she gonna tell me what I can and can't do in her car."

"I meant no disrespect Aunt Ethel. You should thank me. Every cigarette you smoke shortens your life by eleven minutes," Veronica said.

"If you could see the patients that I see at work with lung and throat cancer, you would put those things away," Cecelia said.

"Now here's another little heifer trying to tell me what to do."

"It's just that we care about you Aunt Ethel Fay. We want you to be around a long time. You know cigarettes aren't good for you."

Aunt Pearl said, "The child is right. It's bad for you and it will make my hair stink. I might meet a man over here and you messing up my chances. No man wants a woman that smells like smoke."

"Honey, I think them fifty pounds on your hips is what's messing up your chances of finding a man, not my cigarette. If you got the right stuff, a man don't care what your hair smells like," Aunt Ethel Fay said, blowing smoke out of a crack in the window.

Cecelia and I cut our eyes at each other. Once these two got tuned up, they took no prisoners. They made our sibling rivalry look like patty-cake. Mama said they fussed so much because they were just alike.

When I awoke from my short nap, my aunts were still fussing.

"Baby, can you drop us off at the door?" Aunt Ethel Fay asked Veronica.

"Go ahead and park," Aunt Pearl said. "Her fat behind needs to get some exercise."

"I'm getting ready to exercise my right arm on those money machines in there. Don't come asking my fat behind for any money either," Aunt Pearl chuckled as she unraveled a roll of twenties she had stashed in her bosom.

We agreed to meet in two hours near the main entrance ladies room. Aunt Pearl and Aunt Ethel Fay headed for the fifty-cent slot machines. Veronica headed for the nonsmoking floor. Cecelia and I were in line to get change behind an interracial couple.

"Carolyn, I know what you're thinking and don't even start," Cecelia warned.

"What? I wasn't going to say a word about you know what. To each his own," I said.

"Good. Then you should say something to Paul. His feelings were hurt by the things you said about Julia."

"I'm tired of hearing about his precious Julia. What did he bring her for if he doesn't want her subjected to the family?"

"It's not the family. It's you. For some reason, you have a hang-up about her and you don't try to hide it."

"Why should I? I hide my feelings all week long at work. She's in our world now. Let her adapt and assimilate for a change," I said looking through my purse for a twenty-dollar bill.

We were next and Cecelia stepped to the window and handed bought two hundred-dollar bills to the Cashier. I thought about my American Express bill, and was about to ask Cecelia about my two hundred dollars when I spotted a familiar profile in the aisle. I whispered in Cecelia's ear. "Isn't that the guy from the club standing over there?"

His ears must have been burning, because he turned around and came toward us. "Fancy meeting you ladies here, maybe you should have invited me to your reunion."

He held a polite conversation with both of us, but was obviously interested in Cecelia. This was deja vu. Boys were always interested in one of my sisters. I was a little envious, but we weren't going to end up on Jenny Jones or anything like that. We had different tastes in boys and men, so I didn't mind acting as a matchmaker or messenger. I also knew when to make myself scarce.

"I'm going to find the roulette tables," I announced. I was actually glad we ran into Maurice. Maybe he would distract Cecelia from overspending. I was afraid Cecelia's gambling was changing from recreation to addiction. She used to ask me to go with her to Trumps or The Empress. I went a few times, but I always ended up waiting for her. I usually lost my money quickly and was first to the designated meeting place. If I won, I'd quit while I was ahead. It made no sense to me to win, then give it back. Once after waiting for Cecelia, I found her at an ATM machine.

"Girl, don't you know I have been waiting for you an hour? Let's go." I must have really been loud, because people turned to look at me.

"Is it time to go? I guess I lost track of time," she said.

"You must have lost your money too. Let's go." I ordered. "I know you weren't getting money out of that machine to gamble with?"

"I didn't bring much money with me. I was doing pretty well, until I hit a bad run at the black jack table," she answered gaily.

"You're grown, I'm not going to lecture you. Although I will say, you look like some desperate wino with your tongue hanging out waiting for money to spit out of that machine. Go broke on your own time."

"Oh, now you're Miss Holy Roller on a gambling crusade?" Cecelia said.

"No, I don't have a problem with gambling. But I've seen scores of gambling casualties. They come in to discuss their payment plan for back taxes. People get in over their heads and then can't pay their bills. Most file bankruptcy, some don't even have the money to file. But you can't run from the taxman. Bankruptcy does not wipe out IRS debt. I hear all the sob stories. Most of the time, it's people who should have known better, like you. Working people out for a little fun, like you, and before they know it, they are out of control, *like you*."

She attempted to reassure me that my concerns were unnecessary, but I'm still not convinced. Hopefully, Mr. Tall, Dark and Handsome will be enough of a diversion to keep Cecelia from overdoing it... with my two hundred dollars.

"I was starting to worry that you weren't coming. What's your pleasure?" Maurice asked.

"Excuse me?" Cecelia answered.

"What game do you play? You said you liked black jack, want to start there?"

"I told you that? I guess that wine loosened my tongue. Are you here alone?" Cecelia asked.

"Not anymore." Maurice said as he grabbed her arm and headed toward the black jack tables.

Time sped by. Cecelia had lost four hands in a row, when Maurice cashed in his chips. "I'm hungry, let's grab something to eat."

"You must be a good luck charm." Cecelia beamed as the cashier counted out six one hundred-dollar bills. She had been tired when they arrived at the casino. She had only slept a few hours in two days and had been on the go all day. But entering the casino, revitalized her like a shot of vitamin B. She couldn't believe it was time to go already. She was just getting started.

"Maybe we're good luck for each other," he said as he led her through the crowd.

Now what did he mean by that? Cecelia wondered. Is this man trying to hit on me? Should I go eat with him? It's just a friendly gesture. He hasn't said anything inappropriate. I must be reading too much into this. Michael has several female friends. I probably won't ever see him again anyway.

"Let's go to the snack bar. I don't have time for a sit-down meal. We're supposed to meet in about thirty minutes," Cecelia said.

"Don't tell me you have to go already. I thought we were going to check out the show. Tickets are still available."

"I wish I could. This was just a quick get-a-way from the reunion. We still have a full agenda. Actually, I'm AWOL right now," Cecelia said looking at her watch. "I'm supposed to be helping my mother get ready for the banquet tomorrow."

"That's too bad. I didn't get to spend much time with you. Can you stay if I take you home?"

"I hope I'm not jumping to conclusions, but you seem to have forgotten a little matter called my husband. Besides, Eden is over an hour's drive from here. You seem pleasant, but I don't think I should get in a car with you on a highway. You could be a well-dressed ax murderer," Cecelia said, as she scanned the menu.

"That's why we need to spend more time together. Then you'll find out I'm as pleasant as I seem. As for your husband, he's not here today, and he wasn't with you last night. I believe in destiny. Our paths crossed for a reason, and I'm content just to enjoy the crossing. Whatever else happens is meant to be."

Cecelia feigned fanning herself with her hand. "Whew. That's a pretty smooth line. I bet you say that to all the girls."

"Cecelia, listen---"

She cut him off. "I see Aunt Pearl and Carolyn, I'll be right back. Order a taco salad for me."

"Where is everyone?" Cecelia asked as she joined her relatives near the door.

"Uncle Henry and Aunt Ethel Fay are going to stay longer. Are you ready to go?" Carolyn asked with a slight grin, as she spotted Maurice sitting in the snack bar.

"Well, if they're staying, I could ride back with them. Do you think they will mind?" Cecelia asked.

"They're meeting here at ten. Your gentleman friend in there looks like he wouldn't mind you staying a little while longer," Aunt Pearl whispered.

"He's just a friend. We had a streak of good luck together," Cecelia said.

"Child please, I wasn't born yesterday. I've been where you're trying to go. You be careful, and keep some mad money," Aunt Pearl advised.

It's been ages since I've heard that one. That's what mama used to tell us before dates. Always take enough money, so if you get mad, you can get home. But I'm not on a date.
"Yes ma'am. I'll be careful," Cecelia answered.

Carolyn stopped Cecelia as she turned back toward the snack bar. "I'm not trying to get in your business, but do you think you should --- "

Cecelia waved her off. "Carolyn, I don't want to hear it. He's a nice guy. It's not like we're rushing off to a hotel room. We're only talking. I'm coming back with Uncle Henry and I'll be home before midnight. You tell me to give Sheree some space, I hate to see what you'll be like with your kids."

Aunt Pearl tugged Carolyn's arm. "Veronica's out there, we better hurry up. Give your sister a break. Let her have some fun. Sometimes a woman likes to see that she still has it even if she doesn't plan to use it. Men get to try their tired raps out all the time. A woman has to wait until she's approached. Although I was never one to wait myself," Aunt Pearl stated.

Cecelia returned to her seat just as the waitress brought their food.

"So you got permission to stay? I thought I was going to get stuck with two taco salads," Maurice said.

"Yes, I got permission to stay, but I turn into a pumpkin at ten o'clock," Cecelia said.

"That should be enough time to convince you I'm not an ax murderer."

"Do you realize we have been sitting here almost two hours?" Cecelia asked. She couldn't believe how much fun she was having. At home, she never ate at the casino. She figured that was a waste of precious gambling time; she could eat when she got home. But she and Maurice had eaten, and were lingering over espresso. She'd heard all about his divorce, his job, and his daughter that he didn't get to see because his ex moved to Los Angeles. She'd spilled her guts about her job, her kids, and Michael's scheme to open yet another business.

"I guess that means you're ready to gamble some more," Maurice said.

I'm gambling already, Cecelia thought. Why in the world am I telling this man all of my business? I've never done anything like this before.

They went back to the casino floor and roamed among the ringing slot machines, video poker games and roulette tables. Ordinarily, Cecelia preferred to gamble alone. When she went with a group, they set a time and place to meet; then split up. She couldn't concentrate with someone looking over her shoulder, and she disliked watching others gamble. But tonight, the team approach was working.

The appointed hour soon arrived and they made their way to the meeting place. "This has been a fun and profitable evening," Cecelia said. "Call me if you're ever in Chicago. You can go on to the show, you don't have to wait with me."

"I've enjoyed spending time with you, too. I'll wait with you," Maurice said.

Cecelia led the way to a bench by the front door. "We can see the entrance and the elevator. There should be no way to miss them from here."

Another hour flew by. They solved the world's problems, the black man's problem, or rather the white man's problem with the black man- as Raymond would say, and predicted the outcome of the next election. Maurice caught Cecelia checking her watch. "Maybe you should call home. We've already paged them and gotten no response."

Cecelia called home and spoke with Julia. "This is Cecelia. Is Carolyn or Veronica over there? I'm stranded in Tunica. I was supposed to meet Uncle Henry and Aunt Ethel Fay and I haven't seen them."

"Everybody is on the porch. Let me go check," she answered.

Cecelia returned to their bench. "It seems we have had a failure to communicate. When Aunt Ethel Fay told me to meet them at ten o'clock, she meant by her watch, which is Eastern Standard Time. My watch is Central Standard Time. Julia called them on the car phone and they are almost back to Eden. I hope I'm not being presumptuous, but I told her I had a friend who would take me to Beverly's house. I can ride back to Eden in the morning with her. Would you mind taking me to Memphis?"

"I'll do better than that. I'll take you home."

"I couldn't ask you to do that," Cecelia replied.

"You didn't ask, I volunteered. Since you're already late, let's go catch the show," Maurice said as he grabbed Cecelia's hand.

Cecelia looked over her shoulder to see if there were any familiar faces. They were just friends, but she didn't want any one to get the wrong idea. Michael was gone anyway, why not enjoy the rest of the evening?

22

This may have been the reunion weekend, but one thing never changed. Saturday meant wrestling. Even if Martin Luther King Jr. himself came to the house, he would have to sit with Mama and Aunt Belle and watch wrestling. We knew not to mess with Mama or Aunt Belle on Saturday evenings. Aunt Belle always came to our house to watch wrestling with Mama. Charles still comes over and watches with them. Today he only stayed for the first two matches before he went home.

We all loved wrestling when we were young. Junk Yard Dog was a favorite, because he was one of the first and few black wrestlers then. Mama, usually the epitome of self-control, loosened up on Saturday nights. She would yell, "get up off that floor, boy" or "kick his butt." 'Butt' back then was a curse word, so it was shocking to hear Mama saying it. As we got older, wrestling was put aside for boys, parties and ball games. But Mama remained a loyal fan.

The wrestling match was the center of attention in the house. A few brave souls were still outside, but ferocious mosquitoes had run off most picnickers. Beverly, Paul, Julia, and Raymond were on the back porch playing spades. It was supposed to be a friendly game, although it was more like a slaughter. Julia had never played before and was learning under fire. The Washington family were serious card players and had no sympathy for amateurs.

"Partner, I hope you kept your eyes on these two," Beverly said as she returned from the rest room. "These brothers of mine will cheat if you don't watch them."

"I never knew Paul was so competitive," Julia said.

"We need to talk girlfriend. I can tell you some stories---"

"Don't believe a word she says," Paul said.

"Paul's mouth was always getting him in trouble," Raymond said. "He was too smart for his own good."

"Remember when Paul told Mama wrestling was fake?"

Beverly asked shaking her head.

"Big mistake," Raymond said. "He was about eleven and had gone to a wrestling match at the high school with me and Carl. He asked why they didn't wrestle like that on television and we told him the wrestling on television was staged. We had sense enough not to say that within earshot of Mama."

"But not Paul. That's one of the few times I remember Paul getting in trouble. He was the baby and got away with more stuff than we did," Beverly said.

"He was arguing with Mama about it being fake. Then she asked if he was calling her a liar. She made him wash dishes and mop, for arguing with her," Raymond remembered.

"Well, I still don't see how she watches that stuff," Paul said.

"Let her have her fun," Beverly said, as she shuffled the cards. "This gives us a chance to talk. We don't have much time. So, Paul, don't play dumb. I know you've been looking at Daddy's papers. We need to present a united front when we discuss this with Daddy."

"Who is 'we' and what are 'we' discussing?" Paul asked.

Beverly leaned over the card table and stated in a low voice, "Okay, listen, Daddy asked Carolyn to help get his affairs in order. Cecelia said Daddy is getting six hundred thousand dollars from the black farmers lawsuit. As it stands right now,

Charles has power of attorney and if something happens to Daddy, Charles gets everything. Can you believe that?"

"Well, that's not exactly how things are set up, but if Daddy wants Charles to handle everything, we should respect his wishes," Paul said. "After all, we've been gone. Charles has stuck right here with Mama and Daddy."

"You can't be serious," Beverly said. "I love my big brother, but he is not the one to handle money. Look what happened with the fish fry, and we sure don't want Brenda handling our family business. We need to find out what Daddy plans to do with the farm."

"Even if you were right, what could we do about it?" Paul asked.

"We need to have a family meeting. We go to Daddy and talk, like we are now. We list reasons why his present plan is unacceptable and give him our suggestions," Beverly said calmly, while studying her cards.

"And our suggestion is that he keep the farm. Right?" Raymond asked.

"Or will it to Charles and let him buy each of us out," Beverly said.

"Since Carolyn is the one that's supposed to be looking at all of this, can't she make the suggestions to him?" Raymond asked.

"That's an idea, but I think we should do it together," Beverly said.

"As much as I hate to admit it, Daddy's affairs do need to be cleared up as soon as possible. I'm not even sure Daddy ever divorced Charles' mother. Think what would have happened if Daddy hadn't made it last fall. This would have been a big mess," Paul said.

"I thought it was strange, that Charles hasn't been around much this weekend," Beverly said.

Brenda appeared in the kitchen screen door. "Beverly, can you check that cooler next to you for a Miller Lite, please?"

Beverly opened the cooler and handed her a beer. Brenda politely thanked her and headed across the field toward her trailer.

"I wonder how long she was standing there," Raymond said.

The answer wasn't hard to figure out. Within ten minutes Charles and Brenda were marching across the field with grim faces, toward Mama's back porch. This was not a social visit.

"I hear y'all are planning a family meeting. I guess my invitation is still in the mail. Was anybody planning to tell me?" Charles asked.

"Okay, I see things are getting out of hand," Raymond said as he stood.

"That's because a certain person ran off at the mouth without knowing what she was talking about. Some people are always trying to stir up mess," Beverly said, while rearranging her cards.

"I went to tell my husband about your plans, since you obviously were not. Everybody doesn't go around shooting their husbands. I look out for my man, even if his family doesn't," Brenda said.

"Now did I mention any names?" Beverly asked while surveying the other card players. "There you go again jumping to the wrong conclusion. If you would spend more time looking out for your man as you say, instead of looking for mine, I would appreciate it."

"Beverly, don't start nothing. I can save everybody a lot of time and misery," Charles said. "C.W. put everything in my name for a reason. I'm the oldest son and I've worked with him all my life."

"Then you should buy us out," Beverly said.

"You don't own nothing for me to buy. My mother helped C.W. get started in the first place. Miss Lois moved in on C.W. while my Mama was sick. She used the oldest trick in the book, coming up pregnant," Charles said.

"Now wait a minute, I am not going to sit here and let you scandalize my mother," Paul said.

"I can not believe my ears. I am standing here speechless," Mama said through the screen door. "You all are out here arguing about your Daddy's money. You think he's ready to die or something? And what about me? I guess if something had happened to C.W. you would have shuffled me off to the nursing home."

"Mama, of course not," Raymond said as he opened the screen door for her to come on the porch. "This is a big misunderstanding."

"I'm no fool, boy. I understand very well. I want to say this, then I don't want to hear nothing else about it this weekend. C.W. worked too hard on this reunion for it to be ruined by your greediness. Charles, I never made no difference between you and these other kids. I treated you just as I would if I had birthed you. I did not come between C.W. and your mama. Truth is your mama liked to drink and C.W. did too, back then. I didn't take C.W. from your Mama. If he was hers, me and Lena Horne and nobody else coulda' took him. I'm not saying I did no wrong. That's between me and my God and not your concern. I done more for you than I did for any of these kids, because you were first. If you feel partial to your Mama, I can understand that. But don't be digging up no trash. I don't care how many wives C.W. done had. This is my house and if you can't respect that, you are not welcome in it anymore."

Charles and Brenda silently walked down the back steps.

"Mama, I'm sorry about this whole thing. How could Charles turn on you after all you've done for him?" Beverly said as she put her arm around her mother.

"Beverly, hush," she said shrugging Beverly's arm off. "I'm disgusted with all of you. I don't want to hear another word about it. I'm missing wrestling."

23

The shopping trip and picnic occupied Beverly's mind all day and kept her from thinking about Anthony. He made a brief appearance at the picnic, but they didn't have time alone. To avoid going home, she considered spending the night in Eden. But she could tell her mother was still irritated from the scene on the back porch. Several of her relatives wanted to visit the clubs on Beale Street. Beverly didn't want to drive home, but she didn't know which was worse, her mother's disapproval or her husband's betrayal. She decided to stay out of her mother's way for awhile, so she led the caravan of cousins to Memphis. As she exited the freeway near her house, she pasted on her best hostess smile. She saw Anthony's truck in the driveway, and dreaded going inside.

He met them in the driveway. Beverly walked right past him, while Sheryl, Willie and others greeted him like the prodigal son. Sometimes she felt like Anthony was the relative and she was the in-law. Everyone knew of his indiscretions and seemed to love him even more. Her sisters weren't under his charming spell, but they were in the minority.

"I heard you got a new car," he said, admiring Sheryl's Lexus.

"Now what does anybody in Eden need with a Lexus?" Willie asked. "I wish Cousin Edward had given me some of that money. I've been trying to tell her, I have the perfect business venture for her. Then she could write off the Lexus on her taxes. You and Beverly need to check it out. If you get four people to sign up, you could make even more money. Let me show you this brochure ---"

"Ain't nobody interested in no vitamins," Sheryl said.

"Quit bugging folks," Willie's wife said.

"These women don't know nothing," Willie said. "I'm trying to get my piece of the rock. Hey Anthony, I forgot you got a barbershop over there now. How about hooking up your favorite cousin? I just need a line and my mustache trimmed."

"Anthony does not feel like cutting your nappy hairs," Willie's wife said, as she grabbed his arm. "Let's go in the house. I don't want to get West Nile Virus standing around out here."

"Come on in. Did you bring some barbecue with you?" Anthony asked.

"We've been eating all day. We're ready to party," Willie said. "We want to go to Beale Street. Which club should we go to first?"

"Stop at B.B. King's. If you hurry, you won't have to pay a cover charge. Go to Isaac Hayes' too. Tonight is steppers night," Anthony said

"These folks down here don't know nothing about stepping. Me and my baby will blow them off the floor," Willie said, as he crisscrossed his feet and spun around. "Why don't you and Beverly come with us? Maybe you'll learn something."

"I don't think so," Beverly said. "Anthony worked today and I've been on the go all day. We need to rest. And, we've got to leave early to make it to church in the morning."

"We need someone who knows the directions. These country folks down here can't drive," Willie said, helping himself to a handful of mints from the candy dish.

"I know the way," Sheryl said.

"Lord help us," Willie said. "That girl can barely find her way around Eden. It's early. Come on and go."

Anthony turned to his wife, "Let's go. We haven't gone out in a long time."

"I'm tired. Do what you want," Beverly said, as she closed the living room curtains.

"Well… I probably do need to show them the way. Those one way streets can be tricky if you don't know your way around."

"I'll keep him out of trouble," Willie said.

"Who's going to keep you out of trouble?" Willie's wife asked.

Sheryl whispered to Beverly, "I think he's had enough trouble for one weekend. Jackie told me what happened. You did the right thing, girl. Let him and his hussy know you mean business."

Anthony grabbed his keys and put his wallet in his pocket. "I won't stay out too late," he said.

"Sheryl, are you coming or not?" Willie asked as they went out the door.

Anthony backtracked and kissed Beverly on the cheek. "I love you, baby."

What's love got to do with it? Beverly thought as she watched them pull out of her driveway. She unsnapped her eighteen-hour long line bra and grabbed a beer out of the refrigerator. She had been looking forward to this weekend all year, and now that it was here she was alone.

She went in Tony's room to change the sheets. She didn't venture into his room much anymore. It wasn't the same with him gone. He went to Eden to help C.W. last fall. She had hoped her father and brothers would convince him to return home and go back to school. Tony was an adult now, but he was still her baby. Her mind replayed his last night at home countless times. She wondered what she could have done differently.

Tony was a college freshman at the local community college. He wanted to attend Tennessee State University in Nashville, but he also wanted a new car.

"You said I could get a new car when I went to college."

"That was before you decided to slack off. You barely graduated with C's and D's. You can do better. College is expensive, and you need to be serious," Anthony said.

"It ain't doing me no good. I still can't get a new car."

"You act like we deprived you. You got more stuff than I ever thought about having at your age. If that car out there ain't good enough for you, get your behind a job and work for one."

"I want to work, but y'all want me to go to college."

"Boy, you can run that line on your Mama, but it ain't working on me. You don't want to do the work we ask you to do in the shop. I know you don't want no *real* job. You carry your behind to college so you can get one of them sit down jobs."

"But I need a new car, Daddy. I don't see why . . . "

Beverly had been looking in the classified pages for a car for her son. She felt he had learned his lesson. But her husband said Tony hadn't shown any sign of taking responsibility for the accident. He didn't want to shell out money for tuition, room and board, a new car and a computer for Tony if he wasn't serious. He had to go to summer school just to graduate from high school.

Tony and his friends had an automobile accident the last week of summer school. Tony wasn't driving, and the accident wasn't fatal. The driver suffered a broken wrist, while the others received cuts and bruises. The police said the driver was legally drunk and there were several open bottles of wine in the car. The officer said he smelled marijuana, but didn't find any drugs. Tony admitted to his parents that some of the guys were smoking weed, but swore he wasn't.

Beverly attributed his problems to normal teen mischief and felt he had learned his lesson. Beverly was thankful the accident wasn't worse. Anthony was concerned that their son would resume his antics if he were away from home, and told Tony he had to attend college in Memphis for a year. If he maintained good grades, they would let him go out of town and help him get a car.

Tony enrolled in Memphis Community College. He worked in the salon three days a week and was supposed to save his paychecks for his car. They thought their plan to help their son become mature and responsible was working.

Then Beverly discovered an opened letter from Memphis Community College, while putting laundry away in Tony's drawer. It was a cancellation notice for failure to pay tuition due. The letter was dated September fifteenth.

That was almost three weeks ago, Beverly thought. I know his Daddy gave him the money to pay for school. What happened to it? Where has he been going every day?"

Anthony and Beverly discussed the approach they would take and waited for their son to come home. He didn't get home until almost midnight.

"How was school today, son?" Anthony asked.

"I'm holding my own," Tony said while rummaging through the refrigerator.

"Tell us about your classes. Have you made any new friends?" Beverly asked.

"I'm not trying to make friends. I just go there and leave."

"This game is going to stop right now," Anthony said. "You have not been going to school. Not only have you not been going to school, you've been lying about it and stood right here and lied to my face. Not only that, you spent the money we gave you to register for school. What is wrong with you?"

"Okay, so you trapped me. I'm glad it's all in the open. I'm sorry, college ain't my thing and I didn't want to hurt your feelings."

"You didn't think lying and scheming would hurt our feelings?" Beverly asked.

"I said I was sorry. What more do you want?" Tony said as he poured a glass of orange juice.

"For starters, I want the twelve hundred dollars we gave you," Anthony said.

"I'll get your money. Are you finished?"

"What have you been doing all day?" Beverly asked.

"Just hanging out."

"Hanging out where? Baby, are you doing drugs?" Beverly asked.

"No. You searched my room. Did you find any drugs? I knew y'all would trip like this. That's why I didn't tell you." Tony walked out of the kitchen.

"We're not finished talking to you," Anthony said. He rose and walked behind Tony and snatched his jacket. "Dammit, don't walk away from me when I'm talking to you."

"Damn, this is an eight hundred-dollar jacket you're pulling on."

"You *must* be smoking dope if you think you can talk to me like that. Sit down until I tell you to get up. As long as you live in my house, you will treat your mother and me with respect. Don't walk away from us when we're talking to you and don't ever curse around your mother again. If you can't follow our rules, then it's time for you to go. "

"Cool. I've been thinking about moving out anyway," Tony reached for the car keys on the table.

His father grabbed his arm and pulled Tony back from the table. Tony tried to take the keys from his father. Anthony shoved him and sent him stumbling across the kitchen floor.

"What are you doing?" Beverly screamed and rushed to Tony's side.

"Beverly leave him alone. Don't you *ever* raise your hand to me, boy. I don't care how old you are. If you want to leave, then leave. But leave my car here. I paid for it. I paid for that jacket you cursed me about, too and that college you don't like. You're man enough to curse me, then you're man enough to pay your own way."

Tony got up and walked out.

"Where are you going?" Beverly cried, looking back at Anthony. "You can't let him walk out in the middle of the night like this. He's bleeding."

"Beverly, let him go."

Anthony went to bed, while Beverly lay on the couch in the living room. The doorbell rang two hours later. Beverly peeked out of the curtains to see a police car in the driveway.

"Oh, my God. Oh, my God. Anthony, Anthony!" she yelled.

He rushed to the living room in his boxer shorts. "What is it?"

"It's the police. I knew something would happen to him. I knew it. I should not have let him go."

Anthony opened the door.

"Are you Anthony Townsend?" the officer asked.

"Yes I am."

"Anthony Townsend, I have a warrant for your arrest. Please get dressed so you can come with me."

"Man, what are you talking about?" Anthony asked as the officer read his rights.

"Charges of domestic battery are being filed against you by Shelby County in the interest of Anthony Townsend Jr."

"Where is my son?" Beverly asked.

"He's at the police station downtown."

"I don't understand," Beverly cried.

"Your son claims that you attacked him. I suggest you get dressed sir."

"This is a mistake. We just had a family squabble," Beverly said.

"You can post bail for your husband in the morning, ma'am," the officer said as he led Anthony away.

Beverly, the unofficial therapist, psychologist, marriage and family counselor for all her clients knew everyone's business and darkest secrets and always had an answer. For her own problems, she didn't know what to do other than call her trusted confidante: Daddy.

Anthony spent one night in jail. She asked her parents if Tony could stay with them until things cooled down. She was afraid something regrettable would happen with the next confrontation between her husband and son. Tony stayed there until Daddy got sick and had been staying with Raymond since Daddy came home from the hospital. Beverly was torn. Tony was clearly wrong, but he was her child. She usually tried not to intervene in their clashes. Tony could get out of hand at times, but they had managed to get him out of high school, keep him out of jail and he didn't have any babies. Beverly attributed much of that to Anthony, who kept a tight rein on his son. This time he may have gone too far.

Beverly smoothed the bedspreads and thought of the countless times she had tucked Tony into bed. It seemed like yesterday. But it wasn't. Yesterday, she found her husband in the arms of another woman. She was reuniting with relatives from across the country, but those closest to her were slipping away. My family is falling apart, she thought, as she turned the light out in her son's room.

Beverly's hopes that this reunion would reunite her family were fading. Her strategy to send Tony to Eden to make him homesick, had backfired. She had barely seen Anthony today, and he wasn't trying very hard to get back in her good graces after getting caught with Tanya. After going out tonight, there was no need to ask if he would go to church with her tomorrow. He had told her he loved her, but those words rang hollow without any actions to back them up. And how did he know so much about the Beale Street clubs? He hadn't taken her.

She didn't have the answer to her problems, but she knew how to make things feel better. She went to the freezer and grabbed the tub of butter pecan ice cream. She unwrapped the slice of sock-it-to-me cake she brought from the picnic and placed it in the tub. She found a tablespoon, kicked off her sandals and sat down to gorge her troubles away.

24

We survived Aunt Pearl's snoring and Uncle Willie's smoking and made it back to Eden just after dark. Mama and her crew were watching wrestling and they didn't notice me come in. I headed to the kitchen in search of leftovers.

"Hey Big Spender, how did you do?" Paul asked.

"Let's just say I contributed to the Mississippi economy," I said. "Losing money is hard work. I'm ready to go to bed."

"Well, let me warn you, we got big trouble," Paul said lowering his voice. "Beverly and Brenda exchanged a few words about Daddy's estate and --- "

"How did Brenda find out?"

"I'm afraid I mentioned to her that Paul was working on something for you and C.W. I had no idea it was a secret," Julia confessed.

I rolled my eyes at her. "It's not anymore."

"To be honest, I don't see what the big deal is. Your father can handle his affairs any way he chooses. People pick one person to handle their affairs all the time. There can only be one executor, it's just an administrative position. Your father still dictates who gets what. Why the secrecy?" Julia asked.

"It is a big deal for a black person to have any affairs to handle. Most of the time there is only some old raggedy furniture to argue over for sentimental value. It may be common in your world for people to pass on an inheritance, but few black people my father's age were able to overcome Jim Crow and lynching to amass any assets of value. I wouldn't expect you to understand," I said.

"Carolyn, don't get mad at Julia. It's not her fault," Paul broke in.

"No, it's your fault. If you had kept it to yourself like I asked you to, this wouldn't have happened. I may as well have put it in the paper," I said as I opened the refrigerator.

Paul told Julia, "Don't take it personally. She gets like that around her time of the month. I would give her this phone message, but she's so crabby and tired she needs to go on to bed."

"What phone message?" I asked.

"Don't worry about it. Go ahead and get your rest. Julia and I will sit here and lick our wounds from your tongue lashing."

"Okay, I'm sorry. Now, who called?"

"I don't think that apology rates very high on the sincerity scale. What do you think?" Paul said to Julia.

"I think she sounds sorry."

"All right, you got me. I'm sorry, guys. I guess this is really my fault. I shouldn't have said anything to anyone."

"It's not anyone's fault, but I do agree with Julia. We can avoid problems if we discuss everything in the open. Why don't you suggest it to Daddy?"

"I think I will. Especially since we're all here together. Who knows the next time we'll all be home? I'll ask him about it first thing in the morning. I'm going to bed."

"Oh, yeah, Derrick called. He said to call him at his grandmother's," Paul said.

"Did he leave a number?" I asked trying not to sound excited.

"Yes, but since you're so tired, you can call him in the morning. He won't mind," Paul said, looking over the paper with the phone number on it.

I snatched it out of his hand. "I'll return his call. I wouldn't want to be rude."

"You're so considerate," Paul said. "Aren't you robbing the cradle?"

"There's only a few years difference in our ages. That hardly qualifies as robbing the cradle. We're just friends anyway."

"That's a sexist statement, honey," Julia said. "You're three years older than I am and you didn't think anything was unusual about that."

"The girl is right, Paul."

"I know I'm in trouble now. You're both ganging up on me. Let's go, I see my sister is a bad influence on you," Paul said. "We'll be at the motel."

"See you tomorrow," I said. "Hey Paul, you really need to work on that sexist attitude of yours."

Derrick answered the phone on the first ring. "I tried to wait until you got back, but I got tired of being beat by Big Mac and Mr. Nap. Your family shows no mercy in cards. Let's go for a ride. I'll be there in ten minutes," he said and hung up before I could reply.

I tiptoed past the ringside crowd on my way to the front door, being careful not to block the view of the loyal Washington family fans. Mama and Aunt Belle were rooting for Big Buster, while Cousins Sally Jean and Essie were pulling for Pretty Boy Roy. They barely looked up, although Aunt Belle did tell me to tell Derrick to say hello to his grandmother. How she knew where I was going, I don't know.

Derrick guided his car to Highway 29 and turned on Lake Council Road. He turned the headlights off as we approached the water's edge. The moon illuminated our path and its reflection shimmered on the water. When I was in school, the Lake was the hang out for girls that were lucky enough to have boyfriends with cars, and for boys who were lucky enough to have girlfriends that went 'all the way'. I could see the dark outline of several new houses across the lake, instead of the woods I remembered. The cars were newer and I heard rap instead of Stax and Motown, but for the most part, the Lake was the same.

Derrick parked as far away from the other cars as he could. We still could barely hear the smooth sounds of Derrick's Phil Perry CD over the booming bass in someone's car.

"A smart person would invest in Miracle Ear, because these kids are going to need hearing aids before they're twenty-five," I observed.

"It seems like yesterday, we were the ones sneaking out here," Derrick said.

"Speak for your mannish self. I was at home or at church. My visits to Lake Council were in the daytime with Girl Scouts or some other wholesome activity."

"I guess I wasn't that frequent a visitor out here myself. If I had been, I would know not to bring a pretty lady to the lake in a car with bucket seats. It makes kissing very awkward," Derrick said as he put his hand behind my head and leaned over and kissed me. "I wanted to do that all day." He kissed me again, and it was not an 'old friend' kiss. His lips were full and soft and his breath was warm.

I couldn't believe Bucky was kissing me. I couldn't believe I was kissing him back. When we came up for air, neither of us said a word for what seemed like an eternity. I don't know if it was the humidity from the lake or the steam from Derrick's kiss, but I could feel my edges napping back up. Even though I couldn't have asked for a more romantic setting, I couldn't free myself and enjoy the kiss. The Lake held bad memories. My thoughts went to that night. I had buried the incident so deep in my subconscious; sometimes I almost forgot that it happened.

Mama and her Missionary Sisters were tidying the church for the upcoming Sunday School conference. I didn't want to wait because I had to study for a test, so I told her I would walk home. Our house was about two miles from the church. Back in those days, walking alone was safe for a teenage girl - at least we thought it was.

As I walked, a familiar car pulled up along side me. "Hey Chubby, you need a ride?" the driver asked.

"Sure," I said as I hopped in the car.

As soon as we swerved back onto the road, I knew I had made a mistake. There were three beer cans on the floor, and now that I was close enough, I could smell the alcohol on his breath. Rather than make the turn to my house, he kept straight.

"You missed the turn. Just let me out, I can walk from here," I said.

He ignored me and increased his speed.

"You know this isn't the way to my house. Quit playing."

"I like you. I just want to spend some time with you," he said. "Go for a little ride with me and then I'll take you home." He turned down the road that led to Lake Council, but turned on a pathway that ran through the woods around the lake. He turned the car off and without a word, immediately began putting his hands under my blouse.

"If you don't get your hands off me and take me home ---"

"What? What will you do? Tell my mama, or get your sister or brothers to beat me up? You know you want it. Come on now, don't fight it," he said while pulling up my skirt. "I've seen you watching me."

I struggled, screamed, cried, scratched, hit and kicked. Our heads kept bumping the window, and he pinned my arm behind my back. He tore my underwear, and as he fumbled with his belt, I put both feet in his chest and thrust him off of me. As he tried to recover from his head hitting the rear view mirror, I found the car door handle, got out and ran. I felt like a runaway slave as I found my way through those dark woods. I finally emerged from the maze of trees and found the main road. I had gone about a mile when a car pulled up behind me. I took off running again. Then I heard a voice say, "Chubby, what are you doing out here? Get in this car girl."

I stopped and turned around. The headlights blinded me, but I recognized Charles' voice. I had never been so happy to see my big brother. He asked me what happened, who brought me out there, but I wouldn't say. He didn't ask any more questions and just drove me home.

Luckily, Mama was still at church and Daddy was in the shed, working on a tractor. Paul and Carl were at a basketball game. I got out of the car and headed straight for the bathroom and ran a bath to wash off his smell and touch.

I don't know why I didn't tell anyone. I should have told my parents and we should have called the police. Charles quizzed me a few times, but I wouldn't tell. At the time, I didn't define what happened as attempted rape. I willingly got in the car. I knew him, he wasn't some wild stranger that jumped out of the bushes. I was afraid people would agree with him, that I had brought the whole thing on myself. He was almost like family, and, everyone liked him. We're more enlightened now, and statistics show that most victims know their rapists. I didn't know that then, and the best thing to do seemed to be to avoid Anthony and forget it. So I did. Most of the time.

But this night, as hard as I tried, I couldn't suppress my feelings. These circumstances; being in a car, at the Lake, in the dark, with a man, were too similar. My body tensed and Derrick sat back in his seat.

"I hope I didn't offend you," he said.

"No, you didn't. You surprised me," I said.

"I'm full of surprises, girl. I'm just getting started," he said. "Let's go for a walk."

"You don't appreciate things until you don't have them. I love this lake," I commented, feeling better once I got out of the confining car. Waves lazily lapped the shore and a warm, gentle breeze floated through the air.

"You're right. Every now and then, Sheriff Rhodes comes out here and rounds up the marijuana smokers, but for the most part it's pretty quiet. You live on Lake Michigan. That should be nice."

"It's not the same. It costs money to do anything and you have to deal with parking, traffic and panhandlers. This is so serene and we drove right up to the water's edge. Folks in Chicago drive for hours and spend big money to get a view like this."

"Well, I've never been to Chicago, other than through the airport. I guess you'll have to invite me for a visit."

The lake was peaceful, but the mosquitoes were fierce, so we left. As we slowly rambled along the gravel path that led to the main road, I spotted Tony in a crowd of young men. I told myself not to jump to conclusions, but the stench of marijuana answered the question I was afraid to ask.

We rode home and Derrick parked in front of my parent's house, where we talked for two hours. We debated the politics of Paul's marriage, whether blacks were better off in the North or South, why the divorce rate is so high, and who should replace Sheriff Rhodes, who was finally retiring after thirty-five corrupt years.

"I really should go in now," I said for the fourth time. "We're going to church in the morning. There will be a line for the bathroom, and I want to get in it early. Maybe you can join us at church."

"Well, I hope I don't sound like a wayward sinner, but I'm going fishing in the morning. I've only taken my boat out a couple times this year."

"That sounds relaxing. I haven't been fishing in years," I said.

"You mean *you* like to fish?" Derrick asked as he opened my car door.

"Sure. Daddy used to take me all the time. I had my own rod and everything."

"Miss Washington, you have a date. I'm warning you. I like to go out early."

"That's the best time to go," I said.

"Okay. Be ready at five," Derrick said as he walked me to the porch. He put his arm around my waist and was about to kiss me when I pointed toward the bedroom window next to the porch. The curtain in Mama's bedroom moved and I surmised that they were up to their old tricks again. They pretended to be asleep when we came in, but they knew exactly what time we drove or walked up and how long we lingered outside. I guess those things come natural to parents and it doesn't matter if the child is sixteen or forty-six. Derrick glanced at the window and smiled and pecked me on the cheek. "I'll see you in the morning," he said and walked back to his car.

I peeked in on Mama and Daddy before I went to bed. "Goodnight, you two," I said.

"Good night, Chubby," Mama said.

"You can take my short, blue rod," Daddy said. "It's lightweight and will be easier for you to cast."

I smiled and closed the door.

25

The pungent odor of mothballs floated out of Mama's junk drawer as I searched for pantyhose. In my rush to dress for church, I snagged both my pair. If I had been in Chicago, I would have gone barelegged. Most churches didn't have much of a dress code anymore and sandals without hose would have been fine. But they didn't play that in Eden, Arkansas. I considered skipping church service. I had gotten into the habit of sleeping in on Sunday mornings and watching church services on television. Cecelia nagged me about going to church. I told her I was tired of hypocritical church members and greedy preachers, I could pray at home. But I didn't do much praying because Warren often came over while Terri and the kids went to church. This morning the pews would be filled with family members, but Mama wanted her children there too. Daddy could get away with fishing on Sunday morning, but not the rest of us.

Derrick and I had been fishing on the bayou since five in the morning. Daddy used to take us bank fishing when we were kids, but I had never been fishing on a boat. We were the only ones on the water and seemed to have the world all to ourselves. We caught a cooler full of catfish and sunbrim, which Derrick said he would clean. We went to Jackson's Diner for breakfast and I was home by ten o'clock. Just enough time for me to get ready for eleven o'clock service and squeeze in a ten-minute power nap. That nap turned into a forty-minute snooze. Now I'm sleepy, I'm third in line for the bathroom and I don't have the right hose.

Mama kept her extra hose in the bottom drawer. Unfortunately, all of Mama's stockings were that ugly, milky brown color black women were forced to wear before Madison Avenue realized we came in different shades of brown and tan. She's got to have some darker stockings hiding in here somewhere, I thought, as I fumbled through the hodgepodge of papers, pink hair rollers, bobby pins and mismatched socks.

My eye caught a familiar blue card with a pink bouquet of roses on the cover. I can't believe Mama still has this. I gave her this card for Mother's Day when I was in college. Rubber bands held together other stacks of cards. Yellowed envelopes with twenty cents stamps and Vietnamese postmarks were banded separately. Seeing Walter's neat penmanship brought back memories of the protective big brother I adored. Recent additions to Mama's collection were letters from Carl. He had written me a few times, but stopped when I didn't write him back. To anyone else, this would have been clutter that needed to be purged. But these were precious love letters to our mother. How sad to think that two of my gifted brothers had been snatched away in their prime

A noise from the hall startled me. "I've been looking everywhere for you," Beverly announced peering around the door.

"I need some stockings, and all of Mama's hose are too light. Do you have an extra pair with you?" I asked as I guiltily closed Mama's drawer.

"I'll check for you later. Right now I need to talk to you. Raymond, Paul and Charles are meeting us here. No telling what time Daddy will be back, so we need to hurry up," Beverly said hurriedly.

"I hope you're not doing what I think you're doing," I said.

"Carolyn, we need to make everything clear. Come on," she ordered, ushering me into the back bedroom. Daddy added this room to the house to give the boys more space. It ran the length of the back of the house and had been shared by Raymond, Carl and Paul. The bunk beds were now pushed together to make a king-size bed. The paneled walls made the room dark.

"Hurry, we don't have much time," Cecelia said as she stood watch at the door. "Mama went to Sunday School and Daddy took the kids fishing."

Paul and Raymond were present. She had even gotten Charles and Brenda to come, defying Mama's orders for them not to come in her house.

"Let's get right to it," Cecelia said as she closed the door. "I've called a family meeting to discuss the disposition of Daddy's property. Carolyn has looked over the papers and she says ---"

"Stop right there," I interrupted. "Do not put me in the middle of this. I told you I wouldn't discuss this with you. I don't have time anyway, I promised Mama I was coming to church," I said, as I put on my earrings.

Cecelia ignored me and began her report. "It seems Charles has finagled things so that all of Daddy's property goes to him. This is unfair and totally unacceptable. Don't take it personally Charles. I'm just speaking for what is right."

"Cecelia thinks Daddy should sell while he has a good offer," Beverly said. "She has a valid point. I know we love this place, but times have changed. Equipment is expensive, and workers are hard to find. Of course, we hope Daddy lives a long time. But we need to be practical."

"I thought you called us over here to apologize," Brenda stated. "We do not have time to listen to your schemes. Let's go, honey."

"Wait," Charles said. "I'm interested in hearing what they have to say. I know how Cecelia feels. I want to hear what everybody else has to say. Whose side are you on?" he challenged, looking around the room.

"What do you think, Raymond? Did you know Charles was scheming to cheat us out of everything?" Beverly asked.

This was one of the few times I've seen Raymond at a loss for words. He started slowly while fingering his mustache. "I'm not on anyone's side. I love all of you and I want us to love each other. Families need to---"

"Save the speech," Beverly said. "What do you think we should do about Daddy's estate?"

"Well ... I don't think Daddy wants everything to go to Charles, or he wouldn't have Carolyn looking over his papers. And even Carl thinks Daddy shouldn't sell the land. Let's forget this meeting and let Daddy come to us in his own time, in his own way."

"Since when are you and Carl the voices of wisdom?" Charles asked. "For twenty-five years you didn't want no part of Eden and now that you lost your big-time job in Chicago, you come back and try to take over."

Raymond rose and put his finger in Charles' face. "Who do you think you're talking to? And I did not lose my job, I came home to---"

Brenda jumped in front of Raymond. "I don't understand why you all are so upset. None of you even wanted this land. You couldn't wait to take off your cap and gown to catch the first thing headed up Highway 55 and away from here. You come down here once a year out of obligation and act like we should be grateful. Now, you've been here six months and think you're running things. Since C.W.'s been sick, who's been taking care of him? We have. Who helps your Mama? We do." Brenda's voice was getting louder and louder.

Beverly stood. "Listen, Brenda, you need to be quiet, talking about what you do for my Mama and Daddy. That's the least you could do. You don't work, and you live here rent-free.

No telling how much you and Charles have socked away while you're supposedly looking out for them. As soon as Daddy got sick, you and Charles couldn't wait to start spending money. Charles goes out and wastes money on some fancy tractor and I heard you're planning to build a house."

I thought about the loan documents I discovered at the courthouse. The loan had been repaid, but what other unknown transactions were lurking out there?

"You think you're the only one that deserves a new house? And that tractor was for ---"

Charles cut his wife off. "That's none of their business. All of you can go to hell. Go right back to your integrated neighborhoods and your flunkie jobs where you kiss the white man's behind all day. Always coming down here like you such big stuff, when you're a paycheck away from having your lights cut off. That's why you so worried about this land, because you ain't got none. Well, you know what? You still won't have none. I helped C.W. build this farm for the last thirty years. When you left this was two hundred acres of worn out dirt. Now we got more than six hundred acres, irrigated fields, the latest machinery and three men working for us. I worked for this like you worked for your stuff in Chicago and Memphis and California. You don't see me coming up there trying to claim anything. I put every one of you through school working on this farm. You should be thanking me. I stayed here when you couldn't look white folks in the eye. You couldn't even buy a new car because the sheriff would give you a hard time. So I'll be damned if I'm gonna let any of you cheat me out of what's mine," Charles said as he headed for the door.

"We're not trying to cheat you out of anything," Cecelia said.

"It doesn't look that way to me. All these years, I took a pitiful salary so we could reinvest everything back into this place. Now you want C.W. to cash out and leave me with nothing?"

"Charles, we only want what's fair. No one is trying to leave you out. But how can having you get everything be fair?" Beverly asked.

"It's fair because I helped build it, and my mother helped C.W. get started. Nobody is selling anything around here, if I have anything to do with it," Charles said.

"Well, I'll just have to make sure you have nothing to do with it. I see this is pointless. I'm going to church," Cecelia said as she reached for the door.

Raymond stepped in front of the door as Charles stood. "Wait a minute. This is crazy. We're supposed to be enjoying each other this weekend and strengthening our family. We're supposed to be on one accord."

Paul walked over to Charles, "Raymond is right. I can't believe we're acting like this. We are family."

Brenda stepped in. "Well, how are we supposed to be on one accord when you've practically accused us of stealing. No one has done more for this family than Charles and me."

"Excuse me, but this is family business and I invite you out of our conversation," Beverly turned her back on Brenda.

"When it's convenient or profitable, then its family," Brenda said. "But when it's work, it's only me and Charles. Well guess what, you got no claim to nothing from C.W. anyway. Your *real* daddy is over in Star City with his wife. So if you want to talk about family, you hop your trigger-happy tail over there."

Before she could say another word, Beverly slapped her. She hit her so hard, we could see her hand print on Brenda's pale peach skin. Brenda fell back into the grandfather clock, shattering the glass. Brenda must have had a death wish, because everyone knows not to mess with Beverly, especially about that subject. She was always sensitive because she didn't favor anybody in the family. We heard rumors, but that was grown folks business, and Mama and Daddy never discussed it with her or us. When we were kids, we'd tease her by telling her she was left in a basket on the porch, but as we got older and learned bits and pieces of the truth we left her alone.

Brenda tried to get up and Beverly pushed her back down. "What are you saying about my Mama? Just because you are a trifling, low-life ---"

Charles came over and grabbed Beverly's arm. "Leave her alone. I don't want to have to hurt you."

"Well, why did she say that?" Beverly cried. "She thinks because she's your wife, she belongs here and I don't? You already had one wife and you could have another one tomorrow."

Raymond was helping Brenda up. I was picking shards of glass off the floor when Mama Mary and Julia came in.

"I don't know what's going on in here, but it ain't nothing but the devil," Mama Mary said slowly. "All of you is kin, so it cain't be over no woman or man, so it must be money. The Bible says money is the root of all evil. We gonna pray about this. Fix up this room and act like grown mens and womens."

Everyone mumbled 'yes ma'am' and tried to straighten the room. This was a flashback to when we were kids and one of us got caught playing in the house. We'd all have to clean up even if you weren't the guilty party.

Charles grabbed Brenda's hand and headed for the door. "I'll see you later Mama Mary. I got to go."

She leaned on the dresser, and popped him in the behind with her purse. "Did you hear me, boy? I said help clean up in here. You ain't grown enough to disrespek' me. Y'all didn't go to church and the devil got busy. Well, I say the devil is a liar, and we gonna rebuke him right now."

She sat on the bed and opened her Bible. "We living in the last days chil'ren. Instead of fussing and fighting over nothing you need to be getting your soul right with the Lord, and raising your babies to be God-fearing. The first chapter in the book of Joel says, "Tell ye your children of it, and let your children tell their children, and their children another generation. That which . . . Oh, Carolyn, you can go. I see you're the only one dressed for church."

I hurried out of there, torn stockings and all. How was I going to explain any of this to Daddy? Maybe Cecelia was right. Daddy needs to make some decisions. But he was looking to me for advice. What in the world could I tell him? Can we find a solution that doesn't split the family? The way things were going, our next reunion would be in front of Judge Judy.

By and By

26

A sense of déjà vu enveloped me as I entered Friendship Missionary Baptist Church. I knew Mama would be on the third row, right side, and I went to sit beside her. This had been her seat as long as I could remember. Sister Carter was still on the piano leading the choir in Amazing Grace. Brother Jones and Brother Clark still take up the offering. The Steward Mothers still sat on the front row in their snow-white dresses. They even still had those fans in the pews with pictures of Dr. Martin Luther King Jr. or that cute, caramel-colored family that looks like Easter Sunday in 1965. Hats aren't as common as they used to be, but count on Aunt Belle to model an eye-catching number. Cecelia always sent unique hats to her from Chicago. The white Jesus is still on the stained-glass windows. Reverend Handley has gray hair now, but he still preaches like he's having an asthma attack.

Some things are different. For one thing, the church is air-conditioned. It always seemed a waste of time to spend half of Saturday pressing and curling our hair, only to sweat it out Sunday. Reverend Handley hasn't officially retired, but Mama says his son Marvin is actually running the church now. It's hard for me to imagine him delivering a sermon. I still see him as a mannish boy trying to talk me into doing 'it'.

Marvin was sugar sweet and respectful in public and had all the ladies of the church fooled, including my mother. She even asked him to take me to the junior prom. At first I was mortified, having my mother find me a date. But, eventually we became a couple and dated all of my senior year in high school. Marvin's innocence was a facade, and he was always trying to get me to "do it." The end of the school year was approaching and I wanted to make sure he took me to prom, so I finally gave in.

We were in Little Rock at a church conference and somehow Marvin finagled permission to take me to a movie. We didn't go to a movie. We went to another motel. I don't know whose room it was but he had a key. He went in first and told me to wait fifteen minutes then come to room 344. We watched Soul Train and then we did it. The fireworks and violins I expected weren't there, but he seemed satisfied so I was happy. We went to prom and were both accepted at Tennessee State University. Marvin was going to major in business and I planned to major in prelaw.

We had sex four times before I got pregnant. Marvin said he didn't like rubbers, but he would pull out in time. It's the oldest line in the world and I fell for it.

I was pregnant when I graduated. I didn't tell Mama and Daddy because I didn't want to upset them. I really wasn't upset. We had planned to get married anyway. We would do it sooner, that's all.

I told Marvin the day after graduation. He said something stupid like "How did this happen?"

"I think you know how this happened," I responded.

"Maybe you're just late."

"No. I'm never late. I've missed two cycles and Mama will be asking questions soon."

"Okay. Let me think."

"What is there to think about? You're going to be a father and we need to get married." That was back when boys usually married the girls, and getting pregnant out of wedlock was a major embarrassment to the family.

Marvin didn't call me for four days. I was terrified. Luckily I had a full time job that summer so I didn't have to spend much time at home. When I came home, I stayed in my room. He finally showed up one day after work and announced that he had joined the Army. He was going to Basic Training in three weeks. He'd be gone for thirteen weeks. Then they would assign him to a base and he would send for me. We'd be together by the time the baby was born.

I wanted to get married and I wanted to have the baby but hadn't ever considered not going to college. What if they stationed him in some cold, faraway place like Montana or Maine? Who would help me with the baby? I was relieved that he still wanted me, but I was furious that he had made such an important decision without talking to me first. I didn't see what choice I had. We went over to Sheldon County and got married. We agreed to wait until almost time for Marvin to leave before telling our parents.

Our timetable was pushed up when an Army recruiter called Marvin's house to discuss his assignment. We returned from choir practice to find Reverend Handley standing in the door. To say he was upset is an understatement. He didn't sound like a reverend that day.

He called my house and summoned my parents. Mama was out of town, helping her sister recover from surgery, so Daddy came alone. Reverend Handley said I wasn't good enough for his son and that I was loose like my sister. Daddy backed off, told me to come on and we left. He spat out of the car window and we drove off.

Daddy was quiet. I didn't know what to say. After the initial shock, I figured our parents would get over it. Marvin and I had done the right thing. We had gotten married and Marvin had come up with a way to support us.

Daddy and Reverend Handley arranged our divorce, and Daddy arranged the abortion. Marvin stayed in the Army and I went to Tennessee State. In retrospect, I guess things worked out. I could never have been a preacher's wife. I would have been a terrible single mother, and I wouldn't have been happy as a military wife.

"Stand up, Chubby," Mama whispered, kicking my leg. Visitors had been asked to stand, and everyone around me was already standing. Sister Carter welcomed us, and recited the same speech she'd given for the past thirty years. She gave a special acknowledgment to those attending the Washington reunion. Most family members had attended Grace Christian Fellowship Church, which was the official church of the reunion. It was a new church started last year by Cousin Sarah's son, when he got out of prison. But Mama said she wasn't missing her church for anyone. Reverend Handley also welcomed the visitors, then invited my cousin Amos, who pastored a church in St. Louis, to join the ministers in the pulpit. Then he asked Aunt Pearl to "bless the congregation with a song." She has a rich alto voice and toured professionally before she married. Cecelia says Reverend Handley always asks Aunt Pearl to sing because they had a thing going on back in the day, and some say he is Veronica's father. Cecelia knew gossip that happened before she was even born.

Marvin, or rather, Reverend Handley Jr. led the altar call. He caught my eye and nodded my way. His father then stood and began his asthma attack. My eyelids were becoming heavy as the impact of a late night and an early morning caught up with me. My head nodded a few times and I could feel Reverend Handley's eyes boring through me. I didn't know if he was looking because I was nodding to sleep, because of my past with his son, or if my conscience was working on me. Once Warren started coming over on Sunday mornings, I had drifted out of the habit of going to church. Maybe Reverend Handley was God's messenger to me. Even though, I didn't think my transgressions were any worse than anyone else's.

My mind wandered as I thought about Daddy's papers. This afternoon would be my last chance to work on them. Daddy had been intent on me not taking anything home, but there was no way I could finish everything. I did have a few suggestions already about titling his land and preparing a living will. These were minor things that would prevent a family showdown should something happen to Daddy.

I looked around to avoid Reverend Handley's glare and noticed Sheree leave the sanctuary. That's the second time she's gone to the bathroom since I've been here, I thought. I saw Cecelia smiling contently; engrossed in the preacher's message. I was glad she was finding solace in God's word. I said a silent prayer for Sheree and her mother. That was one showdown that couldn't be prevented.

"Slide it to the left," Beverly ordered.

"Make up your mind," Raymond said as he pushed the desk back against the wall.

"I'm only trying to keep the wall from looking so bare."

"That clock has been here forty years, you're not going to camouflage that it's gone," Raymond said, wiping his brow.

"Brenda gets on my nerves, but I shouldn't have let her get to me like that. It's just that I've always felt different. Me and Charles are the only dark skinned ones. And you all are so smart."

"You're the one with your own business. I think you're the smart one. And you know we come in all colors. Don't worry about what she says. You know who you are. Hey Daddy's here," Raymond said as he looked out the window. "Let's meet them at the door and avoid questions about this room as long as we can."

"I know Lois is going to be mad at me," C.W. announced, as he and his grandchildren invaded the house. "I was supposed to have these kids back in time for church. We were having so much fun, we lost track of time."

"Granddaddy, you said we could have our own church outside and you were coming back when you got good and ready," Mike blabbed.

"Go change those fishy-smelling clothes," he said as he ushered the kids in the house. "You didn't hear that."

"My lips are sealed," Beverly said as she fixed a bowl of left over peach cobbler.

"I sure did have fun with them children," C.W. said, as he removed his cap. "Children these days is smart, and they can carry on a conversation like a grown person. I was working a lot when you all were coming up. We didn't spend as much time together as I would have liked. But I always found time to take all of you fishing. Cece wasn't too crazy about going, but you and Carolyn hung right in there. You were the best hunter of all of my children. I remember Lois got so mad at me for taking you hunting. She said it wasn't lady-like. It doesn't hurt for a gal to be good with a gun. You never know what you'll run into . . . like an unfaithful husband."

"Ok, don't be cute, Daddy. I know you heard what happened."

"I didn't hear it from you. I want to hear what you have to say for yourself."

"Nothing. I caught Anthony screwing around and I snapped."

"Beverly, I don't usually get in your private business. You are grown and you have to live your own life. But I already got one child locked up and that's one too many. I don't think your mother could stand it if it happened again. You and Anthony work it out if you can, and split if you can't. He ain't worth going to prison over."

"I know. I wasn't thinking," Beverly said, spooning the remainder of the cobbler into her bowl.

"You can't afford not to think. Black folks ain't got that luxury. You got to be thinking all the time. Think about what you're going to do next. Think about what you just did. Think about what the other guy is thinking. Be smart. They could have charged you with attempted murder, and put you in jail. At a minimum, you would lose your license. Anthony would have your shop and get another woman to run it. You can't mix your personal life and your business."

"I know you're right. Sometimes I wonder why I even stay with him."

"Only you can answer that. All I can say is, he's the same way he's always been. You knew he was whorish when you married him," Daddy said, washing his hands in the sink.

"I always thought you liked Anthony."

"I didn't say I didn't like him. I don't like him messing around on you, but I'm not married to him. He has always messed around, he's like his Daddy."

"So shouldn't he be tired of running around by now? You're a man, why do married men chase women?"

"Hmmmm, let me see how I can say this and keep myself out of trouble. I think most men do it because they can. Women make them feel good."

"That's it? No deep seated love/hate complex with their mother, or a constant need for approval or some other Freudian reason?"

"It's not as complicated as all that. Anthony likes women and women like him. If you're going to be with him, you have to accept that," Daddy said as he hung his fishing cap on the porch.

"I never thought I would be divorced. But I can't be a fool and keep taking him back."

"Think carefully about that. Is that what you want, or are you worried about what people think? There would be very few married folks, if every wife left every wandering husband. It's most men's nature."

"What about women?" Beverly asked.

"It's different when a woman messes around. I know it ain't fair, but that's the way it is. Most men can't tolerate their woman stepping out on them."

"You stayed with Mama. Everybody says you're not my real father," Beverly said softly as she looked away.

C.W. was quiet while he poured a glass of orange juice. "You know, I was never one to pay too much attention to what 'everybody' says. Things was going on between me and your Mama that you don't need to worry about. As far as I'm concerned you're my daughter. That's what it says on your birth certificate, that's what it says in my heart, and that's all that matters to me. If you feel the need to dig further, I can't stop you. It won't change how I feel, and it won't change all the good times we've had together. I changed your diapers, I taught you to ride a bike, I whipped your butt when you got out of line, and I escorted you down the aisle when you got married. Won't none of that change. I have three daughters, and you're the oldest. Of all my children, you're the most like me. So that's what I would tell 'everybody' next time 'everybody' has something to say about things that ain't they business."

Beverly hugged C.W. "Thanks, Daddy. You always give good advice. So what do you think I should do about Anthony? Should I give him one more chance or should I leave him this time?"

"I can't make that decision for you. Do what's right for you. I didn't mess around, but I drank a little too much to suit your Mama. No one can live your life for you. I will tell you to be smart. Don't mix your honey with your money. If you're planning to make a move, get a lawyer to check everything out first. Put you a little something to the side. If you can tolerate Anthony's courting, then stay where you are. He will eventually wear out and you'll grow old together. Don't do anything because you're worried about what 'everybody' says. I just want you to be happy. If you're happy, that's your answer."

"You're right Daddy. I think I know what I have to do."

Cecelia glanced at her watch, only 12:05, she thought. She escaped Mama Mary's Bible class at the house and made it to church in time to march around for the offering. Reverend Handley selected a scripture from the book of Revelation as the text for his sermon. Why so much talk about the 'by and by', she wondered, as she rubbed her temples. In her rush she had forgotten to take her pills. What about the here and now? These people seem to think God's word speaks against prosperity. Reverend Handley wasn't waiting for the by and by. Mama brags about his new home on the lake like it's hers. He never drives a car more than two years old and his whole family is on the church payroll. My Bible says Jesus came so we can have life more abundantly. I don't want to wait for the 'by and by'.

What are Mama and Daddy waiting on? They should be enjoying their money, traveling, shopping, and dining out. What was the point of working hard and saving, just to hand it over in an inheritance? An inheritance. That was something only rich, white folks had. The thought of an inheritance was as remote as a purple polka-dot sun. Mama and Daddy live so frugally, it's hard to imagine them having money, she thought. She knew Daddy owned a lot of land, but never considered it valuable. Who would want land in Eden? She figured if something happened to Daddy, Charles would continue to live and work on the farm. He would be entitled to any income from it. She hadn't thought past that, but Carolyn's revelation put a new spin on things.

If there was a sizeable estate, of course they should divide it. And since Charles was being so devious and trying to maneuver the rest of them out of anything at all, he could buy them out. It was a good thing Daddy asked Carolyn to look over his papers. If something had happened to Daddy, there would have been an ugly scene. Now they could get everything in order and have an understanding.

Oh, I hope I'm not being sacrilegious by thinking about this, especially right here in church, Cecelia thought. I'm not looking forward to Daddy's passing. He ought to live a good while longer. Men like Bob Hope and George Burns were vital well into their nineties. Daddy is very fit, he's never smoked, he drinks moderately and gets regular checkups. That's why his stroke surprised everyone. The doctors told him to lay off red meat and fried foods and gave him a clean bill of health. Even so, he won't live forever. It's wise to prepare for things like this, Cecelia rationalized. Relatives start coming out of the woodwork when they smell money. We never saw Walter's daughter when she was growing up. It seems like more than a coincidence that she shows up at this reunion when she never has before.

I really need to talk to Daddy. He needs to know what Charles is up to. His conniving wife acts like she already owns the place. The chick barely made it out of high school and never worked a day in her life. Yet she was in position to benefit more from her father's hard work than his own daughters.

And Daddy can't be serious about leaving property to Carl. I know his letters say that he's saved now and plans to turn his life around. Hey, they always say that when they're in jail. I wish him no ill will, but you can't hand things over to irresponsible people. Daddy may as well flush it down the toilet. It's almost a reward for going to prison and it's not fair to the rest of us. We've scuffled and worked hard and even pooled our money to pay his attorney and back child support. Yet he'll come out debt-free, with money in the bank. My basement leaks and my mortgage is past due. Carl probably even has good credit, Cecelia thought.

Cecelia noticed Sheree leaving the church sanctuary. Good thing Mama and Aunt Belle sat close to the front, she thought. They wouldn't notice her leaving. They would rather see you die or pee on yourself than walk out while the preacher gave the sermon. That child knows walking during the sermon is not proper church etiquette. She probably waited until he started talking to get up, just to be contrary, Cecelia thought.

Maybe she was feeling bad again. She was sick on the way down here. Then I rushed her out of bed this morning. She didn't even have time to eat breakfast. Her stomach is probably still unsettled.

Cecelia was proud of Sheree. She had inherited the best of both her parents' personalities. Assertive and smart like her mother, some said that's why they bumped heads all the time. She's creative and personable like Michael.

Sheree - a senior in high school! Where had the time gone? She still hadn't picked a college. Well, actually she had. Her first choice was Spelman. Even with the scholarships she'd been offered, Cecelia knew they couldn't afford it. "Don't put all your hopes on one choice." Cecelia told her. "Don't limit yourself."

If Daddy was as well off as Carolyn said, maybe she could go to Spelman. What good would the money do when she and Michael were ready to retire? We need it now. Why not take Daddy up on his offer of a loan? He co-signed for Beverly's beauty salon. Lord knows, he threw away a fortune on lawyers and bail trying to keep Carl out of jail. Charles and his silly wife were living rent-free on Daddy's land. When Mr. Slaughter fell behind in his payments, Daddy lowered the rent, and Slaughter wasn't even family. Everyone is benefiting from Daddy's largesse except my family, Cecelia thought. Yes, I will take him up on his offer of a loan. That will tide us over until his settlement comes in. Who knows, once I help him see the benefits of retirement, he may be so grateful, he'll offer me more than enough to pay Sheree's tuition. Then I can get a few things done to the house and catch up on some bills before Michael discovers how behind we are. The money would give Michael and me some breathing room, she thought. We never fought this much before. Maybe if we didn't have to worry so much about bills, our marriage would be better. I could go back to days and we could resume a more normal life.

"The doors of the church are open." Reverend Handley announced, as the deacons placed two chairs in front of the audience. "Tomorrow is not promised. Decide now, where you will spend eternity."

There they go again with that 'by and by' stuff. I'm tired of waiting and worrying. I'll worry about the 'by and by' later. I'm going to spend some time on Michigan Avenue. I'm ready to buy and buy, Cecelia smiled to herself and stood to join in the invitational hymn. It won't be long now.

27

As we exited the sanctuary, Mama nudged me. "Chubby, isn't that Bucky on the back row?" He waved as Mama caught his attention.

"He must have arrived late. He should have come to sit with the family," I commented.

"That boy ain't a bit more interested in this family than the man in the moon. He came here to see you," Mama said. We stood outside the door like a wedding reception line greeting so many that had been my role models and offered encouragement during my days in Eden.

Derrick finally made it to us as the crowd was breaking up. "Bucky, I'm so glad to see you!" Mama exclaimed.

"Good afternoon, ladies. I crashed everything else this weekend, I figure if I keep hanging around, you will adopt me."

"In the Lord's house, everyone is at home, and all are welcome. I would love to have a fine, handsome young man like you as a son," she said. "You sure do look nice. I've never seen you in a suit. Some folks say men don't have to wear suits to church anymore. I want to look my best on the Lord's Day. Doesn't he look nice, Chubby?" she said, pushing me closer to him.

Yes, yes, yes, he does look good. But that's not the kind of thing you proclaim on the church steps, I thought. Clad in a tan suit, cream shirt, brown and gold tie, and camel brown shoes so shiny the sun reflected off them, he *did* look good.

One of Aunt Belle's sayings is that " you can tell a lot about a man from his shoes. If he takes care of his shoes, he'll take care of you." You can supposedly tell other things by looking at a man's feet, but we *were* still on the church grounds.

"I need to turn in my Missionary dues since I missed last week's meeting. Come with me Cecelia. Derrick, would you mind giving Chubby a ride home?" Mama asked. They were gone before Derrick could answer.

"Miss Lois has given me my orders. Shall we go?" Derrick asked.

"My mother is not very subtle," I said as he opened the passenger door for me.

"You don't hear me complaining. I wish I could spend more time with you, but I'm going to the nursing home this afternoon."

"I'll tag along if you don't mind. I would love to see your grandmother. She was always my favorite Sunday School teacher," I said. "And I'd like to visit Aunt Millie." I also wasn't looking forward to going back to the house. I didn't want to answer questions when Mama found her S&H Green Stamps clock broken.

"Why don't I come to your house after I leave the nursing home? I'm not sure how long I'll be there. Sometimes my grandmother wants me to take her visiting, or to the store. That would be terribly boring for you," Derrick said. "I'll come by your house when I leave the nursing home."

"Sounds good. I'll see you later," I said. I can use the time to go through more of Daddy's papers. This will be a good chance for me to talk to him.

Cecelia, Sheree, Aunt Belle, and Mama came home shortly after Derrick dropped me off. "Seems like we hugged and kissed every person in Eden after church," Sheree said.

"Ouuuuweee, these shoes hurt my feet," Mama announced, kicking her white pumps off as soon as she made it to the couch.

"You should have let me buy you a pair yesterday," Cecelia said. "It's bad for your feet to wear shoes that are too tight. I saw a teal pair that would match your dress perfectly."

"That's a waste of money, girl. I only have one dress this color."

"You know, there's no law that says you're allowed to have only black or white shoes. I swear Aunt Vera Mae has a different pair of shoes for each outfit. I wonder what happened to her? I thought she was coming over here after church," Cecelia said.

"My sister doesn't have time for us common folks. I was surprised to even see her at church, fashionably late, of course, so she could parade down the aisle."

"Lois, you and Vera Mae need to stop all this foolishness and act like sisters supposed to act," Aunt Belle said.

"Well, you're talking to the wrong sister. I'm not the one who let the family down, and I really don't feel like talking about it. I'm going to soak my corns in Epsom salt. I have to wear these shoes again tonight."

Cecelia and I shook our heads as Mama left the room. I leaned my head back on the couch and closed my eyes.

"Don't get too comfortable," Cecelia warned me. "Remember we said we were going to the nursing home after church to see Aunt Millie?"

"Derrick's gone over there to visit his grandmother, and he's coming here on his way home," I said.

"Well, you can save him a trip and meet him there. We promised Aunt Millie we'd come see her. Let's hurry and change clothes so we can get going. We still have to decorate for the banquet. I'm sure you'll see Bucky later. Don't start planning your life around him already."

"What do you mean by that?" I asked.

"All I'm saying is don't be so available for men. That's why you always get taken advantage of in your relationships."

"Oh, really? I don't remember asking for your advice, and Derrick and I are not in a relationship. He's just an old family friend."

"Then you don't need to wait around for an old family friend. I'll meet you and Aunt Belle on the porch in ten minutes."

I tried to catch Derrick before he left his house, but there was no answer. I left a message that I would meet him at the nursing home. I searched the refrigerator for a quick snack and was headed to the porch when the phone rang.

"Well, it's about time I caught up with you," Warren said, when I answered. "I've talked to everyone in your family but you."

"Sorry I didn't call. I forgot my cell phone charger."

"What time does your plane get in tomorrow? I'll pick you up."

"I thought you and Terri were taking the boys to the circus."

"That's why I've been trying to call you. I've got some news. I've moved out."

"What?" I asked, sitting down at the kitchen table.

"I've moved out. Terri and I are putting an end to this charade. I should be sad, but I'm not. Baby, now we can be together."

"Warren, what are you saying?"

"I'm saying we're free to be together. I've already taken some of my things to your place. Right now, they're lying on the couch. You have clothes in every closet."

"This is really a surprise," I said softly.

"I thought your response would be more enthusiastic."

I was quiet for a moment as I digested his news. "You caught me off guard. What about your boys?"

"They were upset when we told them, but I'll still see them every day when I pick them up from school. And they can spend weekends with us. I'm not going to abandon them. Our relationship will probably be better, because there won't be tension in the air."

"Warren, are you sure this is the right thing to do? You and Terri have been together a long time. Is this another a spat or are you really through?" I asked looking around to be sure I was alone.

"My marriage has needed work a long time."

"Then why didn't you work on it? How could you give one hundred percent to your marriage, when you were slicing off ten percent for me?"

"That ten percent is what's kept me going. Terri and I grew apart, and I'm tired of trying."

"How do I know you won't get tired of me? I don't want us to be a divorce statistic," I said.

"Divorce? I thought you didn't believe in marriage. You and I don't need a piece of paper to validate our feelings. That's why you're so special to me."

I saw Cecelia go to the porch and pushed my chair back from the table. "I really need to go. Folks are waiting on me."

"So what time do you get in?"

"Eight-thirty."

"I'll be there. I can't wait to see you."

Cecelia was honking the horn as I reached the porch. She and Aunt Belle were already in the car. Ordinarily I would have fussed at her for rushing me, but I was still in a daze from Warren's news. Had I heard him right? He and Terri were splitting for good and he was at my place waiting for me. This was what I always wanted. Wasn't it?

Garden Homes Convalescent Center is one of the largest employers in Dwight County. Though the path from the parking lot is lined with flowers in every shade of the rainbow, the landscaping is impeccable and the lawn is flawlessly manicured, an aura of dread still surrounds the place. The view of the grounds served to remind residents and visitors that the next stop would be another well-manicured site- the cemetery.

A man in a wheel chair sat outside the entrance. His back was curved and he appeared to be leaning forward in the chair. Two other men rested on a park bench on the lawn, smoking.

Aunt Belle patted the man in the wheelchair on the back. "How you doin', Mr. Woods? Sure is a pretty day," she said loudly. "But my joints been aching, so I know a storm is coming. Cece and Carolyn are home. Don't they look fine? We been to church this morning. Sure do miss seeing you in the choir. *Precious Lord* doesn't sound the same when someone else sings it. C.W. still carrying on his heathen ways. He went fishing this morning."

Aunt Belle carried on the conversation for both of them. Mr. Woods had been Daddy's fishing buddy. His deep, baritone voice had driven many a good sister to shout, dance and cry. He had a stroke a few years ago that left him paralyzed and he couldn't talk. He was a widower and all of his children had moved away. They used to visit regularly, but as the weeks turned into months, and the months turned into years with no sign of improvement, their visits slowed. Although he couldn't answer, his rheumy eyes followed us as we walked by.

"We're going in here to sit with Millie awhile. We'll holler at you on the way out," Aunt Belle said.

An imitation leather sofa and two chairs filled the foyer. Dusty, silk flowers hung from the ceiling in wicker baskets. A piano that I had never seen anyone play sat in the entryway. The odor of old people filled the air. Everyone knew Aunt Belle, and they waved and spoke to her as we went by. Aunt Millie was in a newer section of the nursing home. We passed through the community room, which was a gathering place for residents to watch television, visit or leave their rooms while the staff cleaned. A baseball game that no one was watching blared on the television.

Aunt Millie was diagnosed with Alzheimer's disease when we were in college. Her condition worsened until she didn't recognize anyone or remember much of her life. Uncle Nap kept a close eye on her and refused to put her in the nursing home, even after she accidentally set their house on fire. But her diabetes also gave her problems and when her leg was amputated, Uncle Nap could no longer take care of her alone. He and Bryan fixed up her room and placed family photos all around, hoping to trigger her memory. Uncle Nap visited daily. Mama, Daddy and Aunt Belle visit regularly too. Aunt Millie who didn't know anyone had many visitors. While some of the residents, whose minds were sharp, but had physical ailments, rarely had visitors.

Aunt Millie was napping when we entered her room. Her chocolate brown skin was smooth and blemish free. Beverly kept her silver-gray hair cornrowed. She was still a beautiful woman.

"Since she's sleep, let's go speak to a couple folks," Aunt Belle said.

"You and Carolyn go. I'm going to read Aunt Millie's charts and talk to the nurses to see how she's progressing," Cecelia said.

I followed Aunt Belle down the corridor. Our first stop was right across the hall. "This is your Uncle Joe," Aunt Belle said, as she hugged the fair-skinned man.

He was glad to see us and flashed a toothless smile. I was cordial while they laughed and talked, but I couldn't remember an Uncle Joe.

"Who was that again?" I asked as we left the room.

"Joe Wilson, my brother-in-law."

Aunt Belle has more in-laws than some people have relatives. I could barely keep track of her husbands. I don't know how she expected me to keep track of her in-laws too.

"You never knew your Uncle Roebuck. Joe is his brother. Roebuck was a sweet, pretty man. His people in Louisiana were part Creole. You know, his ole' mama didn't want him to marry me. She said I was too dark. But guess who take of her the last years of her life? Me and my black self, that's who. But I didn't even feel bitter, cause it made me feel like I still had a part of Roebuck here with me."

"What happened to him?" I asked.

"There was an accident at the mill. That morning, when he left for the mill, I had a feeling he wouldn't be coming home. I begged him to stay home with me, but he didn't miss no work. He usually took his lunch, but I promised to make him something special and bring it to him. I was on my way out the door with two pork chop sandwiches, an apple and an RC Cola, when I saw Beau and Mr. Moore driving up to the house. I knew what they were going to say before they got out of the car."

"How did you know Aunt Belle?"

"A woodpecker was knocking on our porch early that morning. Everybody knows that means death," she said as she took a handkerchief from her purse.

"It's still hard after all these years, isn't it?" I asked.

"We was together eighteen years and I loved him. I'm not saying I didn't love my other three husbands," she said, wiping her eyes. "Or is it four? But Roebuck was the one. We were so young. He's the only one I had children with. He was such a good man. I guess that's why I kept marrying, trying to find another Roebuck. But there wasn't no more."

"You had eighteen good years. Not many people can say that." We stopped at Miss Johnson's room, my old English teacher, but the nurse was giving her medication, so we waved and kept walking.

"I know. And it won't be long before I see Roebuck again."

"Don't say that Aunt Belle."

"Baby, I've lived my three score and ten. I'm on borrowed time. But I have a few more things left to do. One of them is find you a husband. I don't like you being alone."

"You may be able to scratch that off your 'to do' list now," I said. We stopped in Miss Green's room. The orderly said she would bring her from the community room and for us to wait. She didn't get many visitors and would be glad to see us. I explained my situation with Warren to her while we waited.

"He's not good for you," she said before I even finished my story.

"Please don't lecture me about dating a married man."

"Most folks that lecture you don't know what they're talking about. I'm not telling you what I heard, I'm telling you what I know. My third husband was married when I met him. We was both working with the NAACP and courting was the last thing on our minds. But we was spending so much time together, his wife got real jealous. A woman can nag so, she'll run her man off. Eventually we did start courting and she left him and went to Chicago. We got married and within six weeks, I knew I had made a mistake. I realized I had been with him because he was convenient and I didn't want to be alone. But believe me, alone is better than cleaning up someone else's mess. And that's what you'll be doing. Tell him to get his own place and let him get his mind and money straight before he gets with you. Then things will work out. Right now he got too much confusion in his life."

"You're probably right."

"Ain't no probably to it. And one other thing; I ain't once heard you say you love him."

"What's love got to do with it, Aunt Belle? He probably loved his wife, and see what happened to them."

"I'm talking about you, not him. You haven't had the great love of your life yet. You shouldn't settle until you find it."

Luckily, the orderly finally appeared with Miss Green. I was approaching forty with no husband, children or prospects. This didn't seem like the time to get choosy.

When we left Miss Green, Aunt Belle went to see one of her old neighbors. I headed back to Aunt Millie's room. Cecelia was sitting in the straight-backed chair, looking out the window.

"Just think, this could be us one day, sitting in an old folks home waiting for someone to come visit," I said as I came in and sat in the rocking chair.

"Speak for yourself. I intend to be one of those classy, little old ladies that strut in church and still drive. You've lost weight, that's a good step. If you want to hang with me, you need to start taking the vitamins I bought you, so your bones will be strong and your memory will stay sharp. We can be like the Delaney sisters."

"Neither of those sisters married. You have a husband, and you'll have Sheree and Mike, and probably some grandchildren to visit you. I'll be all alone."

"Carolyn, you won't ever be alone. Husband or no husband, I'll be there for you. I know we don't always see eye to eye, but---" Cecelia stopped in midsentence and walked up to the window. "Carolyn, come look at this."

I joined her at the window just in time to see a petite woman step out of Derrick's car as he held the door open for her.

"What exactly did Bucky say his plans were?" Cecelia asked.

"He said he had to come see his grandmother and maybe take her visiting for awhile. He didn't know when they would be finished and he would pick me up after he left the nursing home."

"It looks like he's done some visiting on his own," Cecelia said. "I think that's Karen Jones with him. You should go out there and confront him. Let him know you caught him in a lie."

"Why? It's not like he's my man or anything."

"I know, but you should let him know he's not as slick as he thought."

"Why bother," I said. "I don't know why he felt the need to lie. I didn't ask him to start hanging around." Aunt Belle was going to live a long time, if she was conjuring up a true love for me.

"Let's go find Aunt Belle. We have a lot of work to do this afternoon," Cecelia said. "I guess you knew what you were talking about. Beverly and I were both wrong. We were sure Bucky would be a good catch."

"Well, it looks like he's still on somebody else's line." Our circumstances may not be ideal, but at least with Warren, I knew what I was getting.

28

The banquet was the highlight of the reunion. For the first time this weekend, we were all together in the same place. Some folks hadn't made it in time for the Friday night fish fry and some skipped the picnic, claiming they couldn't take the heat. We had even gone to different churches. But no one wanted to miss the banquet.

Daddy reserved the old Lincoln High School annex for the banquet. The annex which had housed the gymnasium, science labs and home economics classes, was all that remained of the Colored high school. The other buildings mysteriously burned down when Black residents recommended that the school board reopen the vacant school as a middle school rather than build a new school in the newer, mostly white outskirts of the county. The annex was now used for Head Start classes, after school programs and storage. Since many of us were Lincoln alumni, the setting evoked fond memories.

Cecelia decorated the gym in Lincoln High School's colors. She draped the tables with gold tablecloths, and set royal blue vases filled with white and gold silk gardenias on each table. Places were reserved at the head table for Cousin Amos, who would say the opening and closing prayer, Mama Mary as the oldest family member, Mama, Daddy, Raymond, Aunt Belle, and Cousin Edward as the host committee members. Raymond was the Master of Ceremonies. My cousins Genetta and Jesse, would also sit at the head table. Even the nametags were blue and gold. Raymond did have some input on the decor and draped a kente cloth over the head table. Luckily, the cloth had blue and gold tones, so Cecelia didn't object.

Next to the head table were posters with pictures of previous reunions. The reunion had been in Orlando a few years ago. There were pictures of Aunt Ethel Fay and Uncle Henry with Mickey Mouse ears. My old boyfriend's reunion was at the same time. So I went with him to meet his parents. The last reunion was in Detroit, but I went to the Essence Festival in New Orleans. Other reunions had been in Atlanta, Milwaukee, Kansas City and Dallas. I had missed them all. I did finally spot me and a pregnant Geneva at Maywood Park in Chicago. I couldn't believe it had been twelve years since I had been to a reunion.

This may have only been the Lincoln High gym, but we dressed in our Sunday best. I finally got to wear my white silk dress. Raymond had on an African outfit and wore a kufu on his bald head. Cecelia wore a new dress she picked up Saturday in Memphis. Mama wore what she had on at church, although Cecelia did get her to spice it up with a pair of Cecelia's earrings and one of her gold bags. Daddy even had his funeral suit on.

Veronica and Jackie were the hostesses. While Cecelia and I added finishing touches to the decorations, Beverly helped Mama and Miss Emma in the kitchen. It was only five o'clock, but people were already arriving. For once 'CP' time was not the rule. As I put door prize numbers under the plates, I heard raised voices coming from the door.

Aunt Vera Mae stood at the hostess table. She possessed a regal aura and always smelled like the cosmetics section of Macy's. Everything about her was correct from her matching shoes and handbag to her perfect diction. For this occasion, she wore a sleeveless jumper made of brown and burnt orange mudcloth, gold sandals, gold bag and dangling elephant earrings. She completed the ensemble with a peach silk scarf draped around her neck. We always admired her style and tried to get Mama to jazz up her own wardrobe. She resented the comparisons to Aunt Vera Mae and we learned to tread lightly where Mama's sister was concerned. Aunt Vera Mae was my favorite because she was the only adult in the family to call me Carolyn. She taught high school in Memphis for forty years. Her husband, Uncle Ted worked at the post office. In the fifties and sixties, those professions were royalty in the black community. They never had children and lavished us with toys and clothes. Uncle Ted died ten years ago just as he was to retire.

Raymond had prepared a family tree and placed it on an easel next to the head table. The Washington family tree was an old oak with many branches and deep roots. Raymond had interviewed Mama Mary and other older residents and identified relatives back to the 1850's. My Grandfather Beau came from a family of nine children and cousins were plentiful. I spotted my place on the tree and was amazed to see the lineage that preceded me.

Mama's family tree was small like a sassafras tree. She, her sister and a few distant cousins were the only remnants of the Jones family. Technically, Aunt Vera Mae was not a member of the Washington clan, but the Washingtons didn't observe such technicalities. We were like the Mafia, once you were in, you were in for life. If you had ever been a neighbor, you were family. We even had a few double-cousins, who were related on both sides of the family. If you were an ex-spouse, we still claimed you. Cousin Larry brought his fiancée from St. Louis with him to the reunion. His first wife still lived in Eden and she came too. This made for some interesting family gatherings, and there was never a dull moment.

The voices from the door were getting louder and I saw Aunt Vera Mae shaking her finger in Veronica's face. People were lined up behind her. I grabbed Raymond and headed for the table. "I'm not going over there alone," I whispered in his ear.

"Chicken," he whispered back.

"Hello, Aunt Vera Mae, you look stunning as usual," I said.

"Oh, please drop the Mae. Aunt Vera will suffice," she said as she air-kissed me on the cheek. "Losing weight has done wonders for you. Raymond, give me a hug! I missed you at church service this morning."

"I didn't go. I had last minute preparations for the banquet," Raymond explained.

"Well you overlooked something. This child says my name is not on the list," she said, glaring at Veronica.

"Aunt Vera Mae, I've searched this list and your name is not on it," Veronica said. We definitely had the right person on the door. Veronica wouldn't admit her own mother if her name was not on the list.

"Then someone has made a mistake. I don't appreciate being detained at the door like a common gate-crasher."

"Aunt Vera, I'm sure you're right. Veronica, add her name to the list. We'll clear this up later," I said as I led her into the gym.

"Where is your mother? I want this fixed now."

"She's in the kitchen. I'm sure she'll be glad to see you."

Mama was filling tea glasses as we came in. "Hey, Vera Mae. Did you come early to help us?"

"No. I need to clear something up. My name was not on the list at the door."

"Vera Mae, you know you never sent your money. We sent notices in the mail, but you were probably on a cruise somewhere."

"I told you I promised C.W. I would be here."

"You never returned your confirmation notice, so I didn't know whether you were coming or not," Mama said.

"You should know if I said I was coming, I was coming."

"I wasn't sure if you would be able to squeeze us common relations into your busy schedule," Mama said.

"Lois, how long are you going to be mad about Mama's funeral? You know I would have come if I could have."

"I'm not mad at anyone. You and your conscience have to live with that," Mama said, placing glasses on a tray.

"My conscience is fine because I know I did all I could for her while she was alive."

Aunt Vera was in Greece last year when Grandmama Jean died. Aunt Vera said it would have cost thousands of dollars for her to arrange a last minute flight from overseas. She was on a three month, around the world cruise that was her retirement present to herself. Mama never forgave her sister for missing the funeral. And, Aunt Vera never forgave Mama for packing up Grandmama's house and belongings before she returned. She said she and Mama should have gone through their mother's things together. Their already cool relationship, turned to ice. Cecelia kept me posted on the status of the feud and thought they might make up at this reunion. If there was a chance for reconciliation, it didn't look like it was going to happen tonight. It would take a Herculean effort to get them to sit in the same room.

"You know, I'm going to be the big one and pay the seventy-five dollars. Both of us can't be petty. However, it's not what we agreed upon," Aunt Vera Mae said as she left the kitchen.

"Now Mama, don't you feel bad?" I asked.

"Be quiet and take these glasses to the tables before the ice melts," she ordered.

Despite a few more mishaps at the door with people saying they had paid and their name was not on the list, the banquet finally began. We honored Mama Mary as the oldest person present. She could be long winded, and we worried that she might get cranked up and forget to sit down. She was brief and wished everyone a long healthy life. We lit candles and Raymond read a brief eulogy of each of the family members that died since the last reunion. Jackie's youngest brother, Ricky won a prize for traveling the farthest. He came from his Naval base in Guam. Those who were at their first reunion were also recognized. All those who graduated from high school or college since the last reunion were congratulated. To my surprise, Charles was listed as having received his GED. Daddy stood for him, since he was absent and led everyone in giving him a standing ovation.

After the preliminaries, it was finally time to eat. Miss Emma, who cooks for all the funerals at church, did the catering. She outdid herself. The buffet consisted of ham, turkey, dressing, greens, corn, yams, dirty rice and potato salad. She baked a tiered cake with white frosting and blue and gold flowers. The frosting was so creamy, you could taste the butter. My Stairmaster is going to get an extra workout when I get back, I thought as I looked around to be sure Cecelia wasn't spying on me as I fixed my plate.

Midway though dinner, Cousin Genetta began her sermon. She lives in Memphis and is an Associate Minister at Beverly's church. She spoke about the prodigal son and his return home and compared his story to ours. We were all returning home to Eden, to Lincoln High and to our family's roots. She reminded us to remember the foundation laid right there in Eden. Most important, she didn't talk too long.

We had a family meeting after dinner. At the family meeting we select the next reunion site and the host family submits its report of money spent. If any money is leftover, it's submitted to the new host family for the next reunion. We also take up a collection to add to the fund.

"Could I have everyone's attention, please?" Raymond was at the microphone. "We can do this quickly and get on with the festivities. I want to thank everyone for coming. I know we have all enjoyed ourselves. I want to thank all those who helped in any way with any of the activities. I won't call names, because I don't want to leave anyone out. Except, I must recognize Miss Emma for that delicious dinner. Everything was superb, but we will have to discuss that pork." Everyone laughed at that comment. "The official family count this weekend is one hundred forty-three." Everyone clapped when he announced the number. "Some of you didn't register, I'm not calling any names, so we really had even more. The official count at the last reunion was ninety-six. This is a valuable tradition and I know the numbers will continue to grow, especially if David and Freda keep it up." Our cousin David and his wife Freda live in Eden and have eight children, with another on the way. "At this time, we will take nominations for the next reunion site."

Sacramento and St. Louis were nominated and put on the slate for the vote. Mama Mary stood and asked to speak.

Raymond held a microphone in front of her as she leaned on the table. "I cain't describe how I feel seeing all of you. Y'all know the Lord took my child, but he gave me all of you. I'll be at the next reunion even if you have it at the North Pole. The places mentioned are nice, but there's no place like home. Can we have the next reunion here in Eden again? After that the Lord will probably have called me to glory and you can go where you want." She took her seat to a chorus of "amens" and applause.

"Well, I guess Mama Mary settled it," Raymond stated. "The next reunion will be in Eden. But knowing you Mama Mary, you'll be at many more reunions. It wouldn't be the same without you. If there is no further business, this meeting is adjourned."

Cecelia, Jackie, Veronica and I cleared the tables during the family meeting. After the meeting we moved the tables and cleared space for a dance floor. Tony and Cousin Booker T. were the disc jockeys. They played a good mixture of music and kept the dance floor full. The Temptations, Lakeside and James Brown were everyone's favorites, with a few rap records thrown in every now and then. It was fun attempting to do old dances. Beverly was still the queen of the 'popcorn'. Uncle Henry was still mashing those potatoes. We coaxed Mama to the floor for the Electric Slide and Aunt Belle put her cane to the side to show us how they used to 'ball and jack'. Daddy and Uncle Nap had a card game going in the corner. The corner was also the undercover bar since liquor wasn't allowed on the premises. Daddy brought some of his homemade plum wine for the occasion. Paul was on the prowl with the video camera again.

At the official ending time of 10:00 p.m., no one was ready to leave. People gathered getting and giving the last bit of family news and hugs, before we went our separate ways. Even though tomorrow was the actual holiday, most people would be traveling on Monday.

I was ready to go, since I still had to organize Daddy's papers. I planned to finally talk to Daddy tomorrow morning about his affairs. He and Mama needed a living will. I planned to get Raymond to print one off the Internet for me. He should move most of his cash from savings accounts to money market mutual funds. And I thought Raymond should have Power-of-Attorney along with Charles. There were still some items I would have to research when I got home, but hopefully Daddy would be satisfied with my progress.

Raymond was finally able to clear the room, when he solicited help for the clean up committee. Only Miss Emma and her son Lester were left in the kitchen packing up her dishes. Raymond caught Cecelia as she gathered vases off the tables.

"Cecelia, I need you to stay and help straighten up the gym," he said.

"You must be kidding," she said as she continued clearing the tables. "I helped set up. I thought you and your kids were going to clean up."

"I let Tony take them and some other kids to Cedric's house. They said they wanted to hear some music made in this century. I figured since Michael wasn't here you wouldn't mind."

"You should have asked some of the folks that were here earlier. There shouldn't be that much to do once I pack the tablecloths and decorations. The kids and I are going to call it a night. We have a long drive ahead of us tomorrow," Cecelia said.

"Your kids are gone, too. I told Sheree and Mike they could go with the others."

"Raymond, you had no right to let them leave without consulting me," Cecelia declared. "Who is this Cedric? What do you know about his family?" Cecelia stormed off to the ladies room, shaking her head.

"I didn't think it was that big a deal. You'd think I asked her to fly to the moon," Raymond mumbled.

Beverly turned to Raymond. "Go ask Paul to help you. I'll talk to Cecelia. Don't pay her any attention."

Raymond scratched his head and turned in Paul's direction. "Man, Michael deserves a medal for putting up with my sister," he said.

"I appreciate you helping me clean up," Raymond said to Paul as they folded chairs.

"Glad to do it. Looks like your clean up crew deserted you."

"Yeah, it's hard to get good help these days," Raymond laughed. "I'm not complaining. This way we get to spend some time together before you leave."

"Yeah, you've been HNIC this weekend and I haven't talked to you much. Everything turned out great. You did a good job pulling this together. I know it wasn't easy dealing with Daddy's stroke and everything else at the same time."

"Thanks. It was worth it to see everyone together. And, I'm glad to see you haven't changed. I thought you might go 'Hollywood' on us, living out there with the stars and rich folks, especially when I heard about Julia."

Paul stopped folding chairs to ask, "What did you hear about her?"

"Nothing bad, Mama gave her a glowing report. It's just, you know, marrying a white girl seems to be the thing to do out there."

"Do you have a problem with her being white?" Paul asked.

"I don't if you don't. Just remember who and what you are."

"What does that mean?"

"It means you're a black man in America, and that ain't a safe thing to be, little brother. It doesn't matter how many degrees you get or how many white women you have, you can't escape that. As soon as you forget it, you'll be in trouble."

"I'm not trying to escape anything. Julia and I don't see race when we're together."

"Spare me the Pollyanna crap. You may not see race, but I bet she does. And I bet she also sees dollar bills. How many white women do you see with an average brother? Do you think Julia would be interested in you if you weren't driving that Lexus, and didn't have them letters behind your name? I'm not saying she doesn't care about you, I'm saying don't forget who you really are."

"I know what you're saying and I don't like it."

"See that's what I'm talking about. You're all sensitive and got your feelings hurt because I told you about yourself. You won't last very long in this world wearing your feelings on your sleeve."

"I'm not talking about the world. I'm talking about you and me, I thought you were cool about me and Julia."

"You're taking this all wrong, Paul, I have no quarrel with Julia. Just don't become one of those self-proclaimed 'colorblind' black folks. America is not colorblind."

"Raymond, my wife and I---"

"Look, I don't want to talk about you and your wife. I'm happy for you. I need to talk to you about something else. I know you and Carolyn have been looking into Daddy's affairs, and I know he's expecting a large settlement. I've already talked to Carolyn about a bank a group of us are organizing. She was noncommittal, but if you talk to her, and both of you talk to Daddy, I know he'll support it."

"Slow down, slow down. What do you mean support it? What kind of bank?" Paul asked.

"A bank that you put your money in, that's what I'm talking about. I want you and Daddy to invest in it. Most of the other organizers have their share already. I'm the smallest investor, but I have the most banking experience. I can raise my stake though, if I get help from Daddy." Raymond said softly while looking over his shoulder to see if anyone was near. "You should get some of those athletes and entertainers you know to get in on it. This is the kind of investment they need. Something that will appreciate even after their career fades. Shawn said he was interested."

"Send me a prospectus and I'll look it over," Paul said, as he began to stack chairs again.

"No, man, I have a short time line. I really need you to talk to Daddy before you leave," Raymond insisted.

"How can I do that? I can't recommend something I haven't even looked at. I wouldn't do that to any client, let alone my father."

"I can fill him in on the particulars. I need you to convince him that he's actually losing money, by letting it sit in the bank. He needs to invest it, and this isn't just for me. It's a good deal for the whole family and he will be leaving behind a great inheritance."

"I can tell him that, but I can't recommend your bank deal either way."

"You know, that's why the black man can't get ahead. How do you think the Goldbergs and Silversteins of the world made money? They helped each other. Your business may not be my thing, but I'm confident that you know your stuff so I'll invest in you and next time around you invest in me. Black folks act like they're scared of prosperity. I don't understand it," Raymond said shaking his head.

"Black folks never had much, so they try to hold on to what they have. Suggesting that Daddy put his hard-earned money in something that I wouldn't invest in would be irresponsible of me. I may invest, but I need to research everything carefully first; brother or no brother. So you can talk that black man line if you want to, I'm only telling you how I feel," Paul said walking toward the door.

"I guess I was wrong when I said you hadn't changed. I bet you'd invest if it were Julia's family, no questions asked."

Paul turned and walked back toward Raymond. "This has nothing to do with Julia. Everything is not a black vs. white issue."

"As soon as you think that, they've got you right where they want you and you're headed for misery. They may let you taste a little piece of the action, they may even let you sleep with a few of their women, but when the deal goes down, see who's on your side and see where Miss Julia sits."

Paul headed for the door again. "I'll talk to you later."

"Yeah, check you later, O.J. Washington," Raymond said.

"Well, Carolyn, looks like you and I are the clean-up crew," Raymond said as I swept the gym floor. We heard loud voices coming from the ladies room. "Cecelia must really be giving Beverly a hard time about helping with the clean up."

"This is getting embarrassing," I said. "I know Miss Emma and Lester can hear them in the kitchen."

"You better go in there," he said.

I shook my head. "Not without a bulletproof vest."

29

"Come on, Cece. Raymond worked hard on the banquet, the least we can do is help straighten this place up," Beverly said as she checked her hair in the ladies room mirror. "If we all help, we can have everything clean in no time. You'll get in before midnight and still get a good night's rest. If you leave before ten, you will have mostly day driving and get to Chicago before it gets too late," Beverly said.

"Oh, really? You don't know what I have on my agenda, so I thank you not to make plans for me. The van needs work and we're praying we make it home. I want to take the kids to visit Aunt Millie on the way out of town. Besides, Sheree hasn't been feeling well this trip. I don't want her to stay out late and overdo it, then be sick all the way home."

Beverly cut her off. "Let the child have some fun. Tony knows some girls here Sheree's age. You had your fun last night, just let her ---"

"Stay out of my business, if you don't mind," Cecelia snapped.

"Don't get touchy. I won't tell Michael. I don't blame you. Boyfriend was fine. I heard you got home at a rather late hour, or very early hour, depending on how you look at it."

"Beverly, you don't know what you are talking about."

"I say more power to you. I should find a part-time lover and let Anthony worry about keeping up with me for a change.

But don't go acting like you're so prim and proper and better than everyone else."

"I don't think I'm better than anyone, and don't spread lies about me. I don't let my children roam the streets at all times of the night. Maybe you need to get a little more control over your own son instead of worrying about my children."

"Now what does that mean?"

"Nothing. Can you take me where Sheree and Mike are or not?"

"What do you mean, control my son?" Beverly asked as she put her hands on her hips.

"I said *nothing*."

"You said nothing, but I know that's not what you meant. If you have something to say, say it."

"It's no secret that Tony has been drinking and smoking weed. He only graduated because he went to summer school. He flunked out of college and then Anthony kicked him out of the house. He came to stay with Mama and Daddy and was probably the reason for Daddy's stroke. No, I don't think I want my children to hang out with Tony or his friends," Cecelia grabbed her purse and headed for the door.

Beverly stepped in front of Cecelia, "Well someone finally said it. I knew everyone blamed Tony for Daddy's stroke. Mama said he had nothing to do with it."

"What else would she say? It's called *stress*. No one wanted to tell you that your spoiled son almost killed Daddy. What were you thinking, pawning your hard-headed, pot-smoking son on Mama and Daddy?"

"Daddy wanted him to come here. They asked me to send Tony."

"You should have said no, thank you. What made you think he would listen to Mama and Daddy when he wouldn't listen to his own parents? You know drugs are as rampant here-if not more so. You're supposed to be a parent all the time, not give up when the going gets rough."

Beverly continued to block Cecelia's exit. "I have had about as much of this that I'm gonna stand. People that live in glass houses shouldn't throw stones, *grandmother*."

My eyes grew wide at Beverly's last comment. I couldn't avoid entering the combat zone any longer. I had swept the floor outside the bathroom until it was spotless.

"What are you talking about? Move out of my way. I need to go get my kids, no telling what kind of mess your son has them mixed up in."

"Maybe he's helping Sheree pick baby names. Or maybe they're trying to decide if the kid should call you Granny, Ma'Dear or Grandmama. Which do you prefer?"

"I'm not even going to ask what you're talking about. I don't have time to listen to your rambling. Move!" Cecelia ordered trying to walk around Beverly.

"That's exactly what Sheree said. You never have time, or don't want to hear what anyone else has to say. That's why she confided in me. She couldn't talk to you."

"She couldn't talk to me about what? What did she say to you?"

"Your precious daughter is pregnant. That's why she hasn't been feeling well."

Cecelia dropped her bags on the floor. "Are you sure? Is she sure? When did she tell you this?"

"She took a home pregnancy test. She said she's missed two periods. That would make her due about January."

"January? No, she'll be in school then. This is her senior year. Having a baby is out of the question. I need to talk to her right away," Cecelia said, rubbing her temples.

"She's young, but she's old enough to take care of a child," Beverly said.

"She can't have a baby now. We'll have to take care of this."

"What do mean 'take care of this'? Don't you think this is a decision she needs to make for herself? She'll be eighteen next year."

"Beverly, I'm tired of you butting in. Sheree has always looked up to you. Your hair is always in the latest style and she thinks you are so hip or flyy or whatever word they use now. I'm trying to instill values and get her in college. You go around talking about beef and 'getting some', filling her head with romantic notions about being a single mother."

"Instead of being mad at me, you need to check yourself. I'm not the one with the pregnant daughter."

"Will you two hold it down? Your voices are echoing off the walls," I said as I stepped in the ladies room.

"Carolyn, I told her about Sheree. I didn't mean to---"

Cecelia whirled around to face me. "What the hell is she talking about? You know about this?"

"I think you need to talk to Sheree," I said.

Cecelia grabbed her purse. "You're right. Apparently she's talked to everyone but me."

I grabbed her arm. "Wait. You need to calm down. If you confront her now you may say something you'll regret."

"You have no children. What makes you think you can tell me how to talk to mine?" she said, as she walked out and slammed the bathroom door.

"Beverly, *why* did you do that?" I asked. "You have to stop her. She's too upset to talk to Sheree right now."

"I know, I know," Beverly sighed. "She was getting on my last nerve talking about Tony. He's not perfect, but her kids aren't saints either. Do you think he caused Daddy's stroke too?"

"Why bring up that old news? Daddy's fine. We need to concentrate on Sheree right now."

"You're right. I should have walked away. Now she's going to catch poor Sheree off guard."

"Well, she won't get too far," I said. "She rode with me." Beverly and I emerged from the ladies room like defeated soldiers returning from the battlefield.

"What in the world is going on?" Raymond asked, with a puzzled look.

Cecelia came back inside and marched across the gym like a woman on a mission. "Raymond, I need to borrow your car. Where did you say Sheree was?"

"Will someone tell me what happened in there?" Raymond asked.

"Don't worry about it. Arc you going to lct mc usc your car or not?"

"First you and Beverly are screaming like you're crazy. I send Carolyn to see what's wrong and the screaming increases. Now Cece is demanding my car. Whatever it is, remember why we're here. We can work it out."

"Shut up, Raymond. If you're not going to let me use your car, then go get Sheree, since you're the one that let her go in the first place."

"Raymond, please pick up Sheree," Beverly said. "Carolyn and I will take Cecelia and be at Mama's waiting for you."

"You know if we don't get this place cleaned up, we forfeit our three hundred dollar deposit," Raymond informed us.

"I don't care about your deposit. Go pick up my child."

"It's not *my* deposit. It's our deposit. I don't know who you think you're talking to, but I am not Michael. You can throw tantrums with him, but I don't want to hear it," Raymond said.

I reached for his hand. “Come on, Raymond. Beverly and I will come back and help you clean up.”

“Will you please tell me what is going on?” Raymond asked, as we left the gym.

“Sheree is pregnant and she told Beverly because she was afraid to tell her mother. Now Cecelia is upset with me and Beverly because we knew and she’s upset with Sheree for getting pregnant.”

“What? I can’t believe it. Cecelia must be devastated. Having a baby is the least of Sheree’s worries. Facing her mother will be the biggest hurdle.”

“I know. Believe me, I know.”

“What’s going on?” Sheree asked, as I opened Raymond’s car door for her. “Why does Mike get to stay and not me?”

“Your mother wants to talk to you. I know you asked Beverly not to say anything. I don’t even know how it came out, but---”

“You *told* my mother? I knew Aunt Bev shouldn’t have told you!”

“Look, I didn’t tell your mother. It doesn’t matter how she found out. We’ll be here for you. Your mother just wants to be sure you’re okay.”

The ride from Raymond’s house seemed agonizingly long and Route 4 seemed darker than ever. Aunt Belle’s prediction came true, as fat raindrops began splattering the car. We parked behind Beverly’s SUV and sat in the car a few minutes. I turned to Sheree, who was crying in the back seat. “You may as well get this over with. Let’s get in the house before the storm gets worse.”

We dashed through the storm outside, only to run into hurricane Cecelia, "Sheree, why? How could you do this?"

"Mama, don't cry."

"Why didn't you come to me?"

"I don't know. I guess I wanted to avoid a scene. I never meant to hurt you," Sheree said between sniffles.

"Your father and I have given you everything. You know how babies get here. You know about AIDS. I even offered to let you get birth control pills. What happened?"

"I couldn't talk to you about it."

"When were you going to tell me?"

"I don't know," Sheree said, as she wiped her tears with the back of her hand.

"Well, how far along are you?"

"I think I'm two months."

"Good. Then it's not too late."

"Too late for what?"

"To get an abortion of course. Surely you don't think I'm going to let you have this baby? This is not like the Barbie dolls you played with. You are talking about a person."

"We haven't decided what to do yet."

"*We*? *We* who? Have *we* decided how *we're* going to feed and clothe this child? Who's going to take care of it while you go to school, and pay for shots and hospital bills? I assume Greg is the father. And when were you and Greg going to make your big decision?"

"He doesn't want the baby. He gave me one thousand dollars to pay for an abortion." More tears dropped from Sheree's eyes.

"Well, he and I finally agree on something. You can't take care of a baby. I can't take care of a baby. And the father doesn't want it. I don't see what choice you have."

"Other people have their babies. Look at Aunt Bev. She was young when she had Tony and she's doing fine."

"She had Mama to babysit and a man who wanted to marry her."

"Mama, I don't want to kill my baby."

Cecelia cleared her throat and said in a low voice, "Wake up Sheree. You are seventeen years old, with no job and a boyfriend who's telling you he doesn't want this responsibility. They're cutting out welfare, so you can't count on that. What choice do you have?"

"Mama, how can you tell me to kill your grandchild?" Sheree cried.

"Lower your voice. I thought you didn't want a scene."

"I just want you to leave me alone. I wish I were dead."

"Sheree, baby, listen to me. You have the opportunity to be anything you want to be. We'll get the money for college. I thought you wanted to be a lawyer like Carolyn. Don't ruin your life," Cecelia pleaded.

"I can still do those things. I know it will be hard, but my life isn't over."

"I see this is going nowhere. I'm going to make an appointment for you to see Dr. Turner as soon as we get home. I will not stand by and let you fall into this trap."

"Mama, you're not listening to me. You never listen to me! Leave me alone!" Sheree cried, as the phone rang.

"Leave you alone? I'm all you got. Do you know what you're asking me to do? Your Daddy is talking about quitting his job. So who is going to take care of this baby? Me. Well, I don't think so. You'll thank me for this one day."

"No, I *won't* do it," Sheree wailed.

Raymond met Mama at the door. "What going on in here?" Mama asked. "I can hear you all the way to the road. Somebody answer the phone."

Sheree ran to Mama and hugged her waist. "Mama's trying to make me have an abortion. Do I have to?"

Mama and Daddy blinked wide-eyed, then looked at Cecelia.

"That's right Mama. It seems Sheree is going to have a baby. Or should I say she's pregnant. Because she's not going to have this baby," Cecelia stated.

"Let's not make these decisions right now. We need to pray about this. Then we'll go to bed. It will be better in the morning," Mama said, rubbing Sheree's back.

"Mama, you know, I don't feel like praying to God right now. Somehow I think he missed me while he was watching that sparrow."

"Mama's right," Raymond said. "You'll feel differently after a good night's rest. You don't really mean you want Sheree to have an abortion," Raymond said.

"Yes, that's exactly what I mean. Whether I go to bed or not, whether I pray or not, I will feel the same. Tuesday morning, Sheree and I are going to take care of this foolishness."

"I know this is not what you planned for Sheree, but our children are all we have. You are playing right into the white man's plan of genocide if you do that. Our people---"

"Raymond, spare me the brother man speech. I don't think black people need another illegitimate child that doesn't know its father. I will not let that happen to my daughter. I won't."

"Cecelia, you're only thinking about yourself. How hard it will be for you, and what you want Sheree to do. Stop being so self-centered and think about your daughter."

"How can you call me self-centered? You don't even live with your children anymore. I doubt if you would be so calm and concerned about the black race if Rayven were pregnant."

"I feel blessed that the Lord let me live long enough to be a great-grandmother," Mama said as she wiped Sheree's face. "We may think Sheree doesn't need a baby. The Lord must think so, he gave it to her. We don't always understand the Lord's plan."

"Mama, *please*! Don't go putting that on the Lord. Greg gave her a bastard and I'm going to see that she gets rid of it."

Mama slapped Cecelia. "Cecelia Denise, I can't believe my ears!" Mama said with tears in her eyes. "I never thought the day would come when a child of mine would blaspheme the Lord, and right here in my own house. You think you know more than God? Who gave you the right to decide which children are born?"

Daddy spoke for the first time. "A table or a chair is an 'it'. A baby is a 'he' or a 'she'. There will be no more talk of getting rid of babies, like she has a rash or a cold. Maybe college will have to wait. You all need to think about this and talk to Michael. Your Mama and I will help in any way we can. Don't let me ever hear you call my grandchild a bastard. That baby got me and Michael, that's plenty enough daddies. People think they can throw babies away like garbage. Not if I have anything to say about it. Your Mama and I raised eight children and none of you went hungry or naked. We made it, and Sheree will too. For now, Sheree go home with Raymond. We're all tired. Let's go to bed."

"I don't want her to leave," Cecelia cried.

"Let her go," Daddy said.

"I'm sorry about all of this. I should never have blurted it out to you like that," Beverly said as she sat on the couch.

"At least it's in the open," Cecelia said, looking out the window as Raymond and Sheree drove away. "I wonder when she was planning to tell me."

Mama stood next to Cecelia and put her arm around her. "You've probably heard us talk about my Granny. My great-grandmother often told us stories of her childhood. She was the youngest child and the first one born free. Her mother bore twelve babies and they were all sold, except Granny. We kids tried to hide whenever she came in. She always made us hug and kiss each other. She said it was a blessing to have brothers and sisters. She's probably turning over in her grave to see me and Vera Mae carrying on this way," Mama said as she shook her head.

"Did she ever try to find her brothers and sisters?"

"No. They didn't keep records on Black folk back then, and neither she or my grandmother could read anyway. Granny was born and raised in Mississippi. Her first husband was lynched, and she had to get out of town when she told the sheriff she knew who done it. That's when she came to Arkansas."

"Well, I wouldn't have kept having babies, just so the white man could take them from me. Some women threw their babies overboard the slave ships or suffocated them rather than bring them to a life of slavery," Cecelia stated as she paced the floor.

"If that had happened, my Granny wouldn't have been born. Neither would I and neither would you. We don't know God's plan. The old folks used to say; "we'll understand it better by and by." It's not the end of the world. A baby is a gift from God," Mama said softly as she patted her daughter's shoulders. "Lord, time sure is marching on. I don't feel old enough to be a great-grandmother," she laughed. "Everything will work out. You'll see. When that baby gets here, you'll be the main one trying to spoil her. But don't let Sheree pick one of them made-up names. Pick a simple name I can pronounce."

I left Mama and Cecelia in the front room and joined Daddy in the kitchen. "All this drama has given me an appetite," I said.

"Help yourself. Look in the icebox and fix you a plate. Lord knows Lois and I can't eat all this food. Once you all leave, we'll end up throwing it away. It bothers me to think somebody sweated in the hot sun, growing a crop, just for it to be thrown away. I remember we didn't used to throw nothing away. We made jelly from watermelon rinds and dumplings from chicken feet. We cooked every part of the pig except the 'oink'," Daddy reminisced. "I guess things is different now."

"Yeah, a lot of things are different. Did you feel the same way when I had the abortion?" I asked. "I know we've never discussed it, but after hearing you say those things to Sheree, it sounds like you feel I made a mistake. Do you think I threw my baby away?"

"Sometimes I think I threw him away, but I never blame you," Daddy answered.

"But I was the one that had it done," I said.

"Yeah, but I arranged it. You would never have done it if I hadn't let you. You were only a child. You didn't know what you wanted. I put my own desire and pride ahead of an innocent baby and ahead of what was best for you. You've done well, but who is to say what would have happened? That child may have been a genius."

"So you think I should have had the baby?" I asked as I searched the refrigerator.

"There's nothing we can do about it now. Life is about choices, and you have to live with the ones you make. What you done was my choice, not yours. So don't be beating yourself up about it."

"Looks like I'm not going to get that choice again. I don't think I'll ever have children."

"Don't count yourself out. You never know what's around the corner. I would rather see you by yourself than stuck with some no-count rascal like some of these gals. I'm so glad my daughters didn't get messed over. Edward's daughter Sheryl got five babies, with different daddies, and none of them belong to that man she's shacking with."

"Your daughters may be married, but I don't know how happy they are. Michael doesn't say much, but I think he's getting fed up with Cecelia's gambling and her attitude. I can't say that I blame him."

"They'll work through their problems. Married folks have ups and downs. They just have to struggle through them."

"Well, after Friday night, Beverly and Anthony are probably hanging on by a thread. I know you heard what happened," I said.

"Yeah, well that's another one of them downs I was talking about."

"Daddy, I hate to say this, but Anthony is a dog. I wish Beverly would wake up and leave him."

"That's Beverly's life. It's not up to us."

"What if I knew something that would make her leave him for sure? A secret I've kept for a long time, but that she has a right to know?"

"I would say if you've kept the secret so far, take it to your grave. Don't start no mess now. Beverly's got enough to deal with."

"But Daddy, if she knew this, she would leave him for sure," I said as I put two ribs in the microwave.

"Maybe she would, and maybe she wouldn't. It's best not to meddle in married folk's business. Let her figure it out on her own," Daddy advised. "You concentrate on Carolyn. I noticed you and Bucky been spending a lot of time together this weekend. He called you this afternoon."

"When Daddy?" I asked, trying not to sound excited.

"He called while you were at the nursing home, and he came by right after you left for the banquet. He's a nice young man."

"Don't go throwing any hints, Daddy. He's just a friend."

"He didn't look like he wanted to be 'just a friend' to me. He looked sadder than a hungry hound dog, when I told him you were gone to the banquet. Bucky's a good boy. He takes care of his grandmama and keeps her place up. He got a good job and been real helpful to the farmers around here. He don't whore around, least I ain't never heard tell of him doing nothing. I think he was married a while back, but---"

"Daddy, are you trying to match me up?"

"No, you can do your own matching. I'm only being observant," he said.

"Derrick is probably one of the most eligible bachelors around here. Why would he want me?"

"Why not you? Girl, you been bounced around so much by them jokers in Chicago, you don't recognize a good man when you see one," Daddy said as he left the kitchen.

I glanced at my watch- eleven-fifty. Maybe I should call Derrick, I thought, licking barbecue sauce off my fingers. Then I swung the other way. "Why even bother? It's obvious he's playing games, and I did not come to Eden, Arkansas to get played. But he did call. And he came by. I could call just to tell him good-bye. I'm leaving tomorrow and probably won't ever see him again. It would be nice to leave things on a positive note.

Despite being up since five a.m., I wasn't sleepy. I dialed five digits, then hung up. I dialed six digits, then hung up and cut a slice of pecan pie. Then, I dialed the seven digits.

The phone rang twice before he answered. "Carolyn, I'm so glad you called. I tried to get your attention at the nursing home, but you were already turning out of the parking lot."

"I saw you. I saw your girlfriend too," I said. "I figured she must have been who you were referring to when you said you had to go visiting."

"Carolyn, you've got it all wrong. She is not my girlfriend. I've spent the whole evening trying to catch up with you. I called you on my way to the nursing home and they said you had already left. Later, I tried to get into the banquet, but your cousin wouldn't let me in without a ticket. Now let me explain."

"Derrick, you don't owe me an explanation. I do wish you had been honest with me. You said you weren't in a relationship."

"I'm not . . . yet. Things between Karen and I have been over a long time. She called and wanted to deliver some pies to my grandmother and a few other members from her church. I picked her up and that was it. Carolyn, really, that's all there was to it. You haven't gone to bed yet, have you?"

"No."

"Then I want to come pick you up. I'd like you to come over for a while."

"I don't know if that's a good idea," I said thinking about Warren waiting for me at home.

"Why not? We're at least friends. Friends visit friends."

"Derrick, to be honest, I don't know what we are."

"Then that's why you need to come see me. So we can figure that out."

"But it's so late," I protested halfheartedly.

"Listen, I'm won't attack you. I'll be a perfect gentleman. You're leaving tomorrow and I can't let you leave without seeing you again. I'm on my way."

"No, let me drive over there. I'll take Mama's car. Tongues will wag for sure if you pick me up this late."

I tried to decide what to wear. If I changed into something too nice, it would seem that I was trying to impress Derrick. If I put on something sexy, it would be like I was expecting something to happen. What did I expect? I thought about Daddy's endorsement of Derrick. He's not wrong about too many things. Then I thought about Derrick and Karen at the nursing home and reminded myself that he was just an old friend.

30

"Charles, thanks again for the battery," Michael said. "With the air and the battery fixed, the van should make it home with no problems. We can put the battery in early tomorrow."

"Don't worry about it. They make cars these days out of plastic and you need a computer to fix anything. I'm glad to see you got an American van. They're easier to work on."

"I'll send your money as soon as we get home. I don't know what the problem was with the credit card."

Charles chuckled. "You don't have to try to fool me. I bet my sister was the problem with the credit card."

Michael hated to admit that he was right. They had an agreement. After Christmas, they took a second mortgage on the house to pay off bills, and agreed not to use the credit cards. Michael wanted to tear them up, but Cecelia said they might need them for emergencies or to travel. Michael hadn't used them all year. Cecelia paid the bills, so he assumed she was sticking to their plan as well. His futile attempt to charge his purchase at Walmart was evidence that his assumptions were wrong. He tried four credit cards and each was denied.

Michael hurdled in the house and threw open their bedroom door. Cecelia laid in bed with her face turned toward the wall. Michael turned on the light and jerked the sheet off his wife.

"Get up. We need to talk. Now."

Cecelia snatched the sheet back over her curled up body.

"I want to talk to you," he said.

"Don't you mean you want to yell at me? Will you lower your voice, please?"

"I'm not really concerned about appearances right now. I came back to surprise you at the banquet. Charles agreed to fix the van this evening. I tried to buy a sixty-dollar battery at Walmart and the Visa card was rejected. As a matter of fact, the American Express, MasterCard, and Visa Gold cards were all rejected. I borrowed money from Charles to buy the battery. What the hell have you been doing with the money?"

Cecelia's eyes remained closed.

"Answer me!" Michael said.

Michael opened her suitcase and pulled out the bags from her shopping trip in Memphis. "Why do you need more shoes?" he said as he threw them on the floor. He picked up Cecelia's Fendi bag and threw everything out as he looked for the checkbook. He opened her wallet and several ATM cash withdrawal receipts floated to the floor: Bally's, June 6, $100, Bally's June 6, $150, Trump's, June 12, $200. He threw the rest of them at her. "We took a loan on our house so you could throw money away on this? You want me to keep working, so you can keep playing with money? Have you lost your mind?"

Cecelia sobbed, "I hit a streak of bad luck. I know I sort of overdid it, but things are turning around now. I won last night."

Michael's eyelids narrowed and his nostrils flared. In an instant, he pulled Cecelia out of bed and threw her against the wall. The picture of Jesus fell to the floor. She curled up in a ball on the floor and continued to cry.

"Get up," Michael pulled her up and slammed her shoulders against the wall. He grabbed the collar of her blouse in one fist and raised his other hand, but stopped inches from her face. He stared at her, then let her go.

Cecelia collapsed on the floor and pulled the sheet over her body.

"You are so selfish. It used to be cute. You thought the world revolved around you, and because I was a part of you, that self-centeredness included your children and me. But we're not in your world anymore. You have thrown away our home and your daughter's chance to go to college."

"Sheree is pregnant. She won't be going to college," Cecelia announced.

For the first time, Michael noticed that Cecelia was still dressed. She hadn't removed her makeup and black tears streaked her face. He sat on the bed. "Pregnant? How could you let that happen?"

"Why is it my fault?" Cecelia cried.

"You're her mother. You're supposed to take care of things like this."

"How was I supposed to do that? I couldn't lock her up in the house."

"You could have paid more attention to what was going on, instead of running to the casino every chance you got. Where is she?"

"She's at Raymond's."

"Shouldn't she be with you?"

"She's mad at me and doesn't want to talk to me. Everyone seems to be mad at me."

Michael stood, straightened his clothes and pulled his keys out of his pocket. He reached for the door, then said, "I can't even use these keys because the van won't run." He threw them at her. "Maybe you can win us a new one," he said as he slammed the door.

I tried to hurry and dress and not let the voices on the other side of the wall distract me. As I searched my purse for Mama's car keys, I heard a thud on the wall and the pom poms fell to the floor. I couldn't help hearing their argument, the walls couldn't hide his yelling and Cecelia's crying. I wondered if I should play dumb and not say anything. I know husbands and wives have their problems, but I couldn't act like I didn't hear anything. I stayed in my room until I heard Michael leave the house, then stuck my head through the door. "Cece, can I come in?"

"Didn't your mama teach you to knock before you enter a room?" Cecelia asked. She stood in front of the mirror and modeled a negligee that wasn't much bigger than the price tag hanging from it.

"Did you buy that yesterday?" I asked.

"Yes. And I plan to wear it."

"I hope it does the trick. Michael sounded furious – not that I was listening."

"Please. Who's talking about Michael," Cecelia asked.

"What does that mean?"

"It means I'm tired of being the bad guy. I'll deal with Sheree and Michael tomorrow. I'm wrong for wanting my daughter to go to college and not be saddled with an illegitimate baby. I'm wrong for not wanting my husband to quit his job. I work sixty hours a week and I'm wrong because I go to the casino occasionally. I try to talk to my daughter and instead of supporting me; everyone acts like it's no big deal for a teen-age girl to have a baby. Even Raymond turned on me, after I bugged Geneva for weeks to let me bring his nappy-headed kids down here. Well, I'm going to start putting Cecelia first for a change," she said as she packed the negligee in her Dior bag.

"Cece, I'm afraid to ask what you're talking about."

"I'm talking about life passing me by. I have done everything I was supposed to do. I sat through the dumb Brownie and Girl Scout meetings. I was Team Mom for softball, soccer and basketball. I breast-fed and I have the droopy titties to prove it. I supported Michael through two career changes and two restructurings. What thanks do I get? My daughter who has never worked a day in her life is pregnant. She wants to keep the baby although neither she nor the father has any visible means of support. I am broke. My marriage has fallen apart, and I'm too old to start dating. At least I thought I was until I met Maurice. Being with him reminded me that I still matter. So don't give me a hard time. If I was Beverly, you'd tell me to go for it."

"I don't know what to say. I had no idea you were so unhappy. You've been kind of moody. I thought maybe it was the change. Is there anything I can do?" I asked.

"Actually there is. I know you're talking to Daddy about his affairs. And I know Daddy's expecting a lot of money from some lawsuit. I need you to convince him to sell out. He and Mama can't keep this place up. If he sold now and distributed everything, it would avoid confusion later. Michael and I are in a financial bind, and I don't know if our marriage will survive if we don't get past it," she said while she reapplied her eye makeup.

"I didn't know things were that bad."

"Why do you think we drove down here? We couldn't afford to fly. We can't seem to catch up. We saved a little bit, then we had to get a new roof. Our mortgage is behind and Sheree is talking about having a baby. We can't afford the kids we have, let alone another mouth to feed. Michael is determined to quit his job. Now the van is broke down. It's always something."

I wanted to say, "It's always the casino," but she already felt bad. No way should they have money problems with their salaries. I know Michael feels the same way because I heard him through the paper-thin walls.

"Cece, I'm sure Daddy would help you if you asked him. He probably thinks you're doing great, like I did."

"I don't want special favors. It makes more sense to do it this way. We could all use the money now. Why wait? Daddy should enjoy his money and we should too. We are working ourselves into our graves, waiting for the sweet ‘by and by’. Well, not me. Starting right now, I’m going to stop letting life pass me by,” she said as she applied lipstick.

“Cece, you know you shouldn’t go meet that man. You have a good husband, and he loves you. Don’t make a bad situation worse.”

“You’re an expert on children, but you don’t have any. You’re giving marriage advice and you didn’t stay married long enough to change your name. If you want to help, talk to Daddy. That’s what you can do for me,” she said and walked past me out of the door.

31

Derrick was standing in the door as I drove up. Years ago Mama would send me to his house to relay a message about church business or to fetch Paul. There were only two of them in that big house. They each had a bedroom and they even had a guestroom. We had four times as many people in the same amount of space. As with most things in Eden, time seems to have shrunk them. It wasn't the mansion I remembered, but it was still a nice house.

"You took so long, I thought you changed your mind. Have a seat," Derrick said as he moved pillows to clear a space on the plastic-covered couch. "My grandmother is a pack rat. She took a bunch of things to the nursing home and the house is still crowded. The doctors said she won't be able to live alone again, so I'll probably sell this house and give this old stuff away."

"Don't you dare. What you call 'old' others call 'quaint.' You should go in those antique shops on Main Street and see the prices they ask for things like this. You could be sitting on a gold mine," I said.

"I thought furniture had to be really old to be considered antique."

"It depends on the piece and the condition it's in. Your grandmother was like my mother and saved all her good things. Since there weren't a lot of people running around here, I'm sure everything is in mint condition. An antique dealer will come to your house or you can even post items on auction sites on the Internet. You may have a piece that isn't worth much alone, but it could be the missing item to complete someone's set. Would you mind showing me around? I love looking at antiques. It's like discovering valuable gems everyone else has overlooked."

Derrick showed me around the house. I had never been farther than the living room before. The house was an antique lover's dream. We opened two trunks filled with handmade quilts. "These are worth at least $ 500 apiece, maybe more."

"They're made of rags," Derrick said.

"That may be, but quilting is a dying art. Mama and Aunt Belle used to make them, but they both complain about arthritis now and don't quilt much anymore. You should get some plastic to put them in to better preserve them."

I inspected the curio cabinet and noted several vintage salt and pepper shaker sets with Aunt Jemima and watermelon-eating children caricatures. "These are very rare, they're the originals, given away by Quaker Oats in the 1940s. In Chicago you could get hundreds of dollars for these."

"For real? I hated those things because they made the black people with big red lips and bandanas," Derrick said.

"They aren't very flattering, but it's a part of American culture. We just need to have the last laugh and not throw these things away because we don't recognize their value."

"I'm impressed. You're very knowledgeable about this stuff. Have you ever thought about doing it for a living?"

"I thought about it. Then I decided I like to eat, so I stayed with Uncle Sam."

"Well, you talk about going to antique shops and shows, so somebody is making some money at it. Why not you? The fact that you have a business background would work in your favor. I want you to pick something out to take home with you."

"I couldn't take your grandmother's things."

"She won't mind. She would love for someone who appreciates her things to have them. I only have one request. Don't take a piece and put it away. Pick a piece that you will display and look at everyday, so you will think of me whenever you see it."

"Derrick, I don't know what to say."

"Don't say anything." Derrick took my hand and led me to the couch. I sat, and then stood up again right away.

"Carolyn, I don't mean to move too fast. But after tomorrow you'll be gone. And I---"

"That's exactly right. We've had a great weekend and could top it off with a great night. But I can't do a one night, or in this case a three-night stand. Even though we didn't just meet, it would be the same thing. I'm not trying to 'get my groove back' on a vacation fling."

"I'm not thinking of this weekend as a fling, Carolyn. I have had flings, stands, exclusive relationships and casual friends. I could never put my finger on what I was looking for, but I knew I would recognize it when I saw it. Well, I'm looking at it."

"Derrick, you and I haven't seen each other in years. We've both changed and grown. Even if there was a possibility of a relationship between us, we need more time to get to know each other. You can't do that from five hundred miles away. Besides I thought you were seeing someone."

"I already told you, that's history. Paul told me you're free, so the timing is perfect."

"You discussed me with Paul?"

"I asked a few questions. I found out enough to know that you're dating someone, but it's not serious."

"Sounds like you asked more than a few questions," I said.

"Let's me ask you, is it serious? Do you have a man waiting for you in Chicago?"

I thought about Warren. On Sunday evenings he and Terri usually went to his mother's house. How would that work if he and I were together? Would Warren and his boys go, or would I be invited? Was I now expected to act like a mother? I always said I would never live with a man again. Did he expect to stay at my place permanently, or was this just until he found his own place? Was Warren now 'my man'? He didn't sound like he was interested in marriage again. Maybe he and Terri had reconciled since I talked to him. There was 'a man' waiting for me in Chicago, but I wasn't sure he was 'my man'. Was Warren ready to commit to me, or was he confused like Aunt Belle said? Maybe, I was the confused one.

"If it takes you that long to answer, I'll take that as a 'no'. Carolyn, I've never felt like I belonged with someone. It's so easy to be with you."

"That's because we're practically brother and sister," I said.

Derrick stood and placed my arms around his neck. He placed his finger under my chin and gently kissed me. "What I'm feeling is definitely not brotherly."

No, it wasn't a brotherly kiss. I had to will myself to step back from him.

"You say you've had all types of relationships, well I have too. They all start out this way; sweet words and lust. But it doesn't last. I'm tired of playing the game."

"Carolyn, I wouldn't waste my time or yours playing games. I want to know everything about you and spend more time with you. It's as simple as that."

"But it's not that simple. How are we going to spend more time together when I live in Chicago?"

"We can work around that. The flight from Memphis to Chicago is less than two hours. I don't mind collecting frequent flyer miles," he said, with a smile.

"Derrick, long distance relationships never work."

"Anything can work if you put forth the effort. Don't be so negative. Maybe, I've misinterpreted everything. I thought you were interested in me. I don't have a big bank account. I'm not a lawyer. I'm not from the big city. But I'm honest and hard-working, and I even have good credit."

"Your job and money don't matter. I do like you, Derrick. I like you a lot. To tell you the truth, you seem perfect, so I figure there must be a catch."

"There's no catch. What you see is what you get. No, I take that back. You'll get much more."

"Derrick, this is crazy. I can't believe we're even having this conversation."

"From the moment I saw you at your mother's house, I haven't been able to think of anything else. I'm usually very cautious with women, but I couldn't let you leave town without telling you how I feel."

"Derrick, I don't know ---"

"Look, you're making this more complicated than it has to be. I like you and you like me. That's a start. We'll just see where things go from here. Deal?" Derrick asked while extending his right hand.

Talk about bad timing. I've been unattached for years. Now there were two men interested in a relationship. But even though Warren had moved himself into my house, I didn't see any rings on my fingers. "Deal," I said.

I extended my hand, and planned to work out the details later. But rather than a handshake, he pulled me in his arms.

"Besides, it's not everyday you run into a woman that can bait her own hook," Derrick said while nibbling on my ear. "Now that we got all of that out of the way. I seem to remember you saying you like to discover gems. I have something that's not worth much alone, but I think you can complete the set."

I stepped out of his reach. "Derrick, this is a little too fast for me. How do I know this isn't some smooth rap you use all the time?"

"I know better than to try that with you. For one thing, your father and all your brothers know where I live. I don't want those Washington men hunting me down. And I *really* don't want Beverly after me, I've heard she has a quick trigger finger. Listen, I'm not pressuring you for sex, although I'd be lying if I said it wasn't on my mind. A lot. But I can wait. I've waited twenty years, I suppose I can hold out a little longer."

I picked up my keys and walked toward the front door. Derrick held his hand out and opened the door for me. "On the other hand, why wait if we already know what we want?" he said and grinned, showcasing his perfect teeth.

My mind quickly raced through the pros and cons. Derrick was attractive, available, employed, independent, responsible and a good kisser. The cons … I stepped back inside and closed the screen door. "You may just have the piece to complete my set. I hope you have something to protect those gems."

Independence Day

32

Paul and Julia checked out of the motel before dawn and stopped by the house en route to the airport. He planned to leave an envelope in the mailbox, but C.W. was already sitting on the porch drinking coffee.

"Daddy, we're going to leave early and catch the 8:30 flight back to L.A.," he said.

"I thought you weren't leaving until this evening. You want Lois to fix you some breakfast?"

"No, we'll grab something on the way. I just wanted to drop a little something off for you two before we left," Paul said as he handed his father the envelope.

"Take it in to your Mother. I'll never hear the end of it if I let you get away from here without telling her goodbye."

Paul beckoned to Julia to come to the porch before he went to his parent's room. He leaned over and kissed his mother's forehead.

"What are you doing, boy?" she asked groggily.

"I didn't mean to wake you, but I couldn't leave without kissing my favorite lady."

"What do you mean, leave?" she said as she sat up. "Why so early?"

"We changed our reservation to the first flight. We both have a lot of work to do back home." He took three hundred-dollar bills out of the envelope and handed them to her. "You and Daddy buy yourself something nice."

"Thank you, baby, that's so sweet. I would tell you to keep your money, but I know you won't. I also know you're not leaving to go do any work. Don't let what happened this weekend run you off. This is still your home."

"I know. I'm just tired of all this bickering. Both Charles and Raymond are mad at me. Carolyn won't say two words to my wife. Cecelia is ready to abort Sheree's baby herself. This weekend has been more like a family feud than a family reunion."

"Can't say that I blame you. I hope Julia doesn't think we carry on like this all the time. I sure do hate to see my children all torn apart, and I definitely don't want your father upset."

"Don't worry, it'll be okay. Maybe we had too much togetherness this weekend. To make things easier, you can leave me out of the will. You and Daddy have already given me more than I can repay. Julia and I will be fine. Carolyn's alone and I think Cece's having money problems. They need it more than I do. I won't feel bad at all. I'm just proud to be your son. I'm betting that you'll both live to be at least 100, so all of this uproar is for nothing." Paul hugged his mother one more time before he left the room.

Julia and C.W. were deep in conversation and didn't hear Paul coming. "I guess it's time for us to hit the road, Daddy," Paul interrupted.

"So, your Mother wasn't able to talk you into staying?" C.W. asked.

Mama appeared at the doorway, tying the belt around her pink flowered housecoat. "No, he's ready to get back to the big city. You two take care of . . . each . . . other," she advised between sniffles. She then disappeared from the doorway.

"Your Mama doesn't handle good-byes well. She has to have a good cry, then she'll be okay."

"Thank you for everything, " Julia said.

"Thank you for being a good wife to my son. And I'll remember what you said. You all get on your way so I can go check on your mother. Come back soon." C.W. stood on the step waving, as their taillights disappeared into the rising sun.

"I hope I'm not coming between you and your family. It's hard to believe people are still hung up on race," Julia said as they passed Booker T's barbeque stand.

"We've never run into a problem in California," Paul said. "Or am I really out of touch? Maybe I've been too self-absorbed to notice." This worried Paul. Just because he didn't wear a kufu and quote Malcolm, like Raymond, didn't mean he wasn't aware of his roots. That was part of the reason he chose law and worked for a black firm. Was it hypocritical, like Carolyn said, to extol the virtues of the black woman, yet still be attracted to the 'forbidden fruit?' Was he talking black and sleeping white?

Why am I tripping? he thought. Am I supposed to say, Julia you would be the perfect woman for me if you weren't white?

"I'm sorry things turned out this way," Paul said as they sped past an exit sign. "Raymond is a little overzealous, but his heart is in the right place. You're not saying it, but I know you're thinking 'I told you so', and that you shouldn't have come."

"No, I wasn't thinking that at all. I was thinking about your father's estate."

"Ah-ha, now the truth comes out. You married me for my money," Paul teased.

"Very funny. Listen, I thought of a way for your father to settle his affairs without pitting you all against each other. I'm sure there's a bank close by with a trust department. He can put the assets in a trust and stipulate how he wants them managed and how the income should be distributed."

"You're right. I had no idea Daddy's estate was so sizable, or I would have suggested it earlier."

"With a trust, your father can dictate how the money is spent and invested. You can set it up for one year or one hundred years. You have to pay a fee, but it's better than you all trying to manage things from Chicago and California and wondering what Charles is doing with the money. I'm sure the increased income would offset the management fee."

"I'll call Carolyn from the airport and mention it to her. Brains and beauty too. How did I get so lucky?" Paul said as he patted Julia's leg.

Paul looked in his rear view mirror to see a sheriff's car closing in on his bumper. "Looks like my luck is about to run out."

"Were you speeding, honey?" Julia asked as she turned around to see the flashing lights.

"No, I'm sure I wasn't," he said double-checking his seat belt.

Paul pulled the car over and rolled the window down, as Sheriff Rhodes took his time walking to the car.

"You're out pretty early, aren't you, son?"

"Yes sir. We're headed to the airport in Memphis."

The officer looked them over. "Let me see your license and registration," he said as he turned his head and spat.

"You from California, huh? What're you doing around here?"

"Visiting my parents. Is there a problem, officer?" Paul was starting to get irritated, thinking this was not a routine traffic stop.

The sheriff ignored his question and headed back toward the police car.

After fifteen minutes, Paul turned off the car and rolled down the windows. Cars whizzed by.

"Why do you think he's taking so long?" Julia asked.

"I think he saw a black man in a fancy car and decided to stop him. Then when he stopped him, he saw a white woman and decided to mess with him. Now he knows he's made me mad, and thinks I'll come back there and start something. Then he can take me back to the county seat and hold me for questioning. It's a little game they play down here. They pull this crap all the time. I don't see how Raymond lives here."

"If he doesn't hurry up, we're going to miss our flight," Julia said. "You know there's extra security at the airport because of the holiday. Should I go ask him if there's a problem?"

"That's what I need, my wife going to meet the man for me. No, you stay here. I'll go talk to him. Keep the doors locked."

Paul got out of the car and went to the Sheriff's car and knocked on the passenger side window. "Is there a problem sir? We're trying to catch an early flight."

"Go back to your car. I'm waiting for the DA to call me back."

"What do you need the DA for?"

"I need to search that car. There have been quite a few drug busts in the surrounding counties lately and we've had word to watch for out-of-town licenses," the sheriff said.

"This is ridiculous. You have no reason to suspect me of drug trafficking. Do you stop every car that passes? I grew up only 40 miles from here, and this is a rented car."

"Hold on now. Go wait in the car with your little lady. It's a holiday and it may take him a while to answer his page."

"We've already waited almost thirty minutes. We have a plane to catch. Is your department going to reimburse me for the tickets if I miss my plane? Does your department have extra money sitting around for a harassment lawsuit? I was not speeding and I won't be intimidated. If a light or something is out on the car, give me the ticket and I'll give it to Best Rent-A-Car. Otherwise, it's been nice talking to you, but I'm leaving."

The sheriff got out of his car and walked to the passenger side. He got up in Paul's face and spoke softly. "Boy, if you leave here without my consent, I'm going to arrest you for interfering with an investigation."

Paul felt the heat rise around his temples. His mind flashed back thirty years. He could remember his father being arrested on trumped-up charges. Daddy spent one night in jail, but Uncle Nap got him out. When he casually remarked how thoughtful the officer was for keeping the sheriff's wife company while he was out of town, they miraculously dropped the charges. This was why I became a lawyer, Paul thought. People are always twisting the law to their advantage and the black man is always on the short end of the twisting. He'd considered practicing in Arkansas, but decided to settle in L.A. after visiting a fraternity brother. He managed to put all that old stuff in the back of his mind and believe things were different. Obviously, this clown missed the civil rights movement.

"Excuse me. I am six feet two and I weigh 200 pounds. Do I look like a boy to you? " Paul's voice was rising. "If you see a boy, you---"

"What's going on, Sheriff Rhodes? Is Paul having a problem here?" Raymond interrupted as he walked to the police car.

"Hey, Ray, what you doing out this way?" the sheriff asked.

"I was headed to the airport, to catch my brother. Looks like you already caught him."

"This here's your brother, huh? Well, I guess I don't need to wait for that phone call. I know your people wouldn't be mixed up in no trouble," the sheriff said. "You all be careful, the roads are slick from the rain. Have a nice holiday, Ray."

The sheriff got in his car, turned around and headed back toward Eden. Raymond waved.

"What just happened here? One minute he was ready to get the rope, the next minute he's gone," Paul asked.

"It's part of the scam. He shakes down people with out-of-state licenses. Then promises to dismiss the traffic violation for a small fee."

"He shakes down black people with out of state licenses, you mean. I was this close to---"

"This close to what, going to jail?"

"It would have been bogus and you know it. He had nothing on me."

"That doesn't mean he wouldn't have taken a day or two before he *decided* he had nothing on you. This is not L.A. Nobody's standing around with a video camera. Johnnie Cochran is not here to plead your case. They don't care that you graduated *cum laude* from Tennessee State University, or that you're the youngest partner in your firm. In fact, they probably resent it. This is cracker capital and you still got to play by their rules."

"Let me check my hearing. This can't be Revolutionary Raymond formerly known as Malik Asim I'm talking to. I never expected to hear that nice Negro talk from you."

"I'm not saying he doesn't have a sheet in his closet. I'm not saying we roll over either. We need to pick our battles. Let's say he and I have an understanding and don't cross each other. Look, I don't want to waste time talking about him. What time is your flight?" Raymond asked.

"We planned to catch the eight-thirty flight because the next nonstop isn't until five this evening. The others lay over in Dallas or St. Louis," Paul said looking at his watch.

"It's almost seven, you might make it in time if you put the pedal to the metal. But you've had one run in with the sheriff this morning; you probably shouldn't press your luck. They're really strict about speeding over holiday weekends. I felt bad about you leaving, man. I didn't want things between us to be messed up like that. When Daddy said I had missed you, I headed this way hoping to catch you before you got to the airport. I'm sorry for pressuring you about the bank investment."

"No problem. If you can't nag your relatives, who can you nag? Besides, I know you can get carried away at times."

"Really? That's what Geneva says."

"She's right."

"I'm afraid she's been right about a lot of things. She said my move down here was selfish and I wasn't thinking about Rayven and Malcolm. I think what hurt Cecelia the most was that Sheree felt she couldn't talk to her. I want my kids to know they can come to me. I'm convinced I need to be with them."

"Are you going to ask Geneva for joint custody?"

"No. I'm going home," Raymond said as he waved to a car passing by.

"To Chicago?"

"Yep."

"I thought Chicago was driving you crazy. I thought you loved your new house and being with Mama and Daddy."

"I do, but I need to be with *my* family more. Geneva and I talked this weekend. I think we can work things out."

"What about your plans for black empowerment and opening a bank and lobbying with the BFA?"

"I can lobby in Chicago. I can probably also get investors for the bank in Chicago. But right now, the best thing I can do for the black race is to raise my kids and love their mother. I'm going home. Why don't you take the later flight and let me take you and my sister-in-law to breakfast? Or better yet, come on back and get a fresh start tomorrow. We never did go visit Carl, and you know your crazy sisters will be highly upset if you sneak off without saying good-bye."

Paul gave Raymond one of those quick hugs and pats on the back that men give each other. "Julia and I will follow you," Paul said.

"Stay at my house instead of the motel. You'll still get a chance to see the fireworks tonight."

"That's what I was trying to avoid," Paul said.

33

"Chubby, get up!" Mama said shaking me urgently. I struggled to pry my mascara crusted eyelids open. I had crawled into bed without removing my makeup and it seemed like I had only been asleep a few minutes, when Mama woke me up.

"Chubby, it's Sheree," she said, jerking the pillow from under my head.

"Is she calling again? Tell her to call---"

"They've taken her to the hospital. Tony went in her room this morning and found her on the floor".

"Cecelia mentioned that Sheree has been sickly all weekend. I hope nothing is wrong with the baby," I said.

"It's not the baby. Tony said he found an empty medicine bottle and white pills strewn across the floor. He thinks she took an overdose of something. He said he tried to call us earlier and the line was busy. But no one would be on our phone at that time of the morning, so it must have been off the hook. He phoned Charles and Brenda and they told him to call 911. The ambulance came and they're at the hospital now."

I sat straight up. "What kind of pills? Is she going to be all right?"

"I didn't get all the details, and I can't find anybody. Nap just took your Daddy to the hospital. Raymond's not at home and Beverly has that doggone machine on. I called Michael's mama, and he wasn't there. Cece's not in her room and she didn't stay at Mama Mary's. Where is she?"

"I don't know. Last night when she left I thought she was going over Raymond's to talk to Sheree," I said, hoping Mama's lie detector antennae weren't activated.

"Cece never came back last night," Mama said, pacing the floor. "I've called everywhere. Lord, please don't let anything happen to my children. I'm going to make some more phone calls. Hurry and get ready to go."

Dazed by Mama's news, I wondered if this could all be my fault? The last time I heard Sheree's voice, she was begging me to come get her. The phone had rung as I was getting in bed. I quickly answered, thinking it was Derrick.

"Aunt Carolyn, please come get me," she pleaded.

"It's four o'clock in the morning, honey. What's wrong?" I asked.

"I need to get out of here. I just called Greg's apartment and a girl answered the phone. He told me we were through and hung up. When I called back, he wouldn't answer." Sheree was crying and I could barely understand her. But I did understand that I didn't need to get in her business anymore than I already was.

"Sheree, I know you feel like you haven't got a friend in the world. Sweetie, you have to accept the fact that Greg doesn't feel the same way about you, that you feel about him. Plenty of boys will jump at the chance to have a smart, pretty girl like you. You may not think you can talk to Cecelia, but you really need to talk to your mother. She only wants what's best for you. If I come over there, she'll be mad at me for butting in."

"Forget it. I guess you wish I would disappear. Sorry to be a bother," Sheree snapped.

"You're not a both---" The phone clicked in my ear before I could finish. In my day, that would have been considered rude, I thought as I turned over.

That was my last conversation with Sheree. If something happened to her or the baby, I won't be able to live with myself. Why didn't I go over there? I should have been honored that she felt close enough to me to talk to me. I know how Cecelia is. I hate telling her my problems; I can imagine how Sheree feels. I ignored her cry for help because I was too tired from staying out with Derrick.

It was nearly four a.m. when I got back from Derrick's house. I still can't believe things are happening so fast. I was in Derrick's old bedroom, looking into his eyes as he unbuttoned my blouse, when he sensed something was wrong.

"Is everything all right?" he asked.

"I hope it will be," I said, wondering how he knew to kiss my earlobe.

"What do you mean by that?"

"Derrick, you are almost too good to be true. I know it's not fair to judge you by my experiences with others. But I can't help it. I don't mean to be a tease but my mind is telling me to be smart. Believe me, my body is not in agreement, but I think this is one argument, my mind should win." My mind was also telling me I should get things straightened out with Warren. Aunt Belle said Warren was confused. Right now, I was the confused one.

"I'm sincere, and I will feel the same whether we have sex or not. But I see you're not certain, so we can wait. I'm not just trying to get in your pants. I plan to be in your life for a long time." Derrick buttoned my blouse and kissed my forehead. "At least I got a peek at coming attractions," he said and smiled.

We watched an old movie on television, then I came home. He insisted that I call to let him know I made it home safely and we talked another hour. My parents view call waiting as an extravagance, so Tony couldn't get through when he called. Lord, please, let Sheree pull through this, I prayed while grabbing my reunion T-shirt and shorts. I dressed quickly then met Mama on the porch.

She squeezed my hand as we dashed to the car. We rode in silence, and waited impatiently as what seemed like the longest train in the world crawled by. The hospital was a few miles away in Johnson County and I prayed that the sheriff wouldn't stop me. We finally arrived and ran to the Emergency Room. They directed us to the intensive care unit. As soon as the elevator opened, Charles and Brenda rushed to meet us. Brenda was dressed in a faded paisley housecoat with a striped scarf covering her hair. Anthony and Beverly were right behind them.

"How is she?" Mama and I asked at the same time.

"They say she's holding her own. But they won't tell us anything. They want to talk to her parents. Where are they?" Brenda asked.

"I don't know," I said. "Cecelia left in a huff last night. Michael said he was going to see his mother, but Mama couldn't reach him there."

We were standing outside Sheree's room, when Cecelia, Michael and his mother, stepped off the elevator. Aunt Belle had tracked them down. Cecelia had gone to Pine Bluff to apologize to Michael and they decided to stay at a motel and make up. Mrs. Brown and Mama both started crying when they saw each other and rushed to hold hands. Cecelia discarded her professional bedside manner and cried hysterically, "Where is she? Where's my baby?"

I took her hand and led her to Sheree's bed. Without makeup, Sheree looked like the kid, I guess we all thought of her as. She should be trying to decide which color nail polish to wear, or how to arrange her CDs, not whether or not to have her baby. I kept wondering why I didn't respond differently to her cry for help. Why didn't I recognize how despondent she was?

The doctor finally came and asked all of us to come to the sitting room. "Sheree is severely anemic and her blood pressure is low," he said while reading her chart. "We are concerned because the medicine she was given in the emergency room to counteract the effect of the pills, could put the fetus in distress. The paramedics didn't know she was pregnant when they gave her the medicine. We will be running several tests. We will upgrade her condition from critical to serious, but she is still very sick. Our focus right now is on stabilizing her blood pressure. We can't yet determine if there has been damage to the fetus. Our first priority is to save the mother."

Michael was crying uncontrollably and Daddy led him to a corner of the room.

We were all in shock, trying to comprehend the doctor's message. At the ring of the elevator, we looked up to see Raymond, Paul and Julia. Raymond rushed to Cecelia with outstretched arms.

Cecelia stepped back from his advance. "Why weren't you there?" she shrieked. "I said I didn't want Sheree to stay with you and now look what happened!"

Paul took Cecelia's hand. "You don't mean that. You're being unfair to Raymond."

"I left to go clean the gym. She was fine when I left. I... I don't know what to say," Raymond said as his eyes watered. He turned and walked down the hall.

I looked around and saw Michael with Cecelia, Paul with Julia, Charles with Brenda and Mama with Daddy. I was feeling left out and went to find Raymond. He was at the end of the hall talking to Geneva on his cell phone. I went to the pay phone and called Warren. He was in a rush because he was joining his boys at Terri's parents house for a cookout. I thought about my sister's predictions concerning who a man spends his holidays with as I headed back to the waiting room.

Brenda took her keys out of her housecoat pocket. "Since all of you are here, I'm going back to the house. We left in such a rush I didn't lock up or dress." Brenda walked up to Cecelia. "I know we said some harsh words yesterday, but I want you to know I'm praying for Sheree. Despite our differences, we're still family and if I can do anything---"

Cecelia cut her off. "No, we are not family. You are my brother's second wife, and there is nothing you can do for me. Less than twenty-four hours ago, you were ready to steal Sheree's birthright from her. Now you're acting so concerned. You know, that's exactly what you said when Daddy was sick. If you could help in any way . . . You helped all right, helped yourself to his money."

"Cecelia, don't bring that up here," I said.

Brenda waved her hand. "That's quite all right, Carolyn. That's her problem. This wouldn't have happened if she wasn't so busy counting C.W.'s money and had been paying more attention to her child."

"How dare you judge me," Cecelia shouted. "I pay plenty of attention to my children, and I'm going to be paying attention to you too.

"We just saved your daughter's life and instead of falling on your knees to thank us, you're talking about money. No wonder the child is so unstable."

"Both of you need to hush," Mama ordered. "This is not the time or the place."

"I'm sorry Mama, but I can't stand her phony act. She doesn't give a damn about---"

"I'm going to have to ask you all to hold it down, please." A stern-looking nurse came over to us with her finger over her lips.

"Let's go to the waiting room," I said. "You all are creating a scene out here in the hall."

Michael looked up as we entered the waiting room. "Brenda, I want to thank you. If you and Charles hadn't helped Sheree . . ." He turned and put his head in his hands.

"I'm glad to see Sheree has at least one concerned parent," Brenda sniped.

"Brenda, that was uncalled for. You know Cecelia is upset," I said.

"She's upset because she thinks she's going to miss out on some money."

"This is not the time or the place to go into that Brenda. Didn't you say you were leaving?" I said.

"Don't get an attitude with me. Charles has done everything around here, from seeing after C.W. and Miss Lois to saving his wayward nieces and nephews. Now you come down here and try to take over. Sheree called you last night, and you didn't have time. I suppose you were too busy plotting how to shut Charles out?" Brenda said.

"Charles isn't worried about anybody cutting him out. He's taking care of himself quite well. Isn't that right," I asked. "Charles, tell Daddy how you---"

"Sheree called *you*? Why did she call you?" Cecelia cried. "Why won't she come to me? And how could Raymond leave those kids?"

"Cecelia, be quiet. Shut up. Shut up! Shut up!" Michael screamed.

"Stop it. Stop it right now," Mama said. "All of this mess has nothing to do with praying that little girl gets better. I'm ashamed of all of you."

"Mama, you don't understand what's going on," I said shaking my head.

"Well, I understand," Daddy said, rising to his feet. "You all are fighting because you think I got some money and you're trying to beat each other out of it. Where would an idea like that come from, Chubby?" Daddy gave me a look I hadn't seen in years. The look was usually a precursor to a severe whipping, punishment and lecture. He didn't give the look often. We knew not to push him that far. This time it was too late.

The stern nurse opened the door, flanked by a burly security guard. "I'm sorry, I'm going to have to ask you all to leave. You're disturbing the patients."

"You can't do that!" Cecelia shouted.

"I don't believe this," I said. "We're very upset, we'll be quiet," I said.

"I'm afraid you've been too disruptive. Her parents can stay. The rest of you will have to wait in the lobby downstairs."

"I just rode an hour to get here. I'm not going anywhere," Mrs. Brown declared.

"Lois, you and Juel stay here. Raymond, stop downstairs at the pharmacy and pick up my prescriptions. The rest of us will wait at the house. Carolyn, I'll ride with you," Daddy said, still giving me the look.

"Daddy, you probably need to eat something. Do you want to stop and get breakfast?" I asked as we got in the car.

"No. Let's go home. We should stay close to a phone."

"Daddy, I know you told me not to say anything to anybody."

"Then why did you?"

"I only told Paul because he was helping me look some things up at the courthouse. You gave me more work than I anticipated. Then Cecelia overheard us talking. Paul told Julia to explain to her why he wasn't going to Graceland. Then Julia told Brenda because she didn't know it was a secret. Then Beverly busted in my room while I was working on your papers. One thing led to another and before I knew it things had gotten out of control. I am so sorry," I said as we headed home.

"Drive out to the old house for a minute," Daddy ordered.

"Now? I think we should---" I stopped in midsentence, since Daddy was giving me the look. Many houses along the highway displayed American flags. More than a few also sported Confederate flags. We had to slow down as we ran into the Dwight County, Fourth of July parade down Main Street. With all of the activity surrounding Sheree, I had forgotten today was a holiday. It was still early, but the aroma of barbeque was already in the air. Mama Mary's dog barked as we drove up. There was a narrow dirt road behind her vegetable garden that led to the old house that Daddy grew up in. The road was now overgrown and after the rain last night, was little more than a muddy path. The house was a weathered shotgun shack, with a tin roof, and the outhouse was covered with kudzu. In the winter, you could see them from Mama and Daddy's back porch if you knew where to look.

Daddy got out of the car and headed for the old house. I was always afraid to go to the house because my brothers told us snakes were there. But I followed Daddy. He walked around what was left of the porch and began pulling vines off the shack. I stuck close to him in case those snake threats were real.

"Daddy, I know you're upset but let me ask you something." I figured I was already in the doghouse, so I had nothing to lose. "You and Mama have enough money to live well the rest of your lives. You, yourself have said farming isn't like it used to be. Why not sell the land? I know you savor the notion of this land staying in the family and your sons running it together. But the reality is, Charles is the only one interested and his children have no desire to farm. Raymond and Paul have other careers and Carl is locked up. Are you being realistic?"

"Chubby, this was the first piece of land anybody in our family ever owned. We had everything we needed right here; hogs, chickens, fruit, vegetables. We only went to town to go to church, and to get meal, flour and sugar. Even our little school was in the country, not far from here. We were cotton farmers and proud of it. I can remember when I was a boy, we planted cotton almost right up to the doorstep. We didn't waste land on a yard. By the time I was ten, I could pick almost two hundred pounds a day. Me and Beau used to have contests to see who could pick the most," he said with a laugh. "My daddy left this house and forty acres to me and Beau. That was a lot of land for a colored man to own outright back in those days. Daddy was plowing behind an old white mule, and had a stroke right in the middle of that field," he said, pointing to the west. "You know what me and Beau did? He called me and I drove fourteen hours from Detroit. We buried Daddy the next day. Back then, you didn't keep bodies out very long. That was a Thursday, and Friday, we were planting cotton. We didn't divide the land or talk about selling it and splitting the money. We shared the house, the work and the money. When Beau got called for Korea, it got a little rough. It was a lot for me to do by myself, and I wasn't making enough to hire no help. I even left the farm and went back up North. They say that's why I didn't have to go to the war. The Army lost track of me when I left here, and that was fine with me. I made more money in Detroit than I had seen in all my life. When Beau got out of the Army, he bought a tractor and more land with the money he had earned from the Army and started farming again. Then I got laid off, came home to visit and decided to stay. I even chose this land over Betty. Beau didn't get mad and say I was trying to take something from him. He was glad for me to help him. I sold my car, since he had a truck we could share, took the money and bought more land. We cleared the timber ourselves with nothing but a crosscut saw. We worked side by side for two years before the accident. Don't exactly know how it happened, he was a real careful person, but he fell off the tractor and broke his back. He suffered about two days, then he died.

"Daddy, I never knew that."

"I guess me and your mama just wanted you kids to experience the good things in life. We didn't dwell on the bad times. That's probably why you all don't appreciate this place as much as you should. I always dreamed of working with my brother. Our dream got cut short, but he made it possible for y'all to work together. That's what I been working for all my life. I felt like I was doing it for y'all and for Beau who didn't get to have no children. To see y'all tear each other apart over it breaks my heart. What good did it do for me to build something that's going to tear my family apart? What good did it do for Beau to die?"

I didn't know what to say. "I'm sorry" was so inadequate. "We'll share everything," seemed greedy. I saw Daddy wipe a tear from his cheek. This was only the second time I had ever seen him cry.

"My dream is turning into a nightmare and it ain't worth it. Consolidated has been trying to talk to me for months. I'm calling Lester to tell him to bring those papers to the house. I'm going to sell."

34

I dialed Warren's number for the third time in an hour, and still got no answer. I had left messages for him at my house and on his cell phone. I did some thinking of my own, while Daddy was at the old house this morning. And after Warren's surprising phone call yesterday, I had finally gathered my thoughts and was anxious to talk to him.

Beverly came in with two plates wrapped in foil. "Mama wants you to take these sweet potato pies with you. She says they're frozen, so they should keep until you get home."

"There is no way I'll be able to carry all of this on the plane," I said, surveying all my bags. "How will I get all of this done? My flight leaves in four hours and I haven't finished packing. If I hadn't changed my flight for a rendezvous with Warren, I wouldn't be rushing now."

"Cecelia can bring anything you forget," Beverly said.

"Can you believe I almost skipped the reunion to be with him? I never thought I'd have so much fun in Eden. I'm already looking forward to the next reunion. I wouldn't have missed this for the world."

"Mama was afraid you were going somewhere with Warren. She made me and Cecelia promise to talk you into coming."

"How could I have even considered not coming? Think how miserable I would have been. He's probably already gone back to his wife and I would be sitting alone, watching fireworks on TV."

"Did you say wife?" Beverly asked, raising her eyebrows.

"Yeah, and no lectures please. He was separated when we met."

"Yeah right. You went to school all those years and you still fell for that line?"

"Beverly, it's a long story. I don't feel like getting into it right now."

"It's not a long story at all. He wants you to think it is. Bottom line, he's married and you shouldn't be with him."

"Don't you think I know that? I thought I was being smart by seeing him. I wouldn't have to wonder if he was lying to me, or seeing someone behind my back. He wasn't trying to get money from me and he even gave me a few dollars from time to time. We had a nice, safe relationship and no one was being hurt."

"Someone always gets hurt," Beverly said.

"I know that now. Seeing Tanya and Anthony made me furious. I can only imagine how you must have felt."

"So you decided to break it off?"

"Yes. I was going to tell him the next time I spoke with him. Then he called yesterday and said he left his wife."

"So now he's separated again?" Beverly asked. "And you're happy about that?"

"Yes, I mean no. Yes, he's separated, but no, I'm not happy about it. If I had stayed home this weekend, I would have been jumping for joy at the news. But now I know that's not what I want. He's all set to move in with me, and bring his boys to my house. I'm not ready for all of that. I want someone to want me first, not because it's not working out with his wife. It's taken me awhile to wake up, but him canceling our holiday plans was a blessing in disguise."

"He did you a favor. You and Derrick make a cute couple. Remember what Aunt Belle says, "When one says 'scat cat,' another says 'here kitty kitty'. So when is Derrick coming to see you?"

"Quit trying to pick information from me," I said shaking my finger at her. "If I learned nothing else this weekend, I learned not to tell the Washington family *anything*. Help me pack this suitcase. I don't understand why it won't close."

"Well, let's see, you went shopping, you cleaned out my closet, then Mama loaded you down with preserves and pecans. Even if you get it closed, you might break the handle. I guess you'll have to leave some of your things here, starting with those sandals," Beverly said.

"I'm sure I can find room for them," I answered.

"Well, since you've lost weight, that's the only thing of yours that I can wear. I gave you my small clothes, why don't you send me your big ones?"

"Beverly, you'll just have to come get them."

"I may surprise you. Do you realize this is the first time the three of us have spent together in ages? You need to come home more."

"I came twice last year," I said wrapping a towel around the pies.

"You came for Grandmother Jean's funeral and when Daddy got sick. Those trips don't count."

"That's still two times more than you've been to visit me. Why don't you come up for a long weekend? You are married to that beauty shop."

"I might just do that."

"Girl please, I will believe it when I see it."

"Really, I've been thinking about getting away. Anthony and I could use a vacation."

"I thought you meant you were coming by yourself. I guess you can't leave Anthony home alone," I said as I checked the closet to be sure I wasn't forgetting anything.

"You don't think much of my marriage, do you?"

"Beverly, who am I to judge? If you have to shoot and follow your man to keep your marriage together, that's your business."

"I know you dislike Anthony. Friday's episode lowered your opinion of him even more."

"My opinion doesn't matter. All I want is for him to treat you with respect, if he knows what that is."

"Both of you are always making digs at each other. What's going on?"

What nerve, I thought. He makes digs at me? That degenerate should worship the ground I walk on. One word from me would end his marriage, although she probably wouldn't even believe me.

"Carolyn? Are you listening to me?"

"I've had enough of sticking my nose in other people's business for one weekend. I need to pack my stuff and get out of here. I don't want to spend our last time together talking about your husband."

"Well, I just wanted to tell you that I know."

"You know what?" I asked.

"I know why you dislike Anthony. I know you must think I'm a fool, but that was a long time ago."

"Was Friday a long time ago?"

"He and I have talked about Friday. He was so sorry, and he promised not to ever be unfaithful again. He knows I mean business this time. He could have any woman he wanted and he chose me. Women flirt with him all the time, even when I'm around."

"That doesn't mean he has to sleep with them."

"You're a fine one to talk. Maybe if women like you would leave people's husbands alone, they wouldn't be tempted."

"Touché. I deserved that Beverly," I said as I packed the preserves and pecans in a bag.

"I'm sorry. I shouldn't have said that. I know you don't understand. Anthony is the only man I've ever wanted. He's the only man I've had sex with. I know I talk a lot, but he's all I know. I can't throw twenty years of marriage away because of a fling with some hussy. He has his faults, but he brings his money home and worked two jobs to help me open the beauty salon. He's a good father. He always wanted more children, but I could never have any more. Not too many people know this, but I had an abortion and it messed me up."

"You never told me that."

"I didn't tell anyone but Jackie. She came and stayed with me when I had some complications. I left Anthony, then found out I was pregnant. I didn't want him or his baby, so I got rid of it. When I told him, he cried. He said it was his fault because if he hadn't been messing around on me, I wouldn't have left. He straightened up and we got back together. He was devastated when the doctors said my uterus was too scarred to have more children. I was afraid he would leave me. We considered adoption, but never followed through. Now they have all these fertility drugs and treatments available, but we've accepted it. Tony has been a handful all by himself. Besides, I don't want to end up with seven babies. I know Anthony isn't an angel. But he's mine. We're a family and I'm in it for the long haul."

"Beverly, you don't have to justify yourself to me. What happened between Anthony and me is ancient history. If you've forgiven him, more power to you."

"Then can't you find it in your heart to call a truce? I know you'll never be best buddies, but everyone makes mistakes. Anthony feels terrible about it. He said he was drunk."

"So that makes it okay? Surely, he can come up with a better line than that. I hate to burst your bubble, but he was not drunk. He had been drinking, but he was not drunk. He knew exactly what he was doing." I was near tears. All these years, I've held the feelings in. Now, to hear her excuse the whole ordeal made the dam burst.

"Beverly, even if he were sloppy drunk I can't stand him. I tolerate him, for you. Don't ask for more than that. This is not something you read about in the paper. This is your family, your blood."

"I know. That's why I haven't said anything. Though Charles gets on my nerves most of the time, I don't want to hurt his feelings. He and Anthony are good friends."

"What?" I asked.

"Anthony told me you caught him with Brenda. I know all about it. I never said anything to Charles, because I know he's crazy about that baldhead, gap-tooth, skinny-leg, hag. I don't know what they both see in her. Anyway, that was a long time ago. I'm glad to know you have my back, but you really don't have to worry about it."

I was at a loss for words. She had no idea what I was talking about. I wanted to say, "Beverly, your husband almost raped me when I was all of fifteen. He has never apologized. I've carried the burden of this secret, as if I did something to be ashamed of. I wanted to tell her the truth, but I couldn't. I thought about Daddy's advice. Even with all she knew about Anthony, she still loved him. She was happy and I didn't want to be the one to slap her with reality. I decided to finally let go of the turmoil I felt all these years, but I didn't want to place it on Beverly.

"Fine. If you're happy, I'm happy. Can we finish packing now?" I said.

"Can I come in?" Cecelia asked and pushed the door open.

"How is Sheree?" Beverly and I both asked.

"They have upgraded her condition to stable. Michael is staying with her tonight. Her blood pressure got dangerously low, but she's going to make it."

"That's a blessing," Beverly said. "Sheree is a sweet girl. Everyone makes mistakes."

"I know. But I can't accept my daughter as a teenage mother. I'm still going to encourage her not to have it. Although right now, the priority is to make sure she's okay. How could all of this have been going on and me not know it? I know teen girls are full of angst, but suicide?" Cecelia said, rubbing her temples. "Maybe I need to stop working the night shift."

"Maybe you need to stop visiting the casinos," I said. "Before you jump all over me, think about it. I'm not trying to meddle, it's obvious to everyone but you."

"It's becoming obvious to me too. I knew I was crossing the line when I got a loan from Daddy's bank last fall, but---"

"*You* signed Daddy's name when he was sick? I thought it was Charles," I said.

"I paid it back, but I know I shouldn't have done it. Our property taxes were due and I went to Tunica a few times while I was here ---"

"I owe Charles a huge apology," I said.

"Well, I promised Michael I would stop. I do need to cut back for a while."

"Remember your advice to Carl, you can't cut back an addiction. It's like being a little pregnant," I said.

"I'm not addicted. It's not the same at all."

"Cecelia you are borrowing from me, your credit cards are all at the limit and you forged Daddy's signature. What other evidence do you need?"

"Think about it," Beverly said. "We know you'll do the right thing."

"I already promised Michael I would stop, okay?"

"Okay. We'll drop it," Beverly said. "I'm just glad Sheree's doing better."

"I'm relieved too. I blamed myself and thought if I had stayed here instead of going to see Derrick, I would have paid more attention when she called last night."

"You went to Derrick's last night?" Beverly asked. "You didn't mention that."

"Details, details," Cecelia said, as she leaned toward me. "Tell us all about it."

"Well, we talked and watched a movie."

"And . . . " Cecelia said.

"And that's it."

"You're holding out on us Carolyn. We want all the juicy details," Cecelia insisted.

"The movie was 'A Raisin in the Sun'. It's one of my favorites."

"Forget all that. Did you give him some?" Beverly asked.

"A good girl never tells," I said.

"Good girls don't have anything to tell," Beverly said.

"You can both stop licking your lips," I said. "I'm not telling you anything. I will tell you this - the next man I'm with is going to have to buy the cow. No more free milk here. Help me finish packing. Derrick will be here any minute to take me to the airport."

"She's holding out on us, isn't she?" Cecelia said.

"Girl, you know he wouldn't be taking her to the airport if she had gone over there talking about "no milk," Beverly said.

"Some men like a challenge," Cecelia said. "This could be a good strategy for her. I've always told her she gets too serious too fast."

"I have clients that are celibate, at least they say they are. Aunt Belle says it makes your hair grow."

I looked at my sisters, and smiled, as they mapped my dating strategy. No, I wouldn't have missed this for the world.

35

Cecelia quickly washed her face and changed clothes. She packed a change of clothes for Michael, who was still at the hospital with Sheree. She fished in the bottom of her purse for her brush and noticed a credit card. She pulled it out to return to her wallet. But when she pulled it out, she realized it wasn't her card. It was Carolyn's. Cecelia had called the 800 number and activated the card. She hadn't used it, but was ashamed that she had even thought about using it.

They're right, she thought as she placed the card back in her purse. I was going to use Carolyn's card at the casino. How could this happen to me? A knock at the door startled her.

She opened the door and let her mother in. "Sorry to rush you, my kidneys aren't what they used to be. Have you been crying, Cece?" her mother asked. "Don't worry about a thing, baby. Sheree is going to be fine. She's lucky to have you as her mother. The Lord knows you've done your best. That's all we can do."

Cecelia gathered her bags and told her mother she would call her from the hospital. She didn't want a long conversation with her mother, because she knew she hadn't been giving her best. The only difference between gambling and drug addiction was that gambling is legal. But the financial jeopardy she had placed her family in was criminal. Luckily there was still time to make things right.

She had promised Michael and her sisters she would get help, just to shut them up. But now she realized they were right.

She planned to apologize to her husband as soon as she got to the hospital. As she stepped off the porch, she saw Raymond drive up. I need to apologize to him too, she thought.

"Raymond, I was going to stop by your house on my way to the hospital. I'm sorry I went off on you this morning," Cecelia said as she opened the screen door.

"Okay, okay, don't worry about it. I just saw Lester driving away down the road. What was he doing here?"

"I don't know, he was in the kitchen with Daddy ---"

Raymond dropped the bag he was carrying and rushed in the house. Cecelia picked up the bag and took it inside. It was Daddy's medicine. She was waiting for mama to come out of the bathroom and happened to look at the labels. The prescriptions were for Procrit and dexamethasone. "Why does Daddy need these?" she muttered.

As her mother opened the door, she realized what they were prescribed for. She dropped the bag and rushed to find her father.

36

We had barely taken off before we heard the pilot's voice, "Ladies and gentlemen, if you look on the left side of the airplane, you can see the fireworks display over the Mississippi River. It's not as exciting without the sound, but FAA regulations prohibit me from rolling down the windows."

The sun had set, signaling the start of fireworks shows. Raymond was taking the kids to the fireworks at Lake Council. Mama and Daddy always sat on the porch and caught a glimpse of some of the colorful sparks over the trees. I was on the right side so I couldn't see anything anyway, and the Washington family fireworks had been enough for me. My mosquito bites itched and my nerves were frayed from worrying about Sheree. My calves were sore from double-dutch jumping, and my arms ached from volleyball. The splinters on my hand were getting infected and my face was breaking out from Mama's Dollar Store soap. I had a great time.

The 'fasten seat belt' sign went off and I stood to get one of my bags out of the overhead bin. A surly flight attendant lectured me as I boarded the plane because I had more carry-ons than usually allowed, but she let me bring them all on. I couldn't check Daddy's papers and risk losing them, and I couldn't entrust my precious cargo of peach and pear preserves to baggage handlers. I fumbled through my bag and found the legal papers from the United States Department of Agriculture. I reclined my seat slightly and tried to review the legal document. My efforts were wasted as the words ran together like little ants on a page. Twenty minutes later, I was still on page one. My mind was stuck on Daddy's words earlier today.

Once we got word that Sheree would be ok, Daddy summoned us for a family meeting. It really wasn't a meeting. Daddy spoke and we listened. There was no discussion and no debate.

Mama and Daddy sat at the head of the dining room table. This underscored the seriousness of this gathering since we rarely used the dining room for anything other than a passageway to the two back bedrooms. Charles, Brenda, Paul, Julia, Beverly, Anthony, Tony and Cecelia also sat at the table. Raymond, Mike, Malcolm and Rayven stood against the wall. Daddy had even summoned Aunt Vera Mae, who stood at the door.

We were all there on time and Daddy started promptly. "When I had the stroke, the doctors noticed some unusual growths. They did a biopsy and found cancer. It seems all those years in the sun have given me skin cancer. I had the growths removed and I've been taking chemotherapy, so I feel all right, for an old man."

"Lord have mercy," Mama said. "That's what happened to your hair, and the moles on your face. I thought you were just trying to look younger."

"I thought only white folks got skin cancer," Raymond said.

"Charles and Brenda been taking me over to Memphis every two weeks for my treatments. I asked them not to say anything to the rest of ya'll."

"You should have told me, C.W." Mama said softly. "I could have helped you."

"Lois, you were still grieving over your Mama, and I didn't want to burden you. I had good checkups until the last one. The doctors say the melanoma is starting to spread and want to do surgery. But I told them it would have to wait until after the Fourth of July. My children were coming home.

Besides, I don't know if I want them cutting on me anymore. I may just make the best of whatever time I got left. I want to focus on living, not dying. This may be the last time we are together on this side, and I want to say this in front of everyone so there's no misunderstanding. After I left the hospital this morning, I went out to the old house. I was feeling pretty low, then I realized how blessed we are as a family. Y'all know I don't have too much use for religion, but I do believe in the Man upstairs. I believe He brought us all to this time and place for a reason. I got to see what most folks don't. Ozell told me how folks react to death and how families fight over silly mess. I was disappointed because you were arguing over money that ain't even yours yet. Now, after thinking about it and talking to Lois, I feel lucky. It's like Jimmy Stewart in "It's A Wonderful Life." He got to see what would happen to his family if he wasn't there. Well, I got to see what would've happened if the Lord had taken me last fall. It wasn't a pretty sight. I never thought my children would be so mean-spirited and jealous toward one another. Me and your Mama raised you better than that, and I was ashamed. Just like I know Miss Jean is ashamed and turning over in her grave to see Lois and Vera Mae fighting over nothing. I was so fed up, I made an appointment with Lester and told him to bring those Consolidated papers over here. I figured I couldn't do anything about you all fighting because it's human nature. It's been going on since Cain and Abel. I would sell everything, and give you the money. Then you would be satisfied. But selling out would have been the worst mistake of my life, because I *can* do something to avoid y'all fighting. First thing I plan to do is draw up a will. I'm going to dictate how every dime should be spent. That is if there's any money left. Me and your mama are going to start enjoying ourselves. Vera Mae, I want you to book us on one of them cruises. I'm going to buy your mama a decent wedding ring. And I'm going to buy her a new grandfather clock," he said as he cleared his throat and looked around the room. “I’m even going to get tickets for Wrestle Mania next time it comes to Memphis. We might spend it all,” Daddy said, and winked at Mama.

“I know I need to get this deal with Betty straightened out, too. We didn’t know nothing ‘bout no divorce and lawyers in them days. You just said, ‘I divorce you’ and went on your way. To make sure there’s no question, I’m gonna change everything to specify Lois’, not just ‘wife.’”

“Whatever happens, I don’t want this land sold. We worked too hard and too long to let that happen. My Daddy and my brother both died trying to scratch out a living on a patch of land that wasn’t fit to grow grass. The rich folks around here ain’t rich from no stocks, or some fancy job. They got land, and it’s land that’s been passed from generation to generation. When my Daddy was born, the only thing he could inherit was sharecropper debt. Nobody gave him nothing. He bought his own forty acres and a mule. Now, colored folks get some land they parents worked hard for and they want to sell it and buy some foreign car. Land is the only thing man hasn’t figured out how to duplicate. They cloning sheep and got test tube babies, but they ain’t figured out how to make more land. Most wars been fought over land. Why you think they keep throwing away millions of dollars in outer space, and now talking about going to Mars? They ain’t worried about other life forms, if they find ‘em they’ll just kill ‘em off like they done the Indians. They looking for more land.”

“Chubby’s going to talk to her friend in Memphis and they’re going to put the land and most of the money in a trust. Whenever I get the government settlement, that’s going in there too. You all will get equal distributions from the interest and income earned by the farm. That includes Carl too. Your Mama and I want him to have the house. Whatever he done is in the past and he deserves a fresh start. I want Walter’s part to go to his daughter. We need to get closer to her. I plan to start putting more of my land in timber. Hibernated pine matures in about ten years and Charles can gradually retire from crop farming. Then he won't have to be an old man in the fields like I was. Beverly, I want you to make a list of everything in this house and your Mama and I will decide who gets what. I don't want y'all falling out over a set of dishes or some chipped vase. Me and your Mama's burial and plots is already picked out and paid for. I'm going to start an account for Sheree. She can use it for college and for my great-grandchild. I'm going to lend Cecelia and Raymond some money, but they got to pay it back. If they don't pay it back, deduct it from their portion of the trust. All I ask is that you keep us out of the nursing home as long as you can. I have a few more details to work out, but for the most part, that's it. It ain't a whole lot, but it's more than most got and it's more than white folks around here meant for me to get. Anybody don't like it, too bad."

"The money seems to be all anybody is thinking about, but I'm more concerned about how you treat each other. I know you won't always be best friends. I can remember Beverly beating Raymond so bad I was scared for the boy. Chubby and Cece used to argue so much they were hoarse the next day. Through it all, though, we're family. And Raymond, I want you to take me to see my boy next week. I shouldn't have cut him off like I did. Right or wrong, he's my son. I don't know how much longer I'll be on this earth and I want to see all my children as much as I can. All this talk about who is who's Daddy and who don't belong is ridiculous. You are all my children. Me and Lois won't always be here and you got to take care of each other. Vera Mae, you and Lois got to stop this foolishness. We done what we thought was best. The roof on your Mama's house was leaking bad. I got one of Edward's boys to fix the roof and he said he was getting married and wanted to buy the house. I told Lois we should take the offer. So if you want to be mad at somebody, be mad at me. Lois sent you your share of the money and anything of your Mama's in this house, you want, you can have. I'm counting on you to help Lois, because my time is winding down. Just because you don't like or approve of each other doesn't mean you don't love each other. As long as all of you remember that, you'll be okay."

"One more thing. I heard some of you think Tony caused my stroke. Don't be laying that burden on that boy. I told you, I'm glad this all happened. I was upset with him, true enough. None of my children talked to me the way that boy talked to me that night. I see why Anthony was so upset. But if I hadn't had the stroke, they probably wouldn't have found the cancer until it was too late. You wouldn't have felt guilty enough to show up for this reunion, then you wouldn't have been fighting and I wouldn't be taking the steps I'm taking now to get my affairs in order. And Beverly, let the boy grow up. College ain't for ever body. He say he want to work with Charles, let him. There may be a fourth generation farmer in this family after all. The good Lord has a master plan. Raymond's moving back to Chicago, so Tony can stay in his house. Those babies need you son and you're doing the right thing," he said nodding at Raymond.

"Yeah, cause' he sure ain't no farmer," Charles said. "He sprayed on so much insect repellant before he went in the field, I could smell him a mile away."

"Does anybody have anything that they can't forgive?" Daddy asked as he stood. "If you do, ask the Lord to help you. Jesus forgave and we have to forgive to make it to heaven. I believe there is a heaven, and I believe Walter and Beau and Henrietta are there waiting for us. We got to live right and love each other so we can have another reunion on the other side. We don't know why some things happen, but, as the old folks used to say, we'll understand it better by and by."

"Lord, I've lived with this man fifty years and I didn't know he could preach," Mama said as teardrops fell on her lap. We could barely hear her over Beverly's bawling.

Anthony put his arm around his wife and Tony handed her a box of tissues. "Do you realize this is the first time we've sat together all weekend?" she asked and cried even louder.

Brenda handed Cecelia a notebook, with details of all Daddy's medications and doctor visits. Cecelia told him about clinical trials at her hospital she would try to enroll him in. Raymond urged caution, reminding them of the 'experiments' run on the Scottsboro boys. Cecelia called him paranoid, and they were off on another of their debates.

Charles tapped Mama, who was hugging Aunt Vera Mae, and said he was sorry. Paul and I began discussing Carl's case to see how we could get his sentence reduced. I vowed to write Carl as soon as I got home. I also vowed to talk to Cecelia about Sheree when we returned to Chicago. It's easier to change the weather than Cecelia's mind, but I had to try. I didn't want Sheree to experience the guild and regret I'd felt all these years. Then I thought of something that shouldn't wait until I got home.

"I owe you a big apology," I said to Charles.

"How could you think I would do anything to hurt or take advantage of C.W.?" he asked. "He's my father too, and I love him just as much as you do."

"You're right. I don't know how I let myself think such a thing. Can you forgive me?"

"Let me see," he said as he scratched his chin. Then a big smile cracked his face and he hugged me so tight I had to gasp for air.

I then made my way to Julia and gave her a belated welcome to the family. Even Beverly and Brenda hugged each other. Anthony caught my eye and got up to walk toward me, but I walked away. Some things take more time.

"Now see that's what I'm talking about," Raymond said excitedly. "This is how families are supposed to be. We have enough strife with the white man and the racist power structure of this country, the black man must ---"

We all turned around and said, "Shut-up Raymond."
The Washington family was finally on one accord.

Webster's defines family as 'a group of people of common ancestry or a group related by common characteristics or properties'. I learned a lot about family this weekend. It's people who care about you, regardless of your education, weight or DNA. I felt I did my familial duty by sending my parents money and gifts. The Eden of my memory was stuck in a time warp. I didn't mind missing nosy, trifling relatives and drama. But I was also missing precious time with my parents, the wisdom of my elders and the warmth of a hamlet that holds my history and is part of my soul. I learned I have a place and we'll do what is necessary to keep that place in the family. The census bureau may record Mama and Daddy's land as a 'small farm', but it's big to us.

I also learned the answer to Tina Turner's question. What's love got to do with it? Everything. Love lets me forgive my sister for cutting off my hair and struggle to be civil to her husband. Love lets me forgive my brother for running up my debt. Love lets me overlook Cecelia's lapse in judgment, rather than brand her a thief. Love is what Paul has found, and I'm glad for him. I want someone to love me like that, and if they did, it wouldn't matter what color they were. I haven't found the love of my life, but I know it's not Warren. Derrick seems promising. He volunteered to help Raymond move back to Chicago next month and wants to visit me then. He wants me to come home for Labor Day and for the Southern Heritage Classic football game. He took me to the airport and we agreed not to rush things. We're going to take things as they come. But I do have a secret. Before I sprinted to the plane, I placed the hair Beverly chopped off my head, under the mat in Derrick's car. I learned to listen to my elders.

APPENDIX

Forty Acres and a Mule - A History Lesson

Where's my forty acres and a mule? That's the question that came to mind as I wrote this book. Most African Americans have heard or said at one time or another a comment about getting our "forty acres and a mule." It is generally an inside joke as most of our families didn't get forty acres or a mule. But what is the 'real deal' surrounding forty acres and a mule? Was there a promise of 40 acres and a mule? Is this just a myth passed down through generations? Did anyone actually receive land? I briefly remember learning about the evils of slavery and the challenge of reconstruction in my high school history class. Although I admit, my focus was on learning the newest dance and getting my driver's license. So it is possible that I just missed the lesson on "forty acres and a mule". But I doubt it. I am always amazed at how much I did not learn about my history. But I did learn how to read and reason, so I can find the information for myself. My research uncovered some surprising facts about the "promise" of forty acres and a mule that may surprise you too.

I would like to take you back to your American History high school class for a brief history lesson. But first, let's start with a quiz. Test your knowledge of facts associated with "forty acres and a mule" by answering the following questions (no cheating):

Quiz Select the best answer.

1. Which of the following abolished slavery in the United States?
   A. Emancipation Proclamation
   B. 13th Amendment
   C. Homestead Act of 1862
   D. Freedmans Bureau Bill
   E. None of the above

2. Which is the closest estimate of the number of slaves freed?
   A. one million
   B. four million
   C. ten million
   D. twenty million
   E. fifty million

3. Did the United States government promise 40 acres to freed slaves?
   A. No. This was a trick by southern masters to keep blacks in the south.
   B. Yes. But it was repealed by President Johnson.
   C. No. Frederick Douglass called for 40 acres and a mule in on of his speeches.
   D. Yes. The promise was included in the Emancipation Proclamation.
   E. None of the above.

4. Which document promised 40 acres and a mule to freed slaves?
   A. Emancipation Proclamation
   B. 13th Amendment
   C. Homestead Act of 1862
   D. Freedmans Bureau bill
   E. None of the above

5. Who was the most vocal proponent of land for the freedman?

A. abolitionists
B. President Abraham Lincoln
C. W. E. B. DuBois
D. O. O. Howard
E. None of the above

6. Which of the following proposals for black land ownership was suggested by government officials?

A. place freed slaves on a reservation
B. freed slaves could go to western frontier states and homestead
C. colonize freed slaves in another country such as Liberia or Haiti
D. send them to Columbia to work on Panama Canal in exchange for land
E. all of the above

7. Which is the closest estimate of the number of freedman who received land through the Freedman's Bureau?

A. zero
B. one percent
C. twenty percent
D. fifty percent
E. one million

8.In which state were the freedmen most successful in obtaining land?

A. Alabama
B. Georgia
C. Mississippi
D. North Carolina
E. South Carolina

9. Which of the following is most comparable in size to 40 acres?

A. 1 square mile
B. 3 city blocks
C. 22 baseball fields
D. 32 football fields
E. none of the above

10. Which of the following is the reason for a large part of the present day land loss among African Americans?

A. floods
B. heirs property
C. migration to northern cities
D. eminent domain
E. none of the above

Extra Credit

What is a mule?

A. offspring of a male horse and female donkey
B. offspring of a female horse and a male donkey
C. offspring of a male and female mule
D. offspring of a female mule and a male donkey
E. none of the above

Discussion

1. Correct answer B.

The Thirteenth Amendment was ratified in 1865 and abolished slavery in the United States. President Lincoln is often credited with freeing the slaves via the Emancipation Proclamation. He announced the Emancipation Proclamation in 1862 to become effective January 1, 1863. However, the Proclamation only freed slaves in those parts of the nation that were in rebellion. Slaves in states such as Maryland, Missouri and Tennessee, which were part of the Union were *not* included.

2. Correct answer B:

There seems to be general agreement about this estimate of the number of slaves freed, as several books quoted this same figure. Blacks outnumbered whites in Mississippi and South Carolina at the end of the Civil War, and represented more than forty percent of the population in the states of Alabama, Florida, Georgia and Louisiana.

3. Correct answer: E

Freed slaves were promised the right to *purchase* up to 40 acres. There was no mention of a mule. However, the military was given permission to provide excess animals (i.e. horse or mule) and tools to help the freedmen when they were available.

4. Correct answer D:

A bill to establish a bureau in the War Department for the care of refugees and freedmen was first proposed in 1862. It was finally passed on March 3, 1865. This statute established the Freedmen's Bureau, which was given supervision and management of all abandoned lands, and the control of all subjects relating to refugees and freedmen from rebel states. The statute included language that gave the bureau authority to rent not more than forty acres of land abandoned during the war to every male citizen for three years. At the end of three years, the occupant could purchase the land.

This revealed two interesting facts to me. First of all, the term 'refugees' included whites. Many whites had been displaced and were destitute after the Civil War. The Freedmen's Bureau was responsible for their well-being and hundreds of thousands of whites were served.

The second interesting fact is that the statute did not promise to give us 40 acres and a mule, but the right to rent, then buy the land. However, with four million freed slaves, the Freedman's Bureau did not control enough land to make good on this provision. In addition, the Freedman's Bureau did not have enough funds to carry out it's mandate. Taxes were not initially appropriated and the Bureau had to raise money by employing the freedmen, then selling the crops the freedmen raised on the abandoned lands. It seems the Freedmen's Bureau was doomed from it's inception.

5. Correct answer D:

Oliver Otis Howard was a Major General in the Union Army and was appointed as the first commissioner of the Freedman's Bureau. He advocated that land be allotted for the freedmen to work and purchase. Secretary of War Stanton also felt confiscated lands should be given to Negroes, and since the government freed them, it was "bound to provide for them". General Saxon, a bureau agent appointed by Commissioner Howard was removed from his position by President Johnson because he did not "cooperate" with the President's plans to return land to plantation owners. General Howard himself was investigated twice for fraud and cleared both times.

The Freedman's Bureau was responsible for everything from providing food rations to medical services. Land reform was a low priority when compared with food and health needs. Their greatest success was in the field of education. The Freedman's Bureau was responsible for the establishment of hundreds of grammar schools throughout the south and aided the founding of colleges such as Howard, Fisk, Morehouse, Talledega and Atlanta University. Howard University was named after General Howard, who was the third President of the University.

While abolitionists had been vocal about freedom for the slaves, most were surprisingly silent on the issue of land reform. Many who were in favor of freedom for the slaves, felt justice had been served by ending their bondage. The former slaves were now free to pull themselves up by their bootstraps (never mind that they had no boots). Others expressed sentiments that to give land to the freedmen would make them lazy and dependent on the government. Some Northern whites felt it unfair to give land to the freedmen, when whites had not been given land. But whites had been given land.

The Homestead Act of 1862 encouraged settlement of "new" lands west of the Mississippi River. Anyone could settle a 160-acre parcel. The only requirement was that the settler be 21 years old, pay an $18 filing fee, build a home and live on the land for 5 years. At the end of five years the land belonged to the homesteader. Ten percent of the area of the United States was claimed and settled under this act and many present day landowners are descendents of these settlers. While this opportunity was generally not available to blacks, a few thousand did make successful claims, particularly in Kansas and Oklahoma.

6. Correct answer E:

There were several bills offered by lawmakers to award land to freed slaves. Some were initiated from a sense of retribution and to right a wrong, such as by Pennsylvania Congressman Thaddeuss Stevens, who introduced many bills to provide land to the freedman. Others suggested land ownership for the freedmen as a way to export potential problems associated with having a large block of poor and uneducated residents as neighbors. Orlando Brown, a politician from Virginia proposed that ten thousand freedman stationed in Texas be offered land if they stayed there and sent for their families. He also proposed that the government reserve a separate territory in southern Florida exclusively for them. One General proposed that Negro troops and their families be sent to Columbia to work on digging a canal. This would aid the freedmen and serve the economic interests of the United States. A similar proposal was made by President Lincoln to send the freedmen to Panama to work in coal mines in exchange for land. These proposals were unsuccessful because Latin American states viewed them as imperialistic by the United States. The government briefly aided private groups who sponsored emigration to Liberia. The Freedman's Bureau assisted with transportation for a few hundred, but withdrew its support due to the cost. Commissioner Howard felt the money could be better spent on assistance efforts in the United States. And, just as today, there were differing opinions among black people. While some were eager to leave this country, a convention of Negroes in Virginia in August, 1865, resolved: "That as natives of American soil we claim the right to remain upon it and that any attempt to remove, expatriate, or colonize us in any other land against our will is unjust, for here we were born, and for this country our fathers and brothers have fought, and we hope to remain here in the full enjoyment of enfranchised manhood and its dignities."

7. Correct answer B:

This is the primary answer that I was searching for; did anyone receive their forty acres and a mule? This is a difficult question because all states did not keep records by race. The question is also difficult to answer because thousands initially entered into contracts to work and buy land. However, these contracts were voided by President Johnson's pardon. On May 29, 1865, he granted amnesty to those that participated in the rebellion and declared that confiscated land be returned to the previous landowners. The Freedman's Bureau had control of over 800 thousand acres in 1865, but by 1868 this was down to 139 thousand acres, as land was returned to white landowners. Professor Claude Oubre, author of *Forty Acres and A Mule, The Freedmen's Bureau and Black Land Ownership* states, "by and large, those who secured land during the first years of freedom were the exception rather than the rule, probably less than 5 percent of the total Negro population."

Despite this slow start, by 1900, a quarter of the black farmers in the south owned land. They weren't given forty acres or a mule, but just one generation out of slavery, they made significant progress.

8. Correct Answer: E

The most successful land transfer occurred in the islands off South Carolina. Land there had been confiscated due to rebellion and failure to pay Union taxes. On January 16, 1865, General W. T. Sherman issued Special Field Order No. 15, which set aside the abandoned rice fields from Charleston, South Carolina, across the eastern Georgia shore to the Florida border "for the settlement of the Negroes now made free by the acts of war …" This is often referred to as the Sherman Reservation. The order stated, "Whenever three respectable Negroes, heads of families, shall desire to settle on land …the three parties named will subdivide the land… so that each family shall have a plot of not more than (40) forty acres of tillable ground…" By the end of the war, he reported that approximately forty thousand freedmen had settled on these islands. However, when President Johnson issued his pardon, the former landowners wanted their land back. General Saxton's response was " The freedmen were promised the protection of the Government… I cannot break faith with them now by recommending the restoration of any of these lands." He suggested that Congress appropriate money to purchase the entire reservation. If the former landowners wanted their land back, the money would go to the freedmen to settle elsewhere. Or, the former landowners could take the money as compensation for their land. Needless to say, this bill was never passed and President Johnson removed General Saxton from his position. Eventually most of the freedmen were evicted, although they were given the right to stay and work the land for wages (how nice). While most freedmen declined the offer to stay and returned to the mainland, a significant contingent stayed and their culture, that we know as "Gullah" has been preserved.

9. Correct answer D

An acre is approximately the size of three-fourths of a football field (including the end zones). It was hard for me to appreciate the missed opportunity since I couldn't picture what 40 acres looked like. I won't even try to put a dollar value on this. Rural land today ranges from approximately $500 an acre to millions if the land is near a metropolitan area. This doesn't even consider the impact of lost opportunity cost, inflation, time and present value factors. You do the math. I'm only taking you to history class.

10. Correct answer B

Many Black landowners died without wills, leaving the land to their heirs. This left siblings and their offspring to share a piece of land, but no one knows who owns which part of the land. Because most of the heirs do not live on or near the land, the land was easily lost due to unpaid taxes or to real estate speculators who purchased the land at low prices.

An additional problem is the lack of access to capital. As farming became a more expensive vocation, the ability to get loans became more critical. While my novel is fiction, the Pigford vs. Glickman class action lawsuit that Raymond refers to is real. It was settled out of court in 1999. The Judge writing the opinion acknowledged that the United States Department of Agriculture and the county commissioners "discriminated against African American farmers when they denied, delayed or otherwise frustrated the applications of those farmers for farm loans and other credit and benefit programs". Despite this acknowledgement and financial settlement, many black farmers feel it was "too little, too late" and continue to pursue additional compensation. Detailed information can be found at the Black Farmers and Agriculturalists Association website.

Extra Credit
Correct answer B
A mule is the offspring of a female horse and a male donkey. Mules had more stamina than horses and were valued as work animals. Mules are sterile and do not reproduce.

Additional Background

President Andrew Johnson had a humble background and ran for office as a proponent for the "common man". Prior to the Civil War he felt that " the great plantations must be seized and divided into small farms". The fact that his pardon returned southern lands to their former landowners reminds us that politicians flip-flopping is nothing new. Many blacks were assaulted, intimidated and even killed if they tried to settle on their own lands. The end of the war did not end racist attitudes.

Politics and racism aside, there were other practical hindrances to the newly freed slaves efforts to become landowners. A lack of information was a key hindrance. There was no television, radio, Internet, pager or telephone to spread news. By the time news traveled from Washington DC to other states, it was often distorted or obsolete. Slaves in Texas didn't learn of the Emancipation Proclamation until June, 1865 (origin of Juneteenth celebration). Many were focused on reuniting with family members first, but by the time they did this, or gave up trying, the Freedman's Bureau had lost most of it's power to grant land. Another problem was lack of education. The overwhelming majority of slaves could not read; it was a crime for a slave to read or write. So some of the freedman who were working toward owning the land they were occupying didn't know the terms of their contracts. Even Mother Nature seemed to conspire against the freedmen. There were heavy rains in the spring which retarded planting and too little rain in the summer. From 1864 to 1867 there was an uncontrollable infestation of the armyworm which invaded cotton fields and stripped stalks of their foliage. Then in 1867 the cotton market plummeted. England began receiving large quantities of cotton from it's own colonies (remember there were more slaves in the West Indies and Brazil than in the United States). This reduced the demand for American cotton and the price reached all time lows.

So was there a promise of forty acres and a mule, or is this a myth? It is a myth that the government promised to *give* all freed slaves forty acres and a mule. But the Freedmen's Bureau Bill and Sherman's Order No. 15 did promise freed slaves the right to *purchase* forty acres. However, President Andrew Johnson rescinded that order when he pardoned ex-confederates and ordered that their land be returned to them. So the promise made to freed slaves was broken.

Present Day Implications

Some may say, "Why should I care? Farming is big business today. A forty-acre farm can not support a family and who needs a mule? Besides, the decline in black land ownership is not strictly a racial issue. The number of white farmers declined in the twentieth century as well."

You should care because black land ownership has declined at a faster rate than other groups. This decline has not been by choice. Lack of access to capital and 'heirs property' titles have been the primary culprits.

Some claim to be tired of black people dwelling on the past. It's not news that this government has often dealt unfairly with people of color. Besides, the majority of African Americans live in urban areas. How does this information help anyone in the twenty first century?

This information may influence someone to hold on to their land rather than sell it. Others may consider their congressman's voting records on small farm issues. This information may spark increased interest in local elections. We need to know who is sitting on those zoning boards and county land commissions. Or it may provide additional background and help someone form their opinion on the reparations debate. Someone may decide it's wiser to invest in acreage than to buy twenty-five inch rims. Someone may decide to do additional research, or major in agribusiness, a field where African Americans are underrepresented. Someone may decide to donate to the Black Farmer's Agriculturalists Association or the National Black Farmer's Association to assist their efforts to help and lobby for farmers. Hopefully this information will help someone convince a reluctant relative to prepare a will. And if it's not feasible to keep the land, let's agree on the disposition rather than losing the land for taxes or eating up any profit in attorney's fees. Let's get together and stop fighting. As I speak to people about *Forty Acres,* the stories that I have heard about family fights over land would be comical, if the outcome wasn't so disastrous.

We don't have to be farmers to make the land work for us. Land can be collateral for college educations and business ventures. Land can be rented or placed in timber as a source of wealth for future generations. Also, participation in the Farm Service Agency's Conservation Reserve Program is an option for many land owners. There are even instances of corporations paying families for the right to drill for oil. Many people have been coming back south, to their old home places to retire. The benefits include a network of extended family, a lower cost of living and generally a warmer climate.

Summary

There is good news and bad news. The good news - Blacks own 7.8* million acres of agricultural land, with a value of over $14 billion. This is a significant source of wealth. The bad news - Black land ownership peaked around 1910 at 16 - 19 million acres. The 7.8 million acres owned by African Americans represents less than 1% of all agricultural land in the United States.

Most African Americans were not given forty acres or a mule. A few, like the Washingtons of Eden, Arkansas, struggled to buy their own forty acres. The prospect of the government giving them land was as remote to them as winning the lottery is to most of us today. But like many people dream of what they would do if they won the lottery, many African Americans can't help but wonder where they would be if we had received our "forty acres" or at least been granted the right to purchase land as promised in the initial Freedman's Bureau bill. We can't change the past, but we can prepare for our future.

So, that's our lesson for today. How did you do on the quiz? Hopefully this brief essay shed a little more light on a subject that most know too little about. Most adults know little of this topic because it was generally not covered in school. Most young people know little of this topic because they mistakenly consider slavery and it's aftermath irrelevant. But as Aunt Belle would say, you must know where you been to figure out where you're going.

Class dismissed.

"Land is the basis of all independence. Land is the basis of freedom, justice and equality."

Malcolm X

Sources

This essay just skims the surface of this topic. I encourage you to consult the following books, and articles which served as sources of facts in the preparation of this essay.

--Bennett, Lerone Jr. *Black Power U.S.A. The Human Side of Reconstruction 1867 - 1877* Chicago, Johnson Publishing Co. 1967

--Camejo, Peter. *Racism, Revolution, Reaction 1861 - 1877 The Rise and Fall of Radical Reconstruction* New York, Monad Press 1976

--DuBois, W.E.B. *Black Reconstruction in America 1860 - 1880* New York, The Free Press, 1935

--Dybiec, David *Slippin' Away: The Loss of Black Owned Farms* Atlanta, Georgia Glenmary Research Center, 1987

--Gilbert, Jess Sharp, Gwen and Spencer D. Wood *Who Owns the Land? Agricultural Land Ownership by Race/Ethnicity* Rural America Winter 2002 Volume 17, Issue 4

--Macdonald, William *Select Statutes and other Documents Illustrative of the History of the United States 1861 - 1898* New York, Macmillan 1903

--Oubre, Claude *Forty Acres and a Mule: The Freedman's Bureau and Black Land Ownership* Baton Rouge, Louisiana State University Press 1979

--Internet Sites

http://www.nps.gov/home/homestead_act

http://members.tripod.com/~american_almanac/oohoward.htm

http://www.civilwarhome.com

http://members.aol.com/tillery/llf.html

* This figure includes all rural land owned by African Americans. Land being farmed is much less.

Forty Acres

Group Discussion Guide

Forty Acres is a story of relationships. It explores relationships between family members, between lovers, and our relationship to our past. The following questions can be a starting point for your group's discussion about the relationships in the novel and in your own lives.

1. Which character do you most identify with and why?

2. Should you speak up when you know of infidelity or other dishonest behavior in a close family member's marriage? Would you want to be told, if it were you?

3. Should C.W. pass his inheritance equally to his children? Or should he make his decision based on need or based on who has earned it through service?

4. Is Raymond's Afrocentric focus commendable or a hindrance? Why do you think so?

5. Is C.W.'s insistence that the land be kept in the family a worthy goal or an unrealistic ideal from another era?

6. Since Carolyn has invested so much time in Warren, should she stick with him?

7. Should Sheree have the right to decide on having her baby, even though she currently has no means to support it?

8. Is Beverly's marriage worth hanging on to?

9. How can we instill a sense of history and appreciation for the struggles of our forefathers in young people?

10. Have you had an experience in your family with a dispute over land? What can you do, or could you have done to help resolve the situation?

About the Author

Phyllis R. Dixon is the author of *Let the Brother Go If...* which was published by Pines One Publications of Los Angeles, California. The book appeared on the *Emerge* magazine Best Seller list. She is a graduate of the University of Wisconsin, Milwaukee. She has been employed by the U.S. Treasury Department as a National Bank Examiner for twenty years. She currently resides in Memphis, Tennessee with her family. *Forty Acres* is her first novel. Visit her website at www.phyllisrdixon.com.

About the Cover

Ms. Dixon is honored to feature 'Forty Acres and a Mule' by **Ruth Russell Williams** on the cover. Ms. Williams is an award-winning, internationally recognized folk artist. Her work has appeared on the television shows, 'My Wife and Kids' and 'The Hughleys' and has been featured on the cover of the *Associate* magazine, published by the Smithsonian Institution. This is her first association with a book. She resides in Henderson, North Carolina and runs an art gallery. Visit www.ruthsart.com to see more of her work.